Sword of Kings

BOOKS BY BERNARD CORNWELL

1356

THE FORT

AGINCOURT

Nonfiction

WATERLOO

The Saxon Tales

THE LAST KINGDOM

THE PALE HORSEMAN

THE LORDS OF THE NORTH

SWORD SONG

THE BURNING LAND

DEATH OF KINGS

THE PAGAN LORD

THE EMPTY THRONE

WARRIORS OF THE STORM

THE FLAME BEARER

WAR OF THE WOLF

The Sharpe Novels (in chronological order)

SHARPE'S TIGER
Richard Sharpe
and the Siege of
Seringapatam, 1799

SHARPE'S TRIUMPH
Richard Sharpe and
the Battle of Assaye,
September 1803

SHARPE'S FORTRESS
Richard Sharpe and
the Siege of Gawilghur,
December 1803

SHARPE'S TRAFALGAR
Richard Sharpe and
the Battle of Trafalgar,
21 October 1805

SHARPE'S PREY
Richard Sharpe and
the Expedition to
Copenhagen, 1807

SHARPE'S RIFLES
Richard Sharpe and the
French Invasion of Galicia,
January 1809

SHARPE'S HAVOC
Richard Sharpe and the
Campaign in Northern
Portugal, Spring 1809

SHARPE'S EAGLE
Richard Sharpe and the
Talavera Campaign,
July 1809

SHARPE'S GOLD
Richard Sharpe and the
Destruction of Almeida,
August 1810

SHARPE'S ESCAPE
Richard Sharpe and the
Bussaco Campaign,
1810

SHARPE'S FURY
Richard Sharpe and
the Battle of Barrosa,
March 1811

SHARPE'S BATTLE
Richard Sharpe
and the Battle of
Fuentes de Onoro,
May 1811

SHARPE'S COMPANY
Richard Sharpe and
the Siege of Badajoz,
January to April 1812

SHARPE'S SWORD
Richard Sharpe and the
Salamanca Campaign,
June and July 1812

SHARPE'S ENEMY
Richard Sharpe and the
Defense of Portugal,
Christmas 1812

SHARPE'S HONOR
Richard Sharpe and
the Vitoria Campaign,
February to June 1813

SHARPE'S REGIMENT
Richard Sharpe and the
Invasion of France,
June to November 1813

SHARPE'S SIEGE
Richard Sharpe and the
Winter Campaign, 1814

SHARPE'S REVENGE
Richard Sharpe and the
Peace of 1814

SHARPE'S WATERLOO
Richard Sharpe and the
Waterloo Campaign,
15 June to 18 June 1815

SHARPE'S DEVIL
Richard Sharpe and the
Emperor, 1820–1821

Sword of Kings

A Novel

Bernard Cornwell

An Imprint of HarperCollinsPublishers

Originally published in Great Britain in 2019 by HarperCollins Publishers.

Map © John Gilkes 2019

FIRST HARPERLUXE EDITION

ISBN: 978-0-06-294477-1

HarperLuxe™ is a trademark of HarperCollins Publishers.

Library of Congress Cataloging-in-Publication Data is available upon request.

19 20 21 22 23 LSC 10 9 8 7 6 5 4 3 2 1

Sword of Kings is for
Suzanne Pollak

Contents

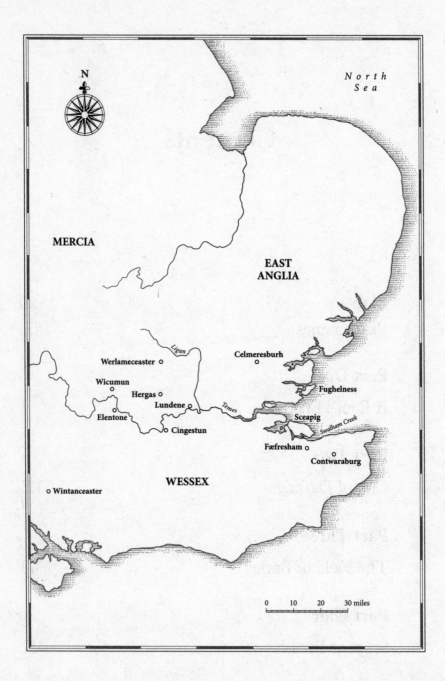

N

North Sea

MERCIA

EAST ANGLIA

Ligan

Werlameceaster ○   Celmeresburh
                                          ○
Wicumun
     ○   Hergas ○   Fughelness
            Lundene ○   *Temes*
Elentone ○   Sceapig
        ○ Cingestun   ○
                                  Fæfresham   *Swalham Creek*
                                          ○
                                      Contwaraburg
                                        ○
WESSEX

○ Wintanceaster

0   10   20   30 miles

Place Names

The spelling of place names in Anglo-Saxon England was an uncertain business, with no consistency and no agreement even about the name itself. Thus London was variously rendered as Lundonia, Lundenberg, Lundenne, Lundene, Lundenwic, Lundenceaster, and Lundres. Doubtless some readers will prefer other versions of the names listed below, but I have usually employed whichever spelling is cited in either the *Oxford Dictionary of English Place-Names* or the *Cambridge Dictionary of English Place-Names* for the years nearest or contained within Alfred's reign, AD 871–899, but even that solution is not foolproof. Hayling Island, in 956, was written as both Heilincigae and Hæglingaiggæ. Nor have I been consistent myself; I have preferred the modern form Northumbria to Norðhymbralond to avoid

the suggestion that the boundaries of the ancient kingdom coincide with those of the modern county. So this
list of places mentioned in the book is, like the spellings
themselves, capricious.

Andefera	Andover, Wiltshire
Basengas	Basing, Hampshire
Bebbanburg	Bamburgh, Northumberland
Beamfleot	Benfleet, Essex
Caninga	Canvey Island, Essex
Ceaster	Chester, Cheshire
Celmeresburh	Chelmsford, Essex
Cent	Kent
Cestrehunt	Cheshunt, Hertfordshire
Cippanhamm	Chippenham, Wiltshire
Colneceaster	Colchester, Essex
Contwaraburg	Canterbury, Kent
Cyningestun	Kingston upon Thames, Surrey
Crepelgate	Cripplegate, London
Dumnoc	Dunwich, Suffolk
East Seax	Essex
Elentone	Maidenhead, Berkshire
Eoferwic	Saxon name for York, Yorkshire
Fæfresham	Faversham, Kent
Farnea Islands	Farne Islands, Northumberland
Fearnhamme	Farnham, Surrey

Ferentone	Farndon, Cheshire
Fleot, River	River Fleet, London
Fughelness	Foulness, Essex
Gleawecestre	Gloucester, Gloucestershire
Grimesbi	Grimsby, Lincolnshire
Hamptonscir	Hampshire
Heahburh	Fictional name for Whitley Castle, Cumbria
Heorotforda	Hertford, Hertfordshire
Humbre, River	River Humber
Jorvik	Danish name for York, Yorkshire
Ligan, River	River Lea
Lindcolne	Lincoln, Lincolnshire
Lindisfarena	Lindisfarne, Northumbria
Ludd's Gate	Ludgate, London
Lupiae	Lecce, Italy
Lundene	London
Mameceaster	Manchester
Ora	Oare, Kent
Sceapig	Isle of Sheppey, Kent
St. Cuthbert's Cave	Cuddy's Cave, Holburn, Northumberland
Strath Clota	Kingdom in southwest Scotland
Suðgeweork	Southwark, London
Swalwan Creek	The Swale, Thames Estuary
Temes, River	River Thames

Toteham	Tottenham, Greater London
Tuede, River	River Tweed
Weala, brook	The Walbrook, London
Werlameceaster	St. Albans, Hertfordshire
Westmynster	Westminster, London
Wicumun	High Wycombe, Buckinghamshire
Wiltunscir	Wiltshire
Wintanceaster	Winchester, Hampshire

PART ONE

A Fool's Errand

One

Gydene was missing.

She was not the first of my ships to vanish. The savage sea is vast and ships are small and *Gydene*, which simply meant "goddess," was smaller than most. She had been built at Grimesbi on the Humbre and had been named *Haligwæter*. She had fished for a year before I bought her and, because I wanted no ship named *Holy Water* in my fleet, I paid a virgin one shilling to piss in her bilge, renamed her *Gydene*, and gave her to the fisherfolk of Bebbanburg. They cast their nets far offshore and, when *Gydene* did not return on a day when the wind was brisk, the sky gray, and the waves were crashing white and high on the rocks of the Farnea Islands, we assumed she had been overwhelmed and had given Bebbanburg's small village six widows and almost three times as many orphans. Maybe I should have left her name alone, all seamen know that you risk fate by changing a ship's name, though they know equally well that a virgin's piss averts that fate. Yet the gods can be as cruel as the sea.

Then Egil Skallagrimmrson came from his land that I had granted to him, land that formed the border of my territory and Constantin of Scotland's realm, and Egil came by sea as he always did and there was a corpse in the belly of *Banamaðr*, his serpent-ship. "Washed ashore in the Tuede," he told me. "He's yours, isn't he?"

"The Tuede?" I asked.

"Southern shore. Found him on a mudbank. The gulls found him first."

"I can see."

"He was one of yours, wasn't he?"

"He was," I said. The dead man's name was Haggar Bentson, a fisherman, helmsman of the *Gydene*, a big man, too fond of ale, scarred from too many brawls, a bully, a wife-beater, and a good sailor.

"Wasn't drowned, was he?" Egil remarked.

"No."

"And the gulls didn't kill him." Egil sounded amused.

"No," I said, "the gulls didn't kill him." Instead Haggar had been hacked to death. His corpse was naked and fish-white, except for the hands and what was left of his face. Great wounds had been slashed across his belly, chest, and thighs, the savage cuts washed clean by the sea.

Egil touched a boot against a gaping wound that had riven Haggar's chest from the shoulder to the breastbone. "I'd say that was the axe blow that killed him," he said, "but someone cut off his balls first."

"I noticed that."

Egil stooped to the corpse and forced the lower jaw down. Egil Skallagrimmrson was a strong man, but it still took an effort to open Haggar's mouth. The bone made a cracking sound and Egil straightened. "Took his teeth too," he said.

"And his eyes."

"That might have been the gulls. Partial to an eyeball, they are."

"But they left his tongue," I said. "Poor bastard."

"Miserable way to die," Egil agreed, then turned to look at the harbor entrance. "Only two reasons I can think of to torture a man before you kill him."

"Two?"

"To enjoy themselves? Maybe he insulted them." He shrugged. "The other is to make him talk. Why else leave his tongue?"

"Them?" I asked. "The Scots?"

Egil looked back to the mangled corpse. "He must

have annoyed someone, but the Scots have been quiet lately. Doesn't seem like them." He shrugged. "Could be something personal. Another fisherman he angered?"

"No other bodies?" I asked. There had been six men and two boys in the *Gydene*'s crew. "No wreckage?"

"Just this poor bastard so far. But the others could be out there, still floating."

There was little more to say or do. If the Scots had not captured *Gydene* then I assumed it was either a Norse raider or else a Frisian ship using the early summer weather to enrich herself with the *Gydene*'s catch of herring, cod, and haddock. Whoever it was, the *Gydene* was gone, and I suspected her surviving crew had been put on their captor's rowing benches and that suspicion turned to near certainty when, two days after Egil brought me the corpse, the *Gydene* herself washed ashore north of Lindisfarena. She was a dismasted hulk, barely afloat as the waves heaved her onto the sands. No more bodies appeared, just the wreck, which we left on the sands, certain that the storms of autumn would break her up.

A week after the *Gydene* lurched brokenly ashore another fishing boat vanished, and this one on a windless day as calm as any the gods ever made. The lost ship had been called the *Swealwe* and, like Haggar, her master had liked to cast nets far out to sea, and the first I knew of the *Swealwe*'s disappearance was when three widows came to Bebbanburg, led by their gap-toothed village priest who was named Father Gadd. He bobbed his head. "There was . . ." he began.

"Was what?" I asked, resisting the urge to imitate the hissing noise the priest made because of his missing teeth.

Father Gadd was nervous, and no wonder. I had heard that he preached sermons that lamented that his village's overlord was a pagan, but his courage had fled now that he was face to face with that pagan.

"Bolgar Haruldson, lord. He's the—"

"I know who Bolgar is," I interrupted. He was another fisherman.

"He saw two ships on the horizon, lord. On the day the *Swealwe* vanished."

"There are many ships," I said, "trading ships. It would be strange if he didn't see ships."

"Bolgar says they headed north, then south."

The nervous fool was not making much sense, but in the end I understood what he was trying to say. The *Swealwe* had rowed out to sea, and Bolgar, an experienced man, saw where she vanished beyond the horizon. He then saw the mastheads of the two ships go toward the *Swealwe*, pause for some time, then turn

back. The *Swealwe* had been beneath the horizon and
the only visible sign of her meeting with the mysterious
ships was their masts going north, pausing, then going
south, and that did not sound like the movement of any
trading ship. "You should have brought Bolgar to me,"
I said, then gave the three widows silver and the priest
two pennies for bringing me the news.

"What news?" Finan asked me that evening.

We were sitting on the bench outside Bebbanburg's
hall, staring across the eastern ramparts to the moon's
wrinkling reflection on the wide sea. From inside the
hall came the sounds of men singing, of men laughing. They were my warriors, all but for the score who
watched from our high walls. A small east wind brought
the smell of the sea. It was a quiet night and Bebbanburg's lands had been peaceful ever since we had
crossed the hills and defeated Sköll in his high fortress
a year before. After that grisly fight we had thought
the Norsemen were beaten and that the western part
of Northumbria was cowed, but travelers brought news
across the high passes that still the Northmen came,
their dragon-boats landing on our western coasts, their
warriors finding land, but no Norseman called himself
king as Sköll had done, and none crossed the hills to
disturb Bebbanburg's pastures, and so there was peace
of a sort. Constantin of Alba, which some men call

Scotland, was at war with the Norse of Strath Clota, led by a king called Owain, and Owain left us alone and Constantin wanted peace with us until he could defeat Owain's Norsemen. It was what my father had called "a Scottish peace," meaning that there were constant and savage cattle raids, but there are always cattle raids, and we always retaliated by striking into the Scottish valleys to bring back livestock. We stole just as many as they stole, and it would have been much simpler to have had no raids, but in times of peace young men must be taught the ways of war.

"The news," I told Finan, "is that there are raiders out there"—I nodded at the sea—"and they've plucked two of our ships."

"There are always raiders."

"I don't like these," I said.

Finan, my closest friend, an Irishman who fought with the passion of his race and the skill of the gods, laughed. "Got a stench in your nostril?"

I nodded. There are times when knowledge comes from nothing, from a feeling, from a scent that cannot be smelled, from a fear that has no cause. The gods protect us and they send that sudden prickling of the nerves, the certainty that an innocent landscape has hidden killers. "Why would they torture Haggar?" I asked.

"Because he was a sour bastard, of course."

"He was," I said, "but it feels worse than that."

"So what will you do?"

"Go hunting, of course."

Finan laughed. "Are you bored?" he asked, but I said nothing, which made him laugh again. "You're bored," he accused me, "and just want an excuse to play with *Spearhafoc*."

And that was true. I wanted to take *Spearhafoc* to sea, and so I would go hunting.

Spearhafoc was named for the sparrowhawks that nested in Bebbanburg's sparse woodlands and, like those sparrowhawks, she was a huntress. She was long with a low freeboard amidships and a defiant prow that held a carving of a sparrowhawk's head. Her benches held forty rowers. She had been built by a pair of Frisian brothers who had fled their country and started a shipyard on the banks of the Humbre where they had made *Spearhafoc* from good Mercian oak and ash. They had formed her hull by nailing eleven long planks on either flank of her frame, then stepped a mast of supple Northumbrian pinewood, braced with lines and supporting a yard from which her sail hung proud. Proud because the sail showed my symbol, the symbol of Bebbanburg, the head of a snarling wolf. The wolf and the sparrowhawk, both hunters and both savage. Even Egil Skallagrimmrson who, like most Norsemen, despised Saxon ships and Saxon sailors, grudgingly approved of *Spearhafoc.* "Though of course," he had said to me, "she's not really Saxon, is she? She's Frisian."

Saxon or not, *Spearhafoc* slid out through Bebbanburg's narrow harbor channel in a hazed summer dawn. It had been a week since I had heard the news of *Swealwe,* a week in which my fisherfolk never went far from land. Up and down the coast, in all Bebbanburg's harbors, there was fear, and so *Spearhafoc* went to seek vengeance. The tide was flooding, there was no wind, and my oarsmen stroked hard and well, surging the ship against the current to leave a widening wake. The only noises were the creak of the oars as they pulled against the tholes, the ripple of water along the hull, the slap of feeble waves on the beach, and the forlorn cries of gulls over Bebbanburg's great fortress.

Forty men hauled on the long oars, another twenty crouched either between the benches or on the bow's platform. All wore mail and all had their weapons, though the rowers' spears, axes, and swords were piled amidships with the heaps of shields. Finan and I stood on the steersman's brief deck. "There might be wind later?" Finan suggested.

"Or might not," I grunted.

Finan was never comfortable at sea and never understood my love of ships, and he only accompanied me that day because there was the prospect of a fight. "Though whoever killed Haggar is probably long gone," he grumbled as we left the harbor channel.

"Probably," I agreed.

"So we're wasting our time then."

"Most likely," I said. *Spearhafoc* was lifting her prow to the long, sullen swells, making Finan grip the sternpost to keep his balance. "Sit," I told him, "and drink some ale."

We rowed into the rising sun, and as the day warmed a small wind sprang from the west, enough of a breeze to let my crew haul the yard to the mast's top and let loose the wolf's head sail. The oarsmen rested gratefully as *Spearhafoc* rippled the slow heaving sea. The land was lost in the haze behind us. There had been a pair of small fishing craft beside the Farnea Islands, but once we were further out to sea we saw no masts or hulls and seemed to be alone in a wide world. For the most part I could let the steering-oar trail in the water as the ship took us slowly eastward, the wind barely sufficient to fill the heavy sail. Most of my men slept as the sun climbed higher.

Dream time. This, I thought, was how Ginnungagap must have been, that void between the furnace of heaven and the ice beneath, the void in which the world was made. We sailed in a blue-gray emptiness in which my thoughts wandered slow as the ship. Finan was sleeping. Every now and then the sail would sag as the wind dropped, then belly out again with a dull thud as the small breeze returned. The only real evidence that we were moving was the gentle ripple of *Spearhafoc*'s wake.

And in the void I thought of kings and of death, because Edward still lived. Edward, who styled himself *Anglorum Saxonum Rex*, King of the Angles and the Saxons. He was King of Wessex and of Mercia and of East Anglia, and he still lived. He had been ill, he had recovered, he had fallen sick again, then rumor said he was dying, yet still Edward lived. And I had taken an oath to kill two men when Edward died. I had made that promise, and I had no idea how I was to keep it.

Because to keep it I would have to leave Northumbria and go deep into Wessex. And in Wessex I was Uhtred the Pagan, Uhtred the Godless, Uhtred the Treacherous, Uhtred Ealdordeofol, which means Chief of the Devils, and, most commonly, I was called Uhtredærwe, which simply means Uhtred the Wicked. In Wessex I had powerful enemies and few friends. Which gave me three choices. I could invade with a small army, which would inevitably be beaten, I could go with a few men and risk discovery, or I could break the oath. The first two choices would lead to my death, the third would lead to the shame of a man who had failed to keep his word, the shame of being an oathbreaker.

Eadith, my wife, had no doubts about what I should do. "Break the oath," she had told me tartly. We had been lying in our chamber behind Bebbanburg's great hall and I was gazing into the shadowed rafters, blackened by smoke and by night, and I had said nothing. "Let them kill each other," she had urged me. "It's a quarrel for the southerners, not us. We're safe here." And she was right, we were safe in Bebbanburg, but still her demand had angered me. The gods mark our promises, and to break an oath is to risk their wrath. "You would die for a stupid oath?" Eadith had been angry too. "Is that what you want?" I wanted to live, but I wanted to live without the stain of dishonor that marked an oathbreaker.

Spearhafoc took my mind from the quandary by quickening to a freshening wind and I grasped the steering-oar again and felt the quiver of the water coming through the long ash shaft. At least this choice was simple. Strangers had slaughtered my men, and we sailed to seek revenge across a wind-rippled sea that reflected a myriad flashes of sunlight. "Are we home yet?" Finan asked.

"I thought you were asleep."

"Dozing," Finan grunted, then heaved himself upright and stared around. "There's a ship out there."

"Where?"

"There," he pointed north. Finan had the sharpest eyesight of any man I've ever known. He might be getting older, like me, yet his sight was as keen as ever. "Just a mast," he said, "no sail."

I stared into the haze, seeing nothing. Then I thought I saw a flicker against the pale sky, a line as tremulous as a charcoal scratch. A mast? I lost it, looked, found it again, and turned the ship northward. The sail protested until we hauled in the steerboard sheet and *Spearhafoc* leaned again to the breeze and the water seethed louder down her flanks. My men stirred, woken by *Spearhafoc*'s sudden liveliness, and turned to look at the far ship.

"No sail on her," Finan said.

"She's going into the wind," I said, "so they're rowing. Probably a trader." No sooner had I spoken than the tiny scratch mark on the hazed horizon disappeared, replaced by a newly dropped sail. I watched her, the blur of the big square sail much easier to distinguish than the mast. "She's turning toward us," I said.

"It's *Banamaðr*," Finan said.

I laughed at that. "You're guessing!"

"No guess," Finan said, "she has an eagle on her sail, it's Egil."

"You can see that!"

"You can't?"

Our two ships were sailing toward each other now, and within moments I could clearly see a distinctive lime-washed upper strake that showed clearly against the lower hull's darker planks. I could also see the big black outline of a spread-winged eagle on the sail and the eagle's head on her high prow. Finan was right, it was *Banamaðr,* a name that meant "killer." It was Egil's ship.

As the *Banamaðr* drew closer I dropped my sail and let *Spearhafoc* wallow in the livening waves. It was a sign to Egil that he could come alongside, and I watched as his ship curved toward us. She was smaller than *Spearhafoc,* but just as sleek, a Frisian-built raider that was Egil's joy because, like almost all Norsemen, he was happiest when he was at sea. I watched the sea break white at *Banamaðr's* cutwater, she kept turn-ing, the great yard dropped, and men hauled the sail inboard, turned the long yard with its furled sail fore and aft, and then, sweet as any seaman could desire, she slewed alongside our steerboard flank. A man in *Banamaðr's* bows threw a line, a second line sailed toward me from her stern, and Egil was shouting at his crew to drape sailcloth or cloaks over the pale upper strake so our timbers did not crash and grind together. He grinned at me. "Are you doing what I think you're doing?"

"Wasting my time," I called back.

"Maybe not."

"And you?"

"Looking for the bastards who took your ships, of course. Can I come aboard?"

"Come!"

Egil waited to judge the waves, then leaped across. He was a Norseman, a pagan, a poet, a seaman, and a warrior. He was tall, like me, and wore his fair hair long and wild. He was clean-shaven with a chin as sharp as a dragon-boat's prow, he had deep eyes, an axe-blade of a nose, and a mouth that smiled often. Men followed him eagerly, women even more eagerly. I had only known him for a year, but in that year I had come to like and trust him. He was young enough to be my son and he had brought seventy Norse warriors who had sworn their allegiance to me in return for the land I had given them along the Tuede's southern bank.

"We should go south," Egil said briskly.

"South?" I asked.

Egil nodded at Finan. "Good morning, lord." He always called Finan "lord" to their shared amusement. He looked back to me. "You're not wasting your time. We met a Scottish trader sailing northward, and he told us there were four ships down there." He nodded southward. "Way out to sea," he said, "out of sight of land. Four Saxon ships, just waiting. One of them stopped him, they demanded three shillings duty, and when he couldn't pay, they stole his whole cargo."

"They wanted to charge him duty!"

"In your name."

"In my name," I said softly, angrily.

"I was on my way back to tell you." Egil looked into *Banamaðr* where around forty men waited. "I don't have enough men to take on four ships, but the two of us could do some damage?"

"How many men in the ships?" Finan had scrambled to his feet and was looking eager.

"The one that stopped the Scotsman had forty, he said two of the others were about the same size, and the last one smaller."

"We could do some damage," I said vengefully.

Finan, while he listened to us, had been watching Egil's crew. Three men were struggling to take the eagle's head from the prow. They laid the heavy piece of wood on the brief foredeck, then helped the others who were unlacing the sail. "What are they doing?" Finan asked.

Egil turned to *Banamaðr*. "If the scum see a ship with an eagle on the sail," he said, "they'll know we're a fighting ship. If they see my eagle they'll know it's me. So I'm turning the sail around." He grinned. "We're a small ship, they'll think we're easy prey."

I understood what he was suggesting. "So I'm to follow you?"

"Under oars," he suggested. "If you're under sail they'll see you sooner. We'll suck them in with *Banamaðr* as the bait, then you can help me finish them."

"Help?" I repeated scornfully, which made him laugh.

"But who are they?" Finan asked.

That was the question that nagged at me as we rowed southward. Egil had gone back to his ship and, with his sail showing a drab frontage, was plunging ahead of us. Despite his suggestion, the *Spearhafoc* was also under sail, but at least a half-mile behind *Banamaðr*. I did not want my men wearied by hard rowing if they were to fight, and so we had agreed that Egil would turn *Banamaðr* if he sighted the four ships. He would turn and pretend to flee toward the coast and so lead the enemy, we hoped, into our ambush. I would drop our sail when he turned, so that the enemy would not see the great wolf's head, but would think us just another trading ship that would prove easy prey. We had taken the sparrowhawk's head from the prow. The great carved symbols were there to placate the gods, to frighten enemies, and to drive off evil spirits, but custom dictated that they could be removed in safe waters and so, instead of being nailed or scarfed into the prow, they were easily dismounted.

"Four ships," Finan said flatly, "Saxons."

"And being clever," I said.

"Clever? You call poking you with a sharp stick clever?"

"They attack ships from Bebbanburg, but only harass the others. How long before King Constantin hears that Uhtred of Bebbanburg is confiscating Scottish cargoes?"

"He's probably heard already."

"So how long before the Scots decide to punish us?" I asked. "Constantin might be fighting Owain of Strath Clota, but he still has ships he can send to our coast." I gazed at *Banamaðr*, which was heeling gently to the west wind and leaving a white wake. For a small boat she was quick and lively. "Somebody," I went on, "wants to tangle us in a quarrel with the Scots."

"And not just the Scots," Finan said.

"Not just the Scots," I agreed. Ships from Scotland, from East Anglia, from Frisia, and from all the Viking homelands sailed past our coast. Even ships from Wessex. And I had never charged duty on those cargoes. I reckoned it was none of my business if a Scotsman sailed past my coast with a ship filled with pelts or pottery. True, if a ship put into one of my harbors then I would charge a fee, but so did everyone else. But now a small fleet had come to my waters and was levying a duty in my name, and I suspected I knew where that fleet had come from. And if I was right, then the four ships had come from the south, from the lands of Edward, *Anglorum Saxonum Rex.*

Spearhafoc plunged her bows into a green sea to shatter a hard white foam along her decks. *Banamaðr* was pitching too, driven by a rising west wind, both of us sailing southward to hunt down the ships that had killed my tenants, and if I was right about those ships, then I had a bloodfeud on my hands.

A bloodfeud is a war between two families, both sworn to destroy the other. My first had been against Kjartan the Cruel who had slaughtered the whole household of Ragnar, the Dane who had adopted me as a son. I had welcomed that feud, and ended it too by killing both Kjartan and his son, but this new bloodfeud was against a far more powerful enemy. An enemy who lived far to the south in Edward's Wessex, where they could raise an army of household warriors. And to kill them I must go there, to where that army waited to kill me. "She's turning!" Finan interrupted my thoughts.

Banamaðr was indeed turning. I saw her sail come down, saw the late morning light reflected from oarblades as they were thrust outboard. Saw the long oars dip and pull, and saw *Banamaðr* laboring westward as if seeking the safety of a Northumbrian harbor.

So the bloodfeud, it seemed, had come to me.

I had liked Æthelhelm the Elder. He had been Wessex's richest ealdorman, a lord of many estates, a genial and even a generous man, and yet he had died as my enemy and as my prisoner.

I had not killed him. I had taken him prisoner when he fought against me, then treated him with the honor that his rank deserved. But then he had caught a sweating sickness, and though we had bled him, though we had paid our Christian priests to pray for him, and though we had wrapped him in pelts and given him the herbs that women had said might cure him, he had died. His son, Æthelhelm the Younger, spread the lie that I had killed his father, and he swore to take revenge. He swore a bloodfeud against me.

Yet I had thought of Æthelhelm the Elder as a friend before his eldest daughter married King Edward of Wessex and gave the king a son. That son, Æthelhelm's grandson, Ælfweard, became the ætheling. Crown Prince Ælfweard! He was a petulant and spoiled child who had grown to be a sour, sullen, and selfish young man, cruel and vain. Yet Ælfweard was not Edward's eldest son, that was Æthelstan, and Æthelstan was also my friend.

So why was Æthelstan not the ætheling? Because Æthelhelm spread the rumor, a false rumor, that Æthelstan was a bastard, that Edward had never married his mother. So Æthelstan was exiled to Mercia, where I had met him and where I came to admire the boy. He grew into a warrior, a man of justice, and the only fault I could find in him was his passionate adherence to his Christian god.

And now Edward was sick. Men knew he must die soon. And when he died there would be a struggle between the supporters of Æthelhelm the Younger, who wanted Ælfweard on the throne, and those who knew that Æthelstan would make the better king. Wessex and Mercia, joined in an uncertain union, would be torn apart by battle. And so Æthelstan had asked me to swear an oath. That on King Edward's death I would kill Æthelhelm and so destroy his power over the nobles who must meet in the Witan to confirm the new king.

And that was why I would need go to Wessex, where my enemies were numerous.

Because I had sworn an oath.

And I had no doubt that Æthelhelm had sent the ships north to weaken me, to distract me, and, with any luck, to kill me.

The four ships appeared in the summer haze. They were wallowing in the summer sea, but as we appeared they hoisted their sails and turned to pursue us.

Banamaðr had dropped her sail so that, as she pretended to flee westward, the four ships would not see the black eagle that now faced aft. And we, the moment we saw *Banamaðr* turn, also dropped our sail so that the enemy would not see the wolf's head of Bebbanburg.

"Now row!" Finan called to the benches. "Row!"

The haze was thinning. I could see the distant sails bellying in the gusting wind and could see they were gaining on Egil, who was only using three oarsmen on each side. To show more oars was to betray that his ship was no merchant's vessel, but a serpent-ship crammed with men. I wondered for a moment whether I should follow his example, then decided that the four distant ships were unlikely to fear a single warship. They outnumbered us, and I did not doubt that these men had been sent to kill me if they had the chance.

So I would give them the chance.

But would they take it? More urgently, they were gaining on *Banamaðr*, driven fast by the brisk wind, and I decided to reveal myself, shouting at my crew to hoist the big sail again. The sight of the wolf's head might give the enemy pause, but surely they must reckon on winning the coming fight, even against Uhtredærwe.

The sail flapped as it rose, boomed in the wind, then was sheeted home, and *Spearhafoc* leaned into the sea as her speed increased. The oars were brought inboard and the oarsmen pulled on their mail coats and fetched their shields and weapons. "Rest while you can!" I called to them.

The sea was white-flecked now, the crests of the waves being blown to spume. *Spearhafoc* was dipping her bow, drenching the deck, then rising, before plunging down into the next roller. The steering-oar was heavy in my hands, needing all my strength to push or pull as it quivered with speed. I was still sailing south to face the four ships, to challenge them, and Egil now did the same. Two ships against four.

"You think those are Æthelhelm's ships?" Finan asked.

"Who else?"

"He won't be on any of them," Finan grunted.

I laughed at that. "He's safe home in Wiltunscir. He hired these bastards."

The bastards were in a line now, spread across our path. Three of the ships looked to be about the size of *Spearhafoc*, while the fourth, which was farthest east, was smaller, no bigger than *Banamaðr*. That ship, seeing us race southward, was lagging as if reluctant to join a fight. We were still far away, but it seemed to me that the smaller ship had very few crewmen.

Unlike the three larger ships, which kept coming toward us. "They're well manned," Finan said calmly.

"Egil's Scotsman said there were about forty men in the ship that stopped him."

"I'd guess more."

"We'll find out."

"And they have archers."

"They do?"

"I can see them."

"We have shields," I said, "and archers like a steady ship, not a boat pitching like an unbroken colt."

Roric, my servant, brought me my helmet. Not the proud helmet with the silver wolf crouching on its crest, but a serviceable helm that had belonged to my father and was always left on board *Spearhafoc*. The metal cheek-pieces had rusted and been replaced with boiled leather. I pulled the helmet over my head and Roric laced the cheek-pieces so that an enemy would see nothing but my eyes.

Three of the ships bore no symbols on their sails, though the craft farthest west, closest to the unseen Northumbrian coast, showed a coiled snake, which, like our wolf, was probably woven from wool. The huge slab of cloth was reinforced with rope that made a diamond pattern through which the black snake showed. I could see the water shattering white at her bow.

Egil had turned *Banamaðr* so, instead of feigning a clumsy flight west toward the harbors of the Northumbrian coast, he was now sailing south next to *Spearhafoc*. Like me he had hoisted his sail, his crew just sheeting it home as we came abreast of him. I cupped my hands and shouted across the churning water. "I'm aiming for the second one!" I pointed to the ship nearest the snake-sailed vessel. Egil nodded to show he had heard. "But I'm going to attack the snake one!" I pointed again. "You too!"

"Me too!" he called back. He was grinning, his fair hair streaming from beneath his helmet's rim.

The enemy had spread into a line so that any two of their ships could close on one of ours. If that notion had worked they could board us from both sides at once and the sword-work would be brief, bitter, and bloody. I let them think that plan would succeed by heading slightly off the wind toward the second ship from the west and saw the other two larger ships slightly change their direction so that they were headed toward the place where they thought we would meet their line. They were still spread out, at least four or five ships' lengths between each, but their line was shrinking. The smaller ship, slower than the others, lagged further behind.

Egil's ship, slower than mine because she was shorter, had fallen behind, and I ordered the steerboard sheet to be loosened to slow *Spearhafoc*, then turned and waved to Egil, pointing to my steerboard side, indicating he should come up on that flank. He understood, and slowly the *Banamaðr* crept up to my right. We would go into battle together, but not where the enemy hoped.

"Christ!" Finan swore. "That big bastard has a lot of men!"

"Which big bastard?"

"The one in the center. Seventy men? Eighty?"

"How many on the snake bastard?"

"Maybe forty, fifty?"

"Enough to frighten a merchantman," I said.

"They don't seem frightened of us," he said drily. The three larger ships were still coursing toward us, confident that they outnumbered us. "Be careful of that big bastard," Finan said, pointing to the middle ship, the one with the larger crew.

I gazed at the ship, which had a lime-washed cross

mounted high on its prow. "Doesn't matter how many they have," I said, "they reckon we only have forty men."

"They do?" he seemed amused by my confidence.

"They tortured Haggar. What could he tell them? They'd have asked how often our ships go to sea and how many men crewed them. What would he have said?"

"That you keep two warships in the harbor, that *Spearhafoc* is the bigger one, and usually has a crew of forty, but sometimes not so many."

"Exactly."

"And that usually it's Berg who takes her to sea."

Berg was Egil's youngest brother, and I had saved his life on a Welsh beach many years before and, ever since, he had served me well and faithfully. Berg had been disappointed to be left behind on this voyage, but with Finan and me at sea, he was the best man to command Bebbanburg's remaining garrison. I would usually have left my son in charge, but he was in the central hills of Northumbria to settle a dispute between two of my tenants.

"They think we're about forty men," I said, "and they'll reckon *Banamaðr* at about thirty." I laughed, then touched the hilt of Serpent-Breath, my sword, before shouting across to Egil. "Turn now!" I heaved the steering-oar to windward and *Spearhafoc* dipped her prow as she slewed around. "Tighten the sail!" I shouted. The trap was sprung, and now the snake would discover how the wolf and the eagle fought.

I had tightened *Spearhafoc*'s sail to quicken her again. She was faster than the enemy's ships. I could see the weed thick on the snake-ship's bottom whenever she reared on a wave. She was slow. We dried our ships out on a falling tide and scraped their lower hulls clean, which kept us fast. I turned back toward *Banamaðr*. "I plan to sink the bastard," I shouted, "then go east after the second one!"

Egil waved, and I assumed he had heard me. Not that it mattered. *Spearhafoc* was pulling ahead, she was as close to the wind as I dared take her, but she was carving her swift path, she was breaking the sea white at her cutwater. She was as deadly as her name now, and Egil would realize soon enough what I planned.

"You're going to ram her?" Finan asked.

"If I can, and I want you in the prow. If I don't hit her right you'll need to get aboard her and kill their helmsman. Then ditch their steering-oar."

Finan went forward, shouting at men to follow him. We were closing on the snake-ship now, near enough to see a group of men in her bow and see the spears they carried. Their helmets reflected the light. One clung to the forestay, another hefted his spear. There was a group of archers in the belly of the boat, arrows already on their strings. "Beornoth!" I shouted, "Folcbald! Come here! Bring your shields!" Beornoth was a stolid, reliable man, a Saxon, while Folcbald was an enormous Frisian, one of my strongest warriors. "You're to protect me," I said. "You see those archers? They'll aim for me."

The helmsman was in the most vulnerable place on a ship. Most of my men were crouched in *Spearhafoc's* belly behind raised shields, Finan had gone to the bow where he and six men also made a barrier of shields, but I had to stand at the steering-oar. The arrows would come soon, we were seething through the green seas and were close enough that I could see the nail heads on the snake-ship's hull. I glanced to my left. The other three enemy ships had seen where we were going and had turned to help, but that turn meant they were now heading directly into the wind and their sails were flattening against the masts. Men were scrambling to lower the sails and to thrust oars through their holes, but they were slow and their ships were being blown backward and pitching hard in the rising seas.

"Now!" Beornoth growled and raised his shield. He had seen the archers loose their arrows.

A half-dozen arrows thumped into the sail, others

flickered past to plunge into the sea. I could hear the waves roaring, the wind's song through the rigging, and then I shoved the steering blade hard, putting all my strength into the oar's great loom, and I saw the snake-ship turning toward us, which is what her helmsman should have done moments before, but now it was too late. We were close, and closing fast. "Spears!" Finan shouted the warning from the prow.

"Brace!" I bellowed. An arrow glanced off the iron rim at the top of Folcbald's shield, a spear-blade scarred the deck at my feet, then *Spearhafoc* heeled into the turn and a gust of wind buried her rail. I staggered, an arrow smacked hard into the sternpost, then *Spearha-foc* recovered, her sail protesting as we turned into the wind, water streaming from her scuppers, and above the sounds of the sea and the howl of the wind I heard the shouts of alarm from the enemy.

"Hold hard!" I shouted at my crew.

And we struck.

We lurched violently forward as we jarred to a stop. There was a huge splintering sound, bellows of fright, a churning of water, curses. The backstay beside me tautened frighteningly and, for an instant, I thought our mast would collapse across the bows, but the twisted sealhide held, even though it vibrated like a plucked harp string. Beornoth and Folcbald both fell. *Spear-*

hafoc had ridden up on the snake-ship's hull and now settled back with a grinding noise. We had turned into the wind to ram the enemy and I had worried that we would lose way and so strike her less hard than if we had rammed her downwind, but *Spearhafoc*'s weight and speed had been enough to shatter the snake-ship's hull. Our sail was now pressed against the mast and was pushing us back, though it seemed as if our bow was tangled with the enemy's hull because the ships stayed together and *Spearhafoc* slewed slowly around to larboard and, to my alarm, she began to go down at the prow. Then I heard a sharp crack and *Spearhafoc* quivered, there was a ripping sound, and she suddenly righted. Her prow had been caught by the broken strakes of the snake-ship's hull, but she had broken free.

The snake-ship was sinking. We had struck her with our prow, the strongest part of *Spearhafoc*'s hull, and we had splintered her low freeboard as easily as cracking an egg. Water was flowing in, she was tilting, and her bilge, which was crammed with ballast stones, was flooding fast. Her crew, dressed in mail, was doomed, except for those few who had managed to cling to our ship, and meanwhile we were being blown backward toward the other enemy boats, who, their oars at last in the water, were straining to reach us. We were wallowing. I bellowed at men to haul in the larboard sheet of the sail and loosen the steerboard sheet. To my right the snake-ship was on her side in a maelstrom of white water, surrounded by flotsam, and then she vanished, the last sight of her a small triangular banner at the peak of her canted mast.

I thrust the steering-oar over, praying that *Spearhafoc* would gain enough way to make the oar's big blade bite, but she was still sluggish. Our prisoners, there were five of them, had been hauled inboard, and Finan had men stripping them of mail, helmets, and sword belts. "Watch behind, lord!" Folcbald said, sounding alarmed.

The nearest enemy ship, the vessel with the lime-washed cross on her high prow, was closing on us. She was as large as *Spearhafoc* and looked much heavier. Her crew was bigger than the snake-ship's doomed crew, but her commander had only ordered twenty-four men to the oars, a dozen on each side, because he wanted the rest ready to leap aboard *Spearhafoc*. There were helmeted warriors in the bows and more crammed into her waist. At least seventy of them, I thought, maybe more. The first arrows flew, and most went high to slap into our sail, but one whipped close beside me. I instinctively made sure Serpent-Breath was at my side and shouted for Roric.

"Lord?" he called back.

"Have my shield ready!" The cross-prowed ship was lumbering toward us, and we were being wind-driven toward her. She was not coming fast because she was rowing into the wind, she was heavy, and she had too few oarsmen, so it was doubtful that she could sink us as we had sunk the snake-ship, but the height of her prow would let her warriors leap down into our wide belly.

Then *Banamaðr* suddenly crossed our bows. She was running before the wind and I saw Egil thrust his steering-oar to turn toward the cross-prowed ship. The helmsman of that ship saw the Norseman coming and, even though *Banamaðr* was half his size, he must have feared being rammed because he shouted at his larboard oarsmen to back water and so slewed to meet Egil's threat bows on. He was close to us now, so close! I shoved the steering-oar, but still it would not bite, which meant *Spearhafoc* was dead in the water and still being wind-driven toward the enemy. I let go of the oar's loom and took my shield from Roric. "Get ready!" I shouted. I drew Wasp-Sting, my seax, and the short blade hissed from the fleece-lined scabbard. Broken waves slopped between our ships. The enemy ship had turned toward Egil and would now crash broadside into us, and her crew, armed and mailed, was standing ready to leap. I saw a half-dozen archers raise their bows, then there was sudden chaos in the belly of the cross-prowed ship as *Banamaðr* slid down her larboard side to shatter the oars. The oar looms were driven hard into the bellies of the rowers, the ship seemed to shiver, the archers staggered and their arrows flew wild, Egil loosed his sail to fly free in the wind as he turned to slide his bows against the enemy's stern. He had men with long-bearded axes ready to grapple the enemy, *Banamaðr*'s bows glanced on the enemy's stern quarter, both ships lurched, the axes fell to draw the two hulls together, and I saw the first screaming Norsemen leap onto the cross-prowed ship's stern.

Then we hit. We crashed into the enemy's steerboard oars first, which cracked and splintered, but also held her off for a moment. One huge man, his mouth open as he yelled, leaped at *Spearhafoc*, but his own ship lurched as he jumped and his bellow of defiance turned into a desperate shout as he fell between the ships. He flailed as he tried to grab our rail, but one of my men kicked his hands and he vanished, dragged down by his armor. The wind drove our stern against the enemy and I jumped onto her steering platform, followed by Folcbald and Beornoth. Egil's savage Norsemen had already killed the helmsman and were now fighting in the belly of the boat, and I was shouting at my men to follow me. I jumped down from the steering platform, and a boy, no more than a child, screamed in terror. I kicked him under a rower's bench and snarled at him to stay there.

"Another bastard coming!" Oswi, who had once been my servant and had become an eager, vicious fighter, shouted from *Spearhafoc*, and I saw the last of the enemy's larger ships was coming to the rescue of the boat we had boarded. Thorolf, Egil's brother, had stayed aboard *Banamaðr* with just three men, and they now loosed their ship and let the wind carry her out of the approaching boat's way. More of my men were leaping aboard to join me, but there was little room for us to fight. The wide belly of the boat was crammed with warriors, the Norsemen grinding forward from bench to bench, their shield wall stretching the full width of the big ship's waist. The enemy crew was trapped there between Egil's ferocious attackers and Finan's men, who had managed to reach the platform on the prow and were thrusting down with spears. Our challenge then would be to defeat the third ship, which was being rowed toward us. I climbed back onto the steering platform.

The approaching ship, like the one on which we fought, had a cross high on her prow. It was a dark cross, the wood smeared with pitch, and behind it were crammed the armed and helmeted warriors. The ship was heavy and slow. A man at the prow was shouting instructions to the helmsman and thrusting an arm northward, and slowly the big ship turned that way and I saw the men in the prow raise their shields. They planned to board us at our stern and attack Egil's men from behind. The rowers on the ship's steerboard side slid their long looms from the holes and the big ship coasted slowly toward us. The rowers picked up shields and drew swords. I noted that the shields were not painted, bearing neither a cross nor any other symbol. If these men had been sent by Æthelhelm, and I was increasingly sure of that, they had clearly been ordered to disguise that truth. "Shield wall!" I shouted. "And brace yourselves!"

There must have been a dozen men on the steering platform with me. There was no room for more, though the enemy, whose prow was higher than our stern, planned to join us. I looked through the finger-width gap between my shield and Folcbald's and saw the great prow just feet away. A wave lifted it, then it crashed down and slammed into us, splintering the top strake, then the enemy's dark bow grated down our stern as I staggered from the impact. I had a glimpse of a man leaping onto me, axe raised, and I lifted the shield and felt the shudder as his axe buried its blade in the willow board.

Almost any fight on shipboard is a confusion of men packed too close together. In battle even the best disciplined shield wall tends to spread as men try to make room for their weapons, but on a ship there is no space to spread. There is only the fetid breath of an enemy trying to kill you, the press of men and steel, the screams of blade-pierced victims, the raw stink of blood in the scuppers, and the crush of death on a lurching deck.

Which is why I had drawn Wasp-Sting. She is a short blade, scarce longer than my forearm, but there is no room to swing a long-sword in the crush of death. Except there was no crush. The ship had struck us, had broken the strake, but even as more of the enemy readied themselves to leap down at us, a heave of the sea lifted and drove their ship back. Not far, scarcely a pace on land, but the first men to leap flailed as the ships drifted apart. The axeman, his blade still buried in my shield, sprawled on the deck and Folcbald, on my right, stabbed down with his seax and the man shrieked like a child as the blade punctured mail, broke ribs, and buried itself in the man's lungs. I kicked the man's shrieking face, stabbed Wasp-Sting into his thick beard, and saw the blood spread across the ship's pale deck planks.

"More coming!" Beornoth shouted behind me. I ripped Wasp-Sting to one side, widening the bloody slash in the axeman's throat, then raised my shield and half crouched. I saw the dark prow loom again, saw it strike our hull again, and then something heavy struck my shield. I could not see what it was, but blood was dripping from the iron rim. "Got him!" Beornoth called. He was close behind me, and, like most of the second rank, was holding an ash-shafted spear that slanted toward the enemy ship's high prow. Men who leaped on us risked being impaled on those long blades. Another heave of the waves parted the ships again, and the dying man slid from my shield as Beornoth tugged the spear-blade loose. The dying man still moved, and Wasp-Sting struck again. The deck was red now, red and slippery. Another enemy, face contorted in rage, made a giant leap, hammering his shield forward to break our line, but Beornoth heaved on me from behind and the man's shield clashed on mine and he staggered back against the rail. He lunged his seax past my shield, his toothless mouth opened in a silent bellow of rage, but the point of his blade slid off my mail and I hammered my shield forward and the man cursed as he was forced backward. I pushed my shield again, and he cried aloud as he fell between the ships.

The wind drove us back onto the big enemy ship. Her prow was a good three feet higher than the stern where we stood. Five men had managed to board us, and all five were dead, and now the enemy on that high prow tried to kill us by thrusting spears at us. The lunges were futile, simply banging into our shields. I could hear a man encouraging them. "They're pagans! Do God's work! Board them and slaughter them!"

But they had no belly for boarding. They had to jump down onto the waiting spears, and instead I could see men going to the waist of their ship where it would be easier to cross to us, except that Egil's men had finished their killing and now waited for the next fight. "Beornoth!" I somehow stepped back, forcing my way through the second rank. "Stay here," I told him, "keep those bastards busy." I left six men to help him, then led the rest down into the blood-spattered waist. "Oswi! Folcbald! We're crossing over! All of you! Come!"

The wind and sea were turning us so that at any moment the two ships would lie side by side. The enemy waited in their ship's belly. They had a shield wall, which told me they did not want to board us, but instead were daring us to leap aboard their ship and die on their shields. They were not shouting, they looked frightened, and a frightened enemy is already half beaten. "Bebbanburg!" I bellowed, stepped onto a rower's bench, ran, and jumped. The man who had shouted that we were pagans was still yelling. "Kill them! Kill them!" He was on the prow's high platform where a dozen men were still thrusting futile spears at Beornoth and his companions. The rest of the crew, and I doubted they numbered more than forty, were facing us in the dark ship's belly. The man in front of me, a youngster with terrified eyes, a leather helmet, and a battered shield, stepped back as I landed. "You want to die?" I snarled at him. "Throw your shield down, boy, and live."

Instead he raised the shield and thrust it at me. He screamed as he thrust, though he had taken no hurt. I met his shield with my own, turned mine so that his turned too, and that opened his body for Wasp-Sting's lethal thrust that took him low in the belly. I ripped her upward, gutting him like a fat salmon. Folcbald was to my right, Oswi to my left, and the three of us broke through the thin shield wall, stepping over dying men, slipping on blood. Then I heard Finan shout, "I've got their stern!"

A man came from my right, Folcbald tripped him, Wasp-Sting sliced across his eyes, and he was still screaming as Folcbald heaved him overboard. I turned and saw that Finan and his men were on the steering platform. They were throwing the dead overboard and, for all I knew, the living as well. The enemy was now split into two groups, some at the prow, the rest between my men and Finan's men who were being joined by Egil's eager warriors. Egil himself, his sword, Adder, red to the hilt, was carving a path between the rowers' benches. Men shrank from his Norse fury. "Throw down your shields!" I called to the enemy. "Throw down your blades!"

"Kill them!" the man on the prow shouted. "God is on our side! We cannot be defeated!"

"You can die," Oswi snarled.

I had twenty men with me. I left ten to guard against the men behind us as I led the rest toward the prow. We made a shield wall, and slowly, obstructed by the rowers' benches and by the discarded oars, we walked forward. We clashed blades against our shields, we shouted insults, we were death approaching, and the enemy had taken enough. They dropped their shields, threw down their weapons, and knelt in submission. More of my men clambered aboard, joined by Egil's Norsemen. A shriek told me that a man died behind me, but it was the last shriek from a defeated crew because this enemy was beaten. I glanced right to see that the fourth enemy ship, the smallest one, had sheeted in her sail and was racing southward. She was running away. "This fight is over," I called to the enemy who were now crammed beneath the cross that decorated the prow of their ship. "Don't die for nothing." We had sunk one ship and captured two. "Throw down your shields!" I called as I stepped forward. "It's over!"

Shields clattered on the deck. Spears and swords were dropped. It was over, all except for one defiant warrior, just one. He was young, tall, and had a thick blond beard and fiery eyes. He stood on the prow where he carried a long-sword and a plain shield. "God is on our side!" he shouted. "God won't desert us! God never fails!" He hammered the blade against his shield. "Pick up your weapons and kill them!"

Not one of his companions moved. They knew they were beaten, their only hope now was that we would let them live. The young man, who had a silver chain and crucifix hanging over his mail, hammered the sword a last time, realized he was alone and, to my astonishment, jumped down from the prow's platform and took two paces toward me. "You are Uhtredærwe?" he demanded.

"Men call me that," I acknowledged mildly.

"We were sent to kill you."

"You're not the first to be sent on that errand," I said. "Who are you?"

"I am God's chosen one."

His face was framed by his helmet, which was a fine piece of work, chased with silver and topped by a cross on the ridged crest. He was good-looking, tall and proud. "Does God's chosen one have a name?" I asked. I tossed Wasp-Sting to Oswi and slid Serpent-Breath from her fleece-lined scabbard. God's chosen one seemed determined to fight, and he would fight alone, so there would be room for Serpent-Breath to work her savagery.

"My name," the young man said haughtily, "is for God to know. Father!" he turned and shouted.

"My son?" a harsh voice answered. It was a priest who had been standing amid the spearmen on the ship's prow and, from his grating voice, I recognized him as the man who had been encouraging our slaughter.

"If I die here I'll go to heaven?" The youngster asked the question earnestly.

"You will be at God's side this very day, my son. You will be with the blessed saints! Now do God's work!"

The young man knelt for an instant. He closed his eyes and made a clumsy sign of the cross with the hand holding his sword. Egil's men, my men, and the surviving enemy watched, and I saw the Christians among my crew also make the sign of the cross. Were they praying for me or were they begging forgiveness because they had captured cross-prowed ships? "Don't be a fool, boy," I said.

"I am no fool," he said proudly as he stood. "God does not choose fools to do his work."

"Which is?"

"To rid the earth of your wickedness."

"In my experience," I said, "your god almost always chooses fools."

"Then I will be God's fool," he said defiantly. There was a clatter behind him and he turned, startled, only to see that another of his companions had thrown down spear and shield. "You should have more faith," he told the man derisively, then turned to me and charged.

He was brave, of course. Brave and foolish. He knew he would die. Maybe not at my hands, but if he had succeeded in killing me then my men would have hacked him down mercilessly, which meant this fool knew he had only minutes to live, yet he believed he would have another life in the sunlit boredom of the Christian heaven. And did he believe he could kill me? Nothing is certain in battle. He might have killed me if he had both the sword-skill and the shield-craft that make a great warrior, but I suspected his faith was not rooted in hard-won craft, but in the belief that his god would reach down and give him victory, and that foolish belief spurred him toward me.

While he had been praying I had slipped my hand out of my shield's leather grips and was now holding it by just the outer loop. He must have noticed, but he thought nothing of it. I held both shield and sword low, waited until he was just six or seven paces away, then I drew my left arm back and threw the shield. I threw it low, threw it hard, and threw it at his feet and, sure enough, he tripped on the shield and a heave of the waves tipped him sideways so that he sprawled on a rower's bench, and I stepped forward, swept Serpent-Breath once, and her blade hit his blade with a dull sound and broke it. Two-thirds of his sword clattered across the deck as he desperately stabbed the remaining stub at my thigh. I reached down and took his wrist and held it firm. "Are you really so eager to die?" I asked him.

He struggled against my grip, then tried to hit me with the iron-rimmed edge of his shield, which banged against my thigh without hurting me. "Give me another sword," he demanded.

I laughed at that. "Answer me, fool. Are you really so eager to die?"

"God commanded me to kill you!"

"Or were you told to kill me by a priest who dripped poison in your ear?" I asked.

He drove the shield against me again so I placed Serpent-Breath in its way. "God commanded me," he insisted.

"Then your nailed god is as big a fool as you," I said harshly. "Where are you from, fool?"

He hesitated, but I squeezed his wrist and bent his arm back painfully. "Wessex," he muttered.

"I can tell that from your accent. Whereabouts in Wessex?"

"Andefera," he spoke reluctantly.

"And Andefera," I said, "is in Wiltunscir." He nodded. "Where Æthelhelm is ealdorman," I added, and saw him flinch at Æthelhelm's name. "Let go of the sword, boy."

He resisted, but I bent his wrist again and he let the broken sword fall. Judging by the hilt that was decorated with gold wire it had been an expensive sword, but it had shattered when it was struck by Serpent-Breath. I tossed the hilt to Oswi. "Take this holy fool and tie him to *Spearhafoc*'s mast," I said. "He can live."

"But *Spearhafoc* might not," Finan said drily. "She's foundering."

I looked across the deck of the intervening ship and saw that Finan was right.

Spearhafoc was sinking.

Spearhafoc had sprung two planks when she struck the first enemy ship, and water was pouring into her bows. By the time I reached her she was already low at the prow. Gerbruht, a big Frisian, had ripped up the deck planking and now had men lifting the ballast stones, which they carried to the stern to balance the ship. "We can plug it, lord!" he shouted when he saw me. "The leak's only on one side."

"Do you need men?" I called.

"We'll manage!"

Egil had followed me onto *Spearhafoc*'s stern. "We'll not catch that last one," he said, looking at the enemy's smallest ship, which was now almost at the southern horizon.

"I'm hoping to save this one," I said grimly. Gerbruht might be optimistic about plugging *Spearhafoc*'s leaks, but the wind was rising and the seas building. A dozen men were bailing the ship, some using their helmets to scoop the water overboard. "Still," I went on, "we can get home in one of those ships." I nodded toward the two we'd captured.

"They're lumps of shit," Egil said, "too heavy!"

"They might be useful for cargo," I suggested.

"Better as firewood."

Gerbruht, his hands under the bilge's water, was stuffing cloth into the gap left by the sprung planks, while other men were hurling water overboard. One of the two enemy ships we had captured was also leaking, the ship with the lime-washed cross, which had been damaged when the last ship joined the fight. Her stern had been hit by the larger boat and her planking had cracked to spring a leak at the waterline. We put most of our prisoners on that ship, after taking their weapons, their mail, their shields, and their helmets. We took their sail, which was new and valuable, and their few supplies, which were meager; some rock-hard cheese, a sack of damp bread, and two barrels of ale. I left them just six oars and then cut them loose. "You're letting them go?" Egil asked, surprised.

"I don't want to feed the bastards at Bebbanburg," I said. "And how far can they go? They've no food, nothing to drink, and no sail. Half of them are wounded and they're in a leaking boat. If they've any sense they'll row for shore."

"Against the wind." Egil was amused at the thought.

"And when they get ashore," I said, "they'll have no weapons. So welcome to Northumbria."

We had rescued eleven of the fishermen who had crewed the *Gydene* and the *Swealwe*, all of them forced to row for their captors. The prisoners we had taken were all either West Saxons or East Anglians and subjects of King Edward, if he still lived. I had kept a dozen to take back to Bebbanburg, including the priest who had so feverishly called on his men to slaughter us. He was brought to me on *Spearhafoc*, which was still bows down, but Gerbruht's efforts were stemming the worst of the leak, and moving much of the ballast aft had steadied the hull.

The priest was young and stocky, with a round face, black hair, and a sour expression. There was something familiar about him. "Have we met?" I asked.

"Thank God, no."

He was standing just below the steering platform, guarded by a grinning Beornoth. We had raised the sail and were going northward, going home, driven by the steady west wind. Most of my men were on the large ship we had captured, only a few were still on *Spearhafoc*, and those few were still bailing water. The young man who had sworn to kill me was still tied to the mast, from where he glowered at me. "That young fool," I said, talking to the priest and nodding toward the young man, "is from Wessex, but you sound Mercian."

"Christ's kingdom has no boundaries," he retorted.

"Unlike my mercy," I said, to which he answered nothing. "I'm from Northumbria," I went on, ignoring his defiance, "and in Northumbria I am an ealdorman. You call me lord." He still said nothing, just looked up at me with a scowl. *Spearhafoc* was still sluggish, reluctant to lift her bows, but she was sailing and she was heading home. *Banamaðr* and the captured ship were keeping us company, ready to take us off if *Spearhafoc* began to sink, though minute by minute I sensed that she would survive to be dragged ashore and repaired. "You call me lord," I repeated. "Where are you from?"

"Christ's kingdom."

Beornoth drew back a meaty hand to strike the priest, but I shook my head. "You see that we're in danger of sinking?" I asked the priest, who stayed stubbornly silent. I doubted he could sense that *Spearhafoc*, far from foundering, was recovering her grace. "And if we do sink," I went on, "I'll tie you to the mast alongside that idiot child. Unless, of course, you tell me what I want to know. Where are you from?"

"I was born in Mercia," he spoke reluctantly, "but God saw fit to send me to Wessex."

"If he doesn't call me lord again," I told Beornoth, "you can smack him as hard as you like." I smiled at the priest. "Where in Wessex?"

"Wintanceaster," he said, paused, then sensed Beornoth moving and hastily added, "lord."

"And what," I asked, "is a priest from Wintanceaster doing in a ship off the Northumbrian coast?"

"We were sent to kill you!" he snarled, then yelped as Beornoth smacked the back of his head.

"Be strong in the Lord, father!" the young man shouted from the mast.

"What is that idiot's name?" I asked, amused.

The priest hesitated a heartbeat, giving the young man a sideways glance. "Wistan, lord," he said.

"And your name?" I asked.

"Father Ceolnoth," there was again a slight pause before he added, "lord."

And I knew then why he was familiar and why he hated me. And that made me laugh. We limped on home.

Two

We took *Spearhafoc* home. It was not easy. Gerbruht had slowed the leak, yet still the sleek hull wallowed in the afternoon seas. I had a dozen men bailing her and feared that worsening weather might doom her, but the gusting wind was kind, settling into a steady westerly, and the fretting sea calmed and *Spearhafoc*'s wolf-sail carried us slowly north. It was dusk when we reached the Farnea Islands and limped between them and a western sky that was a red-streaked furnace of savage fire against which Bebbanburg's ramparts were outlined black. It was a weary crew that rowed the stricken ship through the narrow channel into Bebbanburg's harbor. We beached *Spearhafoc*, and in the morning I would assemble teams of oxen to drag her above the tideline where her bows could be mended. *Banamaðr* and the captured ship followed us through the channel.

I had talked with Father Ceolnoth as we labored home, but he had proved sullen and unhelpful. Wistan, the young man who had believed his god wanted my death, had been miserable and equally unhelpful. I had asked them both who had sent them north to kill me, and neither would answer. I had released Wistan from the mast and showed him a heap of captured swords. "You can take one and try to kill me again," I told him. He blushed when my men laughed and urged him to accept the offer, but he made no attempt to do his god's work. Instead he just sat in the scuppers until Gerbruht told him to start bailing. "You want to live, boy? Start slinging water!"

"Your father," I spoke to Father Ceolnoth, "is Ceol-berht?"

He seemed surprised that I knew, though in truth it had been a guess. "Yes," he said curtly.

"I knew him as a boy."

"He told me," the priest said, a pause, then, "lord."

"He didn't like me then," I said, "and I daresay he dislikes me still."

"Our God teaches us to forgive," he said, though in the bitter tone some Christian priests use when they are forced to admit an uncomfortable truth.

"So where is your father now?" I asked.

He stayed silent for a while, then evidently decided his answer revealed no secrets. "My father serves God in Wintanceaster's minster. So does my uncle."

"I'm glad they both live!" I said, though that was not true because I disliked both men. They were twins from Mercia, as alike to each other as two apples. They had been hostages with me, caught by the Danes, and while Ceolnoth and Ceolberht had resented that fate, I had welcomed it. I liked the Danes, but the twins were fervent Christians, sons of a bishop, and they had been taught that all pagans were the devil's spawn. After their release from captivity they had both studied for the priesthood and grew to become passionate haters of paganism. Fate had decreed that our paths should cross often enough, and they had ever despised me, calling me an enemy of the church and worse, and I had finally repaid an insult by kicking out most of Father Ceolberht's teeth. Ceolnoth bore a remarkable resemblance to his father, but I had guessed that the toothless Ceolberht would name his son after his brother. And so he had.

"So what is the son of a toothless father doing in Northumbrian waters?" I had asked him.

"God's work," was all he would say.

"Torturing and killing fishermen?" I asked, and to that question the priest had no answer.

We had taken prisoner those men who appeared to be the leaders of the defeated ships, and that night they were imprisoned in an empty stable that was guarded by my men, but I had invited Father Ceolnoth and the misery-stricken Wistan to eat in the great hall. It was not a feast, most of the garrison had eaten earlier, so the meal was just for the men who had crewed the ships. The only woman present, besides the serving girls, was Eadith, my wife, and I sat Father Ceolnoth to her left. I did not like the priest, but I accorded him the dignity of his office, a gesture I regretted as soon as he took his place at the high table's bench. He raised his hands to the smoke-darkened rafters and began to pray in a loud and piercing voice. I suppose it was brave of him, but it was the bravery of a fool. He asked his god to rain fire on this "pestilential fortress," to lay it waste, and to defeat the abominations that lurked inside its ramparts. I let him rant for a moment, asked him to be silent, and, when he just raised his voice and begged his god to consign us to the devil's cesspit, I beckoned to Berg. "Take the holy bastard to the pigs," I said, "and chain him there. He can preach to the sows."

Berg dragged the priest from the hall, and my

men, even the Christians, cheered. Wistan, I noticed, watched silently and sadly. He intrigued me. His helmet and mail, which were now mine, were of quality workmanship and suggested that Wistan was nobly born. I also sensed that, for all his foolishness, he was a thoughtful young man. I pointed him out to Eadith. "When we're done," I told her, "we'll take him to the chapel."

"The chapel!" she sounded surprised.

"He probably wants to pray."

"Just kill the pup," Egil put in cheerfully.

"I think he'll talk," I said. We had learned much from the other prisoners. The small fleet of four ships had been assembled at Dumnoc in East Anglia and was crewed by a mix of men from that port, other East Anglian harbors, and from Wessex. Mostly from Wessex. The men were paid well and had been offered a reward if they succeeded in killing me. The leaders of the fleet, we learned, had been Father Ceolnoth, the boy Wistan, and a West Saxon warrior named Egbert. I had never heard of Egbert, though the prisoners claimed he was a famed warrior. "A big man, lord," one had told me, "even taller than you! A scarred face!" The prisoner had shuddered in remembered fear.

"Was he on the ship that sank?" I had asked. We

had not captured anyone resembling Egbert's description so I assumed he was dead.

"He was on the *Hælubearn*, lord, the small ship."

Hælubearn meant "child of healing," but it was also a term the Christians used for themselves, and I wondered if all four ships had carried pious names. I suspected they did because another prisoner, clutching a wooden cross hanging at his breast, said that Father Ceolnoth had promised every man that they would go straight to heaven with all their sins forgiven if they succeeded in slaughtering me. "Why would Egbert be on the smallest ship?" I had wondered aloud.

"It was the fastest, lord," the first prisoner told me. "Those other boats are pigs to sail. *Hælubearn* might be small, but she's nimble."

"Meaning he could escape if there was trouble," I had commented sourly, and the prisoners just nodded.

I reckoned I would learn nothing from Father Ceolnoth, but Wistan, I thought, was vulnerable to kindness and so, when the meal was over, Eadith and I took the boy to Bebbanburg's chapel, which is built on a lower ledge of rock beside the great hall. It is made of timber like most of the fortress, but the Christians among my men had laid a flagstone floor that they had covered with rugs. The chapel is not large, maybe twenty paces long and half as wide. There are no windows, just a wooden altar at the eastern end, a scattering of milking stools, and a bench against the western wall. Three of the walls are hung with plain woollen cloths that block the drafts, while on the altar is a silver cross, kept well polished, and two large candles, which are permanently lit.

Wistan seemed bemused when I led him inside. He glanced nervously at Eadith who, like him, wore a cross. "Lord?" he asked nervously.

I sat on the bench and leaned against the wall. "We thought you might want to pray," I said.

"It's a consecrated space," Eadith reassured the boy.

"We have a priest too," I added. "Father Cuthbert. He's a friend and he lives in the fortress here. He's blind and old and some days he feels unwell and then he asks the priest from the village to take his place."

"There's a church in the village," Eadith said. "You can go there tomorrow."

Wistan was now thoroughly confused. He had been taught that I was Uhtred the Wicked, a stubborn pagan, an enemy of his church and a priest-killer, yet now I was showing him a Christian chapel inside my fortress and talking to him of Christian priests. He stared at me, then at Eadith, and had nothing to say.

I rarely carried Serpent-Breath when I was inside

Bebbanburg, but I had Wasp-Sting at my hip and now I drew the short-sword, turned her so that the hilt was toward Wistan, then slid the blade across the flagstones. "Your god says you must kill me. Why don't you?"

"Lord . . ." he said, then had nothing more to say.

"You told me you were sent to rid the world of my wickedness," I pointed out. "You know they call me Uhtredærwe?"

"Yes, lord," he said, scarce above a whisper.

"Uhtred the priest-killer?"

He nodded. "Yes, lord."

"I have killed priests," I said, "and monks."

"Not on purpose," Eadith put in.

"Sometimes on purpose," I said, "but usually in anger." I shrugged. "Tell me what else you know about me."

Wistan hesitated, then found his courage. "You are a pagan, lord, and a warlord. You are friends with the heathen, you encourage them!" He hesitated again.

"Go on," I said.

"Men say you want Æthelstan to be king in Wessex because you have bewitched him. That you will use him to take the throne for yourself!"

"Is that all?" I asked, amused.

He had not been looking at me, but now raised his eyes to gaze into mine. "They say you killed Æthelhelm the Elder and that you forced his daughter to marry your son. That she was raped! Here, in your fortress." He had anger on his face and tears in his eyes and, for a heartbeat, I thought he would snatch up Wasp-Sting.

Then Eadith laughed. She said nothing, just laughed, and her apparent amusement puzzled Wistan. Eadith was looking quizzically at me, and I nodded. She knew what the nod meant and so went into the windswept night. The candles fluttered wildly as she opened and closed the door, but they stayed lit. They were the only illumination in the small chapel, so Wistan and I spoke in near darkness. "It's a rare day when there's no wind," I said mildly. "Wind and rain, rain and wind, Bebbanburg's weather."

He said nothing.

"Tell me," I said, still sitting beside the chapel wall, "how did I kill Ealdorman Æthelhelm?"

"How would I know, lord?"

"How do men in Wessex say that he died?" He did not answer. "You are from Wessex?"

"Yes, lord," he muttered.

"Then tell me what men in Wessex say about Ealdorman Æthelhelm's death."

"They say he was poisoned, lord."

I half smiled. "By a pagan sorcerer?"

He shrugged. "You would know, lord, not me."

"Then, Wistan of Wessex," I went on, "let me tell you what I do know. I did not kill Ealdorman Æthelhelm. He died of the fever despite all the care we gave him. He received the last rites of your church. His daughter was with him when he died, and she was neither raped nor forced into marriage with my son."

He said nothing. The light of the big candles flickered their reflection from Wasp-Sting's blade. The night wind rattled the chapel door and sighed about the roof. "Tell me what you know of Prince Æthelstan," I said.

"That he is a bastard," Wistan said, "and would take the throne from Ælfweard."

"Ælfweard," I said, "who is nephew to the present Ealdorman Æthelhelm, and is King Edward's second oldest son. Does Edward still live?"

"Praise God, yes."

"And Ælfweard is his second son, yet you claim he should be king after his father."

"He is the ætheling, lord."

"The eldest son is the ætheling," I pointed out.

"And in the eyes of God the king's eldest son is Ælfweard," Wistan insisted, "because Æthelstan is a bastard."

"A bastard," I repeated.

"Yes, lord," he said stubbornly.

"Tomorrow," I said, "I'll introduce you to Father Cuthbert. You'll like him! I keep him safe in this fortress, do you know why?" Wistan shook his head. "Because many years ago," I went on, "Father Cuthbert was foolish enough to marry the young Prince Edward to a pretty Centish girl, the daughter of a bishop. That girl died in childbirth, but she left twin children, Eadgyth and Æthelstan. I say Father Cuthbert was foolish because Edward did not have his father's permission to marry, but nevertheless the marriage was consecrated by a Christian priest in a Christian church. And those who would deny Æthelstan his true inheritance have been trying to silence Father Cuthbert ever since. They would kill him, Wistan, so that the truth is never known, and that is why I keep him safe in this fortress."

"But . . ." he began, and again he had nothing to say. For his whole life, which I guessed was about twenty years, he had been told by everyone in Wessex that Æthelstan was a bastard, and that Ælfweard was the true heir to Edward's throne. He had believed that lie, he had believed that Æthelstan was whelped on a whore, and now I was destroying that belief. He believed me, and he did not want to believe me, and so he said nothing.

"And you believe your god sent you to kill me?" I asked.

He still said nothing. He just gazed at the sword that lay by his feet.

I laughed. "My wife is a Christian, my son is a Christian, my oldest and closest friend is a Christian, and over half my men are Christians. Wouldn't your god have asked one of them to kill me instead of sending you? Why send you all the way from Wessex when there are a hundred or more Christians here who can strike me down?" He neither moved nor spoke. "The fisherman you tortured and killed was also a Christian," I said.

He started at that and shook his head. "I tried to stop that, but Edgar . . ."

His voice tailed away to silence, but I had noted the very slight hesitation before the name Edgar. "Edgar isn't his real name, is it?" I asked. "Who is he?"

But the church door creaked open before he could answer, and Eadith led Ælswyth into the wind-fluttering candlelight. Ælswyth stopped as soon as she entered, she stared at Wistan, and then she smiled with delight.

Ælswyth is my daughter-in-law, the daughter of my enemy, and sister to his son, who hates me as much as his father did. Her father, Æthelhelm the Elder, planned to make her a queen, to exchange her beauty for some throne in Christendom, but my son gained her first and she had lived at Bebbanburg ever since. To look at her was to think that no girl so wan, so pale and thin could survive the harsh winters and brutal winds of Northumbria, let alone the agonies of childbirth, yet Ælswyth had given me two grandsons and she alone in the fortress seemed immune to the aches, sneezes, shivers, and coughs that marked our winter months. She looked frail, but was as strong as steel. Her face, so lovely, lit with joy when she saw Wistan. She had a smile that could melt the heart of a beast, but Wistan did not smile back, instead he just gaped at her as if shocked.

"Æthelwulf!" Ælswyth exclaimed and went toward him with open arms.

"Æthelwulf!" I repeated, amused. The name meant "noble wolf" and the young man who had called himself Wistan might look noble, yet he looked anything but wolflike.

Æthelwulf blushed. He let Ælswyth embrace him, then looked at me sheepishly. "I am Æthelwulf," he admitted, and in a tone that suggested I should recognize the name.

"My brother!" Ælswyth said happily. "My youngest brother!" It was then she saw Wasp-Sting on the stone floor and frowned, looking to me for an explanation.

"Your brother," I said, "was sent to kill me."

"Kill you?" Ælswyth sounded shocked.

"In revenge for the way we treated you," I continued. "Weren't you raped and forced into an unwanted marriage?"

"No!" she protested.

"And all that," I said, "after I had murdered your father."

Ælswyth looked up into her brother's face. "Our father died of the fever!" she said fiercely. "I was with him through the whole illness. And no one raped me, no one forced me to marry. I love this place!"

Poor Æthelwulf. He looked as if the foundations of his life had just been ripped away. He believed Ælswyth of course, how could he not? There was joy on her face and enthusiasm in her voice, while Æthelwulf looked as if he was about to cry.

"Let's go to bed," I said to Eadith, then turned to Ælswyth. "And you two can talk."

"We shall!" Ælswyth said.

"I'll send a servant to show you where you can sleep," I told Æthelwulf, "but you do know you're a prisoner here?"

He nodded. "Yes, lord."

"An honored prisoner," I said, "but if you try to leave the fortress, that will change."

"Yes, lord," he said again.

I picked up Wasp-Sting, patted my prisoner on the shoulder, and went to bed. It had been a long day.

So Æthelhelm the Younger had sent his youngest brother to kill me. He had equipped a fleet, and offered gold to the crew, and placed a rancid priest on the ships to inspire Æthelwulf with righteous anger. Æthelhelm knew it would be next to impossible to kill me while I stayed inside the fortress and knew too that he could not send sufficient men to ambush me on my lands without those men being discovered and slaughtered by Northumbria's warriors, so he had been clever. He had sent men to ambush me at sea.

Æthelwulf was the fleet's leader, but Æthelhelm knew that his brother, though imbued with the family's hatred for me, was not the most ruthless of men, and so he had sent Father Ceolnoth to fill Æthelwulf with holy stupidity, and he had also sent the man they called Edgar. Except that was not his real name. Æthelhelm had wanted no one to know of the fleet's true allegiance, or to connect my death to his orders. He had hoped the blame would be placed on piracy, or on some passing Norse ship, and so he had commanded the leaders to use any name except their own. Æthelwulf had become Wistan, and I learned that Edgar was really Waormund.

I knew Waormund. He was a huge West Saxon, a

brutal man, with a slab face scarred from his right eyebrow to his lower left jaw. I remembered his eyes, dead as stone. In battle Waormund was a man you would want standing beside you because he was capable of terrible violence, but he was also a man who reveled in that savagery. A strong man, even taller than me, and implacable. He was a warrior, and, though you might want his help in a battle, no one but a fool would want Waormund as an enemy. "Why," I asked Æthelwulf the next morning, "was Waormund in your smallest ship?"

"I ordered him into that ship, lord, because I wanted him gone! He's not a Christian."

"He's a pagan?"

"He's a beast. It was Waormund who tortured the captives. I tried to stop him."

"But Father Ceolnoth encouraged him?"

"Yes." Æthelwulf nodded miserably. We were walking on Bebbanburg's seaward ramparts. The sun glittered from an empty sea and a small wind brought the smell of seaweed and salt. "I tried to stop Waormund," Æthelwulf went on, "and he cursed me and he cursed God."

"He cursed your god?" I asked, amused.

Æthelwulf made the sign of the cross. "I said God would not forgive his cruelty, and he said God was far more cruel than man. So I ordered him into *Hælubearn* because I couldn't abide his company."

I walked on a few paces. "I know your brother hates me," I said, "but why send you north to kill me? Why now?"

"Because he knows you swore an oath to kill him," Æthelwulf said, and that answer shocked me. I had indeed sworn that oath, but I had thought it was a secret between Æthelstan and myself, yet Æthelhelm knew of that oath. How? No wonder Æthelhelm wanted me dead before I attempted to fulfill the oath.

My sworn enemy's brother looked at me nervously. "Is it true, lord?"

"Yes," I said, "but not until King Edward dies."

Æthelwulf had flinched when I told him that brutal truth. "But why?" he asked. "Why kill my brother?"

"Did you ask your brother why he wanted to kill me?" I retorted angrily. "Don't answer, I know why. Because he believes I killed your father, and because I'm Uhtredærwe the Pagan, Uhtred the Priest-Killer."

"Yes, lord," he said in a low voice.

"Your brother has tried to kill Æthelstan," I said, "and he's tried to kill me, and you wonder why I want to kill him?" He said nothing to that. "Tell me what happens when Edward dies?" I asked harshly.

"I pray he lives," Æthelwulf said, making the sign

of the cross. "He was in Mercia when I left, lord, but had taken to his bed. The priests visited him."

"To give him the last rites?"

"So they said, lord, but he's recovered before."

"So what happens if he doesn't recover?"

He paused, unwilling to give the answer he knew I did not want to hear. "When he dies, lord," he made the sign of the cross again, "Ælfweard becomes King of Wessex."

"And Ælfweard is your nephew," I said, "and Ælfweard is a sparrow-witted piece of shit, but if he becomes king, your brother thinks he can control him, and he thinks he can rule Wessex through Ælfweard. There's just one problem, isn't there? That Æthelstan's parents really were married, which means Æthelstan is no bastard, so when Edward dies there'll be civil war. Saxon against Saxon, Christian against Christian, Ælfweard against Æthelstan. And long ago I swore an oath to protect Æthelstan. I sometimes wish I hadn't."

He stopped in surprise. "You do, lord?"

"Truly," I said, and explained no further. I drew him on, pacing the long rampart. It was true I had sworn an oath to protect Æthelstan, but increasingly I was not certain that I liked him. He was too pious, too like his grandfather, and, I also knew, too ambitious. There is nothing wrong with ambition. Æthelstan's grandfather, King Alfred, had been a man of ambition, and Æthelstan had inherited his grandfather's dreams, and those dreams meant uniting the kingdoms of Saxon Britain. Wessex had invaded East Anglia, it had swallowed Mercia, and it was no secret that Wessex wished to rule Northumbria, my Northumbria, the last British kingdom where men and women were free to worship as they wished. Æthelstan had sworn never to invade Northumbria while I lived, but how long could that be? No man lives forever, and I was already old, and I feared that by supporting Æthelstan I was condemning my country to the rule of southern kings and their grasping bishops. Yet I had sworn an oath to the man most likely to make that happen.

I am a Northumbrian and Northumbria is my country. My people are Northumbrians, and Northumbrians are a hard, tough people, yet we are a small country. To our north lies Alba, full of ambitious Scots who raid us, revile us, and want our land. To the west lies Ireland, home to Norsemen who are never satisfied with the land they have, and always want more. The Danes are restless across the eastern sea, and they have never relinquished their claim to my land where so many Danes have already settled. So to the east, to the west, and to the north we have enemies, and we are a small country. And to the south are Saxons, folk who speak our language, and they too want Northumbria.

Alfred had always believed that all the folk who speak the English language should live in the same country, a country he dreamed of, a country called Englaland. And fate, that bitch who controls our lives, had meant I had fought for Alfred and his dream. I had killed Danes, I had killed Norsemen, and every death, every stroke of the sword, had extended the rule of the Saxons. Northumbria, I knew, could not survive. She was too small. The Scots wanted the land, but the Scots had other enemies; they were fighting the Norsemen of Strath Clota and of the Isles, and those enemies distracted King Constantin. The Norse of Ireland were fearsome, but could rarely agree on one leader, though that did not stop their dragon-headed ships crossing the Irish Sea bringing warriors to settle on Northumbria's wild western coast. The Danes were more cautious about Britain now, the Saxons had become too strong, and so the Danish boats went farther south in search of easier prey. And the Saxons were getting stronger. So one day, I knew, Northumbria would fall, and it was likely, in my judgment, to fall to the Saxons. I did not want that, but to fight against it was to draw a sword against fate, and if that fate was inevitable, and I believed it was, then it was better that Æthelstan should inherit Wessex. Ælfweard was my enemy. His family hated me, and if he took Northumbria he would bring the whole might of Saxon Britain against Bebbanburg. Æthelstan had sworn to protect me, as I had sworn to protect him.

"He's using you!" Eadith had told me bitterly when I confessed to her that I had sworn to kill Æthelhelm the Younger on King Edward's death.

"Æthelstan is?"

"Of course! And why are you helping him? He's not your friend."

"I like him well enough."

"But does he like you?" she had demanded.

"I swore an oath to protect him."

"Men and oaths! You think Æthelstan will keep his oath? You believe he won't invade Northumbria?"

"Not while I live."

"He's a fox!" Eadith had said. "He's ambitious! He wants to be King of Wessex, King of Mercia, King of East Anglia, king of everything! And he doesn't care who or what he destroys to get what he wants. Of course he'll break his oath! He never married!"

I stared at her. "What has that to do with it?"

She had looked frustrated. "He has no love!" she had insisted and looked puzzled by my lack of understanding. "His mother died giving birth to him." She made the sign of the cross. "Everyone knows the devil marks those babies!"

"My mother died giving birth to me," I retorted.

"You're different," she had said. "I don't trust him. And you should stay here when Edward dies!" That had been her final word, spoken bitterly. Eadith was a strong, clever woman, and only a fool ignores such a woman's advice, yet her anger aroused a fury in me. I knew she was right, but I was stubborn, and her resentment only made me more determined to keep the oath.

Finan had agreed with Eadith. "If you go south I'll come with you," the Irishman had told me, "but we shouldn't be going."

"You want Æthelhelm to live?"

"I'd like to poke his eyeballs out by shoving Soul-Stealer up his rotten arse," Finan had said, speaking of his sword. "But I'd rather leave that pleasure to Æthelstan."

"I swore an oath."

"You're my lord," he had said, "but you're still a bloody fool. When do we leave?"

"As soon as we hear of Edward's death."

For a year I had been expecting one of Æthelstan's warriors to come from the south bringing news of a king's death, but three days after I had first spoken with Æthelwulf a priest came instead. He found me in Bebbanburg's harbor where *Spearhafoc*, newly repaired, was being launched. It was a hot day and I was stripped to the waist, helping the men who pushed the sleek hull down the beach. At first the priest did not believe I was Lord Uhtred, but Æthelwulf, who was with me and who was dressed as a nobleman, assured him I was indeed the ealdorman.

King Edward, the priest told me, still lived, "God be praised," he added. The priest was young, tired, and saddle sore. His horse was a fine mare, but like the rider she was dusty, sweat-soaked, and bone weary. The priest had ridden hard.

"You rode all this way to tell me the king still lives?" I asked harshly.

"No, lord, I rode to bring you a message."

I heard his message, and next day, at dawn, I went south.

I left Bebbanburg with just five men for company. Finan, of course, was one, while the other four were all good warriors, sword-skilled and loyal. I left the priest who had brought me the message in Bebbanburg and told my son, who had returned from the hills and was to command the garrison while I was away, to guard him well. I did not want the priest's news spreading.

I also gave my son instructions to keep Æthelwulf as an honored prisoner. "He might be an innocent fool," I said, "but I still don't want him riding south to warn his brother that I'm coming."

"His brother will know anyway," Finan had said drily. "He already knows you're sworn to kill him!"

And that, I thought as I pounded the long road to Eoferwic, was strange. Æthelstan and I had sworn oaths to each other and agreed to keep those oaths secret. I had broken that agreement by telling Eadith, Finan, my son, and his wife, but I trusted all of them to keep the secret. So if Æthelhelm knew, then Æthelstan must have told someone, who, in turn, had told Æthelhelm of the threat, and that suggested there were spies in Æthelstan's employment. That was no surprise, indeed I would have been astonished if Æthelhelm did not have men reporting to him from Mercia, but it did mean my enemy was forewarned of the threat I posed.

There was one last person I needed to tell of my oath, and I knew he would not be happy. I was right. He was furious.

Sigtryggr had been my son-in-law and was now King of Northumbria. He was a Norseman, and he owed his throne to me, which meant, I thought ruefully, that I was to Sigtryggr what Æthelhelm was to Edward. I was his most powerful noble, the one man he must either placate or kill, but he was also my friend, though when I met him in the old Roman palace of Eoferwic he fell into a rage. "You promised to kill Æthelhelm?" he snarled at me.

"I took an oath."

"Why!" It was not a question. "To protect Æthelstan?"

"I took an oath to protect him. I took that oath years—"

"And he wants you to go south again!" Sigtryggr interrupted me. "To save Wessex from its own chaos! To save Wessex! That's what you did last year! You saved that bastard Æthelstan. We needed him dead! But no, you had to save the miserable arsehole's life! You won't go, I forbid it."

"Æthelstan," I pointed out, "is your brother-in-law."

Sigtryggr uttered one word to that, then kicked a table. A Roman jug of blue glass fell and shattered, causing one of his wolfhounds to whine. He pointed a finger at me. "You must not go. I forbid it!"

"Do you break your oaths, lord King?" I asked.

He snarled again, paced angrily on the tiled floor, then turned on me again. "When Edward dies," he said, "the Saxons will start fighting among themselves. True?"

"Probably true," I said.

"Then let them fight!" Sigtryggr said. "Pray that the bastards kill each other! It's none of our business. While they're fighting each other they can't fight us!"

"And if Ælfweard wins," I pointed out, "he will attack us anyway."

"You think Æthelstan won't? You think he won't lead an army across our frontier?"

"He promised not to. Not while I live."

"And that can't be long," Sigtryggr said, making it sound like a threat.

"And you're married to his twin sister," I retorted.

"You think that will stop him?" Sigtryggr glared at me. He had first been married to my daughter, who had died defending Eoferwic, and after her death King Edward had forced the marriage between Sigtryggr and Eadgyth, threatening invasion if Sigtryggr refused, and Sigtryggr, assailed by other enemies, accepted. Edward claimed the marriage was a symbol of peace between the Saxon kingdoms and Norse-ruled Northumbria, but only a fool did not recognize that the real reason for the marriage was to place a Saxon Christian queen in what was enemy country. If Sigtryggr died then his son, my grandson, would be too young to rule, and the Danes and Norse would never accept the pious Eadgyth as their ruler, and in her stead they would place one of their own on Northumbria's throne and thus give the Saxon kingdoms a reason to invade. They would claim they came to restore Eadgyth to her proper place, and so Northumbria, my country, would be swallowed by Wessex.

And all that was true. Yet still I would travel south.

I took an oath, not just to Æthelstan, but to Æthelflaed, who had been King Alfred's daughter and once my lover. I swore to protect Æthelstan and I swore to kill his enemies when Edward died. And if a man breaks an oath he has no honor. We might have much in this life. We might be born to wealth, to land, to success, and I had been given all those things, but when we die we go to the afterlife with nothing except reputation, and a man without honor has no reputation. I would keep my oath.

"How many men are you taking?" Sigtryggr asked me.

"Just forty."

"Just forty!" he echoed scornfully. "And what if Constantin of Scotland invades?"

"He won't. He's too busy fighting Owain of Strath Clota."

"And the Norse in the west?" he demanded.

"We defeated them last year."

"And they have new leaders, there are more ships arriving!"

"Then we'll defeat them next year," I said.

He sat again, and two of his wolfhounds came to be petted. "My younger brother came from Ireland," he said.

"Brother?" I asked. I had known Sigtryggr had a brother, but he had rarely been mentioned and I had thought he had stayed in Ireland.

"Guthfrith," he said the name sourly. "He expects me to clothe and feed him."

I looked around the big chamber where men watched us. "He's here?"

"Probably in a whorehouse. You're going south then?" he asked grumpily. He looked old, I thought, yet he was younger than me. His once handsome face with its missing eye was creased, his hair was gray and lank, his beard thin. I had not seen his new queen in the palace, reports said that she spent much of her time in a convent she had established in the city. She had given Sigtryggr no child.

"We're going south," I confirmed.

"Where the worst of the trouble comes from. But don't travel through Lindcolne," he sounded unhappy.

"No?"

"There's a report of the plague there."

Finan, standing beside me, crossed himself. "I'll avoid Lindcolne," I said, raising my voice slightly. There were a dozen servants and household warriors within earshot and I wanted them to hear what I said. "We'll take the western road through Mameceaster."

"Then come back soon," Sigtryggr said, "and come back alive."

He meant that, he just didn't sound as if he meant it. We left next day.

I had no intention of going south by any road, but I had wanted any listeners in Sigtryggr's court to repeat my words. Æthelhelm had his spies in Sigtryggr's court, and I wanted him watching the Roman roads that led south from Northumbria to Wessex.

I had ridden to Eoferwic, knowing it was my duty to speak with Sigtryggr, but while we rode, Berg had taken *Spearhafoc* down the coast to a small harbor on the Humbre's northern bank where he would be waiting for us.

Early on the morning after my meeting with Sigtryggr, and feeling sour with the ale and wine of the night before, I led my five men out of the city. We rode south, but once out of sight of Eoferwic's ramparts we turned eastward and that evening we found *Spearha-*

foc, manned by a crew of forty, riding at anchor on a falling tide. Next morning I sent six men to take our horses back to Bebbanburg while the rest of us took *Spearhafoc* to sea.

Æthelhelm would hear that we had been in Eoferwic and would be told that we had left the city by the southern gate. He would probably assume I was heading for Mercia to join Æthelstan, but he would be puzzled that I traveled with only five companions. I wanted him to be nervous and to be watching all the wrong places.

In the meantime I had told no one, not Eadith, not my son, not even Finan, what we were doing. Eadith and Finan had expected me to travel south on the news of Edward's death, but, though the king still lived, I had left in a hurry. "What did that priest tell you?" Finan asked as *Spearhafoc* coasted south under the summer wind.

"He told me that I needed to go south."

"And what," Finan asked, "are we doing when we get there?"

"I wish I knew."

He laughed at that. "Forty of us," he said, nodding at *Spearhafoc*'s crowded belly, "invading Wessex?"

"More than forty," I said, then fell silent. I stared at the sun-glossed sea as it slid past *Spearhafoc*'s sleek hull. We could not have wished for a better day. We had a wind to drive us and a sea to carry us, and that sea was rippled by dazzling light, broken only by small frills of foam curling at the wave crests. That weather should have been a good omen, but I was assailed by unease. I had launched this voyage impulsively, seizing what I thought was an opportunity, but now the doubts were nagging me. I touched Thor's hammer hanging at my neck. "The priest," I said to Finan, "brought me a message from Eadgifu."

For a moment he looked puzzled, then recognized the name. "Lavender tits!"

I half smiled, remembering that I had once told Finan that Eadgifu's breasts smelled of lavender. Eadith had told me that many women infused lavender into lanolin and smeared it on their cleavage. "Eadgifu has tits that smell like lavender," I confirmed to Finan, "and she asks for our help."

Finan stared at me. "Christ on his cross!" he finally said. "What in God's name are we doing?"

"Going to find Eadgifu, of course," I said.

He still stared at me. "Why us?"

"Who else can she ask?"

"Anyone!"

I shook my head. "She'll have a few friends in Wessex, none in Mercia or East Anglia. She's desperate."

But why ask for your help?"

"Because she knows I'm the enemy of her enemy."

"Æthelhelm."

"Who hates her," I said.

That hatred was easy to understand. Edward had met Eadgifu while he was still married to Æfflaed, Æthelhelm's sister and Ælfweard's mother. The new, younger and prettier woman had won that rivalry, usurping Æfflaed's place in the king's bed and even persuading Edward to name her as Queen of Mercia. To make Æthelhelm's hatred even more intense she had given Edward two more sons, Edmund and Eadred. Both boys were infants, yet the eldest, Edmund, had a claim on the throne if, so some believed, Æthelstan was illegitimate, and, as many realized, Ælfweard was simply too stupid, cruel, and unreliable to be the next king. Æthelhelm understood that danger to his nephew's future, which was why Eadgifu, in her desperation, had sent the priest to Bebbanburg.

"She knows what Æthelhelm is planning for her," I told Finan.

"She knows?"

"She has spies, just as he does, and she was told that as soon as Edward dies Æthelhelm plans to carry her off to Wiltunscir. She's to be placed in a nunnery and her two boys are to be raised in Æthelhelm's household."

Finan gazed across the summer sea. "Meaning," he said slowly, "that both boys will have their throats slit."

"Or else die of a convenient illness, yes."

"So what are we going to do? Rescue her?"

"Rescue her," I agreed.

"But, Christ! She's protected by the king's household troops! And Æthelhelm will be watching her like a hawk."

"She's already rescued herself," I said. "She and her children went to Cent. She told her husband she was going to pray for him at the shrine of Saint Bertha, but in truth she wants to raise troops who'll protect her and the boys."

"Dear God." Finan looked appalled. "And men will follow her?"

"Why not? Remember that her father was Sigehelm." Sigehelm had been the ealdorman of Cent until he was killed fighting the Danes in East Anglia. He had been wealthy, though nothing like as rich as Æthelhelm, and Sigehelm's son, Sigulf, had inherited that wealth along with his father's household warriors. "Sigulf probably has three hundred men," I said.

"And Æthelhelm has double that, at least! And he'll have the king's warriors too!"

"And those warriors will be watching Æthelstan in Mercia," I said. "Besides, if Eadgifu and her brother

march against Æthelhelm then others will follow them."
That, I thought, was a slender hope, but not an impossible one.

Finan frowned at me. "I thought your oath was to Æthelstan. Now it's to Lavender Tits?"

"My oath is to Æthelstan," I said.

"But Eadgifu will expect you to make her son the next king!"

"Edmund is too young," I said firmly. "He's an infant. The Witan will never appoint him king, not till he's of age."

"By which time," Finan pointed out, "Æthelstan will be on the throne with sons of his own!"

"I'll be dead by then," I said, and touched the hammer again.

Finan gave a mirthless laugh. "So we're sailing to join a Centish rebellion?"

"To lead it. It's my best chance to kill Æthelhelm."

"Why not join Æthelstan in Mercia?"

"Because if the West Saxons hear that Æthelstan is using Northumbrian troops they'll regard that as a declaration of war by Sigtryggr."

"That won't matter if Æthelstan wins!"

"But he has fewer men than Æthelhelm, he has less money than Æthelhelm. The best way to help him win is to kill Æthelhelm." Far to the east a speck of sail showed. I had been watching it for some time, but saw now that the distant ship was traveling northward and would come nowhere near us.

"Damn your oaths," Finan said mildly.

"I agree. But remember, Æthelhelm has tried to kill me. So oath or no oath I owe him a death."

Finan nodded because that explanation made sense to him even if he did believe we were on a voyage to madness. "And his nephew? What of him?"

"We'll kill Ælfweard too."

"You swore an oath to kill him too?" Finan asked.

"No," I admitted, but then touched my hammer once more. "But I swear one now. I'll kill that little earsling along with his uncle."

Finan grinned. "One ship's crew, eh? Forty of us! Forty men to kill the King of Wessex and his most powerful ealdorman?"

"Forty men," I said, "and the troops of Cent."

Finan laughed. "I sometimes think you're moon-crazed, lord," he said, "but, God knows, you've not lost yet."

We spent the next two nights sheltering in East Anglian rivers. We saw no one, just a landscape of reeds. On the second night the wind freshened in the darkness and the sky, which had been clear all day, clouded over to hide the stars, while far off to the west I saw lightning flicker and heard Thor's growl in the night. *Spearhafoc*, even though she was tied securely in a safe haven, shivered under the wind's assault. Rain spattered on the deck, the wind gusted, and the rain fell harder. Few of us slept.

The dawn brought low clouds, drenching rain, and a hard wind, but I judged it safe enough to turn the ship and let the wind carry us downriver. We half-hoisted the sail, and *Spearhafoc* leaped ahead like a wolfhound loosed from the leash. The rain drove from astern, heavy and slanting in the wind's grip. The steering-oar bent and groaned and I called on Gerbruht, the big Frisian, to help me. *Spearhafoc* was defying the flooding tide, racing past mudbanks and reeds, then at last we were clear of the shoals at the river's mouth and could turn southward. The ship bent alarmingly to the wind and I released the larboard sheet and still she drove on, shattering water at the bows. This, I thought, was madness. Impatience had driven me to sea when any sensible seaman would have stayed in shelter. "Where are we going, lord?" Gerbruht shouted.

"Across the estuary of the Temes!"

The wind rose. Thunder hammered to the west. This coast was shallow, shortening the waves that shattered against our hull and drenched the rain-sodden crew with spray. Men clung to the benches as they bailed water. They were praying. I was praying. They were praying to survive, while I was asking the gods to forgive my stupidity in thinking a ship could survive this wind's anger. It was dark, the sun utterly hidden by the roiling clouds, and we saw no other ships. Sailors were letting the storm blow over, but we hammered on southward across the wide mouth of the Temes.

The estuary's southern shore appeared as a sullen stretch of sand pounded by foam beyond which were dark woods on low hills. The thunder came closer. The sky above distant Lundene was black as night, sometimes split by a jagged stab of lightning. The rain teemed down, and I searched the shore for a landmark, any landmark that I might recognize. The steering-oar, taking all my and Gerbruht's strength, quivered like a live thing.

"There!" I shouted at Gerbruht, pointing. I had seen the island ahead, an island of reeds and mud, and to its left was the wide, wind-whipped entrance to the Swalwan Creek. *Spearhafoc* pounded on, clawing her way toward the creek's safety. "I had a ship called *Middelniht* once!" I bellowed to Gerbruht.

"Lord?" he asked, puzzled.

"She'd been stranded on that island," I shouted, "on

Sceapig! And the *Middelniht* proved to be a good ship! A Frisian ship! It's a good omen!"

He grinned. Water was dripping from his beard. "I hope so, lord!" He did not sound confident.

"It's a good omen, Gerbruht! Trust me, we'll be in calmer water soon!"

We plunged on, the ship's hull shaking with every wave that pounded her, but at last we cleared the island's western tip where marker withies were being bent flat by the gale, and once in the creek the seas calmed to a vicious chop and we dropped the sodden sail and our oars took us into the wide channel that ran between the Isle of Sceapig and the Centish mainland. I could see farmsteads on Sceapig, the smoke from their roof-holes being whipped eastward on the wind. The channel narrowed. The wind and rain still beat down on us, but the water was sheltered here and the creek's banks had tamed the ship-killing waves. We went slowly, the oars rising and falling, and I thought how the dragon-boats must have crept down this waterway bringing savage men to plunder the rich fields and towns of Cent, and how the villagers must have been terrified as the serpent-headed war boats appeared from the river mists. I have never forgotten Father Beocca, my childhood tutor, clasping his hands and praying nightly: "From the fury of the Northmen, good Lord, deliver us." Now I, a northerner, was bringing swords, spears, and shields to Cent.

The priest who had brought me Eadgifu's message said that though she had announced her pious intention of praying at Saint Bertha's tomb in Contwaraburg, in truth she had taken refuge in a small town called Fæfresham where she had endowed a convent. "The queen will be safe there," the priest had told me.

"Safe! Protected by nuns?"

"And by God, lord," he had reproved me, "the queen is protected by God."

"But why didn't she go to Contwaraburg?" I had asked him. Contwaraburg was a considerable town, had a stout wall, and, I assumed, men to defend it.

"Contwaraburg is inland, lord." The priest had meant that if Eadgifu was threatened by failure, if Æthelhelm discovered her and sent troops, then she wanted to be in a place where she could escape by sea. From where she could cross to Frankia, and Fæfresham was very close to a harbor on the Swalwan Creek. It was, I supposed, a prudent choice.

We rowed west and I saw the masts of a half-dozen ships showing above the sodden thatch of a small village on the creek's southern bank. The village, I knew, was called Ora and lay a short distance north of Fæfresham. I had sailed this coast with its wide marshes, tide-swamped mudbanks, and hidden creeks often enough, I had fought Danes on its shores and had buried good men in its inland pastures.

"Into the harbor," I told Gerbruht and we turned *Spearhafoc*, and my weary crew rowed her into Ora's shallow harbor. It was a bedraggled, poor excuse for a harbor with rotting wharves on either side of a tidal creek. On the western bank, where the wharves showed signs of being in repair, there were four tubby merchant ships, big- bellied and squat, whose normal duties were to carry food and fodder upriver to Lundene. The water, though sheltered from the gale, was choppy and white-flecked, slapping irritably against the pilings and against three more ships that were moored at the harbor's southern end. Those ships were long, high-prowed, and sleek. Each had a cross mounted on the bow. Finan saw them and climbed onto the steering platform beside me. "Whose are those?" he asked.

"You tell me," I said, wondering whether they were ships that Eadgifu was keeping in case she had to flee for her life.

"They're fighting ships," Finan said dourly, "but whose?"

"Saxon, for sure," I said. The crosses on the bows told me that.

There were buildings on both banks of the harbor.

Most of them were shacks, presumably storing fisher-men's gear or cargo that awaited shipment, but some of the buildings were larger and had smoke streaming eastward from their roof-holes. One of those, the big-gest, stood at the center of the western wharves and had a barrel hanging as a sign above a wide thatched porch. It was a tavern, I assumed, and then the door beneath the porch opened and two men appeared and stood watching us. I knew then who had brought the three fighting ships into the harbor.

Finan knew too and swore under his breath.

Because the two men wore dull red cloaks, and only one man insisted that his warriors wear matching red cloaks. Æthelhelm the Elder had started the fashion, and his son, my enemy, had continued the tradition.

So Æthelhelm's men had reached this part of Cent before us. "What do we do?" Gerbruht asked.

"What do you think we do?" Finan snarled. "We kill the buggers."

Because when queens call for help, warriors go to war.

Three

We swung *Spearhafoc* against one of the western wharves. The two men still watched from the tavern as we secured her lines, and then as Gerbruht, Folcbald, and I came ashore. Folcbald, like Gerbruht, was a Frisian and, also like Gerbruht, a huge man, strong as any two others.

"You know what to say?" I asked Gerbruht.

"Of course, lord."

"Don't call me lord."

"No, lord."

The rain was slashing into our faces as we walked toward the tavern. All three of us were wearing mail beneath sodden cloaks, but we had neither helmets nor swords, just rough woollen caps and the knives any seaman wears at his belt. I was limping, half supported by Gerbruht. The ground was mud, the rain pouring off the tavern's thatch.

"That's enough! Stop there!" The taller of the two red-cloaked men called as we neared the tavern door. We stopped obediently. The two men were standing under a porch and seemed amused that we were forced to wait in the pelting rain. "And what's your business here?" the taller man demanded.

"We need shelter, lord," Gerbruht said.

"I'm no lord. And ships pay for shelter here," the man said. He was tall, broad-faced, with a thick beard cut short and square. He wore mail beneath his red cloak, had an enameled cross on his chest and a long-sword at his side. He looked confident and capable.

"Of course, master," Gerbruht said humbly. "Do we pay you, master?"

"Of course you pay me, I'm the town reeve. It's three shillings." He held out his hand.

Gerbruht was not my quickest thinker and he just gaped, which was the right response to the outrageous demand. "Three shillings!" I said. "We only pay a shilling in Lundene!"

The man smiled unpleasantly. "Three shillings,

grandpa. Or do you want my men to search your miserable boat and take what we want?"

"Of course not, master," Gerbruht found his voice. "Pay him," he ordered me.

I took the coins from a pouch and held them toward the man. "Bring it to me, you old fool," the man demanded.

"Yes, master," I said and limped through a puddle.

"And who are you?" he demanded, scooping the silver from my palm.

"His father," I said, nodding back toward Gerbruht.

"We're pilgrims from Frisia, master," Gerbruht explained, "and my father seeks the blessing of Saint Gregory's slippers at Contwaraburg."

"I do," I said. I had hidden my hammer amulet beneath my mail, but both my companions were Christians and wore crosses at their necks. The wind was tearing at the tavern's thatch and swinging the barrel sign dangerously. The rain was unrelenting.

"God damn Frisian foreigners," the tall man said suspiciously. "And pilgrims? Since when do pilgrims wear mail?"

"The warmest clothes we have, master," Gerbruht said.

"And there are Danish ships at sea," I added.

The man sneered. "You're too old to fight anyone, grandpa, let alone take on some Danish raider!" He looked back to Gerbruht. "You're looking for holy slippers?" he asked mockingly.

"A touch of Saint Gregory's slippers cures the sick, master," Gerbruht said, "and my father suffers ague in his feet."

"You've brought a lot of pilgrims to cure one old man's feet!" the man said suspiciously, nodding toward *Spearhafoc*.

"They're mostly slaves, master," Gerbruht said, "and some of them we'll sell in Lundene."

The man still stared at *Spearhafoc*, but my crew was either slumped on the benches or huddling under the steering platform, and in the day's dull light and because of the sheeting rain he could not tell whether they were slaves or not. "You're slave-traders?"

"We are," I said.

"Then there's customs duty to pay! How many slaves?"

"Thirty, master," I said.

He paused. I could see he was wondering how much he dared ask. "Fifteen shillings," he finally said, thrusting out a hand. This time I just gaped at him, and he put a hand on his sword hilt. "Fifteen shillings," he said slowly, as if he suspected a Frisian could not understand him, "or we confiscate your cargo."

"Yes, master," I said, and carefully counted fifteen silver shillings and dropped them into his palm.

He grinned, happy to have fooled foreigners. "Got any juicy women in that ship?"

"We sold the last three at Dumnoc, master," I said.

"Pity," he said.

His companion chuckled. "Wait a few days and we might have a couple of young boys to sell you."

"How young?"

"Infants."

"It's none of your business!" The first man interrupted, plainly angered that his companion had mentioned the boys.

"We pay well for small boys," I said. "They can be whipped and trained. A plump docile boy can fetch a good price!" I took a gold coin from my purse and tossed it up and down a couple of times. I was doing my best to imitate Gerbruht's Frisian accent and was evidently successful because neither man seemed to suspect anything. "Young boys," I said, "sell almost as well as young women."

"The boys might or might not be for sale," the first man said grudgingly, "and if you do buy them you'll have to sell them abroad. Can't be sold here." He was eyeing the gold coin that I slipped back into the pouch, making sure it clinked against the other coins.

"Your name, master?" I asked respectfully.

"Wighelm."

"I am Liudulf," I said, using a common Frisian name. "And we seek shelter, nothing more."

"How long are you staying, old man?"

"How far to Contwaraburg?" I asked.

"Ten miles," he said. "A man can walk there in a morning, but it might take you a week. How do you plan to get there? Crawl?" He and his companion laughed.

"I would stay long enough to reach Contwaraburg and then return," I said.

"And we crave shelter, master," Gerbruht added from behind me.

"Use one of the cottages over there," Wighelm said, nodding toward the farther bank of the small harbor, "but make sure your damned slaves stay shackled."

"Of course, master," I said, "and thank you, master. God will bless your kindness."

Wighelm sneered at that, then he and his companion stepped back into the tavern. I had a glimpse of men at tables, then the door was slammed and I heard the bar drop into its brackets.

"Was he the town reeve?" Folcbald asked as we walked back to the ship.

It was not a foolish question. I knew Æthelhelm had land all across southern Britain, and he probably did own parts of Cent, but it was most unlikely that Eadgifu would seek refuge anywhere near one of those estates. "He's a lying bastard is what he is," I said, "and he owes me eighteen shillings."

I assumed Wighelm or one of his men was watching from the tavern as we rowed *Spearhafoc* across the creek and moored against a half-rotted wharf. I made most of my crew shuffle as they left the ship, pretending to be shackled. They grinned at the deception, but the rain was so hard and the day so dark that I doubted anyone would notice the pretense. Most of the crew had to use a store hut for their shelter because there was no room in the small cottage, where a driftwood fire blazed furiously. The cottager, a big man called Kalf, was a fisherman. He and his wife watched sullenly as a dozen of us filled his room. "You were mad to be at sea in this weather," he finally said in broken English.

"The gods preserved us," I answered in Danish.

His face brightened. "You're Danes!"

"Danes, Saxons, Irish, Frisians, Norsemen, and everything in between." I put two shillings on a barrel that was used as their table. I was not surprised to find

Danes here, they had invaded this part of Cent years before and many had stayed, married Centish women, and adopted Christianity. "One of those," I said, nodding at the silver shillings, "is for sheltering us. The other is for opening your mouth."

"My mouth?" he was puzzled.

"To tell me what's happening here," I said as I took Serpent-Breath and my helmet from the big leather bag.

"Happening?" Kalf asked nervously, watching as I buckled the big sword at my waist.

"In the town," I said, nodding southward. Ora and its small harbor lay a short walk from Fæfresham itself, which was built on the higher ground inland. "And those men in red cloaks," I went on, "how many are they?"

"Three crews."

"Ninety men?"

"About that, lord." Kalf had heard Berg address me as "lord."

"Three crews," I repeated. "How many are here?"

"There are twenty-eight men in the tavern, lord," Kalf's wife answered confidently and, when I looked inquiringly at her, she nodded. "I had to cook for the bastards, lord. There are twenty-eight."

Twenty-eight men to guard the ships. Our story of being Frisian slave-traders must have convinced Wig-

helm or else he would surely have tried to stop us landing. Or possibly, knowing his small force could not
fight my much larger crew, he was being cautious,
first by insisting we landed on the creek's far side from
the tavern, and then by sending a messenger south to
Fæfresham. "So the rest of the crews are in Fæfresham?" I asked Kalf.

"We don't know, lord."

"So tell me what you do know."

Two weeks before, he said, at the last full moon,
a ship had come from Lundene carrying a group of
women, a small boy, two babies, and a half-dozen men.
They had gone to Fæfresham, he knew, and the women
and children had vanished into the convent. Four of
the men had stayed in the town, the other two had pur-
chased horses and ridden away. Then, just three days
ago, the three ships with their red-cloaked crews had
arrived in the harbor, and most of the newcomers had
gone south to the town. "They don't tell us what they're
doing here, lord."

"They're not nice!" the wife put in.

"Nor are we," I said grimly.

I could only guess what had happened, though it was
not hard. Eadgifu's plan had plainly been betrayed and
Æthelhelm had sent men to thwart her. The priest who
came to Bebbanburg had told me that she had endowed

a convent in Fæfresham, and Æthelhelm might well have assumed she would flee there and have sent men to trap her. "Are the women and children still in Fæfresham?" I asked Kalf.

"We haven't heard that they've left," he said uncertainly.

"But you'd have heard if the men in red cloaks had invaded the convent?"

Kalf's wife made the sign of the cross. "We'd have heard that, lord!" she said grimly.

So the king still lived, or at least the news of his death had yet to reach Fæfresham. It was obvious what Æthelhelm's men had come to do in Cent, but they would not dare lay hands on Queen Eadgifu and her sons until they were certain Edward was dead. The king had recovered before, and while he lived he still possessed the power of the throne and there would be trouble if he recovered again and then discovered his wife had been forcibly detained by Æthelhelm's men. Thunder hammered close and the wind seemed to shake the small cottage. "Is there a way to reach Fæfresham," I asked Kalf, "without being seen from the tavern across the water?"

He frowned for a moment. "There's a drainage ditch back yonder." He pointed eastward. "Follow that south, lord, and you'll find reed beds. They'll hide you."

"What about the creek?" I asked. "Do we need to cross it to reach the town?"

"There's a bridge," Kalf's wife said.

"And the bridge might be guarded," I said, though I doubted any guards would be alert in this filthy weather.

"It'll be low tide soon," Kalf assured me, "you can wade it."

"Don't tell me we're going back into this rain," Finan said.

"We're going back into this rain. Thirty of us. You want to stay and guard *Spearhafoc*?"

"I want to watch what you're doing. I like watching crazy people."

"Do we take shields?" Berg asked, more sensibly.

I thought about that. We had to cross the creek, and shields were heavy, and my plan was to turn back once we were on the far bank and rid ourselves of Wighelm and his men. The fight, I thought, would be inside the tavern and I did not intend to give the enemy time to equip themselves for battle. In a small room the large shields would be an encumbrance, not a help. "No shields," I said.

It was madness. Not just to go into the afternoon's storm and wade through a flooding ditch, but to be here at all. It was an easy excuse to say I was trapped by my oath to Æthelstan, but I could have discharged that oath by simply riding with a handful of followers to join Æthelstan's forces in Mercia. Instead I was wading through a mucky ditch, soaked to the skin, cold, deep inside a country that thought me an enemy, and relying on a fickle queen to let me fulfill my oath.

Eadgifu had failed. If what the priest had told me was true she had come south to raise forces from her brother Sigulf, the Ealdorman of Cent, and instead she was inside a convent that was ringed by her enemies. Those enemies would wait until the king died before they seized her, but seize her they would and then arrange for the death of her two young sons. She had claimed to be making a pilgrimage to Contwaraburg, but Æthelhelm, who was staying close to the dying king, had seen through that pretense, he had sent men to find her, and, I suspected, dispatched more men to persuade Sigulf that any attempt to support his sister would be met with overwhelming force. So Æthelhelm had won.

Except Æthelhelm did not know I was in Cent. That was a small advantage.

The ditch led south. For a time we waded with the water up to our waists, well hidden from Ora by the thick reeds. I tripped twice on eel traps and cursed the weather, but after a half mile or so the ditch bent east to skirt higher ground and we could clamber from the mucky water and cross a soggy pasture only to see the creek in front of us. The track from the harbor to Fæfresham lay beyond the creek. No one moved there. To my left was Fæfresham, hidden behind wind-tossed trees and sheeting rain, and to my right the harbor, still hidden by the small swell of land we had just crossed.

Kalf had said the creek could be waded at low tide, which was soon, but the rain was flooding from a dozen ditches, and the creek's water was running fast and high. Lightning split the dark clouds ahead of us and the thunder crashed across the low clouds. "I hope that's a sign from your god," Finan grumbled. "How in hell do we cross that?"

"Lord!" Berg called from my left. "A fish trap!" He was pointing upstream where water churned and foamed around willow stakes.

"That's how we cross," I told Finan.

It was hard, it was wet, and it was treacherous. The willow stakes with their netting were not made to support a man, but they gave us a tenuous safety as we struggled through the creek. At its deepest the water came to my chest and tried to drag me under. I stumbled in the creek's center and would have gone underwater if it had not been for Folcbald hauling me upright. I was grateful none of us was carrying a heavy iron-rimmed shield. The wind screeched. It was already late in the day, the hidden sun was sinking, the rain was in our faces, the thunder was crashing above, and we crawled out of the water, sodden and chilled. "We go that way." I pointed right, northward.

The first thing to do was to retrieve eighteen shillings and to destroy the ship guards in Ora's tavern. We were between those men and Fæfresham now. It was possible that Wighelm had warned the larger force in the town of our arrival and that his few men would be reinforced, but I doubted it. Weather like this persuaded men to stay near the hearth, so perhaps Thor was on my side. I had no sooner thought that than a deafening clap of thunder sounded and the skies were ripped by jagged light. "We'll be warm soon," I promised my men.

It was a short walk to the harbor. The track was raised on an embankment and floodwaters lapped at the sides. "I need prisoners," I said.

I half drew Serpent-Breath then let her fall back into her fleece-lined scabbard. "You know what this storm means?" Finan had to shout to make himself heard above the wind's noise and the pelting rain.

"That Thor is on our side!"

"It means the king has died!"

I stepped over a flooded rut. "There was no storm when Alfred died."

"Edward is dead!" Finan insisted. "He must have died yesterday!"

"We'll find out," I said, unconvinced.

And then we were in the outskirts of the village, the street lined by small hovels. The tavern was in front of us. It had sheds at the back, probably stables or storage. The wind streamed the hearth-smoke eastward from the tavern's roof. "Folcbald," I said, "you keep two men with you and stop anyone escaping." Kalf had told me the tavern had only two doors, a front and a back, but men could easily escape through the shuttered windows. Folcbald's task was to stop any fugitive from reaching Fæfresham. I could see the masts of Æthelhelm's three ships swaying in the wind above the roof. My plan was simple enough, to burst in through the tavern's back door and overwhelm the men inside, who, I assumed, would be huddled as close to the flaming hearth as possible.

We were about fifty paces from the tavern's back door when a man came outside. He hunched against the rain, hurried to a shed, struggled with the latched door and, as he pulled it open, turned and saw us. For a heartbeat he just gazed, then he ran back inside. I swore.

I shouted at my men to hurry, but we were so cold, so drenched, that we could manage little more than a fast, stumbling walk, and Wighelm's men, warm and dry, reacted swiftly. Four men appeared first, each carrying a shield and spear. More men followed, no doubt cursing that they were forced into the storm, but all carrying shields that showed the dark outline of a leaping stag, Æthelhelm's symbol. I had planned a bloody tavern brawl, and instead the enemy was making a shield wall between the sheds. They faced us with leveled spears, and we had none. They were protected by shields, and we had none.

We stopped. Despite the seething rain and the howl of the wind I could hear the clatter of iron-rimmed shields touching each other. I could see Wighelm, tall and black-bearded, at the center of the wall that was just thirty paces away.

"Wolf trap!" I said, then swerved to my right, beckoning my men to follow, and hurried between two hovels. Once out of sight of Wighelm and his spearmen I turned back the way we had come. We broke down a rough driftwood fence, skirted a dung heap, and filed into another narrow alley between two of the cottages. Once hidden in the alley I held up a hand.

We stopped and none of my men made a noise. A dog howled nearby and a baby cried from inside a hovel. We drew our swords. Waited. I was proud of my men. They knew what I meant by a wolf trap and not one had questioned me or asked what we were doing. They knew because we had trained for this. Wars are not only won on the battlefield, but in the practice yard of fortresses.

Wolves are the enemies of shepherds. Dogs are their friends, but shepherds' dogs rarely kill a wolf, though they might frighten them away. We hunt wolves in Northumbria's hills and our wolfhounds will kill, yet the wolves are never defeated. They come back, they prey on flocks, they leave bloody carcasses strewn on the grass. I offer a bounty to folk who bring in a fresh, stinking wolf pelt, and I pay the bounty often, yet still the wolves ravage livestock. They can be deterred, they can be hunted, yet wolves are a cunning and subtle enemy. I have known flocks to be regularly attacked, and we have beaten the surrounding woods and hills, ridden with our sharpened wolf spears, sent the hounds searching, and found no trace of a wolf, and next day another dozen sheep or lambs are ripped apart. When that happens we might set a wolf trap, which means that instead of searching for the wolves, we invite them to search for us.

My father liked to use an old ram for the trap. We would tether the beast close to where the wolf pack had made its last kill, then wait in ambush upwind of the bait. I preferred to use a pig, which was more expensive than an aging ram, but more effective too. The pig would squeal in protest at being tethered, a sound that seemed to attract wolves, and squeal even louder when a wolf appeared. Then we would release the hounds, lower spears, and spur to the kill. We lost the pig as often as not, but we killed the wolf.

I had few doubts that my men were better fighters than Wighelm's troops, but to ask men to attack a shield wall without shields of their own, and without axes to haul down an enemy's shield or spears to pierce the gaps between the enemy's shields, is to invite death. We would win, but at a cost I was not willing to pay. I needed to break Wighelm's shield wall and do it without leaving a couple of my men gutted by his spears. So we waited.

I had made a mistake. I had assumed Wighelm's men would be sheltering from the storm, and that we could approach the tavern unseen. I should have crept behind the cottages until we were closer, but now I would invite Wighelm to make a mistake. Curiosity would be his undoing, or so I hoped. He had seen us approaching, he had made his shield wall, and then we had vanished into an alley. And we had not reappeared. He would be gazing into the storm, looking past the sheeting rain, wondering if we had retreated southward. He could not ignore us. Just because we had vanished from his sight did not mean we had fled. He needed to know where we were. He needed to know whether we still barred his road to Fæfresham. He waited a long time, nervously hoping we had gone altogether, or hoping he would catch a glimpse that would tell him where we were, but we did not move, we made no noise, we waited.

I beckoned Oswi to my side. He was young, lithe, cunning, and savage. He had once been my servant before growing old enough and skilled enough to join the shield wall. "Sneak up the back of the cottages," I told him, pointing southward, "go as far as you can, show yourself, stare at them, show them your naked arse, and then pretend to run away."

He grinned, turned, and disappeared behind the southern hovel. Finan was lying flat at the street corner, peering toward the tavern through a patch of nettles. Still we waited. The rain was pelting, bouncing in the street, cascading from the roofs, and swirling in the gusting wind. Thunder crackled and faded. I pulled my hammer amulet free, clutched it, closed my eyes briefly and prayed that Thor would preserve me.

"They're coming!" Finan called.

"How?" I needed to know whether Wighelm had stayed in the shield wall or was hurrying to catch us.

"They're running!" Finan called. He wriggled back out of sight, stood and wiped mud from Soul-Stealer's blade. "Or trying to run!"

It seemed that Oswi's insult had worked. Wighelm, if he had possessed an ounce of sense, should have sent two or three men to explore the village, but he had kept his shield wall together and now hurried his men in pursuit of Oswi who, he must have assumed, was running with the rest of us. So Wighelm had broken his own shield wall and now chivvied his men up the street in what he fondly imagined was a pursuit.

And we burst from our alley, screaming a war cry that was as much a protest against the cold and wet as a challenge to the red-cloaked men. They were straggling in the muddy street, miserable because of the weather, and, best of all, scattered. We struck them with the force of the storm itself and Thor must have heard my prayer because he released a sky-splintering hammer of thunder directly over our heads, and I saw a young man turn toward me, terror on his face, and he raised his shield that I hit with my full weight, driving him down into the mud. Someone, I assumed it was Wighelm, was bellowing for the West Saxons to make their shield wall, but it was much too late. Berg passed me as I kicked the youngster's sword arm away and the day's gloom was lit by a bright spray of blood as Berg's savage blade sliced the fallen man's throat. Berg kept running, hamstringing a burly man who was shouting incoherently. The man screamed as Berg's sword sliced through the back of his knees and then shrieked as Gerbruht lunged a sword into his belly.

I was running toward Wighelm who turned his spear toward me. He looked as terrified as his men. I knocked the spear aside with my sword, body-charged his shield, and threw him down into the mud. I kicked his head, stood over him, and held Serpent-Breath at his throat. "Don't move!" I snarled. Finan snatched Wighelm's spear and lunged it left-handed at the shield of a tall man half crouching to meet Folcbald's charge. The spear struck the bottom edge of the shield, tipping it downward, and Finan's fast sword slashed viciously across the man's eyes. Folcbald finished the blinded man with a savage two-handed thrust that pierced mail and ripped up from belly to breastbone. The flooded rut in the street turned red, the rain hammered and splashed pink, and the wind howled over the marshes to drown the agonized sobs.

Berg, usually so lethal in a fight, had slipped in the mud. He fell, sprawling, desperately trying to kick himself away from a red-cloaked spearman who, seeing his chance, raised his spear for the fatal lunge. I hurled Serpent-Breath at the man and the blade, whirling through the rain, struck him on the shoulder. It did no damage, but made him look toward me, and Vidarr Leifson leaped to grab his spear arm then pulled him and turned him, dragging him into Beornoth's sword. Wighelm, seeing I had no weapon, tried to slam his shield against my thigh, but I put a boot on his face and pressed his head into the mud. He began to choke. I kept my boot there, leaned down, and plucked his sword from its scabbard.

I had no need of Wighelm's sword because the fight ended swiftly. Our attack had been so sudden and so savage that Wighelm's miserable, wet men stood no chance. We had killed six of them, wounded four, and the others had thrown down their shields and weapons and were begging for mercy. Three fled into an alley, but Oswi and Berg hunted them down and brought them back to the tavern where we stripped the prisoners of their mail and sat them in a wet, miserable huddle at one end of the biggest room. We fed the hearth with more fuel. I sent Berg and Gerbruht to discover a small boat, then to cross the creek and bring *Spearhafoc* back with the men who had been left to guard her, and Vidarr Leifson and Beornoth were set to watch the road from Fæfresham. Oswi was cleaning Serpent-Breath while Finan was making certain our prisoners were securely tied with sealhide ropes.

I had spared Wighelm's life. I drew him away from the other prisoners and sat him on a bench close to the hearth that was spitting sparks from the driftwood fuel. "Free his hands," I told Finan, then held out my own hand. "Eighteen shillings," I said, "for grandpa." He grudgingly took the coins from his pouch and put them in my palm. "And now the rest," I demanded.

He spat mud from his mouth. "The rest?" he asked.

"The rest of your coins, you fool. Give me all you've got."

He untied the pouch and gave it to me. "Who are you?" he asked.

"I told you, Liudulf of Frisia. Believe that and you're a bigger fool than I already think you are." Thunder sounded loud and the seethe of rain on the roof became stronger. I tipped the coins from Wighelm's pouch onto my hand and gave the money to Finan. "I doubt these bastards have paid the tavern keeper," I said, "so find him and give him this. Then tell him we need food. Not for them," I looked at the prisoners, "but for us." I looked back to Wighelm and drew a short knife from my belt. I smiled at him, and drew the blade across my thumb as if testing the edge. "Now you're going to talk to grandpa," I told him, and laid the flat of the blade on his cheek. He shuddered.

Then he talked and so confirmed much of what I had guessed. Eadgifu's declaration that she was traveling to Contwaraburg to pray at the shrine of Saint Bertha had not deceived Æthelhelm for a moment. Even as the queen and her small entourage traveled south Æthelhelm's men were galloping toward Wiltunscir where they roused a troop of his household warriors. Those men, in turn, went to Lundene where Æthelhelm kept ships that had brought them to this creek on the muddy shore of Cent where, just as Æthelhelm had surmised, Eadgifu had taken shelter. "What are your orders?" I asked Wighelm.

He shrugged. "Stay here, keep her here, wait for more orders."

"Orders that will come when the king dies?"

"I suppose so."

"You weren't told to go to Contwaraburg? To order the queen's brother to stay quiet?"

"Other men went there."

"What other men? Who? And to do what?"

"Dreogan. He took fifty men and I don't know why he went there."

"And Dreogan is?"

"He commands fifty of Lord Æthelhelm's household troops."

"What about Waormund?" I asked.

The mention of that name made Wighelm shudder. He made the sign of the cross. "Waormund went to East Anglia," he said, "but why? I don't know."

"You don't like Waormund?" I asked.

"No one likes Waormund," he replied bitterly, "except perhaps Lord Æthelhelm. Waormund is Lord Æthelhelm's beast."

"I've met the beast," I said bleakly, remembering the huge, vacant-faced warrior who was taller and stronger than any man I had ever met except for Steapa, who was another fearsome West Saxon warrior. Steapa had been a slave, but had become one of King Alfred's most trusted warriors. He had been my enemy too, but had become a friend. "Does Lord Steapa still live?" I asked.

Wighelm looked momentarily confused at the unexpected question, but nodded. "He's old. But he lives."

"Good," I said, "and who is in Fæfresham?"

Again Wighelm looked puzzled by the sudden

change of questioning. "Eadgifu is there . . ." he recovered.

'I know that! Who leads the men there?"

"Eanwulf."

"And how many men does he have?"

"About fifty."

I turned to Immar Hergildson, a young man whose life I had saved and who had served me devotedly ever since. "Tie his hands," I ordered him.

"Yes, lord."

"Lord?" Wighelm repeated the word nervously. "You're a—"

"I'm a lord," I said savagely.

The thunder sounded, but farther away now, carrying Thor's anger out to the turbulent sea. The wind still shook the tavern, but with less anger than before. "Storm's passing, I reckon." Finan brought me a pot of ale.

"It's passing," I agreed. I pulled a shutter open, making the flames in the hearth flicker. It was almost dark outside. "Send someone to tell Vidarr and Beornoth to come back," I said. There was no chance that men from Eanwulf's troop in Fæfresham would come north in the darkness, so there was no need to watch for them.

"And tomorrow?" Finan asked.

"Tomorrow we rescue a queen," I said.

A queen whose feeble revolt against Æthelhelm had failed. And she was my best hope of keeping the oath to kill Wessex's most powerful lord and his nephew, who, if Finan's premonition that the storm was sent to mark the death of a king, was king already.

And we had come to make certain his reign was brief.

Tomorrow.

The storm blew itself out overnight, leaving fallen trees, sodden thatch, and flooded marshland. The dawn was damp and sullen, as if the weather was ashamed of the previous day's anger. The clouds were high, the creek had settled, and the wind was fitful.

I had to decide what to do with the prisoners. My first thought was to put them in a stout shack on the harbor's western side and leave two men to guard them, but Wighelm's men were young, they were strong, they were bitter, and they would surely find some way to break out of the shack, and the last thing I wanted was to have vengeful warriors following me south to Fæfresham. Nor did I want to leave any men behind, either to guard the prisoners or to protect *Spearhafoc*. If we were to go to Fæfresham then I would need all my men.

"Just kill the bastards," Vidarr Leifson suggested.

"Put them on the island," Finan said, meaning Sceapig.

"And if they can swim?"

He shrugged. "Not many can!"

"A fishing boat might rescue them."

"Then do as Vidarr suggests," Finan said, tired of my doubts.

There was a risk in stranding them, but I could think of no better solution and so we herded them onto *Spearhafoc*, rowed a mile eastward down the Swalwan Creek, and there found an island of reeds that, judging by the line of flotsam heaped on the shore, did not flood at high tide. We stripped the prisoners naked and sent them ashore, making them carry their four wounded men. Wighelm was the last to go. "You can reach Sceapig easily enough," I told him. The island of reeds was only a long bow shot from Sceapig's marshes. "But if you hurt anyone ashore I'll find out and I'll come for you, and when I find you I'll kill you slowly, you understand?"

He nodded sullenly. "Yes, lord." He knew who I was now and he was afraid.

"All these people," I said, gesturing at both Sceapig and the mainland, "are under my protection, and I am Uhtredærwe! Who am I?"

"Uhtred of Bebbanburg, lord," he said fearfully.

"I am Uhtredærwe, and my enemies die. Now go!"

It was midday before we were back in the creek's harbor and another hour before we set off on the southward road. We had eaten a poor meal of fish stew and hard bread, cleaned our mail and weapons, and donned the dark red cloaks that were the marks of Æthelhelm's men. We had captured twenty-four of Æthelhelm's shields, all painted with the leaping stag, and I had given those to my men. The rest of us would go to Fæfresham without shields. My pagans, like me, hid their hammer amulets. Ideally I would have sent a couple of men to scout the town, but streets and alleys are harder to explore unseen than woodlands and hedgerows, and I feared the men might be captured, questioned too harshly, and so reveal our presence. Better, I thought, to arrive at Fæfresham in force, even though that force was only half the enemy's number. I did send Eadric, the most cunning of my scouts, to explore the edge of the town, but ordered him to remain hidden. "Don't be captured!"

"Bastards won't get a smell of me, lord."

The sky cleared as we walked southward. The wind was dying, gusting occasionally to stir our borrowed cloaks. There was warmth in the sun, which glittered off the flooded pastures. We met a small girl, maybe eight or nine years old, driving three cows northward.

She shrank onto the road's side as we passed, looking fearful. "Better weather today!" Beornoth called
cheerfully to her, but she just shivered and kept her
eyes lowered. We passed orchards where trees had
been felled by the storm and one stout trunk had been
split and scorched by lightning. I shivered when I saw
a dead swan, lying with a broken neck in a flooded
ditch. It was not a good omen and I raised my eyes in
hope of seeing a better sign, but saw only the storm's
ragged rear-guard of clouds. A woman was digging in
the garden of a small reed-thatched cottage, but seeing
us she went indoors and I heard the locking bar drop
into place. Was this, I wondered, how folk had behaved
when they saw Roman troops approaching? Or Danes?
Fæfresham was nervous, fearful, a small town caught
again at the crossroads of powerful men's ambitions.

I was nervous too. If Wighelm had told me the truth
then Æthelhelm's men in Fæfresham outnumbered
mine. If they were alert, if they were expecting trouble,
then we would be swiftly overwhelmed. I had thought
to use the captured cloaks and shields as a means of
entering the town unsuspected, but Eadric returned
to tell me that a dozen spearmen were guarding the
road. "They're not lazy buggers either," he said. "Wide
awake, they are."

"Just twelve men?"

"With plenty more to back them up, lord," Eadric said grimly.

We had left the road to hide behind the blackthorn hedge of a rain-soaked pasture. If Eadric was right then an assault on the twelve guards would bring more enemy running and I could find myself in a ragged fight far from the safety of *Spearhafoc*. "Can you get into the town?" I asked Eadric.

He nodded. "Plenty of alleyways, lord." He was a middle-aged Saxon who could move through woodland like a ghost, but he was confident he could get past Æthelhelm's sentries and use his cunning to stay undiscovered in the town. "I'm old, lord," he said, "and they don't look at old men like young ones." He discarded his weapons, stripped off his mail, and, looking like a peasant, slipped through a gap in the blackthorn hedge that sheltered us. We waited. The last clouds were thinning and the sunlight offered welcome warmth. The smoke from Fæfresham's cooking fires drifted upward instead of being flayed sideways by the wind. Eadric did not return for a long time and I had begun to fear he had been captured and Finan feared the same. He sat beside me, fidgeting, then went very still as a band of red-cloaked horsemen appeared to the east. There

. were at least twenty of them and for a moment I thought they might be searching for us and I half drew Serpent-Breath, but then the horsemen turned back toward the town.

"Just exercising the horses," I said, relieved.

"They were good horses too," Finan said, "not cheap country nags."

"I'm sure they have good horses here," I said. "It's good land once you're off the marshes."

"But the bastards came by ship," Finan pointed out. "No one told us they brought horses with them."

"So they took them from the townsfolk."

"Or they've been reinforced," Finan said ominously. "It feels bad, lord. We should go back."

Finan was no coward. I am ashamed even to have thought this. Of course he was no coward! He was among the two or three bravest men I have ever known, a swordsman of lightning speed and deadly skill, but that day he had an instinct of doom. It was a feeling of dread, a certainty based on nothing he could see or hear, but a certainty all the same. He claimed the Irish had a knowledge denied to the rest of us, that they could scent fate, and though he was a Christian I knew he believed the world to be seething with spirits and it seemed those unseen creatures had spoken to him. In

the night he had tried to persuade me to board *Spearhafoc* and sail back north. We were too few, he had
said, and our enemies too numerous. "And I saw you
dead, lord," he had finished, sounding grieved to speak
of such a thing.

"Dead?" I had asked.

"Naked, blood-covered, lord, in a field of barley."
He paused, but I said nothing. "We should go home,
lord."

I was tempted. And Finan's vision or dream had
almost convinced me. I touched my hammer amulet.
"We've come this far," I told him, "but I need to speak
to Eadgifu."

"Why, for God's sake?" We had been sitting on a
bench beside the tavern's hearth. All around us men
snored. The wind still rattled the shutters and fretted
at the reed thatch, and rain still fell through the roof-
hole to hiss in the fire, but the storm had gone out to
sea and only the remnants disturbed the night.

"Because that's what I came to do," I had answered
stubbornly.

"And she was supposed to raise a force of Centish
men?"

"That's what the priest told me."

"And has she?"

I had sighed. "You know the answer as well as I do."

"So tomorrow we go inland?" he asked. "We've no horses. What happens if we get cut off from the harbor?"

I had thought of answering him by saying I needed to fulfill my oath, but of course Finan was right. There were other ways to keep my promise to Æthelstan. I could have joined him in Mercia, but instead I had chosen to believe the priest and had hoped to lead a rebellious band of Centish warriors to attack Æthelhelm from within Wessex. "So I'm a fool," I had said instead to Finan, "but tomorrow we find Eadgifu."

He had heard the resolve in my voice and accepted it. "Amazing what a pair of good-smelling tits will make a man do," he had said, "and you should sleep."

So I had slept, and now I was on the edge of Fæfresham, and Eadric was missing, and my closest friend was feeling doomed. "We'll wait till dusk," I said. "If Eadric hasn't returned, we'll go back to *Spearhafoc*."

"God be praised," Finan said, and no sooner had he made the sign of the cross than Eadric appeared at the hedge.

He brought us a loaf of bread and a lump of cheese. "Cost me a shilling, lord."

"You went into the town?"

"And it's swarming with the buggers, lord. It's not good news. Another sixty men came yesterday just before the storm struck. Came from Lundene, all of them in those silly red cloaks. They came on horseback." I swore and Finan made the sign of the cross. "The lady is still in the convent, lord," Eadric went on. "They've not tried to winkle her out, not yet. No news of the king's death, you see? A shilling, lord."

I gave him two. "How did you find all that out?"

"Saw the priest! Father Rædwulf. Nice man. Gave me a blessing, he did."

"Who did you say you were?"

"Told him the truth, of course! Told him we were trying to rescue the lady."

"And he said?"

"He said he'd pray for us, lord."

So my foolish dreams had ended. Here, in the damp grass behind a thorn hedge, reality had smacked me. The town was crammed with the enemy, we had come too late, and I had failed. "You were right," I told Finan ruefully.

"I'm Irish, lord, of course I was right."

"We'll go back to *Spearhafoc*," I said. "Burn Æthelhelm's three ships in the harbor, then go back north."

My father had once told me to make few oaths. "Oaths will bind you, boy," he had said, "and you're a fool. You were born a fool. You jump before you think. So think before you swear an oath."

I had been a fool again. Finan had been right, Sigtryggr had been right, Eadith had been right, and my
father had been right. I had no business here. The fool's
errand was over.

Except it was not.

Because the horsemen came.

Four

There were thirty-six horsemen, all in mail, all with shields and half of them carrying long spears. They came from the east, circling below the small swell of pasture where we were crouched beside the blackthorn hedge. We had seen them, but they had not yet seen us.

My first instinct was to draw Serpent-Breath, and my first thought was that Æthelhelm's men must have seen Eadric and followed him from the town. My second thought was the realization that we had few shields. Men on foot who lack shields are easy meat for horsemen. My third thought was that these men were not wearing red cloaks and their shields did not show Æthelhelm's badge of the leaping stag. The shields seemed to show some kind of animal, but the paint had faded and I did not recognize the symbol.

Then the leader of the horsemen saw us and held up his hand to check his men. The horses turned toward us, their big hooves churning the wet turf to muddy ruin. "What's on the shields?" I asked Finan.

"Some are showing a bull's head," he answered, "with bloody horns, and the rest are crossed swords."

"Then they're Centishmen," I said, feeling relief, and just then the newcomers saw our shields showing the leaping stag, they saw our dark red cloaks, and their swords slid free of scabbards, their spurs went back, and the spears were lowered.

"Drop your weapons!" I shouted to my men. "Drop the shields!" The big horses were lumbering up the damp slope, spear-points glittering. I ran a few paces toward them, stopped, and rammed Serpent-Breath point first into the turf. "No fight!" I shouted at the approaching horsemen. I spread my arms to show that I carried no weapons or shield.

The leading horseman curbed his stallion and held his sword aloft to check his men. The horses snorted and scraped at the wet pasture with heavy hooves. I walked on down the gentle slope as the Centish leader nudged his horse toward me. He stopped and pointed his sword toward me. "Are you surrendering, old man?" he asked.

"Who are you?" I demanded.

"The man who'll kill you if you don't surrender." He looked past me toward my men. If it had not been for the silver cross hanging at his neck and for the symbols on his men's shields I might have taken him for a Dane or a Norseman. He wore his black hair very long, cascading to his waist from beneath his fine silver-chased helmet. His mail was polished, while his bridle and saddle were studded with small silver stars. His tall, mud-spattered boots were of the finest leather and carried long silver spurs. His sword, which he still held toward me, had delicate golden decorations on its crosspiece. "Are you surrendering or dying?" he asked.

"I'm asking who are you?" I said harshly.

He looked at me as if I were a piece of dung while he decided whether or not to answer. He finally did, but with a sneer. "My name," he said, "is Awyrgan of Contwaraburg. And you are?"

"I am Uhtred of Bebbanburg," I said, just as arrogantly, and that answer provoked a satisfying reaction. Awyrgan, his name meant "cursed' so I assumed he had chosen the name himself rather than been christened with it, lowered the sword so that it pointed at the wet grass, then just stared at me in astonishment. He saw a bedraggled, gray-bearded, mud-covered warrior in battered mail and with a scarred helmet. I stared at him and saw a handsome young man with dark eyes, a straight long nose, and a clean-shaven chin. I suspected Awyrgan of Contwaraburg had been born to privilege and could not imagine a life without it. "Lord Uhtred of Bebbanburg," I added, stressing the "lord."

"Truly?" he asked, then hastily added, "Lord."

"Truly," I snarled.

"He is Lord Uhtred," an older man said brusquely. He had walked his horse close behind Awyrgan's stallion and now looked down at me with an evident dislike. He, like Awyrgan, wore fine mail, was well horsed, and carried a drawn sword, which, I could see, had a well-worn edge. His close-cut beard was gray and his hard face crossed with two scars, and I assumed he was an old and experienced soldier entrusted to give advice to the younger man. "I fought alongside you in East Anglia, lord," he said to me. He spoke curtly.

"And you are?"

"Swithun Swithunson," he said, still in a distinctly unfriendly tone, "and you, lord, are a long way from home." He had said "lord" with a marked reluctance.

"I was invited here," I said.

"By?" Awyrgan asked.

"The Lady Eadgifu."

"The queen invited you?" Awyrgan sounded astonished.

"I just said so."

There was an awkward silence, then Awyrgan pushed his sword into its long scabbard. "You are indeed welcome, lord," he said. He might be arrogant, but he was no fool. His horse tossed its head and skittered sideways and he calmed it with a gloved hand on its neck. "Any news of the king?"

"None."

"And of the lady?"

"So far as I know," I said, "she's still in the convent and kept there by Æthelhelm's men who now number well over a hundred. What are you hoping to do?"

"Rescue her, of course."

"With thirty-six men?"

Awyrgan smiled. "Ealdorman Sigulf has another hundred and fifty horsemen to the east."

So Eadgifu's brother had answered his sister's call. I had sailed south with the thought of allying myself with the men of Cent to free Wessex of Ælfweard's kingship, but now that I was face to face with two of Cent's leaders my doubts increased. Awyrgan was an arrogant youth and Swithun plainly hated me. Finan had come to join me, standing just a pace behind and to my right. I heard him growl, a signal that he wanted me to abandon this madness, to go back to *Spearhafoc* and so home.

"What happened to Dreogan?" I asked.

"Dreogan?" Awyrgan responded, puzzled.

"One of Lord Æthelhelm's men," I explained, "he led men to Contwaraburg to persuade Ealdorman Sigulf to stay in his bed."

Awyrgan smiled. "Those men! We have their mail, we have their weapons, and we have their horses. I assume Lord Sigulf will have their lives too if they make trouble."

"And Ealdorman Sigulf," I went on, "sent you to do what?"

Awyrgan gestured to the west. "Stop the bastards escaping, lord. We're to block the road to Lundene." He made it sound easy. Perhaps it was.

"Do that then," I said.

Awyrgan was taken aback by my tone, which had been harsh, but he nodded to me and beckoned to his horsemen. "Will you come with us?" he asked.

"You don't need me," I said.

"True, we don't," Swithun growled, then spurred his horse away. The Centish horsemen were keeping to the lower ground, trying to stay hidden from the town, though I suspected they must have been seen already because there was little cover in this low, damp land.

"So do we help them?" Finan demanded.

I still gazed after the horsemen. "It seems a pity," I said, "to come this far and not smell her tits again."

Finan treated that jest with contempt. "They weren't happy to see us. So why help them?"

"Swithun wasn't happy," I agreed, "and I'm not surprised. He remembers us from East Anglia."

Cent had ever been a restless shire. It had once been its own kingdom, but that was far in the past and it was now a part of Wessex, though every now and then there were stirrings of independence, and that ancient pride had driven Sigulf's grandfather to side with the Danes of East Anglia shortly after Edward became king. That alliance had not lasted, I had shamed the Centishmen into fighting for Wessex, but they had never forgotten the disgrace of their near treachery. Now Sigulf was rebelling again, this time to help Edmund, his sister's eldest son, inherit the throne of Wessex.

"If we join their fight," Finan said, "we're fighting for Eadgifu's boys."

I nodded. "True."

"For God's sake, why? I thought you supported Æthelstan!"

"I do."

"Then . . ."

"There are three claimants for the throne of Wessex," I interrupted him. "Ælfweard, Æthelstan, and Edmund. Doesn't it make sense that two of those should join together to defeat the third?"

"And when he's defeated? What happens to the two?"

I shrugged. "Eadgifu's boy is an infant. The Witan will never choose him."

"So now we fight for Eadgifu?"

I paused a long while, then shook my head. "No."

"No?"

For a moment I did not answer. Instead I was thinking of Finan's omen, his vision of my naked corpse in a field of barley, then I remembered the dead swan I had seen lying in the drab ditch with a broken neck. And that, I thought, was an omen if ever there was one, and at that moment I heard the beat of wings and looked skyward to see two swans flying north. Thor had sent me a sign and it could not have been clearer. Go north, go home, go now.

What a fool I was! To think I could lead a Centish rebellion against Wessex? To defeat Æthelhelm with a ragged band of Centishmen and a handful of Northumbrians? It was pride, I thought, mere foolish pride. I was Uhtred of Bebbanburg and one of my poets, one of the men who compose songs for the winter nights in Bebbanburg's hall, always called me Uhtred the Unbeaten. Did I believe him? I had been beaten often enough, though a kindly fate had always given me revenge. But every man knows, or should know, that fate is fickle. "Wyrd bið ful āræd," I told Finan. Fate is inexorable.

"And fate is a bitch too," he said, "but what's our fate now?"

"To avoid all fields of barley," I said lightly.

He did not smile. "Are we going home, lord?"

I nodded. "We're going back to *Spearhafoc*," I said, "and we're going home."

He looked at me almost with disbelief, then made the sign of the cross. "And thank the living Christ for that."

And so we walked back north. Crows or foxes had savaged the swan's corpse, strewing feathers around the exposed ribs, and I touched Thor's hammer and silently thanked the gods for sending me their signs.

"Those dreams," Finan said awkwardly, "they're not always right."

"They're a warning, though."

"Aye, that they are." We walked on. "So what happens to Lavender Tits now?" Finan asked, anxious not to talk any longer about his premonition.

"That's up to her brother. I tried, now he must."

"Fair enough."

"And Awyrgan," I said, "is guarding the wrong road."

"He is?"

"If Æthelhelm's men retreat they'll likely come down this road. Some of them, anyway. They won't want to lose their ships."

"And that pompous little earsling doesn't know they have ships?"

"Apparently not," I said. "And I didn't think to tell him."

"So let the pompous bastard waste his time," Finan said happily.

It was late in the summer afternoon. The sky had cleared, the air had warmed, and sunlight glittered its reflection from the flooded meadows and marshes. "I'm sorry," I said to Finan.

"Sorry?"

"I should have listened to you. To Eadith. To Sigtryggr."

He was embarrassed by my apology. "Oaths," he said after a few paces, "sit hard on a man's conscience."

"They do, but I still should have listened. I'm sorry. We'll take the ship north and then I'll ride south to join Æthelstan in Mercia."

"And I'll come with you," Finan said enthusiastically. He turned to look back the way we had come. "I wonder how Sigulf is doing?" There was no sound of battle from Fæfresham, but we were probably far enough to be out of earshot of the clash of weapons and the screams of the wounded.

"If Sigulf has any sense," I said, "he'll negotiate before he fights."

"Does he have sense?"

"No more than me," I said bitterly. "He doesn't have a reputation, not that I've heard, and his father was a treacherous fool. Still, he's attacking Æthelhelm and I wish him luck, but he'll need more than a couple of hundred men to fight off Æthelhelm's revenge."

"And that's not your fight, eh?"

"Anyone who fights Æthelhelm is on my side," I said, "but coming here was madness."

"You tried, lord," Finan said, trying to console me. "You can tell Æthelstan you tried to keep the oath."

"But I failed," I said. I hate failure and I had failed.

But fate is a bitch and the bitch had not done with me yet.

Oswi was the first to spot our pursuers. He called to me from behind, "Lord!"

I turned and saw horsemen coming. They were a

good way behind us, but I could see the red cloaks. Finan, of course, saw more than I did. "Twenty men?" he said. "Maybe thirty. In a hurry."

I turned to look southward, wondering if we could reach *Spearhafoc* before the horsemen reached us and decided we could not. I turned again. My worry was that the small group of approaching men was merely a vanguard, that a horde of Æthelhelm's warriors was close behind them, but the distant road beyond the galloping horsemen stayed empty. "Shield wall!" I called. "Three ranks! Red cloaks in the front!"

The horsemen would see their own men barring the road. They might wonder why, but I did not doubt they would think us their allies. "Sigulf must have chased them out," I said to Finan.

"And killed the rest?" he asked. "I doubt it. There were—" He stopped suddenly, staring. "They have women!" I could see that for myself now. Behind the leading horsemen were four or five riders all cloaked in gray except one who wore black. I was not certain they were women, but Finan was. "It's Lavender Tits," he said.

"Is it?"

"Has to be."

So Æthelhelm's men in Fæfresham must have decided to remove Eadgifu and her women before the

Centish forces could reach the town's center. They were now cantering down the road, heading for their ships, and doubtless relying on Wighelm and his men to provide much of the crew, but Wighelm was somewhere on the Isle of Sceapig, naked.

"Don't look threatening!" I told my men. "Rest the shields on the ground! I want them to think we're friends!" I turned back to Finan. "We'll have to be quick," I said. "Name half a dozen of your men to seize the women's bridles."

"And once we've rescued her?" he asked. "What do we do with her?"

"Take her to Bebbanburg."

"The sooner the better," he grunted.

The approaching horsemen were half hidden by a tall stand of reeds and still no one followed them from the town. I closed my helmet's leather cheek-pieces to conceal my face. "Berg," I called. Berg was in the front rank, one of the men cloaked in red and carrying Æthelhelm's leaping stag on his shield. "When they get close, hold up a hand! Make them think we have a message!"

"Yes, lord."

The horsemen emerged from the thick reeds and spurred toward us. "Front rank," I called, "you take care of the leading horsemen!" I had thirty men in three ranks. "Second rank!" I was in the second rank, thinking I was less likely to be recognized than if I stood in the front. "We get rid of the horsemen behind the women. Finan! You take the women, then go where you're needed." Meaning he would reinforce whichever of us needed help. I could hear the hooves now and see dark clods of mud spewing from the racing horses. One of the leading men half stood in his stirrups and shouted, but whatever he said was lost in the noise of hooves and jangling bridles, then Berg took a pace forward and held up his hand and the horsemen had no choice but to curb their beasts. "Wighelm!" the leading man shouted. "Go back!"

"He's at the ships!" I called back.

"Get out of the way!" The man had been forced to a halt, and his followers milled uncertainly behind him. "Get out of the way!" he bellowed again, angrily. "Get out of the way and go back to the harbor!" He spurred his horse straight at my front rank, evidently expecting us to make way for him.

"Now!" I called and drew Serpent-Breath.

Berg slapped his shield hard across the face of the leading man's stallion. The beast slewed sideways, slipped in the mud, and fell. The rest of my front rank was charging into the confused horsemen, using the spears we had captured from Wighelm's men to savage both horses and men. Terrified beasts reared, riders were dragged from their saddles. Berg hauled the man who had shouted at us from beneath his fallen and floundering horse. "Keep that one alive!" I shouted at him. The enemy, at least those closest to us, had not even had the time to draw their swords, and my men were fast and savage. The women, I could now see they were women, were looking terrified. I ran past them to be faced by a horseman leveling his sword as he spurred his stallion toward me. I hammered his blade aside with Serpent-Breath and then rammed her up into his armpit. I felt her pierce mail and grind on bone, then blood flowed down the blade. Gerbruht ran past me, bellowing in Frisian. Two of the horsemen had managed to turn their beasts and were spurring back toward Fæfresham. "Let them go!" I shouted at Oswi who had begun sprinting after them. He would not catch them and I expected to be at sea long before any help arrived from the town. The man whose shoulder I had wounded had switched his sword to his other hand and now clumsily tried to strike down at me from across his saddle, but then he suddenly vanished, tugged down by Vidarr. I pulled myself onto his horse, gathered the reins, and kicked my heels. "Lady Eadgifu!" I shouted, and one of the gray-hooded women turned to me and I recognized her pale face framed with her raven black hair. "Ride on!" I called to her. "Ride on! We have a ship waiting. Go! Beornoth!"

"Lord?"

"Get a horse, protect the ladies!" I could see that three of the women had small children on their saddles. "Go!"

Some of the enemy had spurred off the road and were trying to get past us, but the land was a bog, sodden with water, and the horses struggled. Their riders savaged the poor beasts with spurs, the animals whinnied in protest, but could not move. A half-dozen of Finan's men attacked them with spears that far outreached the riders' swords. Two of the enemy simply threw themselves from their saddles and stumbled into the reeds as the others flung down their weapons in surrender. Back on the road Berg was holding his blade at the throat of the group's leader, who lay flat on his back.

The best ways to win any battle are to surprise the enemy, to outnumber the enemy, and to attack that enemy with such speed and ferocity that he has no idea what is happening until a sword is at his throat or a spear-blade is deep in his guts. We had achieved all three, though at a cost. Immar Hergildson, the least experienced of my men, had seen a red-cloaked rider and thrust up with his spear and so wounded Oswi who had mounted a riderless stallion. Oswi was now cursing and threatening revenge, the horses were still panicking, a woman was screaming, a wounded horse was hammering the road with his hooves, and some of the enemy were scrambling toward the reed beds. "Oswi!" I bellowed. "How badly are you hurt?"

"Scratched, lord."

"Then shut your mouth!"

Some of the West Saxons had escaped, but most were our prisoners now, including the young man who had evidently been their leader. Berg was still holding him on the road with the sword at his throat. "Let him up," I said. I saw that the women were safe, some fifty paces down the road from where they now watched us. "What's your name," I demanded of the young man.

He hesitated, unwilling to answer, but a twitch of Serpent-Breath changed his mind. "Herewulf," he muttered, staring down at his fallen blade.

I leaned down from the saddle and forced his head up with Serpent-Breath's tip. "Do you know who I am?" He shook his head. "I am Uhtred of Bebbanburg," I said and saw the fear in his eyes, "and you call me lord. So what were your orders, Herewulf?"

"To keep the Lady Eadgifu safe, lord."

"Where?"

"Cippanhamm, lord," he said sullenly.

Cippanhamm was a fine town in Wiltunscir and doubtless Herewulf had thought to take the women and children up the Temes, through Lundene, and so to Æthelhelm's shire. "Any news of the king?" I asked him.

"He's still sick, lord," he said. "That's all we know."

"Take off his mail," I ordered Berg. "You're lucky," I spoke to Herewulf, "because I might leave you alive. Might." He just stared at me. "What's happening in Fæfresham?" I asked.

For a moment he was tempted to be defiant, but I touched Serpent-Breath to his cheek and that loosened his tongue. "They're talking," he said reluctantly.

"Talking?"

"To the east of the town."

That made sense. Sigulf had brought warriors to his sister's aid only to discover a force equal to his own guarding her. If they fought then men would die and others would be wounded in an uncertain battle. Sigulf was being prudent, hoping to talk his sister out of her enemy's grip, but that enemy had been clever. Under the cloak of talking they had spirited her out of the convent and sent her north toward their ships. The risk they were taking was that Edward might recover and punish them, but better his anger than an heir to the throne safely out of Æthelhelm's grasp. "You were sent to keep the Lady Eadgifu safe?" I asked the prisoner.

"I told you so," Herewulf was recovering his defiance.

"Then tell Lord Æthelhelm that I'll do that job for him."

"When Ælfweard is king," Herewulf responded, "Lord Æthelhelm will take your fortress and feed your carcass to the pigs."

"His father tried," I said, sheathing Serpent-Breath, "and he's worm-food now. Be grateful I've let you live."

We took the mail from all the prisoners, took their weapons and their horses, then left them on the road where one stallion lay dead, its blood darkening the mud. Two men had been killed, though a dozen others of Æthelhelm's men were bleeding, as was Oswi, though he claimed he could hardly feel the wound. I kicked my horse to where the Lady Eadgifu waited. "We have to move, my lady," I said. "They'll pursue us soon and we need to get to the ship."

"Lord Uhtred," she said in a tone of amazement. "You came!"

"We must go, my lady."

"But my brother!"

"Is talking to Æthelhelm's men, my lady, and I can't wait to find out what they decide. Do you wish to

wait? You can stay here, and I'll go." There were four
women with Eadgifu, I assumed they were her servants
or companions, one of whom was holding a small boy,
just three or four years old, while two carried babes in
arms. There was also a priest who wore a black cloak.

"Lord Uhtred is right, my lady," the priest said nervously.

"But my brother has come!" Eadgifu stared toward
Fæfresham as if expecting men with bulls or swords on
their shields to come to her rescue.

"And a lot of Ealdorman Æthelhelm's men have
come too," I said, "and until I know who's won that
battle we must stay with the boat."

"Can't we go back?" Eadgifu pleaded.

I stared at her. She was undeniably beautiful. She had
skin as pale as milk, dark eyebrows and black hair, rich
lips and an understandable look of anxiety. "Lady," I
said as patiently as I could, "you asked for my help and
I'm here. And I don't help you by taking you back into
a town that is full of brawling men, half of whom want
to kill your children."

"I . . ." she began, then decided not to speak.

"We go that way," I insisted, pointing north. I looked
behind and still saw there was no pursuit. "Let's go!"
I shouted.

Eadgifu kicked her horse alongside mine. "Can we wait to find out what happened in Fæfresham?" she asked.

"We can wait," I agreed, "but only once we're aboard my ship."

"I worry for my brother."

"And for your husband?" I asked brutally.

She made the sign of the cross. "Edward is dying. Maybe he's already dead."

"And if he is," I said, still speaking harshly, "Ælfweard is king."

"He is a rotten soul," she spat, "an evil creature. The spawn of a devil woman."

"Who will kill your children in the time it takes to drown a kitten," I said, "so we must take you somewhere safe."

"Where is safe?" The question had come from one of Eadgifu's women, the only one who was not holding a child. She kicked her horse so that she rode on my left, then asked, "Where will we go?" It was plain that English, which she spoke with a delicate accent, was not her native tongue.

"You are?" I asked.

"I am Benedetta," she said with a dignity that intrigued me.

The unusual name intrigued me too, for it was neither Saxon nor Danish. "Benedetta," I repeated it clumsily.

"I am from Lupiae," she said proudly and, when I said nothing, "you have heard of Lupiae?"

I must have stared vacantly at her, because Eadgifu answered for me. "Benedetta is from Italy!"

"Rome!" I said.

"Lupiae is far to the south of Rome," Benedetta said dismissively.

"Benedetta is my treasured companion," Eadgifu explained.

"And evidently a long way from home," I remarked.

"Home!" Benedetta almost spat the word at me. "Where is home, Lord Uhtred, when slavers come and take you away?"

"Slavers?"

"*Saraceni* pigs," she said. "I was twelve years old. And you have not answered me, Lord Uhtred."

I looked at her again and thought this fine, defiant woman was as beautiful as her royal mistress. "I haven't answered you?"

"Where is safe?"

"If Lady Eadgifu's brother survives," I said, "then she is free to join him. If not, we go to Bebbanburg."

"Sigulf will come," Eadgifu said confidently, though

immediately after speaking she made the sign of the cross.

"I hope so," I said awkwardly, and wondered how I would cope with Eadgifu and her companions in Bebbanburg. The fortress was comfortable, but offered nothing like the luxuries of the palaces at Wintanceaster and Lundene. Then there were the rumors of plague in the north, and if Eadgifu and her children were to die in my fortress then men in Wessex would say I had killed them just as they claimed I had killed Æthelhelm the Elder.

"My brother will come," Eadgifu interrupted my thoughts, "and besides, I cannot go to Bebbanburg."

"You'll be safe there, my lady," I said.

"My son," she said, pointing to the eldest of her children, "should be King of Wessex. He cannot be king if we are hiding in Northumbria!"

I half smiled. "Ælfweard will be king," I said gently, "and Æthelstan will try to be king, so there will be war, my lady. Best to be far away from it."

"There will be no war," she said, "because Æthelstan will be king."

"Æthelstan?" I asked, surprised. I had thought she would press her son's claim to the throne over Æthelstan's. "He'll only be king if he defeats Ælfweard," I added.

"Æthelstan will be King of Mercia. My husband," she said those last two words with venom in her tone, "has made the decision. It is in his will. Ælfweard, horrible boy, will be King of Wessex and of East Anglia, and Æthelstan will be King of Mercia. It is decided." I just stared at her, scarce believing what I had heard. "They are half-brothers," Eadgifu went on, "and they each get what they want, so there will be no war."

And still I stared. Edward was dividing his kingdom? That was madness. His father's dream had been to make one kingdom out of four, and Edward had brought that dream so close to reality, yet now he would take an axe to it? And he believed that would bring peace? "Truly?" I asked.

"Truly!" Eadgifu answered. "Æthelstan will rule in Mercia and the nasty pig boy will rule the other two kingdoms until my brother defeats him. Then my Edmund will be king."

Madness, I thought again, pure madness. Fate, that malevolent bitch, had surprised me again, and I tried to persuade myself that it was none of my business. Let Ælfweard and Æthelstan fight it out, let the Saxons kill each other in a welter of blood and I would go back north. But the malevolent bitch had still not done with me. Æthelhelm lived, and I had made an oath.

We rode on.

Once back in the harbor we piled our captured shields, weapons, and mail in *Spearhafoc*'s belly. They could all be sold. The ship was floating some three or four feet below the level of the wharf and Eadgifu protested that she could not jump down, nor would she be carried. "I am a queen," I heard her complain to her Italian companion, "not some fishwife."

Gerbruht and Folcbald ripped up two long timbers from the wharf and made a crude gangplank, which, after some protests, Eadgifu agreed to use. Her priest escorted her down the perilous slope. Her eldest son, Edmund, followed her down and immediately ran to the heap of captured weapons and dragged out a sword with a blade as long as he was tall. "Put it down, boy!" I called from the wharf.

"You should call him prince," the priest reproved me.

"I'll call him prince when he proves he deserves the title. Put it down!" Edmund ignored me and tried to swing the blade. "Put it down, you little shit!" I bellowed.

The boy did not drop the sword, just stared at me with defiance that turned to fear as I jumped down into *Spearhafoc*'s belly. He began to cry, but Benedetta, the Italian woman, intervened. She stepped in front of me and took the sword from Edmund's hand. "If you are told to drop a sword," she said calmly, "then you drop it. And do not cry. Your father is a king and maybe you will be a king one day, and kings do not cry." She tossed the sword onto the pile of captured weapons. "Now say you are sorry to the Lord Uhtred."

Edmund looked at me, muttered something I could not hear, then fled to *Spearhafoc's* bows where he clung to his mother's skirts. Eadgifu put an arm around him and glared at me. "He meant no harm, Lord Uhtred," she said coldly.

"He might have meant no harm," I answered harshly, "but he could have caused it."

"He could also have hurt himself, my lady," Benedetta said.

Eadgifu nodded at that, she even smiled, and I understood why she had called the Italian woman her treasured companion. There was a confidence in Benedetta that suggested she was Eadgifu's protector. She was a strong woman, as competent as she was attractive.

"Thank you," I said to her softly.

Benedetta, I saw, had a small smile. She caught my eye and the smile stayed. I held her gaze, wondering at her beauty, but then the priest stepped between us. "Edmund is a prince," he insisted, "and should be treated as royalty."

"And I'm an ealdorman," I snarled, "and should be treated with respect. And who are you?"

"I'm the prince's tutor, lord, and the queen's confessor. Father Aart."

"Then you must be a busy man," I said.

"Busy, lord?"

"I imagine Queen Eadgifu has much to confess," I said, and Father Aart blushed and looked away. "And is she a queen?" I demanded. "Wessex doesn't recognize that title."

"She is Queen of Mercia until we hear of her husband's death," he said primly, and he was, indeed, a prim little man with a coronet of wispy brown hair surrounding a bald pate. He noticed the hammer at my neck and grimaced. "The queen," he continued, still looking at the hammer, "wishes that we wait for news from the town."

"We'll wait," I said.

"And then, lord?"

"If she wishes to go with her brother? She can go. Otherwise she goes with us to Bebbanburg." I looked up at the wharf. "Gerbruht!"

"Lord?"

"Get rid of those ships!" I pointed to the three ships that had brought Æthelhelm's men from Lundene to this muddy harbor. "Take what's useful from them first," I called after him.

We salvaged sealhide ropes, new oars made from larch wood, two barrels of ale, three of salted pork, and a faded banner of the leaping stag. We heaped them all in *Spearhafoc*, then Gerbruht fetched a metal bucket of embers from the tavern's hearth and blew the embers to life in the bellies of the three ships. "The crosses," Father Aart said when he realized what was happening.

"Crosses?"

"On the front of the ships! You can't burn our Lord's symbol."

I growled in frustration, but recognized his unhappiness. "Gerbruht," I bellowed, "remove the crosses from the prows!"

All three ships were alight before he and Beornoth managed to knock out the pegs holding the crosses. "What do I do with it?" he asked when the first came loose.

"I don't care! Float it!"

He threw the cross overboard, then jumped to help Beornoth loosen the second cross. They freed it, scrambled aft, and escaped the flames just in time, but were too late to save the third cross, and I wondered what kind of omen that was. My men apparently saw nothing sinister because they were cheering. They always enjoyed destruction and they whooped like children as the flames seared up the tarred rigging, then as the fire reached the sails that were furled tight on the yards and they too erupted in flame and smoke. "Was that necessary?" Father Aart asked.

"You want to be pursued by three shiploads of Æthelhelm's warriors?" I asked in return.

"No, lord."

"It was necessary," I said, though in truth I doubted that any of the three ships could have caught *Spearhafoc*. They were typical West Saxon ships, well made but heavy, brutish to row and sluggish under sail.

The wind had gone around to the southwest. The evening air was warm, the sky almost cloudless, though now smirched by the pyre of dark smoke from the burning boats. The tide was low, but had turned and the flood had begun. I had moved *Spearhafoc* well away from the blazing ships and moored her to the most northerly wharf, close to the entrance channel. Fisherfolk watched from their houses, but they stayed well clear both of the fire and of us. They were wary, and with good reason. The sun was low in the west, but the summer days were long and we had two or three hours of daylight left. "I won't stay here overnight, my lady," I told Eadgifu.

"We'll be safe, won't we?"

"Probably. But we still won't stay."

"Where do we go?"

"We'll find a mooring on Sceapig," I said, "then if we've heard nothing from your brother we go north tomorrow." I watched the village through the shimmer of fire. No one had appeared from Fæfresham, so whoever had won the confrontation in the town was evidently staying there. Two ravens flew high above the smoke. They were flying north and I could not have wished for a better sign from the gods.

"Æthelstan might be in Lundene," Eadgifu told me.

I looked at her, struck as ever by her loveliness. "Why would he be there, my lady?"

"Lundene belongs to Mercia, doesn't it?"

"It did once," I said. "Your husband's father changed that. It belongs to Wessex now."

"Nevertheless," she said, "I heard that Æthelstan would garrison Lundene as soon as he heard of my husband's death."

"But your husband still lives," I said, though whether that was true or not I did not know.

"I pray so," she said entirely unconvincingly. "Yet surely Prince Æthelstan must have forces near Lundene?"

She was a cunning bitch, as clever as she was beautiful. I say cunning because her words made absolute sense. If she was right and Edward had divided his kingdom then Æthelstan, who was no fool and who must have heard of the will's contents, would move quickly to take Lundene and so sever East Anglia from Wessex. And Eadgifu, who well knew of my long friendship with Æthelstan, was trying to persuade me to take her to Lundene rather than to Bebbanburg.

"We don't know that Æthelstan is in Lundene," I said, "and we won't know until after Edward is dead."

"They say the prince has put his troops just north of Lundene," Benedetta said.

"Who's they?"

She shrugged. "Folk in Lundene say that."

"A king is dying," I said, "and whenever a king dies there are rumors and more rumors. Believe nothing you cannot see with your own eyes."

"But if Æthelstan is in Lundene," Eadgifu persisted, "you would take me there?"

I hesitated, then nodded. "If he's there, yes."

"And he will let my children live?" she asked. Besides Edmund she had two babies, a boy called Eadred and a girl named Eadburh.

"Æthelstan is not a man to kill children," I said, which was not the answer she wanted, "but if you have a choice between Ælfweard and Æthelstan, choose Æthelstan."

"What I want," she said angrily, "is Ælfweard dead and my son on the throne."

"With you ruling for him?" I asked, but she had no answer to that, or at least none that she wanted to speak.

"Lord!" Immar called. "Lord!" and I turned to see three horsemen appear in the shroud of smoke that drifted from the burning boats. The horsemen saw us and spurred toward us.

"Awyrgan!" Eadgifu shrieked the name with alarm. She stood and gazed at the men who flogged their tired horses toward our wharf. Behind them came a score of red-cloaked men in pursuit. "Awyrgan!" Eadgifu shouted again, fear for him plain in her voice.

"Gerbruht!" I called. "Cut the forward line!"

"You can't leave him here," Eadgifu screamed at me.

"Cut it!" I bellowed.

Gerbruht sliced through the bow line with an axe and I drew Serpent-Breath and moved to the aft line. Eadgifu clutched at my arm. "Let me go!" I snarled, shook her off, then sliced through the sealhide rope. *Spearhafoc* trembled. The tide was pushing her onto the wharf, but the wind was against the tide and there was just enough wind on the furled sail to float us out into the channel. Beornoth helped by seizing an oar and thrusting against a weed-thick piling. The three horsemen had reached the wharf. They threw themselves from their saddles and ran. I saw the terror on Awyrgan's face because Æthelhelm's men were close behind, their horses' hooves drumming loud on the wharf's timbers. "Jump!" I shouted. "Jump!"

They jumped. They made a desperate life-saving leap, and two collapsed sprawling on *Spearhafoc*'s rowing benches while Awyrgan fell just short, but managed to grasp *Spearhafoc*'s low midships rail where two of my men took hold of him. The pursuing horsemen reined in and two of them threw spears. One blade thumped into the balks of timber supporting our mast, the second missed Awyrgan by a finger's breadth, but the men in *Spearhafoc*'s bow were using oars to pole her off the channel's muddy bank and north toward the wider waters of the Swalwan Creek. More spears followed, but all fell short.

"If we'd stayed," I told Eadgifu, "those horsemen would have rained spears on us. Men would have been wounded, men would have been killed,"

"He almost drowned!" she said, her eyes on Awyrgan, who was being hauled aboard.

So that, I thought, was why she had come to Cent? "And they'd have aimed their spears at your sons," I said.

She seemed not to hear me, but instead went forward to where the half-drenched Awyrgan was sitting on a bench. I turned and caught Benedetta's gaze. She held my eyes, as if daring me to speak aloud of what I suspected, and I thought again what a beauty she was. She was older than Eadgifu, but age had added wisdom to beauty. She had a dark skin, which gave her gray-green eyes a striking intensity, a long nose in a slender, grave face, wide lips, and hair as black as Eadgifu's.

"Where to?" Gerbruht distracted me. He had come aft and taken the steering-oar.

The sky was darkening. It was dusk, a long summer dusk, and no time to begin a long voyage. "Cross the creek," I said, "find somewhere to spend the night."

"And in the morning, lord?"

"We go north, of course."

North to Bebbanburg, north to home, and north to where no kings died and no madness ruled.

We crossed the creek in the dying light and found an inlet that twisted deep into Sceapig's reeds where we could spend the short summer night. The ships we had set on fire burned bright, throwing lurid shadows on the small harbor, their last flames only extinguished as the first stars showed.

We could have sailed that evening, but we were tired

and the shoals around Sceapig are treacherous and best tackled in daylight. We were safe for the night, we could sleep under the watch of our sentries, and there was a hummock of dry ground where we could make a fire.

The wind died in the darkness, then came again with the dawn, only now it was a west wind, brisk and warm. I wanted to leave, wanted to be sailing *Spearhafoc* north along the East Anglian coast, wanted to leave Wessex and its treachery far behind, but Benedetta asked me to wait.

"Why wait?" I asked her.

"We have things to do," she said distantly.

"So do I! A voyage!"

"It will not take long, lord." She still wore the gray cloak and hood, her face shadowed from the sun that rose behind her to gloss the Swalwan Creek with a shimmer of red gold.

"What won't take long?" I asked irritably.

"What we must do," she said stubbornly.

I understood then. "There's privacy under the steering platform," I told her, "and buckets."

"Eadgifu is a queen!" Benedetta said with a touch of anger. "Queens do not crouch in a stinking space over a dirty bucket!"

"We can wash the buckets," I suggested, but received nothing in reply but a scornful look. I sighed. "You want me to find her a palace?"

"I want you to give her some privacy. Some dignity," Benedetta said. "She is a queen! We can go to the alehouse, yes?" She pointed across the creek.

"That harbor will be full of Æthelhelm's troops," I said. "Better to piss in a bucket than fall into their hands."

"Then the reeds will do," she said stiffly, "but your men must stay away."

Which meant I had to order two of the rowing benches to be loosened and fashioned into a makeshift gangplank, then post sentries to guard the reeds from anyone approaching whatever place the women chose, and finally threaten death by dismemberment if any of those sentries were within sight of the women. Then we waited. I talked to Awyrgan as the sun rose higher, but he could tell me little of what had happened in Fæfresham the previous day. He had posted his men as guards on the road that led to Lundene, then been surprised by Æthelhelm's horsemen who had attacked him from the south. "We fled, lord," he confessed.

"What of Sigulf?"

"I don't know, lord."

"The last I heard," I said, "they were negotiating."

"Which only bought them time to take her ladyship from the convent," Awyrgan said bitterly.

"Then you're fortunate I was here," I said.

He hesitated, then nodded. "Indeed, lord."

I looked across the reed beds, wondering what on earth took the women so long, then back over the creek. At first light the harbor had appeared deserted, but now I could see men there, red-cloaked men. I pointed to them. "Æthelhelm's men," I told Awyrgan, "which suggests Sigulf lost. And they can see us. They'll be coming for us."

"You burned their ships, lord."

"But I didn't burn their fishing boats, did I?" I cupped my hands and bellowed at the reeds, "My lady! We have to go!"

And it was then I saw the ship. A small ship, coming from the west, rowing down the Swalwan Creek. I could not see the hull, which was hidden by the tall reeds, but there was a cross on the prow, and the distance between that cross and the high mast suggested it could not hold more than ten or twelve benches on each side. The approaching ship's crew had lowered their sail, presumably for fear that a sudden gust of wind might drive them onto a mudbank and leave them waiting for the tide. Oars were slower, but much safer. "Gerbruht!" I bellowed.

"Lord?"

"We have to stop that ship! Get us under way!"

"The women!" Awyrgan protested.

"We'll come back for them. Oars! Hurry!"

I threw off the only mooring line, which we had tied to a massive log that had drifted ashore, then men began poling the ship out of the narrow inlet. "Mail!" I called, meaning that men should don their armor. I pulled my own mail coat over my head, holding my breath as the stinking leather liner scraped my face. I buckled Serpent-Breath to my waist. The bow oars were in clear water now and *Spearhafoc* lunged ahead. I shoved the steering-oar over, held my breath again as the hull touched mud, but a heave of the oars pulled her free. We turned westward and more oars found purchase as we slid into deeper water. I could see the approaching ship now and see she was half the size of *Spearhafoc* and with fewer than twenty men aboard. I had suspected she might be a trading ship, but she had a lean hull and a high prow, a ship made for swift passage. Her oars checked as they saw us and I could see a man in a red cloak shouting from the stern, perhaps wanting his oarsmen to turn the ship so they could flee, but *Spearhafoc* was too close and too threatening. "Put on red cloaks!" I shouted at Finan who had assembled a group of mailed and armed men at *Spearhafoc*'s bows. He waved in reply and called for a man to bring the cloaks. "Don't kill the bastards!" I bellowed. "I just want to talk to them!"

I had asked Finan's men to wear the red cloaks so that the approaching ship would believe that we, like them, served Æthelhelm. I did not think they would fight us, we were too big, but they could have veered into the southern bank and fled across the marshes if they thought we were enemies. The pretense must have worked because the ship began rowing toward us again, their panic over.

"Lord!" Vidarr Leifson, who was standing on one of the rowing benches closest to the stern, called to me. He pointed behind and I turned to see that a fishing boat crammed with red-cloaked men was being laboriously rowed from the harbor entrance. I glanced across the reed beds, but could see neither the stranded women nor the five sentries we had posted. A pair of cranes flew from the reeds, their huge wings beating laboriously and the red feathers of their heads bright in the morning sun. They slowly gained height, long legs trailing, and one of the men on the fishing boat hurled a spear at the closest bird. It missed and plunged harmlessly into the creek. A good omen, I thought. "We'll deal with that fishing boat soon," I told Vidarr, hoping that the men on that boat had no idea that the women and children they had come to recapture were almost unguarded on Sceapig, then I called to the oarsmen to stop rowing as *Spearhafoc*'s prow loomed above the smaller ship. We coasted for a few paces, then I felt a quiver in the hull as we touched her. Finan and two men jumped onto the stranger's deck. "Hold her here," I told Gerbruht, meaning he should try to keep *Spearhafoc* next to the smaller ship, then I went forward to see that Finan was arguing with the red-cloaked man. No swords had been drawn. "What is it?" I called down.

"A hired boat," Finan answered laconically, "bringing messengers from Æthelhelm."

"Bring them on board."

"This fellow doesn't like that idea," Finan said with a grin. "He doesn't believe I serve that piece of shit Æthelhelm!"

The red cloaks had at least made them believe we were friends until Finan and his men boarded their small ship. "You have a choice," I snarled at the man facing Finan. "You either come aboard my ship or we practice our sword-skill on you. You choose."

"And you are?" he demanded.

"Uhtredærwe," I said, and was rewarded with a visible shudder. Reputation is sometimes enough to end a confrontation, and the red-cloaked man, whoever he was, had no desire to add his death to my reputation. He clambered up onto *Spearhafoc*'s prow, urged on by a slap from Finan, and was followed by a priest. I judged both men to be middle-aged, while the one who had argued with Finan was richly dressed and had a silver chain at his neck. "Throw your oars overboard!" I called to the smaller ship's master. "Finan! Cut his halyards!" The twenty oarsmen watched sullenly as Finan slashed through every line he could find. By the time he was done the smaller ship could neither row nor sail, while the flooding tide would take it gently away from Fæfresham. "When we're gone," I called to the master, "you can swim for your oars and splice your lines." His only answer was to spit overboard. He was unhappy and I could not blame him, but I did not want him returning to Lundene to spread news of my arrival in Wessex.

I let Gerbruht turn *Spearhafoc*, a tricky task in the narrow and shallow channel, but one he did with his usual skill as I went forward and confronted our two visitors. "First, who are you?"

"Father Hedric," the priest answered.

"You're one of Æthelhelm's sorcerers?"

"I serve in his household," the priest answered proudly. He was a small tubby man with a wisp of white beard.

"And you?" I asked the well-dressed man who wore the silver chain. He was tall, thin, with a long jaw, and dark, deep-set eyes. A clever man, I thought, which made him dangerous.

"I am Halldor."

"A Dane?" I asked, his name was Danish.

"A Christian Dane," he said.

"And what does a Christian Dane do in Æthelhelm's household?"

"I serve at Lord Æthelhelm's wishes," he answered icily.

"You have a message?" They were both silent.

"Where to, lord?" Gerbruht called from the stern.

I saw that the fishing boat was waiting. She was too small and the number of men aboard too few to dare challenge us, but even as I watched I saw a second and equally heavily laden boat come from the harbor. "Pick up the women!" I called to Gerbruht. "We'll deal with those boats after." I turned back to our two prisoners. "You have a message?" I demanded a second time.

"King Edward is dead," Father Hedric said, then made the sign of the cross. "God rest his soul."

"And King Ælfweard reigns," Halldor the Dane added, "and may God give him a long and prosperous reign."

The king was dead. And I had come to kill the new king. Wyrd bið ful āræd.

PART TWO

City of Darkness

Five

Eadgifu, her women, and her three children must all have been waiting for us because they were crouched with the sentries just inside the tall reeds at the creek's edge, hidden from Æthelhelm's men, who rowed clumsily to confront us. We steered *Spearhafoc* into the muddy bank, feeling the hull touch bottom. "Come on!" I called to the women. "Hurry!"

"We'll get wet!" Eadgifu protested.

"Wet is better than dead, my lady, now hurry!"

She still hesitated until Awyrgan leaped overboard then waded ashore and held out his hand. I saw her smile as she took it, then Awyrgan, along with the sentries, helped them all into the creek. Eadgifu squealed as the water came over her waist, but Benedetta calmed her. "Lord Uhtred is right, my lady. Better to be wet than dead." Once at the ship's side we unceremoniously lifted Eadgifu into the ship. She scowled as she reached the deck. "Your husband's dead," I told her with deliberate brutality.

"Good, may he rot in peace," was her curt answer, though I suspect her anger was delivered more toward me for soaking her rich clothes than at her husband. She turned and offered a hand to help Awyrgan into the boat, but Beornoth gently edged her aside and lifted the man by himself. Then Eadgifu saw Halldor and the priest at the stern of the boat and she spat toward them. "Why are they here?"

"Prisoners," I said curtly.

"Kill the Dane," she said.

"He has to answer questions first," I told her, then reached down and took one of the babies from Benedetta's grasp.

"Bastards are coming!" Finan warned me from *Spearhafoc*'s stern.

The two small fishing boats crammed with Æthelhelm's men were rowing toward us, though they were still a long way off. They were rowing hard, but their boats were clumsy, heavy, and sluggish. We pulled the last woman and child aboard, then poled *Spearhafoc* off the bank and out into deeper water. "Oarsmen! Pull!" I shouted. "Finan! Put the bird on the prow!"

That made my men cheer. They liked it when our sleek sparrowhawk carving crested the prow, though in truth she looked more like an eagle than a sparrowhawk because her beak was far too long, but she had savage eyes and a menacing presence. Finan and two other men slotted her into place and hammered home the two pegs that held her firm. The crews of the two fishing boats, seeing us coming eastward toward them, had stopped rowing and were now standing with spears in their hands. But either the sudden appearance of the sparrowhawk's feral head or the sight of the small waves beginning to break white and quick at *Spearhafoc*'s cutwater persuaded them to sit and pull desperately for the southern shore. They feared a ramming. "Pull!" I bellowed at the oarsmen.

The rowers dragged on the oars' looms, thrusting *Spearhafoc* still faster. Gerbruht and two other men hauled on the main halyard to hoist the sail. The fishing boats were still trying to escape us and I heard a man scream at his oarsmen to pull harder. I was steering toward them, and, as the sail caught the wind, our ship seemed to leap ahead, but then, just before we reached spear-range, I hauled the steering-oar toward me, and *Spearhafoc* turned to slide past them on the creek's farther side. We could easily have sunk both fishing boats, but instead I would avoid them. Not because I feared them, but in the closing moments before we rammed the first boat we were likely to be assailed by spears, and I had no wish for a single man of *Spearhafoc*'s crew to be wounded or worse. We had escaped and that was victory enough.

A dozen spears were hurled as we passed, but all fell far short, and then we were coursing eastward toward the open sea. We brought the oars inboard and lashed them down. Gerbruht had tied down the sail's last sheet and so I gave him the steering-oar. "Just follow the creek," I told him, "then steer north. We're going home."

"God be praised," he said.

I jumped down from the steering platform. Our two prisoners, the tall, well-dressed Dane and the smaller priest, were under guard by the mainmast. Awyrgan, his clothes soaked, had been joined by the two men who had escaped pursuit with him, and was standing over the prisoners with a drawn sword. He was taunting them. "Leave us," I told him.

"I—"

"Leave us!" I snarled. He irritated me.

He went to join Eadgifu and her ladies at the stern, and I drew the short knife from my belt. "I don't have time to persuade you to answer my questions," I told the two men, "so if either of you don't answer straightaway I'll blind you both. When did the king die?"

"A week ago?" the priest, shivering with fright, answered quickly. "Maybe six days. I've lost count, lord."

"You were with him at the end?"

"We were in Ferentone," the Dane said stiffly.

"Where he died," the priest added quickly.

"And Æthelhelm was there?"

"Lord Æthelhelm was with the king to the end," Halldor said.

"And Æthelhelm sent you south?" The priest nodded. The poor man still looked terrified, and no wonder. I was holding the short knife near his left cheekbone and he was imagining the blade slicing into his eye. I twitched it. "He sent you south to do what?" I demanded.

The priest whimpered, but Halldor answered. "To remove the Lady Eadgifu and her children to a place of safety."

I left that lie unchallenged. Eadgifu might have been safely walled up in a convent, but the two boys would be lucky to see another autumn. The girl, who had no claim to the throne, might have lived, but I doubted it. Æthelhelm would probably wish to cull the whole brood. "And the king," I said, "divided the kingdom?"

"Yes, lord," the priest muttered.

"Æthelstan is king in Mercia?" I asked. "And that piece of weasel shit, Ælfweard, rules in Wessex?"

"King Ælfweard rules in Wessex and East Anglia," the priest confirmed, "and Æthelstan is named King of Mercia."

"But only if the Witan confirms the king's dying wishes," Halldor said, "which they will not."

"They won't?"

"Why would they consent to the bastard being King of Mercia? Ælfweard must be made king of all three kingdoms."

And that, I thought, was probably true. The West Saxon and East Anglian Witans, both firmly under Æthelhelm's influence, would never vote to accept Æthelstan as a rival king in Mercia. They would claim all three kingdoms for Ælfweard.

"So you don't feel bound by the king's last wishes?" I asked.

"Do you?" Halldor asked belligerently.

"He wasn't my king," I said.

"It is my belief," Halldor said, "that King Edward was of unsound mind when he dictated his will. So no, I do not feel bound by his final wishes."

I agreed with Halldor that Edward had been a lackwit when he divided his kingdoms, but I was not going to admit that. "Where was King Æthelstan when his father died?" I asked instead.

Halldor bridled at my calling Æthelstan a king, but managed to suppress his indignation. "I believe that Faeger Cnapa was still in Ceaster," he said coldly, "or maybe in Gleawecestre."

"Faeger Cnapa?" I asked. He had said it as a name, but it means "pretty boy." Faege, though, also means "doomed." Whatever he meant it was plainly an insult.

Halldor looked at me coldly. "Men call him that."

"Why?"

"Because he's handsome?" Halldor suggested.

His answer had been fatuous, but I let it pass. "And Æthelhelm?" I asked. "Where is he now? Lundene?"

"God, no," the priest answered with a shudder, earning a scowl from the tall Dane.

"No?" I asked, and again neither man replied so I touched the knife's sharp tip onto the priest's left cheek, just beneath the eye.

"Mercian forces occupied Lundene," the priest said hurriedly. "We were lucky to escape unnoticed."

Gerbruht shouted orders from *Spearhafoc*'s stern. We were leaving the Swalwan Creek, turning northward, and the ship pounded into the first of the wide estuary's larger waves. "Loosen that sheet!" Gerbruht pointed to the windward sheet. "And haul in on that line!" he pointed to the other sheet, and the sail turned to drive the boat north. The wind was freshening, the sea sparkled with reflected sunlight, and our white wake spread as we left Wessex behind and headed northward. Father Aart, the priest who accompanied Eadgifu, suddenly lurched to the ship's leeward rail and vomited. "There's only one cure for seasickness, father!" Gerbruht bellowed from the stern. "Sit under a tree!"

My men laughed at the old joke. They were happy because they were sailing north. North to home, north to safety. We would soon be in sight of the estuary's farther shore, the vast mud expanse where the East Saxons had settled. Then, if this wind held, we would sail up the East Anglian coast and so to the wilder shores of Bebbanburg.

Except Æthelstan's men were in Lundene. For a few moments I was tempted to ignore that news. What did it matter to me if Æthelstan's men had captured Lundene? I was going home to Bebbanburg, but Æthelstan's forces were in Lundene?

"You saw Æthelstan's men?" I asked the two prisoners.

"We did," Halldor answered, "and they have no right to be there!"

"Lundene is part of Mercia," I said.

"Not since King Alfred's day," the Dane insisted.

Which was probably true. Alfred had made certain that his West Saxon troops garrisoned Lundene and, despite Mercia's legal claim to the city, it had been effectively ruled from Wintanceaster ever since. But Æthelstan had acted fast. Eadgifu had been right; he must have had troops north of the city, waiting for his orders, and those troops now separated Wessex from East Anglia. "Was there fighting?" I asked.

"None," Halldor sounded disappointed.

"The garrison wasn't strong, lord," the priest explained, "and the Mercians came suddenly and in great numbers. We were not expecting them."

"That was treachery!" Halldor snarled.

"Or cleverness," I said. "So where is Æthelhelm now?"

Both men shrugged. "He's probably still in Wintanceaster, lord," Halldor said grudgingly.

That made sense. Wintanceaster was the capital of Wessex and in the heartland of Æthelhelm's lavish estates. I had no doubt that Ælfweard was there too, hungry for the Witan to announce that he was truly king. Edward's body, escorted by his own household troops, would be traveling south to Wintanceaster so he could be buried beside his father, and that funeral would assemble the West Saxon lords whose troops

Æthelhelm would need. And Æthelstan, wherever he was, would be sending messengers to the Mercian lords demanding warriors to preserve his Mercian throne. In brief, both Æthelhelm and Æthelstan would be gathering the forces necessary to unpick Edward's division of his kingdoms, but at least Æthelstan had shown forethought and sense in capturing Lundene before Æthelhelm could reinforce the city's small garrison.

"Is King Æthelstan in Lundene?" I asked Halldor.

Again he grimaced at the word "king," but made no comment on it. "I don't know," he said.

"But you're quite sure his men are?"

He nodded unwillingly. By now the coast of East Seax was in sight, a low, dull brown streak of mud topped with a fringe of summer green. The few trees were small and wind-bent, the mud speckled with the white of seabirds. The tide would soon be ebbing, which made any landfall on that coast treacherous. We could be stranded on a falling tide for hours, yet I was determined to nose *Spearhafoc* into the shore. I pointed ahead. "That's Fughelness," I told the two prisoners. "There's little there except sand, mud, and birds. And soon you too, because I'm putting you ashore there." Fughelness was a bleak place, windswept and barren, locked in by tidal creeks, marshes, and mudbanks. It would take Halldor and the priest the rest of the day to find a way to firmer ground, and then more time to work their way back to Wintanceaster if that was, indeed, where Æthelhelm was.

We lowered the sail as we neared the shore, and then, using a dozen oars, nosed our way gently through small breaking waves until *Spearhafoc*'s cutwater slid onto mud. "It would be easier to kill them," Awyrgan said as Berg, grinning, prodded the two captives off the bows toward the water.

"Why would I kill them?" I asked.

"They're enemies."

"They're helpless enemies," I said, "and I don't kill the helpless."

He looked at me defiantly. "And what about the priests you killed?"

I wanted to kill Awyrgan at that moment. "Anger leads to savagery," I said curtly, "and to stupidity." He must have felt my anger because he backed away. The priest was protesting that jumping into the water would give him a fever, but every moment we waited the wind was nudging *Spearhafoc* further onto the mud. "Get rid of him!" I called to Berg.

Berg more or less threw the priest overboard. "Wade ashore!" Berg called. "You won't drown!"

"Pole her off!" I called, and the men in the bows shoved their oars into the sticky mud and heaved. For a heartbeat *Spearhafoc* seemed reluctant to move, then to my relief she lurched and slid back into safer, deeper water.

"Same course, lord?" Gerbruht asked me. "Hoist the sail and up the coast?"

I shook my head. "Lundene."

"Lundene?"

"Oars!" I shouted.

We turned west. We were not going home after all, but upriver to Lundene.

Because King Æthelstan's troops were there and I had an oath to keep.

It was a hard row against the wind, against the tide, and against the river's current, but it would become easier when the tide turned and the flood would carry us upriver. I knew these waters, knew the river, because when Gisela was alive I had commanded the Lundene garrison. I had become fond of the city.

We passed Caninga, a marshy island on the East Seax shore, beyond which was Beamfleot where, in Alfred's reign, we had stormed the Danish fort and put a whole army to the sword. I remembered Skade and did not want to remember her. She had died there, killed by the man she had betrayed, while all around them the women screamed and the blood flowed. Finan stared and he too was thinking of the sorceress. "Skade," he said.

"I remember," I said.

"What was her lover's name?"

"Harald. He killed her."

He nodded. "And we captured thirty ships."

I was still thinking of Skade, remembering. "War seemed cleaner then."

"No, we were younger then, that's all." The two of us were standing in the prow. I could see the hills rising beyond Beamfleot, and I remembered a villager telling me that the god Thor had walked the ridge there. He was a Christian, yet he had seemed proud that Thor had walked his fields.

We had taken the sparrowhawk's head from the prow so that to a casual glance we were just another ship rowing upriver to the wharves of Lundene. Low hills of ripening wheat rose beyond the muddy banks. The oars creaked as they pulled. A man stretching a net to catch marsh birds stood from his task to watch us pass. He saw we were a ship of warriors and made the sign of the cross, then bent to his task again. As the estuary narrowed we began passing close to ships coming downriver, their sails bellying in the southwest wind, and we shouted for news as passing ships always do. Were there Mercian troops in Lundene? There were. Was

King Æthelstan there? No one could say, and so, still
largely ignorant of what happened in Lundene, let alone
Wessex, we rowed on toward the wide smear of dark
smoke that always hung above the city. The tide had
turned and we were using just six rowers on each side to
keep the boat's heading. Berg had the steering-oar now,
while Eadgifu, her children, and her companions were
huddled under the prow platform where Finan and I
stood. "So it's over," Finan said to me.

I knew he had been brooding over my sudden decision to go west to Lundene instead of north to Bebbanburg. "Over?" I asked.

"Æthelstan's men are in Lundene. We join him. We
fight a battle. We kill Æthelhelm. We go home."

I nodded. "That's my hope."

"The men are worried."

"About a battle?"

"About the plague." He crossed himself. "They have
wives and children, so do I."

"The plague wasn't at Bebbanburg."

"It's in the north. Who knows how far it's spread?"

"Rumor said it was at Lindcolne," I said, "but that's
a long way from Bebbanburg."

"That's small consolation to men worrying about
their families."

I had been trying to ignore those rumors of the plague. Rumors are just that and most are not true, and the days around a king's death provoke many rumors, but Sigtryggr had warned me of the sickness in Lindcolne, others had spoken of death in the north, and Finan had been right to remind me. My men wanted to be reunited with their families. They would follow me into battle, they would fight like demons, but a threat to their wives and children was far more important to them than any oath of mine. "Tell them," I said, "that we'll be home soon."

"What's soon?" Finan demanded.

"Let me find the news in Lundene first," I said.

"And what if Æthelstan's there?" Finan asked. "And what if he wants you to march with him?"

"Then I march," I said bleakly, "and you can take *Spearhafoc* home."

"Me!" Finan said, sounding alarmed. "Not me! Berg can sail her."

"Berg can sail her," I agreed, "but you'll command Berg." I knew Finan was no seaman.

"I'll command nothing!" he retorted fiercely. "I'll stay with you."

"You don't have to—"

"I took an oath to protect you!" he interrupted me.

"You? I never asked any oath of you!"

"You didn't," he agreed, "but I still swore an oath to protect you."

"When?" I asked. "I don't remember any such oath."

"I took it two heartbeats ago," he said, "and if you can be tied by a stupid oath, so can I."

"I release you from any oath—"

Again he interrupted me. "Someone has to keep you alive. Seems God gave me the task of keeping you away from barley fields."

I touched the hammer and tried to convince myself that I was making the right decision. "There are no barley fields in Lundene," I told Finan.

"That's true."

"Then we shall live, my friend," I said, touching him on the shoulder, "we shall live and we'll go home."

I walked to the stern where the lowering sun cast a long rippling shadow behind *Spearhafoc*. I sat on one of the low steps that led to the steering platform. A swan flew northward and I idly worried it was an omen that we should also go north, but there were other birds, other omens. Sometimes it is hard to know the will of the gods, and even when we do know we cannot be certain they are not toying with us. I touched the hammer again.

"You believe that has power?" a voice asked.

I looked up and saw it was Benedetta, her face shadowed by the hood she wore. "I believe the gods have power," I answered.

"One god," she insisted. I shrugged, too tired to argue. Benedetta stared at the slow passing bank of East Seax. "We're going to Lundene?" she asked.

"We are."

"I hate Lundene," she said bitterly.

"It's a lot to hate."

"When the slavers came . . ." she began, then stopped.

"You told me you were twelve?"

She nodded. "I was to be married that summer. To a good man, a fisherman."

"They killed him too?"

"They killed everyone! *Saraceni!*" She spat the word. "They killed anyone who fought back or anyone they didn't want as a slave. They wanted me." There was a terrible savagery in the last three words.

"Who are the *Saraceni?*" I asked, stumbling over the unfamiliar word.

"Men from across the sea. Some even live in my land! They are not Christian. They are savages!"

I patted the step beside me. She hesitated, then sat. "And you came to Britain?" I asked, curious.

She was silent for a while, then shrugged. "I was sold," she said simply, "and taken north, I don't know where. I was told this is valuable," she touched a finger to her skin, which was lightly brushed with a golden darkness, "it is valuable in the north where the skin is pale like sour milk and in the north I was sold again. I was still just twelve years old," she paused to look at me, "and I was already a woman, not a child."

Her voice was bitter. I nodded to show I understood.

"A year later," she went on, "I was sold again. To a Saxon from Lundene. A slave-trader. He paid much money and his name," she was speaking so softly that I almost could not hear her, "his name was Gunnald."

"Gunnald," I repeated.

"Gunnald Gunnaldson." She was gazing at the northern bank where a small village came down to the water. A child waved from a decaying wharf. I watched the oars, dipping, pulling, then rising slowly with water dripping from the long blades. "They brought me to Lundene where they sold their slaves," Benedetta went on, "and both raped me. Father and son, both, but the son was the worst. They would not sell me, they wanted to use me, so I tried to kill myself. It was better than being used by those pigs."

She had said the last few words very softly so she

could not be overheard by the men on the nearest rowing bench. "Kill yourself?" I asked just as quietly.

She turned to look at me, then slowly, without a word, pushed back the hood and unwound the gray scarf she always wore about her neck. I saw the scar then, a deep scar across the right side of her slender neck. She let me look for a moment, then replaced the scarf. "I did not cut deep enough," she said bleakly, "but it was enough to make them sell me."

"To Edward."

"To his steward. I would work in his kitchens and in his bed, but Queen Eadgifu rescued me, so I serve her now."

"As a trusted servant."

"As a trusted slave." She still sounded bitter. "I am not free, lord." She pulled the hood back over her raven black hair. "Do you keep slaves?" she asked belligerently.

"No," I said, which was not strictly true. Bebbanburg had many estates where my household warriors farmed and I knew many of them had slaves, and my father had kept a score in the fortress to cook, clean, sweep, and warm his bed, and some of those were still there, aged now and paid as servants. I had taken no new slaves because my own experience as a slave, when I had been condemned to pull an oar through wintry seas, had soured me against slavery. But then, I thought, I did not need slaves. I had enough men and women to keep the fortress safe, warm, and fed, and I had enough silver to reward them. "I've killed slave-traders," I remarked, knowing as I said it that it was only spoken to attract Benedetta's approval.

"If we go to Lundene," she said, "you may kill one for me."

"Gunnald? He's still there?"

"He was two years ago," she answered bleakly. "I saw him. He saw me too, and he smiled. It was not a good smile."

"You saw him? In Lundene?"

She nodded. "King Edward liked to visit. The queen liked it too. She could buy things."

"King Edward could have arranged Gunnald's death for you," I said.

She sneered at that. "Edward took money from Gunnald. Why kill him? I meant nothing to Edward, rest his soul." She made the sign of the cross. "What happens to us in Lundene?"

"We meet with Æthelstan, if he's there."

"And if he's not?"

"We go to meet him."

"And what will he do to us? To my lady? To her children?"

"Nothing," I said flatly. "I'll tell him you're under my protection."

"He will honor that?" She sounded skeptical.

"I have known King Æthelstan since he was a child," I said, "and he is an honorable man. He will send you under escort to my home at Bebbanburg while we fight our war."

"Bebbanburg!" She pronounced the name in her strange accent. "What is at Bebbanburg?"

"Safety. You'll be under my protection there."

"Awyrgan says we are wrong to accept a pagan's protection," she said flatly.

"Awyrgan doesn't have to go with the queen," I said.

I thought she would smile for a heartbeat, but the impulse left her and she just nodded. "He will go with her," she said in a tone of disapproval, then turned her large gray-green eyes on me. "Are you truly a pagan?"

"I am."

"That is not good," she said seriously.

"Tell me," I said, "is Gunnald Gunnaldson a pagan?"

She did not answer for a long while, then she shook her head abruptly. "He wears the cross."

"Does that make him a better man than me?"

She hesitated for a brief moment. "No," she finally admitted.

"Then maybe," I said, "if he's still in Lundene, I'll kill him."

"No," she said firmly.

"No?"

"Let me kill him," she said and, almost for the first time since I had met her, Benedetta looked happy. We rowed on.

We reached Lundene at dusk, a dusk made darker by the city's canopy of smoke. At least a score of other ships were lumbering upriver, most laden with the food and supplies that a city's horde of people and horses need, one ship so heavily laden that it looked like a floating hayrick as it rode the flooding tide about the river's great bends. We passed the smaller settlements built to Lundene's east; the shipbuilders with their stacks of timber and the smoking pits where they burned pine to make stinking pitch, and the tanners who made a stink all their own as they cured pelts with shit. Above it all was Lundene's own thick stench of woodsmoke and sewage. "It's not a river," Finan complained, "it's a cesspool."

"You get used to it," I said.

"Who'd want to?" He looked down at the water flowing past *Spearhafoc*'s hull. "Those are turds!"

We left the marshy banks for the two low hills of Lundene. It was getting dark now, but there was still just enough light to show three spearmen standing on the high stone rampart of the small Roman bastion that guarded the eastern end of the city. None of the three was wearing a dark red cloak and no leaping stag banners hung against the wall. Nor did the three men show any interest as we passed. The wharves, packed with ships, began just beyond the small fort, and in their center, still downstream of the great bridge, was the stone wall I knew so well. The wall had been made by the Romans and protected a masonry platform on which they had built a lavish house. I had lived there with Gisela.

No ship was tied to the stone wall and so I pushed the steering-oar over and the tired rowers dragged their last strokes. "Oars in!" I called, and *Spearhafoc* slid gently against the massive stone blocks. Gerbruht threaded the bow line through one of the vast iron rings set in the wall and waited as *Spearhafoc* coasted the last few yards. Her stern thumped against the stone and Berg seized another of the rings. I tossed him the stern line and our ship was hauled in to grate her hull against the wall. When I had kept a ship here before I had packed canvas sacks with straw to cushion the hull, but that was a task that could wait for the morning.

A narrow flight of steps was inset into the stone to allow folk to climb the wall at low tide. "Wait," I told my crew and passengers, then Finan and I jumped onto the steps and climbed to the wide river terrace where, on evenings when the wind came from the north to blow away the Temes's stench, Gisela and I had liked to sit. Night was falling fast now and the house was dark except for a dim light behind one of the shutters and the glimmer of flames in the central courtyard. "Someone's living here," Finan said.

"The house belongs to the king," I said. "Alfred always gave it to the garrison commander, though most never used it. I did."

"But which king?"

"Æthelstan's now," I said, "but the West Saxons will want it back." Lundene was valuable, the city's customs dues alone could finance a small kingdom, and I wondered if Edward, in his will, had declared which of his sons, Ælfweard or Æthelstan, was to rule here. In the end, of course, it was whichever half-brother could muster the most spears.

The house door opened.

Waormund walked out.

I did not recognize him at first, nor did he recognize me. Behind him the passage that led to the courtyard was lit with torches, so his face was in shadow, while I was probably the last person he had ever expected to see in Lundene. At first all I was aware of was the man's size; a huge man, a head taller than myself, broad-shouldered, shaggy haired, with booted legs like tree trunks. Light from the torches flickered off the links of a mail coat that fell to his thighs. He was eating meat that he tore off the bone with his teeth. "You can't leave your poxy ship there," he growled, then went utterly still. "Christ!" he said, threw the bone away and drew his seax, then leaped at me with a surprising speed for such a huge man.

I had not brought Serpent-Breath from the ship, though my own seax, Wasp-Sting, hung at my waist. I stepped fast to my right, away from Finan so that Waormund would have an enemy on two sides, and dragged the short-sword from her scabbard. Waormund's first slash missed me by a finger's breadth, I ducked the second, a wild swing aimed at my head, and parried the third with Wasp-Sting, catching his blade at the root of the short-sword. The blow jarred up my arm. His strength was prodigious. Like me, Finan only had a seax, but he moved behind Waormund, who somehow sensed the Irishman's approach, turned, and swept his short blade to drive Finan back. I went to my right, stepping past Waormund and dragging Wasp-Sting's blade across the back of his left leg. I was trying to slice his hamstring, but Wasp-Sting was a short stabbing weapon, not made for cutting, and the blade hardly pierced his tall leather boot. He turned on me, roaring, and I stepped back, lunged Wasp-Sting to strike and pierce his thigh, then fell sideways to avoid his savage response. Wasp-Sting had wounded him, I had felt the blade pierce, but Waormund did not seem to notice the injury. He turned back, snarling, as Finan attacked again to distract him, but we were like terriers assaulting a boar, and one of us, I knew, must be gored soon. Waormund had driven Finan back and now came for me, launching a massive kick that should have crushed my ribs. I was still getting to my feet, raised Wasp-Sting and, by luck or by the favor of the gods, she parried Waormund's blade that he had hacked down at me. Once again the shock of the impact seared up my arm. Finan stabbed at Waormund, and the huge man again had to turn away from me, back-handing his sword, but Finan was lightning fast and danced back. "This way!" he called to me.

I had scrambled to my feet. Finan was still shouting at me to go toward *Spearhafoc*, but Waormund prevented that by running at me. He was roaring. There were no words, just a bellow of rage and a stench of ale on his breath. I stepped to my right, toward Finan, Waormund reached with his free hand and grabbed the neck of my mail coat and hauled me toward him. I saw him grin, teeth missing, knew I was about to die, felt his enormous strength as he dragged me effortlessly into his close embrace and I saw his seax coming from my right, the blade's point aimed at the base of my ribs. I tried to tear myself free and could not. But Finan was just as fast and his lunge at Waormund's back must have wounded the big man because he roared again and twisted away to drive Finan back. He still held my coat and I sliced at his arm with Wasp-Sting. She did not break his mail, but the force of the blow made him let go of me and I back-handed Wasp-Sting across his neck. The blade's edge hit the base of his skull, but he was still moving, which robbed the blow of almost all its force and, for all the good it did, I might as well have stroked his neck with a feather. He turned back, his scarred face a grimace of rage, and suddenly a spear flashed across my sight, the blade reflecting the small flame-light, and it struck Waormund's blade and glanced off. My men had come from *Spearhafoc*. A dozen were running toward us and more were coming up the narrow stone steps.

Waormund might have been in a rage, he might have

drunk too much ale, but he was no fool when it came to a fight. He had stood in too many shield walls, had felt the shadows of defeat and the imminence of death too often, and so he knew when to retreat. He spun away from me toward the house where, just as my men came from the ship, three of his companions burst through the door with their long-swords drawn.

"Back!" Waormund bellowed. He was suddenly out-numbered and he and his men went through the door, which they slammed shut. I heard the locking bar drop into place.

"Dear God," Finan said, "he's a brute. Are you wounded?"

"Bruised," I said. It had been stupid to approach the house so lightly armed. "I'm not hurt," I went on as Berg handed me Serpent-Breath, "you?"

"I'm alive," he said dourly.

Alive, but in confusion. Every person we had spoken to had been certain that Æthelstan's troops occupied Lundene, yet here was one of Æthelhelm's most feared warriors at the very heart of the city. I went to the house door, knowing it would not pull open, nor did it. A woman screamed from somewhere inside. "Get an axe," I ordered.

I knew the house all too well, and knew there was no way in from the river terrace except by this door. The stone walls were built to the very edge of the masonry platform, so there was no way to walk down the sides of the house, while the windows were guarded with iron bars.

Beornoth brought the axe and struck a giant blow that made the stout door shudder. A woman screamed again. I could hear other noises inside the house, footsteps and muttered words, but what they meant I could not tell. Then the axe fell again with another mighty blow and the noises beyond the door faded away. "They've gone," Finan said.

"Or they're waiting to ambush us," I answered.

Beornoth's axe crashed through the thick wood. I stooped to peer through the hole and saw the passageway beyond was empty. Torchlight still flickered in the courtyard at the passageway's end. "Keep going," I told Beornoth, and two more blows were enough to let him reach through the shattered door and lift the locking bar.

The house was empty. The great rooms, closest to the river, had six straw mattresses, some cloaks, a litter of ale pots and half-eaten bread, and an empty scabbard. Waormund or one of his men had kicked over a pail of shit and piss that was smeared across the tiled floor of the room where Gisela and I had once slept. The servants' rooms, across the courtyard, still had a simmering cauldron of bean and mutton stew and a heap of firewood stacked against one wall, but no servants. I went to the front door, opened it cautiously, and stepped onto the street with Serpent-Breath in my hand. There was no one in sight.

Finan pulled me back into the house. "You stay here," he said. "I'll go talk to the sentries at the bastion." I began to protest, but Finan cut me off. "Stay here!" he insisted, and I let him take a half-dozen men along the dark street. I locked the door and went back to the larger rooms where Eadgifu was spreading her own cloak on one of the mattresses. Edmund, her eldest son, was peering into the other room with its stinking floor, but I dragged him away and thrust him back to his mother. Father Aart, who had vomited helplessly for almost all of *Spearhafoc*'s voyage, had recovered, and opened his mouth to protest at my treatment of the prince, but one look at my face persuaded him to stay silent. He was frightened of me.

"The straw has fleas," Awyrgan complained.

"Lice too, probably," I said. "And don't be in too much of a hurry to make beds."

"I'm not making a bed," Eadgifu said, "just a place to sit. We're going to the palace, surely? In Lundene I always stay in the palace!"

"We'll go to the palace, my queen," Awyrgan reassured her.

"Don't be a bloody fool," I snarled at him. "Those were Æthelhelm's men. If we're wrong and they're still occupying the city, then we leave. We leave tonight. Finan's gone to discover what's happening."

Awyrgan stared at me. "Leave tonight?"

It would be difficult. The Temes was wide, and though the current would help us downstream there were shoals in the river that would make it a perilous journey in darkness. But if Æthelhelm's men were still holding the city we would have no choice. "How long do you think we'll all live," I asked Awyrgan with a patience I did not feel, "if Æthelhelm's troops are here?"

"Maybe they're not?" Eadgifu asked.

"Which is what Finan is finding out, my lady," I said, "so be ready to leave in a hurry."

One of the babies began crying and a maidservant hurried the child out of the room. "But if Æthelstan's men are here," Eadgifu pleaded, "we can go to the palace? I have clothes there! I need clothes!"

"Maybe we'll go to the palace," I said, too tired to discuss it. If the city was safe then I would let her find her luxury, but till then she could scratch her flea-bites.

I went back to the river terrace to escape the stench

of the house and there sat on the low wall that fronted the Temes and gazed down as Berg and two men turned *Spearhafoc* so that her prow was pointing downstream. They did it efficiently, made her fast again, and so ready to leave the city in a hurry if Finan brought bad news, then all three settled into the ship's wide belly. They would guard the ship from the night thieves who could strip rigging and steal oars.

I watched the river swirl and tried to make some sense of the day. I reckoned Waormund must have sailed straight back to Lundene when he saw our ships destroying his small fleet off the Northumbrian coast, but if Æthelstan controlled the city, as we had been told, then why was Waormund still here? Why had the big West Saxon not left with the rest of Æthelhelm's men? And why only six warriors? I had seen four men, but there had been six straw beds, and that too was strange. Why would six men quarter themselves in this riverside house when presumably the rest of Æthelhelm's men would be lodged in the old fort or guarding the palace at Lundene's northwestern corner?

Night had fallen now. There were buildings on the Temes's south bank, and the torch flames that lit the entrance to a church flickered their shimmering reflections on the river. A three-quarter's moon slid behind a cloud. The ships moored at the nearby wharves groaned in the wind, their halyards slapping lazily against masts. I heard men laughing from the Dead Dane, a nearby tavern.

The house door opened and I turned, expecting Finan, but it was Roric, my servant, who brought a flaming torch that he put into a bracket by the door. He glanced at me, seemed to be about to speak, then thought better of it and went back into the house, first holding open the door for a hooded figure who walked slowly and carefully toward me carrying two beakers. One of the beakers was held toward me. "It is wine." It was Benedetta who offered me the drink. "It is not good wine, but it is better than ale."

"You don't like ale?"

"Ale is sour," she said, "and so is this wine."

I sipped it. She was right, it was sour, but I was used to sour-tasting wine. "You like sweet wine?" I asked.

"I like good wine." She sat beside me. "This vinegar was found in the kitchens of the house. Maybe they cook with it? It stinks!"

"The wine?"

"The river."

"It's a city," I said. "All cities make their rivers stink."

"I remember this smell," she said.

"Hard to forget it."

Benedetta sat to my left and I remembered the heavy wooden bench where Gisela and I would sit, with Gisela always on my left. "The queen is not happy," Benedetta said, "she wants her comfort."

I grimaced. "She wants a mattress filled with feathers?"

"She would like that, yes."

"She asked for my help," I said harshly, "and I gave it to her. When I get her to a safe place she can have all the damned feathers she wants, but till then she can suffer fleas like the rest of us."

"I shall tell her," Benedetta said, sounding as if she looked forward to giving that piece of bad news. "You think Lundene is not safe?"

"Not till I know who controls the city," I said. "Finan should be back soon." I had heard no shouts in the night, no sound of running feet, no clash of swords. That lack of sounds suggested that Finan and his men had met no enemies.

Benedetta had half pushed back her hood and I gazed at her in the night. She had a strong-boned face with large eyes that looked bright against her bronze-darkened skin. "You are looking at me," she said flatly.

"I am."

"Men look at women," she went on, "and take what

they want." She shrugged. "But I am a slave, so what can I expect?"

"You serve a queen. You should demand respect."

"I do demand it! But that does not make me liked or make me safe." She paused. "Edward looked at me too." I said nothing, but I suppose the question was written all over my face. She shrugged. "He was kinder than some."

"How many men do I have to kill for you?"

She smiled at that. "I killed one myself."

"Good."

"That one was a pig, a *porco*! He was on top of me, and I put a knife into his ribs while he was grunting like a pig." She turned to look at me. "Will you really let me kill Gunnald Gunnaldson?"

"Is that what you want?"

"That would be good," she said wistfully. "But how can I kill the *porco* if you send us to your home in the north?"

"We don't know what we're doing yet."

"If Gunnald Gunnaldson lives," Benedetta went on, "then I think it is not far from here. It is by the river, I know, because the smell was always there. A big building, dark. It had a private place where their ships tied up."

"A wharf."

"A wharf," she repeated the word, "with a wooden wall. And two ships were kept there. And there was a courtyard with a fence, another wall. He would show the slaves there, or his father would show us. I thought I was in hell. Men would laugh as they fingered us." She stopped abruptly. She was staring toward the house and I saw the glint of a tear. "I was just a child."

"Yet the child went to a palace," I said gently.

"Yes." She stopped after that one word and I thought she would say no more, then she spoke again. "Where I was a toy till the queen wanted me to serve her. That was three years ago."

"How long ago—" I began, but she interrupted me.

"Twenty-two years, lord. I count the years. Twenty-two years since the *Saraceni* took me from my home." She looked upriver to where the gaunt storehouses stood above the wharves. "I would enjoy killing him."

The house door opened again and Finan appeared. Benedetta started to stand, but I put a hand on her arm to keep her seated. "Finan," I greeted him.

"Æthelstan's men are here," Finan said.

"Thank the gods for that."

"But Æthelstan isn't. They think he's still in Gleawecestre, but they're not sure. Is that ale?"

"Wine."

"Devil's piss," Finan said, "but I'll drink it." He took the beaker from me and sat at the angle of the wall. "Your old friend Merewalh commands here."

And that news was a relief. Merewalh was indeed an old friend. He had led Æthelflaed's household warriors, he had fought beside me many times, and I valued him as a sober, sensible, and reliable man.

"Only he's not here either," Finan went on. "He left yesterday. He took most of his men to Werlameceaster."

"He took them to Werlameceaster! Why?" It was as much a protest as a question.

"God alone knows why," Finan said. "The fellow I talked to just knew Merewalh was gone! Didn't know why he left, but it was all done in a hurry. He left a man called Bedwin in command here."

"Bedwin," I repeated the name. "Never heard of him. How many men did Æthelstan take?"

"Over five hundred."

I swore, briefly and uselessly. "And how many did he leave here?"

"Two hundred."

Which was not nearly enough to defend Lundene. "And most of those," I said bitterly, "are probably the oldest and weakest men." I gazed up, seeing a star wink between two hurrying clouds. "And Waormund?" I asked.

"The devil only knows where that bastard is. I saw no sight or sound of him."

"Waormund?" Benedetta asked with alarm in her voice.

"He was in the house when we arrived," I explained.

"He is a devil," she said angrily and made the sign of the cross. "He is vile!"

I could guess why she spoke so fiercely, but did not ask her. "He's gone," I reassured her instead.

"He's disappeared," Finan corrected me grimly, "but the bastard must be lurking somewhere."

And Waormund only had five men, which surely meant we were safe from him. And he had evidently taken the women servants from the house, which suggested he had other plans for the night rather than attacking us. But why, I wondered, was Waormund even in the city? And why had Merewalh taken most of the garrison north? "Has the war started?" I asked.

"Probably," Finan said, then drained the wine. "God, that's swill."

"Where is this place?" Benedetta asked, then tried to pronounce it, "Werla . . ."

"Werlameceaster?"

"Where is that?"

"A day's march north of here," I said. "It's an old Roman town."

"A Mercian town?" Benedetta asked.

"Yes."

"Maybe they attack it?" she suggested.

"Maybe," I said, but I thought it far more likely that Merewalh had taken men to garrison Werlameceaster, because the town, with its strong Roman walls, lay across one of the main roads from East Anglia, and the lords of that kingdom were now firmly allied with Wessex.

Finan must have thought the same. "So maybe he's stopping an East Anglian army from reinforcing Æthelhelm?" he suggested.

"I'd guess as much. But I have to find out." I stood.

"How?" Benedetta asked.

"By asking Bedwin," I said, "whoever he is. He'll be at the palace, I suppose, so I'll start there."

"Don't forget Waormund is here," Finan warned me.

"I won't go alone. You're coming. It's a mess," I said angrily. But in truth it was a mess of my own making. Because I had sworn an oath. "Let's go."

"I'm coming!" Benedetta said, standing.

"You're coming!" I turned to her, startled.

My surprise had made me speak too harshly and she looked frightened for a heartbeat. "The queen wants me to go," she said uncertainly, and then, like a mare going from a stumbling walk into a smart trot, she went on more confidently, "she wishes me to fetch some robes she left in the palace. And some slippers." Finan and I still just stared at her. "Queen Eadgifu," Benedetta went on with dignity now, "keeps clothing in each royal house. She has need of some. When those pigs took her from Fæfresham they would not let us carry clothes." She paused, looking at us. "We need clothes!"

There was another awkward pause as Finan and I digested that. "Then you'd better come," I said.

I left Berg in charge of the house and the ship. I would rather have taken the young Norseman with me because he was invaluable in a fight, but after Finan he was my most reliable man. "Keep the doors barred," I told him, "and put a larger guard on *Spearhafoc*. I don't want her burned in the night."

"You think Waormund will come back?"

"I don't know what Waormund will do," I told him. So far as I could tell Waormund only had the five men, far fewer than I did, but his presence in the city still troubled me. My reason said that he was helpless, trapped and outnumbered in a city possessed by his enemies, but my instinct was screaming that there was danger. "Maybe Æthelhelm has others hidden in the city," I told Berg. "Your job is to keep the queen and her sons safe. You don't fight a battle if Waormund comes, you get everyone on board *Spearhafoc* and you take her out into the river where the queen will be safe."

"She will be safe, lord," Berg promised me.

"And you hold the ship in the river till we come back," I ordered him.

"And if you don't come back?" Berg asked, hastily adding, "Which you will, lord. Of course you will."

"Then you go home to Bebbanburg and you take Queen Eadgifu with you."

"I go home?" he sounded appalled that he would have to leave without me.

"You go home," I said.

I took Finan and six other men, all in mail, all helmeted, and all carrying long-swords. We walked east, following the wall the Romans had built to face the river, a wall that was now much pierced by ragged holes to give access to the busy wharves. I suspected we passed the slave house where Benedetta had been treated so brutally, but if we did she said nothing. The narrow street was dark except where flame-light was cast through a door or window, and as we approached any such building the noise inside would cease at the sound of our footsteps. Babies were hushed and dogs quieted. Any person we saw, and they were very few, scurried out of our path into the shadows of a doorway or alley. The city was nervous, frightened of becoming the victim to men's ambitions.

We turned into the wider street that led uphill from Lundene's bridge. We passed a big tavern called the Red Pig, an ale-house that had always been popular with Æthelhelm's troops when they were in the city. "Remember the Pig?" I asked Finan.

He chuckled. "You hanged a man from the tavern sign."

"A Centishman," I said. A fight had started in the street and had looked as if it might turn into a riot, and the quickest way to end it had been to hang a man.

A torch burned outside the Red Pig, but despite that flickering light Finan tripped on a slab and almost fell. He swore, then wiped his hand on his cloak. "Lundene," he said bitterly, "where the streets are paved with shit."

"Saxons are dirty people," Benedetta said.

"Cities are dirty," I said.

"They do not wash," Benedetta went on, "even the women! Most of them."

I found I had nothing to say. Lundene was indeed dirty, it was filthy, yet it fascinated me. We passed pillars that had once graced great buildings, but which were now surrounded by wattle and clay. Shadows lay beneath arches that led to nowhere. New buildings had been made since I left, filling the gaps between the Roman houses, some of which still had tiled roofs above three or four stone-built stories. You could see, even in the night, that this had once been a glorious place, proud with pillars and gleaming with marble. Now, except for the streets closest to the river, it was largely abandoned and gone to ruin. Folk had always believed that the ghosts of the Romans stalked these ancient streets and so they preferred to settle in the new Saxon city built to the west and, though Alfred and his son Edward had encouraged people to move back inside the old walls, much of Lundene was still a wasteland.

We passed a newly thatched church and turned left at the top of the hill and, ahead of us, on the city's western hill, flaming torches lit the palace, which lay close by the cathedral that Alfred had ordered to be rebuilt. We had to cross the shallow valley where the Weala brook flowed south to the Temes. We crossed the bridge and walked uphill toward the palace that had first been built for Mercia's kings. The entrance was a Roman arch carved with spearmen who carried long oblong shields, and it was guarded by four men who had round shields painted with Æthelstan's symbol, the dragon holding a lightning bolt. That symbol was something of a relief. Finan had assured me that

Æthelstan's men still occupied the city, but the dragon with its jagged lightning was my first proof. "They're old men," Finan grunted.

"Probably younger than you and me," I said, which made him laugh.

The old men at the gate were evidently alarmed by our approach because one hammered on the closed doors with the butt of his spear and, a moment later, three more men appeared. They pulled the doors shut behind them then lined beneath the arch and leveled their weapons. "Who are you?" one of the newcomers demanded.

"Is Bedwin in the palace?" I asked.

The man who had spoken hesitated. "He is," he finally said.

"And I'm the Jarl Uhtred of Bebbanburg, here to see him." I rarely used the Danish title, but the man's surly tone had angered me, and my men, hearing the arrogance in my voice, drew their swords.

There was a brief pause, then at a signal, the spears were lowered. Six of the men just gaped at me, but the surly man still wanted to keep his authority. "You have to surrender your weapons," he demanded.

"Is there a king here?"

The question seemed to confuse him. "No," he managed to say.

"No, lord," I snarled.

"No, lord."

"Then it isn't a king's hall tonight, is it? We keep our weapons. Open the doors."

He hesitated again, then relented and the high doors creaked open on their ancient iron hinges and I led my men into the lantern-lit corridor beyond. We passed the stairs where, so often, I had climbed to meet Æthelflaed, and that memory was as sharp and painful as the recollection of Gisela on the river terrace. Where were they now? I wondered. Did Gisela wait for me in Asgard, the home of the gods? Did Æthelflaed watch me from her Christian heaven? I have known many wise men, but none who could answer those questions.

We walked through a courtyard where a wooden chapel stood above the remnants of a Roman pool, then through a broken arch into a passage made of thin Roman bricks. "You can put your swords in their scabbards," I told my men, then pushed open the crude wooden door that had replaced some piece of Roman magnificence. The feasting hall beyond was lit by a myriad rushlights and candles, but there were only a dozen men seated about the one table. They looked alarmed as we entered, then stood, not in welcome but to give themselves space to draw their swords. "Who are you?" a man demanded.

I had no chance to answer because another man answered for me. "He is the Lord Uhtred of Bebban-burg." It was a tall, stern priest who had spoken and who now offered me a slight bow. "It is good to see you again, lord. Welcome."

"Father Oda," I said. "It's a surprise to see you."

"A surprise, lord?"

"I thought you were in Mameceaster."

"I was, and now I am here." His words were touched by a Danish accent. His parents had come as invaders to East Anglia, but the son had converted to Christianity and now served Æthelstan. "And I am surprised to see you too, lord," he went on, "but glad of it. Now come," he gestured me toward the table, "there's wine."

"I came to see Bedwin."

Father Oda indicated the man at the head of the table who had challenged us when we entered and who now walked toward us. He was a tall man, dark haired, with a long face and long mustaches that hung down to the ornate silver cross at his breast. "I am Bedwin," he said, sounding anxious. Two wolfhounds growled when he spoke, but quieted at a gesture from him. He stopped some paces away, his face still showing puzzle-ment at our arrival, an expression that swiftly changed to resentment. Did he think I had come to usurp his place as commander of the city? "We were not told of your coming, lord," he said, and it was almost a reproof.

"I came to see King Æthelstan."

"Who is in Gleawecestre," Bedwin said, almost as if he was ordering me to go across Britain.

"You say there's wine, father?" I asked Oda.

"Which needs drinking," the priest answered.

I gestured for my men to follow me, then sat on the bench and allowed Oda to pour me a generous beaker. "This," I held a hand toward Benedetta, "is one of Queen Eadgifu's attendants. She's come to collect some of the queen's robes. I'm sure she would like some wine too."

"Queen Eadgifu?" Bedwin asked as if he had never heard of her.

"Who is here in Lundene," I said, "with her children. She'd like to use her old chambers in this palace."

"Queen Eadgifu!" Bedwin sounded angry. "What is she doing here? She should be with her husband's corpse!"

I drank the wine, which was much better than the swill I had drunk earlier. "She fled from Mercia," I said patiently, "because Lord Æthelhelm threatened her life and those of her children. I rescued her from his forces and she now seeks the protection of King Æthelstan."

That was not quite true, Eadgifu trusted Æthelstan almost as little as she trusted Æthelhelm, but Bedwin did not need to know that.

"Then she must travel to Gleawecestre," Bedwin said indignantly. "There's no room for her here!"

"Merewalh might have a different opinion," I suggested.

"Merewalh has gone north," Bedwin said.

"To Werlameceaster, I hear?"

Bedwin nodded, then frowned as Father Oda refilled my beaker. It was Father Oda who answered me, his voice smooth. "We had a report that an East Anglian army was coming, lord," he explained, "and Merewalh thought the danger sufficient to take most of his men to Werlameceaster."

"Leaving Lundene almost defenseless," I said unhappily.

"Indeed, lord," Father Oda spoke calmly, but could not hide his disapproval of what Merewalh had chosen to do. "But Merewalh will return when he has dissuaded the East Anglians."

"When he's beaten the shit out of them, you mean?"

"No, lord. Dissuaded them. King Æthelstan insists that we do not begin the fighting. Lord Æthelhelm must kill first. King Æthelstan will not have the blood of fellow Christians on his hands unless he is attacked."

"Yet he captured Lundene! Are you telling me there was no fighting?"

Bedwin answered. "The West Saxons abandoned the city."

I stared at Bedwin with astonishment. "They abandoned it?" It seemed unbelievable to me. Lundene was Britain's largest city, it was the fortress that joined East Anglia to Wessex, it was the place where a king could earn a small fortune in fees and taxes, and Æthelhelm had simply given it up?

Father Oda again offered an explanation. "We came, lord, they numbered fewer than two hundred men, they asked for a flag of truce, we described in some detail what fate awaited them if they insisted on defending the city and, seeing the sense of our proposals, they left."

"Some stayed," I said.

"No, lord," Bedwin insisted. "They left."

"Waormund is here," I said. "I fought him not two hours ago."

"Waormund!" Bedwin made the sign of the cross. I doubt he was even aware of doing it, but the fear that Waormund's name aroused was plain on Bedwin's face. "You know it was Waormund?" he asked.

I did not answer because none of this made sense. Æthelhelm knew as well as any man that Lundene was a prize, and not a prize to be given up lightly. Even if Ælfweard and Æthelstan agreed to keep to the terms of their father's will, and Ælfweard would rule Wessex while Æthelstan was King of Mercia, they would still fight over Lundene, because whoever ruled Lundene was the richest king of Britain, and riches bought spears and shields. Yet Æthelhelm's men had simply abandoned the city? Now, astonishingly, Merewalh had done the same.

"You're sure it was Waormund?" Oda repeated Bedwin's query.

"It was Waormund," Finan said curtly.

"He had men with him?" the priest asked.

"A few," I said, "maybe only five."

"Then he's no danger," Bedwin remarked.

I ignored his stupidity. Waormund was a one-man army, a destroyer, a killer, a man who could dominate a shield wall and change history with his sword. So why was he here? "How," I asked, "did you discover this East Anglian army? The one Merewalh has gone to stop."

"News came from Werlameceaster, lord," Bedwin said stiffly, "and it told of an East Anglian army ready to march into the heart of Mercia."

There was some sense in that. Æthelstan would

be watching southward, guarding the Temes's crossing places, and an enemy army at his back would be a distraction at best and a looming disaster at worst, but though it all became clear to me, I could still feel the prickle of instinct telling me it was all wrong. Then, suddenly, like a mist lifting from the morning land to reveal hedgerow and spinney, it all made sense to me. "Have you sent patrols eastward?" I asked Bedwin.

"Eastward?" he asked, puzzled.

"Toward Celmeresburh!" Celmeresburh was a town to the north-east, a town on one of the main Roman roads leading from East Anglia's heartland to Lundene.

Bedwin shrugged. "I have few enough men to hold the city, lord, without sending men away."

"We should have sent patrols," Oda said quietly.

"Priests should not concern themselves with such matters," Bedwin snapped, and I realized the two men had disagreed.

"It is always wise," I said acidly, "to listen to a Dane when he talks of warfare." Oda smiled, though I did not. "Send a patrol in the morning," I ordered Bedwin. "At dawn! A strong patrol. At least fifty men, and give them your fastest horses."

Bedwin hesitated. He did not like me giving him orders, but I was a lord, an ealdorman, and a warrior

with a reputation. Even so he bridled and was searching for the words to argue with me, but those words
never came.

Because a horn sounded in the night. It blew again
and again, an urgent, even desperate call. And then it
stopped abruptly.

A church bell clanged. Then another. And I knew
that my orders had been given too late because Æthelhelm's trap was sprung.

Because surely Waormund had been left behind to
do just one thing; to open a gate in the dead of night.
And somewhere along the city's eastern ramparts there
must already be slaughtered guards and an open gate,
which meant that Æthelhelm's East Anglian army
was nowhere near Werlameceaster. It was coming into
Lundene.

And so the screaming began.

Six

I swore. Much good that did.

Bedwin was gaping, the other men about the table were looking equally confused, each of them just waiting for someone to tell them what to do.

"This way," I snarled at my men and grasped the sleeve of Benedetta's robe, "come!"

At that moment, of course, I did not know what was happening, but the insistent horn and the clangor of bells spoke of an attack. The only other event that might have started such an alarm was a fire, but as we ran from the palace door there was no glow in the sky. The guards were just standing there, staring eastward. "What do we do, lord?" one called to me.

"Go inside, join Bedwin!" The last thing I needed was nervous half-trained men trailing me. The bells announced that there would be killing in the city this night, and I needed to reach *Spearhafoc*. I shouted at my men to follow me down the hill, but before we were halfway to the river I saw horsemen pouring from a nearby street, the points of their spear-blades catching and reflecting the light of a torch. I was still holding Benedetta's arm and she gasped in alarm as I veered sharply right to dive into an alley. I would have preferred to go left, to head eastward toward *Spearhafoc*, but there was no alley or street close enough.

I stopped in the alley and swore again, and it did no more good than the first curse. "What is it?" Beornoth asked.

"The enemy," Vidarr Leifson answered for me.

"Coming from the east by the look of it," Finan said quietly.

"I told the fool to send scouts," a voice said, "but he refused! He said he had too few men, but he'll have even fewer now."

The alley was dark and I could not see the speaker, but his Danish accent betrayed him. It was Father Oda. "What are you doing here?" I asked harshly.

"Seeking safety," he answered calmly, "and I trust you to protect me, lord, more than I trust that fool Bedwin."

For a moment I was tempted to order him back to the palace, then relented. One more man would make no difference to us, even if the man was a Christian priest and carried no weapon. "This way!" I said. I still went downhill, but now using backstreets and alleys. The sound of the horses' hooves was muffled, but I heard a scream, then heard the clash of sword on metal. We kept running.

The horsemen I had seen had been coming from the east. The riverside house where I had left Berg, the rest of my men, and Eadgifu were all to the east, and the house was not far from the city's easternmost gate. Waormund, I thought, must have attacked that gate to let in the approaching troops who now spread through the city. Worse, Waormund would know exactly where to find me, and he had doubtless led men straight to the house. So had Berg managed to escape? If he had, then he would have taken *Spearhafoc* into the river's center and would be holding her there, but as we stumbled down the alleys I wondered how we would ever reach her.

"Down here, lord!" Oswi called.

Oswi was young, clever, and a good warrior. I had met him when he was an orphan haunting the streets of Lundene and making a living by theft. He had tried to steal from me, had been caught and, instead of giving him the whipping he deserved, I had pardoned him and trained him as a fighter. He knew the city, and he must have known what was in my mind because he led us downhill through a maze of alleys. The footing was treacherous in the dark and I almost fell twice. Father Oda was guiding Benedetta now, the rest of us all had drawn swords. The noise in the night was louder, the roar of men, of screaming women, of howling dogs and the hammer of iron-shod hooves, but no enemy had yet pierced these narrow alleys in the western part of the city.

"Stop!" Oswi held up a hand. We had reached the street that ran just inside the old river wall, and the bridge was close to our left. We were hidden by dark shadow, but the approach to the bridge was lit by torches and there were men there, too many men, men in mail and helmets, men with shields, spears, and swords. None wore the dull red cloak of Æthelhelm's men, but nor did any of them carry Æthelstan's symbol on their shields.

"East Anglians?" Finan asked me.

"Who else?"

The East Anglians were barring our way eastward, and we shrank back into deep shadow as dozens of horsemen came into sight. They came from the east, were led by a man wearing a red cloak, and were carrying long spears. I heard laughter, then a command to go uphill. The hoofbeats sounded again as we shrank into the alley, hidden there by shadow and fear.

I swore for the third time. I had hoped to get down to the tangle of wharves and work my way along the river bank to the house, but that had always been a forlorn ambition. Berg and his men had either been overwhelmed and slaughtered, or else they had reached *Spearhafoc* and were even now out in the river's darkness. But had this East Anglian army come by boat too? That seemed unlikely. It would take a seaman of uncanny ability to negotiate the seaward twists of the Temes in the moon-shrouded darkness, but one thing was sure; the eastern part of the city, the part I needed to reach, was swarming with the enemy.

"We go north," I said, and knew I was trying to lead us out of a mistake. There had never been a real chance of reaching *Spearhafoc* and in taking my men and Benedetta down the hill I had gone in the wrong direction.

"North?" Oswi asked.

"If we can leave the city," I said, "we have a chance to reach the road to Werlameceaster."

"We have no horses," Father Oda pointed out calmly.

"Then, damn it, we walk!" I snarled.

"And the enemy," he went on, still speaking calmly, "will send horsemen on patrol."

I said nothing, nor did anyone else speak until Finan broke the silence. "It is always wise," he said drily and using the words I had spoken to Bedwin not long before, "to listen to a Dane when he talks of warfare."

"So we won't stay on the road," I said. "We'll use the woods where the horsemen can't find us. Oswi, get us to one of the northern gates."

The attempt to reach the northern city wall also failed. Whoever led the East Anglian army was no fool. He had sent men to capture and then guard each of the seven gates. Two of those gates pierced the walls of the Roman fort built at the city's northwestern corner and, when we drew close, we heard the sound of men fighting. There was an open space in front of the fort and to the west of the ruined amphitheater, and a score of bodies lay on that paved square that was lit by the torches burning on the palace walls. Blood had run on the stone and trickled into the weed-thick gaps between the old paving slabs where men in red cloaks were stripping the corpses of mail. The fort's southern gate, one of the two that led into the city, was wide open, and six horsemen came through the arch. They were led by an imposing man who rode a great black stallion, wore a white cloak, and had a mail coat of brightly polished metal. "That's Varin," Father Oda whispered.

"Varin?" I asked. We were again hidden in the deep shadow of an alley.

"An East Anglian," Father Oda explained, "and one of Lord Æthelhelm's commanders."

"Varin is a Danish name," I said.

"He is a Dane," the priest said, "and like me he is a Christian. I know him well. We were friends once."

"In East Anglia?" I asked. I knew that Father Oda's parents had settled in East Anglia, sailing there from their home across the North Sea.

"In East Anglia," Father Oda said, "which is as much a Danish land as it is Saxon. A third of Lord Æthelhelm's East Anglian troops are Danes. Maybe more than a third?"

That should not have surprised me. East Anglia had fallen to the Danes before Alfred had come to the throne and had long been ruled by Danish kings. Their sovereignty ended when Edward's West Saxon army defeated them and, though many had died in the fighting, the Danes who survived had known which way fate's wind was blowing and so had converted to Christianity. They then swore loyalty to the new Saxon lords who took over the wide estates. Æthelhelm the

Elder, who had died while my prisoner, had been given vast tracts of East Anglia and had raised an army of hard-bitten Danes to defend it. Those were the men who, with their Saxon comrades, had come to Lundene this night.

"We'll not be getting out of the city this way," Finan said sourly.

Varin's men had captured the gates, the bridge, and the Roman fort, which meant Lundene had fallen. Merewalh had been lured northward, Bedwin had failed to guard the eastern roads, and now squads of Æthelhelm's warriors began to probe into the deep alleys and streets of the city to end any hope of resistance from Bedwin's defeated troops. We were trapped.

And I had made a second mistake that night. The first was the vain attempt to reach *Spearhafoc*, the second was to try to leave by a northern gate, and my best hope now was to find a boat and escape downriver. "Get us back to the wharves," I told Oswi, "east of the bridge." I wanted to be downriver of the bridge, which had perilous narrow gaps between the stone piers where the water seethed, churned, and had capsized many a smaller boat.

"Bastards were swarming down there," Finan warned me.

"Then we hide!" I snarled. My anger was with myself, not with Finan. I felt like a rat trapped by terriers;
still fighting but with no place to run.

No place to run, but there were places to hide, and
Oswi knew Lundene like a rat knows a stable yard.
He led us quickly, keeping to the small alleys that the
enemy had not yet reached. We went eastward now
and, though we had still not met the enemy, we could
hear them. We could hear shouts and shrieks, the clash
of blades, the laughter of men enjoying an easy victory.
Some people had fled to the churches to seek sanctu-
ary and, as we skirted one wooden church, I heard a
woman wailing and a baby crying.

We had to cross the wide street that led from the
bridge to the big market square at the top of the hill.
Torches burned on either side of the street, spewing
dark smoke into the troubled air. There were groups
of men beneath the flames, their swords sheathed and
their shields stacked against walls. One group had rolled
a barrel from the Red Pig tavern and an axeman stove
in the lid to provoke cheers. A woman screamed, then
abruptly went silent. Lundene had fallen and the captors
were enjoying the spoils, but then a red-cloaked horseman spurred up from the river. "To the palace, lads!" he
called. "Leave that ale, there's plenty more!"

The street emptied slowly, but it was still dangerous. I peered downhill and saw there were men guarding the bridge and some of them began to climb toward us. I guessed that this main street would stay busy all night, yet we had to cross it if we were to find a ship on the wharves to the east of the bridge. "We just stroll across," I said.

"Stroll?" Father Oda asked.

"We don't run. We don't look frightened. We just stroll."

So we did. We walked across the street slowly, as if we had not a care in the world. Benedetta was still with Father Oda, and one of the men coming from the bridge saw her. "You found a woman?" he shouted.

"A woman!" a half-dozen voices echoed.

"Share her!" the first man called.

"Keep going," I said, and followed Oswi through a half-broken arch that led into another alley. "Now hurry!" I called, but hurrying was treacherous because it was pitch dark, the alley was narrow, and its footing nothing but earth and broken stone. I heard our pursuers shout again. They had reached the arch and were following us into the darkness. "Finan," I said.

"A pleasure," he answered grimly, and the two of us let the others go past.

"Bring her here!" a man shouted. He received no answer, he could hear nothing but stumbling footsteps. "You bastards!" he called again. "Bring the bitch here!"

Again he received no answer and so he came toward us, followed by four men. We could see them outlined against the small light from the main street, but they would have seen little of us because their looming shadows obscured our drawn swords. "Bring her here!" the man bellowed again and then made a mewing sound as Serpent-Breath pierced his mail, tore through the muscles of his belly, and then twisted in his guts. He collapsed into me, his sword clattering on the ground, his right hand clutching at my mail coat. I brought my right knee up into his chin and the scream that had just begun became a bloody gurgle. I stepped back and wrenched Serpent-Breath free. Finan, with his usual lightning speed, had put his man down with no noise except for the hoarse bubbling gasp of a cut throat. I saw the blood spurt black across the alley and some splashed on my face as I stepped over the gut-slit man to thrust my blade into another. He tried to twist aside, but Serpent-Breath sliced across his ribs, tearing mail, then he tripped on the first dying man, and Beornoth, behind me, hammered down with his sword's pommel to break the man's skull open like an egg. Finan had taken a man's eyes, and that man was screaming, hands clutched to his bloody face.

The last man stopped, then fled from the alley. Finan started after him, but I seized his arm. "Back," I said, "back! Leave him!" The fugitive had already reached the wider torch-lit street.

We ran, looking for Oswi. I turned right into another alley, tripped, skinned my left hand on a wall, turned left again. Sudden shouts came as men discovered the carnage we had made. Finan tugged my sleeve and I followed him down three stone steps. The moon had come from behind cloud and I could see again, except that we were in the black shadow of gaunt stone walls. Ruins, I thought, then we crossed a moonlit space and turned into another alley. Where the hell was Oswi? I could hear shouts behind us. The last bell in the west of the city stopped tolling, then a voice called near us, "This way! This way!" I saw a shadow within a shadow on top of a mound of broken stone. We clambered over and dropped down into bleak darkness. I trod on someone, Benedetta, who gasped, then I dropped beside her. "Quiet, lord!" Oswi whispered. "Quiet!"

Like hunted beasts we had gone to ground, but the hunters wanted more blood. One of our pursuers carried a flaming torch and the blundering shadows of big men were thrown onto a broken wall beside us. The hunters stopped, I held my breath and heard voices muttering. "This way!" one said, and the shadows faded as the footsteps went farther east. None of us moved, none of us spoke. Then a woman screamed terribly from not far away and men roared in triumph. She screamed again. Benedetta whispered something bitter. I did not understand a word, but I sensed she was trembling and I reached out to touch her and she seized my skinned hand and held it tightly.

And so we waited. The noises subsided, but we could still hear the woman whimpering. "Pigs," Benedetta said softly.

"Where are we?" I whispered in Oswi's direction.

"Safe, lord," he murmured, though our refuge seemed anything but safe to me. We appeared to be in the ruins of a small stone house with no way out except to go back the way we had entered. Other houses nearby were still being used. I saw flame-light appear and vanish at a shuttered window. Another woman screamed and Benedetta's hand gripped mine hard. Oswi whispered something and I heard Finan grunt in reply.

Then flint struck on steel, there was a puff of breath, another spark, and the small kindling from Finan's pouch caught fire. The flame was tiny, but just enough to show what looked like a small cave mouth in the rubble at the base of the broken wall, the dark opening supported by a shattered and tilted pillar. Oswi crawled into the hole, Finan handed him a scrap of burning wood, and the small flame vanished inside the hole. "This way!" Oswi hissed.

Finan followed, then one by one we wriggled into the cave. Finan had lit a larger piece of wood and in its light I saw we were in a cellar. I dropped down to a stone floor and almost gagged at the stench. The cellar had to be close to a cesspit. Benedetta held her scarf to her mouth and nose. Thick pillars of narrow Roman bricks supported the ceiling. "We used to hide here," Oswi said, then clambered through a gap in the stone wall on the cellar's far side. "Be careful here!"

Again Finan followed him. The flame of the makeshift torch flickered. Beyond the gap was another cellar, but deeper, and to my right was the cesspit. A narrow ledge led to a brick arch and it was through that last opening that Oswi vanished. A boy's voice challenged him, more voices added to the sudden noise, then Finan handed the torch to Vidarr and drew his sword. He stepped through the arch and shouted for silence. There was immediate quiet.

I followed Finan to discover a dozen children in

the final cellar. The oldest might have been thirteen, the youngest only half that age. Three girls and nine ragged boys, all of them looking starved, their eyes big against pale, wild faces. They had beds of straw, their clothes were rags, and their hair hung lank and long. Oswi had lit a small fire, using straw and scraps of wood, and in its light I could see that one of the older boys held a knife. "Put it away, boy," I snarled and the knife vanished. "Is this the only entrance?" I asked from the brick arch.

"The only one, lord," Oswi said, tending his fire.

"He's a lord?" a boy asked. None of us answered him.

"Who are they?" I asked, though it was a stupid question because the answer was plain to see.

"Orphans," Oswi said.

"Like you."

"Like me, lord."

"Aren't there convents?" Benedetta asked. "Places to look after motherless children?"

"Convents are cruel," Oswi said harshly. "If they don't like you they sell you to the slavers on the river."

"What's happening?" the boy who had hidden the knife asked.

"Enemy troops," I answered. "They took the city. You'd best stay hidden till they calm down."

"And you're running from them?" he asked.

"What do you think?" I asked, and he said nothing. But I knew what he was thinking, that he could earn a small fortune by betraying us, which is why I had asked Oswi if there was another way out of this stinking, dark cellar. "You'll stay here till we say you can leave," I added. The boy just looked at me and said nothing. "What's your name, boy?"

He hesitated, as if wanting to challenge me, then muttered his name. "Aldwyn."

"Aldwyn, lord," I corrected him.

"Lord," he added reluctantly.

I crossed to him, stepping over rags and straw. I crouched and stared into his dark eyes. "If you betray us, Aldwyn, the enemy will give you a shilling. Maybe two shillings. But if you do me service, boy, I will give you gold." I took a coin from my pouch and showed it to him. He stared at it, looked up into my eyes, and then back to the coin. He did not speak, but I could see the hunger in his gaze. "Do you know that man?" I asked, nodding toward Oswi.

He glanced at Oswi, then back to me. "No, lord."

"Look at him," I said. The boy frowned, not understanding, but obediently looked at Oswi who was lit by the flames of the small fire. Aldwyn saw a warrior with a trimmed beard, a fine mail coat, and a sword belt thick with embroidery and small silver panels. "Tell him who you are, Oswi," I commanded, "and what you were."

"I'm a warrior of Northumbria," Oswi said proudly, "but I was once like you, boy. I lived in this cellar, I stole my food, and I ran from the slavers like you do. Then I met my lord and he became my gold-giver."

Aldwyn looked back to me. "You are really a lord?"

I ignored the question. "How old are you, Aldwyn?"

He shrugged. "I don't know, lord. Twelve?"

"You lead these boys and girls?"

He nodded. "I look after them, lord."

"Are you cruel?" I asked.

"Cruel?" He frowned.

"Are you cruel?" I asked again.

He still seemed puzzled by that question and, instead of answering, glanced at his companions. It was one of the girls who responded. "He can hurt us, lord," she said, "but only when we do something wrong."

"If you serve me," I said, "I will be a gold-giver to you all. And yes, Aldwyn, I am a lord. I am a great lord. I have land, I have ships, and I have men. And in time I will drive the enemy from this city and the streets will run with their blood and the dogs will gnaw their flesh and the birds will feast on their eyes."

"Yes, lord," he whispered.

And I hoped I had told him the truth.

———————

Spearhafoc **was** gone, the stone wharf was empty, and no corpses lay on the terrace.

My new troops brought me the news, or rather Aldwyn and his younger brother went as my scouts and came back bubbling with happiness at a successful mission. Father Oda had tried to warn me against employing them, saying that the temptation for them to betray us was too great, but I had seen the hunger in Aldwyn's young eyes. It was not a hunger for treachery, nor for the satisfaction of greed, but a hunger to belong, to be valued. They returned.

"There were soldiers there, lord," Aldwyn said excitedly.

"What was on their shields?"

"A bird, lord." These were city children and would not know a crow from a kittiwake, but I assumed the bird, whatever it might have been, was a symbol from East Anglia.

"And no corpses?"

"None, lord. No blood either."

That was a sensible observation. "How close did you get?"

"We went inside the house, lord! We said we were beggars."

"What did they do?"

"One hit me around the head, lord, and told me to piss off."

"So you pissed off?"

"Yes, lord." He grinned.

I gave him silver and promised him gold if he continued to serve me. So *Spearhafoc* was gone, which was a relief, but there was always the chance that an East Anglian fleet had been waiting in the sea reach of the Temes to reinforce the men who had captured the city, and that fleet could have captured Berg and my ship. I touched my hammer amulet, said a silent prayer to the gods, and tried to plan a future, but could see no hope beyond the immediate need to find food and ale.

"We steal," Aldwyn said when I asked him how his small band fed themselves.

"You can't steal enough food for us," I said. "We'll have to buy."

"They know us in the markets, lord," Aldwyn said gloomily. "They chase us away."

"And the best markets," one of the girls said, "are outside the city." She meant in the sprawling Saxon-built town to the west of the Roman walls. Folk preferred living there, far from the ghosts of Lundene.

"What do you need?" Father Oda asked me.

"Ale, bread, cheese, smoked fish. Anything."

"I will go," Benedetta said.

I shook my head. "It's not safe for a woman yet. Maybe tomorrow, when things calm down."

"She'll be safe in the company of a priest," Father Oda remarked.

I looked at him. The only light in the cellar came from a crack in the roof that also served as the smoke-hole. "But we only have a fire at night, lord," Aldwyn had told me, "and no one has ever noticed the smoke."

"You can't go, father," I told Oda.

He bristled. "Why not?"

"They know you, father," I said, "you're from East Anglia."

"I've grown a beard since then," he said calmly. It was a short beard, neatly cropped. "You either starve or let us go," he went on. "And if they take me captive? What can they do?"

"Kill you, father," Finan said.

A flicker of a smile touched the priest's face. "My lord Uhtred is known as the priest-killer, not Lord Æthelhelm."

"What will they do to you?" I asked.

He shrugged. "Either ignore me or, more likely, send me to Lord Æthelhelm. He is angry with me."

"You! Why?"

"Because I served him once," Father Oda said calmly. "I was one of his confessors. But I left his service."

I stared at him in surprise. When I had first met Father Oda he had been in the company of Osferth, an ally of Æthelstan's, and now I discovered he had been in Æthelhelm's service.

"Why did you leave?" Finan asked.

"He demanded we all give an oath to Prince Ælfweard, and in conscience I could not do so. Ælfweard is a cruel, unnatural boy."

"And King of Wessex now," Finan added.

"Which is why Lord Uhtred is here," Oda went on, still calm. "Soon the priest-killer will be a killer of kings too." He looked away from me to Oswi. "You will come with us, but no mail coat, no weapons. I am a priest, the lady Benedetta will say she is my wife, and you are our servant, and we go to buy food and ale for the brethren of Saint Erkenwald." I knew there was a monastery dedicated to Saint Erkenwald in the east of the city. "You, boy," Father Oda pointed at Aldwyn, "will follow us as far as the city gate and come back here if you see we are in trouble with the guards. And you, lord," he smiled at me, "will give us money."

I always carried a pouch of coins, a heavy pouch,

though I suspected it would lighten fast unless I could devise a way of escaping the city. I gave Father Oda a handful of silver shillings. I was hesitant to allow Benedetta to go with him, but as Oda pointed out the presence of a woman and a priest would allay suspicions. "They are looking for warriors, lord," Oda said, "not for married couples."

"It's still dangerous for a woman," I insisted.

"And only men may face danger?" Benedetta challenged me.

"She will come to no harm," Oda said firmly. "If any man offends her I will threaten him with the eternal furnaces of hell and the endless torments of Satan."

I had been raised with those threats hanging over me and, despite my belief in the older gods, I still felt a shiver of fear. I touched the hammer. "Go, then," I said, and so they did and returned safely three hours later with three sacks of food and two small barrels of ale.

"No one followed them, lord," Aldwyn told us.

"There was no trouble," Oda reported with his usual calm. "I talked to the commander of the gate and he tells me there are now four hundred men in the city and more are coming."

"By sea?" I asked, fearing for *Spearhafoc*.

"He did not say. Lord Æthelhelm is not here, nor is

King Ælfweard. Those two remain in Wintanceaster as far as he knows. The new garrison is commanded by Lord Varin."

"Who we saw yesterday."

"Indeed."

"It was good to breathe proper air," Benedetta said wistfully.

She was surely right because the stench of the cesspit was overwhelming. I was sitting on the damp floor, leaning my head against the dank bricks, and I thought that Jarl Uhtred, Lord of Bebbanburg, had come to this. I was a fugitive in a Lundene cellar leading a handful of warriors, one priest, a royal slave, and a band of ragged children. I touched the hammer hanging at my neck and closed my eyes. "We have to leave this damned city," I said bitterly.

"The walls are guarded," Father Oda warned me.

I opened my eyes to look at him. "Four hundred men, you say. It's not enough."

"No?" Benedetta looked surprised.

"Lundene's wall must be near two miles around?" I said, looking at Finan, who nodded agreement. "And that doesn't count the river wall," I went on. "Four hundred men can't defend two miles of wall. You'd need two and a half thousand men to fight off any attack."

"But four hundred men can guard the gates," Finan said quietly.

"But not the river wall. Too many gaps in that."

"Reinforcements are coming," Father Oda reminded me, "and there's more."

"More?"

"No one can move in the streets after sunset," he said. "Varin sent men to announce that edict. Folk must stay indoors until sunrise."

No one spoke for a moment. The children were tearing into the bread and cheese that Benedetta had given them. "No!" she cried sternly, stopping their squabbling. "You must have manners! Children without manners are worse than animals. You, boy," she pointed at Aldwyn, "you have a knife and you will cut the food. You will cut it evenly, the same for everyone."

"Yes, lady," he said.

Finan grinned at the boy's obedience. "You're thinking," he said to me, "of stealing a boat?"

"What else? We can't drop over the wall into the city's ditch, we won't fight our way through a gate without starting a pursuit by horsemen, but a boat might serve."

"They'll have captured the wharves," Finan said, "and be guarding them. They're not fools."

"There were soldiers on the wharves, lord," Aldwyn put in.

"I know where we might find a boat," I said, and looked at Benedetta.

She looked back, her eyes glinting in the cellar's darkness. "You are thinking of Gunnald Gunnaldson?" she asked.

"You told me his wharves are protected by fences? They're separate from the other docks?"

"They are," she said, "but maybe they captured his ships too?"

"Maybe," I said, "or maybe not. But I made you a promise."

"Yes, lord, you did." She offered me one of her rare smiles.

No one else understood what we spoke about, nor did I explain. "Tomorrow," I said, "we go tomorrow."

Because Uhtred, son of Uhtred, the killer of priests and the would-be killer of a king would become a killer of slavers too.

Aldwyn and his younger brother, who everyone called the Ræt, were my scouts again. They were gone for much of the day, and the longer they stayed away the more nervous I became. I had two men standing guard outside the cellar mouth, concealed there by the mounds of rubble. I joined them at noon to escape the fetid stench of the cesspit and found Benedetta with one of the smaller girls. "She's called Alaina," she told me.

"Pretty name," I said.

"For a pretty girl." Benedetta was cuddling the child, who had very dark hair, frightened eyes, and skin the same light golden color as Benedetta. I guessed she was seven or eight years old, and I had noticed her in the cellar's gloom because she was both better dressed and looked to be in better health than the other children. She had also looked more miserable, her eyes red from crying. Benedetta stroked the girl's hair. "She came here just before us!"

"Yesterday?"

Benedetta nodded. "Yesterday, and her mother is like me. From Italy." She said something in her own language to Alaina, then looked back to me. "A slave." She spoke defiantly, as if it were my fault.

"The child's a slave?" I asked.

Benedetta shook her head. "No, no. Nor is the mother anymore. Her mama is married to one of Merewalh's men and she left the house to take food to her husband and the other sentries. That's when the enemy came."

"The girl was alone?"

"Alone." She bent to kiss the child's hair. "Her mother said she would be home soon, but she never came home. And the poor child heard screaming and she ran from the sound. Aldwyn found her and here she is."

Alaina stared at me with wide eyes. She looked scared. She saw an older man with a scarred, hard face, a battered mail coat, a gold chain, and a brace of swords at his waist. I smiled at her and she looked away, burying her face in Benedetta's clothes. "Maybe," Benedetta said, "the two boys are caught?"

"They're cunning," I said, "they won't be caught."

"Gunnald would like to have them as slaves. Especially the young one. He can sell small boys almost as easily as little girls." She leaned down and kissed Alaina's forehead. "And this poor one? She would fetch a good price."

"The boys will come back," I said, touching the hammer and so earning an Italian scowl.

"You think?"

"I think." I touched the hammer again.

"And what will you do with them?"

"Do?"

"What will you do with them!" she repeated the question aggressively as if to suggest I had willfully misunderstood it the first time. "You take them with you?"

"If they want to come."

"All of them?"

I shrugged. I had not really thought about the children's future. "I suppose so. If they want to come."

"Then what do they do if they come?"

"There's always a need for servants at Bebbanburg," I said. "The girls will work in the kitchen, the hall, or the dairy. The boys in the stables or armory."

"As slaves?"

I shook my head. "They will be paid. The girls will grow and be married, the boys become warriors. If they don't like it they can leave. So no, they won't be slaves."

"You will not teach them?"

"Sword-skill, yes."

"To read!"

I hesitated. "It's not a very useful skill for most folk. Can you read?"

"A little, not much. I would like to."

"Then maybe you can teach them what little you know."

"Then Alaina can read her prayers," Benedetta said.

"I can pray!" Alaina said.

"You speak Ænglisc!" I said, surprised.

"Of course she does!" Benedetta said scornfully.

"Her father is Saxon. We will find her father and her mother? Yes?"

"If we can."

Though what we could do, or rather what I hoped we could do, had to wait for Aldwyn and the Ræt to return, which they did in the late afternoon, slithering down the rubbled slope and grinning proudly. I took them into the cellar where Finan and the rest of my men could hear what they had to say.

"There are not many guards on the wharves," Aldwyn said. "They walk up and down in three groups. Six men in each."

"With spears and shields," the Ræt added.

"The bird on most shields," Aldwyn said, "and some with just a cross."

"Not many men for that length of wharves," Finan said.

"The slaver's house is near the bridge," Aldwyn said. "He has a wharf there, but we couldn't get there."

"Which side?" I asked.

"Toward the sea, lord," Aldwyn said.

"We couldn't reach the wharf," the Ræt explained, "because there's a wooden fence."

"But there was a gap in the wood," Aldwyn said, "and a ship there."

"We looked through!" the Ræt, who I guessed was seven or eight years old, said proudly.

"How big?" I asked.

"A big gap!" the Ræt said, and held his grubby hands maybe two finger-widths apart.

"The ship," I said patiently.

"The ship? Oh, big, lord," Aldwyn said, "long!"

"And just one ship?"

"Just one."

"And the entrance from the street?" I asked.

"A big gate, lord. Big! And men with spears inside."

"You looked through the gate?"

"We waited till they opened it, lord, and men came out. We could see the guards inside."

"Big guards," the Ræt said open-eyed, "three of them."

"Three guards are nothing, lord," Beornoth put in.

"But the noise we make breaking down a big gate will bring the East Anglians," I said. "It's close to the bridge and the bastards are thick there."

"There must be other ships to steal," Finan suggested.

"We saw no oars on the other ships, lord," Aldwyn said.

"They usually lie between the rowers' benches," I said.

Aldwyn nodded. "That's where you told us to look and we saw none." Which meant, I thought, that the East Anglians had confiscated the oars to stop men escaping. "Except in the slave ship," Aldwyn added.

"She had oars?"

"I think so, lord." He sounded uncertain.

"Like thin logs, lord," the Ræt said. "I saw them!"

"We need oars," I said, and wondered how my few men were to row a big ship downriver. "There was a sail?"

"Bundled on the stick, lord, like you said." Aldwyn meant the yard. But unless the gods were kind and sent us a westerly wind we would have a hard time taking a stolen ship downriver under sail. We needed oars, and I was relying on the report of an eager boy who was not entirely sure of what he had seen.

"We can't stay here," I said. No one spoke. The East Anglians, I thought, could not close down the city forever. Merchant ships would arrive and others would want to leave, and Æthelhelm would want the riches that customs dues could bring him. That meant there would be more shipping and perhaps, if we waited, a chance would come to seize one of those vessels. Yet I kept going back to the thought of Gunnald the slave-trader. Was that because of the promise I had made to Benedetta? I looked at her long solemn face and just then she looked back to me and our eyes held each other. Her expression did not change and she said nothing. "We don't have a choice," I said, "we go tonight."

"Lord Varin has forbidden people to walk the streets at night," Father Oda pointed out.

"We go tonight," I insisted, "just before dawn."

"Sharpen your swords, lads," Finan said softly.

I had said we had no choice, but of course we did. A lifetime of war had taught me that fighting a battle without forethought was usually to invite defeat. Some battles start by accident, but most are planned. It can still go horribly wrong, even the best plans can be ripped apart by the enemy's plan, but a good leader does his best to scout the enemy, to learn all he can about that enemy, and all I had was the report of two boys. They had seen a ship that they thought had oars and they had seen three guards. Beornoth was right, three guards were nothing, but the noise we made in breaking into the slaver's yard and defeating his men could bring the bridge garrison running. Then there was Varin's order that no one was to be in the streets at night. So first we must reach the slaver's yard without being seen and then we must break into the yard silently before stealing a ship. So yes, there was a choice, and a sensible man would wait until the city fell back into its daily routine, would wait until folk could walk the streets at night, and wait until the guards on the wharves were bored and careless.

But could we wait? The stench of the cesspit alone was reason to leave. Varin had captured the city, but he had yet to search it thoroughly, and there was the ever looming danger that he would send men to rake through Lundene's ruins and cellars in search of the enemies he must know had survived the city's capture. And soon he would have more men as reinforcements arrived from East Anglia and from Wessex. "The guards patrolling the streets," I asked, "do they carry shields?"

"The men on the wharves had shields," Aldwyn said, "but they weren't carrying them."

"The shields were stacked?"

"Yes, lord."

"And the men we saw patrolling the streets didn't have shields," Father Oda said.

"The guards at the city gate did," Benedetta added.

That made sense. Iron-rimmed willow-board shields are heavy. The sentinels on Bebbanburg's walls did not carry shields, though they were always close at hand. A shield is the last thing a warrior picks up before battle and the first to be discarded after. Men patrolling streets only faced townsfolk, not screaming mail-clad warriors, so a shield was merely an encumbrance. "And we don't have shields," Finan said with a crooked grin.

"So we won't look strange walking the streets without shields," I said, "but we do have children."

For a heartbeat Aldwyn looked as though he would protest that he was no child, then curiosity defeated his indignation. "Children, lord?"

"Children," I said grimly, "because I'm going to sell the lot of you. Tonight."

We waited until the night was almost gone, until the first hint of wolf-gray light edged the east; we waited until the time when men who have stayed awake all night are tired and when they yearn for their replacements to come on duty.

Then we marched. We did not sneak through the city, edging from shadow to shadow, but instead walked boldly down the main street toward the bridge. We carried drawn swords and wore our helmets and mail. We were eight warriors who surrounded the children. Those youngsters were excited, knowing they were going on an adventure, but I had told them to look miserable. "You're captives!" I snarled at them. "You're going to be sold!"

Benedetta walked with them, her head covered by a dark hood, while Father Oda was beside me wearing his long black robe and with a silver cross gleaming in the feeble light of the guttering torches. Ahead of us a fire burned in a brazier at the bridge's northern end and, as we went nearer, two men strolled toward us. "Who are you?" one of them asked.

"Lord Varin's men," Father Oda answered, and his Danish accent only made the lie more believable.

"Crossing the bridge, father?" the man asked.

"Going that way," Father Oda pointed to the street that led eastward along the back of the wharves and warehouses.

"We're taking these little bastards to be sold," I explained.

"They're vermin!" Father Oda added, cuffing Aldwyn's head. "We found them stealing in the palace storerooms."

"Selling them are you?" the man seemed amused. "Best thing for them!"

We wished him a good day and turned down the street. "Not this gate," Aldwyn muttered, "but the next."

Gunnald's slave-yard was perilously close to the bridge where a dozen men stood guard beside the brazier. Whatever we did would have to be done quietly, though it began noisily enough when I hammered on the gate with Serpent-Breath's hilt. No one answered. I hammered again and kept beating the gate until a small hatch was pushed open and a face appeared in the shadow. "What is it?" the man growled.

"Lord Varin sending you merchandise."

"Who's Lord Varin?"

"He commands the city. Now open the gate."

"Jesus Christ," the man grumbled. I could see a slight gleam of one eye as he stared into the street, seeing children and warriors. "Couldn't it wait?"

"You want the little bastards or not?"

"Any girls?"

"Three ripe ones."

"Wait." The hatch closed and we waited. I assumed the man had gone to wake his master, or perhaps an overseer. The gray wolf-light seeped into the east, turning the sky brighter and touching the edges of the high-flying clouds with a silvery gleam. A door opened farther down the street and a woman appeared with a pail, presumably to fetch water. She looked nervously at my warriors and went back into her house.

The hatch opened again and there was just enough light to see a bearded face. The man stared and said nothing. "Lord Varin," I said, "does not like being kept waiting."

There was a grunt, the hatch closed, and I heard locking bars being lifted, then one of the two heavy gates was dragged open, scraping on the paving stones, which,

I suspected, had been there since the Romans first laid the yard. "Bring them in," the bearded man said.

"Inside!" I snarled at the children.

There were three men in the yard, none wearing mail, but with thick leather jerkins over which they wore short swords in plain wooden scabbards. One man, tall and lank-haired, had a coiled whip hanging at his waist. He was the man who had opened the gate and now watched the children file in, then spat on the stones. "Miserable-looking bunch," he said.

"They were caught in the palace storerooms," I said.

"Thieving little bastards. Not worth much."

"And you need Lord Varin's goodwill," I said.

The man grunted at that. "Shut the gate!" he ordered his companions. The gate scraped shut and two locking bars dropped into place. "Make a line!" he snapped at the children, and they obediently shuffled into a rough line. They looked terrified. They might have known this was all pretense, but the lank-haired man with his coiled whip was frightening. He began inspecting them, lifting Aldwyn's face to look closer.

"I know none of these men," Benedetta whispered close to me.

"They need feeding," the man said, and stopped to look at Alaina. He tilted up her face and grinned. "Pretty little thing." I felt Benedetta stiffen beside me, but she said nothing. "Very pretty," the man said and put his hand to the neck of Alaina's dress as if he was about to rip it down.

"She's not yours yet," I growled.

The man looked at me, surprised to be challenged. "Something wrong with the bitch?" he asked. "Got pox rash, has she?"

"Leave her alone!" Father Oda and I said at the same time.

The man snatched his hand away, but scowled. "If she's clean," he said grudgingly, "she might be worth something, but not this little bastard." He had moved on to the Ræt.

I was looking around the yard. The entrance gates faced a high building as large as any mead hall. The lowest floor was made of big blocks of dressed stone, while above that the higher floors were constructed of tarred timber. There was only one door, and a single window that was a small shuttered opening set very high on the forbidding black gable. To the right was a smaller shed, which, from the horse-droppings in the yard, I suspected was a stable. That too had a closed door. "How many men are usually here?" I asked Benedetta in a low voice.

"Ten? Twelve?" she whispered, but her memory was from twenty years before and she sounded uncertain. I wondered how Gunnald Gunnaldson, if he still lived, manned his ship, which, if Aldwyn was right, must have benches for at least twenty rowers. Presumably he hired men for each voyage or, more likely, used slaves. Finan and I had been slaves aboard just such a ship, chained to the benches and scarred by the whips.

The other two guards now stood beside the door of the larger building, lounging there with bored expressions. One yawned. I strolled along the line of children with Serpent-Breath still in my hand. "This one should be valuable," I said, stopping beside a tall, thin girl who had straggly brown hair framing a freckled face. "She'll be pretty if you clean her up."

"Let me look." The lank-haired man walked toward me and I brought Serpent-Breath up and lunged her into his throat and I kept pushing her as his blood brightened the dawn, and one small boy screamed in fright before Aldwyn silenced him with a hand, then the boy just watched wide-eyed as the dying man went backward, hands fumbling at the blade in his torn gullet, and his bowels opening to foul the morning with his stench. He went down hard onto the red-slicked stones and I wrenched the blade left and right, opening the savage cut, and pressed again until the blade jarred against his spine. Blood was still pulsing, spurting, but each spurt was smaller, the gurgling noise of his dying fading with each gasping breath, and by the time his twitching stopped my men had crossed the yard and had butchered one guard and captured the other. We had killed two and seized the third without making too much noise, but then some of the smaller children started wailing.

"Quiet!" I snarled at them. They went silent in terror. I glanced up as a movement caught my eye and wondered if it had been the shutter on the small window, which appeared to be open a crack. Had it been like that before? Then a kite launched itself from the high gable and flew westward. Maybe that bird was all I had seen moving. An omen? Alaina ran and buried herself in Benedetta's skirt. I pulled Serpent-Breath free and wiped her tip on the dead man's jerkin. Aldwyn was grinning at me, excited by the death, but the grin vanished when he saw my glowering face that was spattered by the dead man's blood. "Finan," I said, and pointed to the shed.

He took two men, dragged the door open, and went inside. "A stable," he reported a moment later. "Two horses, nothing else."

"Take the children in there," I told Benedetta. "Shut the door, wait till I send for you."

"Remember your promise," she said.

"Promise?"

SWORD OF KINGS · 269

"To let me kill Gunnald!"

I walked her to the stable. "I have not forgotten," I said.

"Make sure he is alive," she said bitterly, "when you send for me."

I looked up. Night was fading and the sky was a dark blue, not a cloud in sight.

Then the dogs started howling.

Seven

So we had been heard. The crying of frightened children had alerted Gunnald's men inside the warehouse and they had loosed dogs that now barked frantically. I heard footsteps, a shouted command, and a woman's yelp of protest. I was standing at the door where the man we had taken captive was pinned against the wall with Vidarr's sword at his throat. "How many men inside?" I snarled at him.

"Nine inside!" he managed to say despite the blade's pressure.

He had already been disarmed. I now kicked him hard between the legs and he crumpled, yelping as Vidarr's blade sliced a shallow cut on his chin as he fell. "Stay there," I snarled. "Finan?"

"Lord?" he called from the stable door.

"Nine men left," I called as I beckoned him.

"And dogs," he said drily. I heard paws scrabbling furiously on the door's far side.

The door was barred. I lifted the heavy latch and tried pulling and pushing, but it would not budge. And now, I thought, the men inside would be sending for help from the East Anglians on the bridge. I cursed.

And then the door opened. It seemed that the men inside wanted to loose the dogs on us.

Two dogs came, both big dogs, both black and tan with slavering mouths, both with yellow teeth and matted hair. They leaped at us. The first one tried to take a bite from my belly and got a mouthful of mail instead. Serpent-Breath sliced once, Vidarr cut from my left, then I stepped over the poor dying beast, saw Finan dispatch the other, and both of us charged into the huge warehouse. It was dark inside. A spear flashed by my left side and thumped into the doorpost. There were screams.

The men defending the warehouse had loosed the dogs, and fighting dogs are formidable beasts. They attack savagely, apparently without fear, and though they are easily enough dispatched their attack will force men to break ranks, so the skill of using war dogs is to attack at the same time. Let the dogs distract the enemy and, while that enemy is fighting off tooth and claw, hit him with spears and swords.

But the warehouse defenders thought the dogs could do all the work and, instead of attacking us, they just waited in a line that stretched between two cages. Women were screaming to my right, but I had no time to look because the defenders faced me, men with small shields and long-swords. I could not count them, it was too dim, so I just charged them and bellowed a war cry. "Bebbanburg!"

I teach my young warriors that caution is a virtue in warfare. There is always the temptation to attack blindly, to go screaming at the enemy's shield wall and hope that sheer anger and savagery will break it. That temptation comes from fear and sometimes the best way to overcome fear is to shriek a war cry, charge, and kill, but the enemy is likely to have the same impulse and the same fear. He will kill too. Given a choice I would rather be attacked by men maddened by fear than make the attack myself. Men in a rage, men acting on mindless impulse, will fight like wolves, yet sword-skill and discipline will almost always beat them.

Yet here I was, screaming a war cry and charging straight at a group of men who blocked the whole width of the passage between the cages. They had not made a shield wall, their shields were too small and merely meant to parry a blow, but they were a wall of swords. But they were also a slaver's guards, which meant they were paid to keep order, paid to frighten, and paid to use their whips on helpless victims. They were not paid to face Northumbrian warriors. Some, I was sure, had seen service in the shield wall. They had learned their skills, they had beaten down an enemy's shield, they had killed, and they had survived, but since then I doubted they had practiced as my men practiced. They no longer spent hours with heavy swords and shields because their enemies were unarmed slaves, many of them women and children. The worst they expected was a truculent man who could easily be cudgeled senseless. Now they faced warriors; my warriors.

Finan was beside me, shouting in his own language, while Beornoth was to my left. "Bebbanburg!" I bellowed again, and doubtless it meant nothing to them, but they saw warriors in mail and helmets, warriors who seemed fearless in the fight, warriors who screamed for their deaths, warriors who killed.

I was running toward a man in a leather jerkin, a man as tall as I was with a stubby black beard and a sword held like a spear. He took a pace backward as we came near, but still held the sword straight in front of him. Did he hope I would impale myself? Instead I cuffed his blade aside with my mail-clad left arm and sank Serpent-Breath in his belly as I smelled the stink of his breath. He was big, but I threw him backward into the man behind. To my right a man was screaming because Finan's quick sword had taken his eyes and Beornoth was beside me, blade red, and I twisted to my right, dragged my blade free of the falling man, and stepped into the next man, who carried a seax. My mail stopped his blade. He pushed, but he was already stepping back in terror and his thrust had no power. He began to whimper, tried to shake his head, and perhaps he was trying to surrender, but I slammed my helmeted head into his face, the whimper turned to a grunt, then his eyes opened wide as Beornoth's blade took him in the ribs. They were the eyes of a man about to sink into the torments of hell. He fell, I took one more step and I was behind the makeshift line of enemies, ahead of me was an open door beyond which sunlight glittered on water and on the ship we needed. I turned back, still shouting, and dragged Serpent-Breath's hungry edge across a man's neck and suddenly there were no enemies, just men shouting for mercy, men twitching in agony, men dying, blood on the stone floor, and one heavy man fleeing in panic up a stairway that was built beside the women's cage.

We are warriors.

"Gerbruht!"

"Lord?"

"Fetch Benedetta and the children."

We had faced nine men, I counted them. Five were dead or dying, three were on their knees, and one had fled upstairs. Women were crying with fear behind the bars on one side, there were men cowering in the gloom on the other. "Beornoth!" I pointed to the three men on their knees. "Bring the bugger we captured in the yard to join those three, strip them all of their mail, lock them up, and see if any of the slaves want to be rowers!"

I had been given a mere glimpse of the man who had fled up the stairway. A big man, not big like Beornoth or Folcbald who were tall and muscled, but fat. I had glimpsed him panicking, scrambling up the stairs, his footsteps thumping loudly, and now I followed with Serpent-Breath naked in my hand.

The stairs must have been built by the Romans because the first few steps were stone, though above those neat masonry steps was a more recent wooden flight that led to a small landing where dust motes danced. I climbed slowly. There was no noise from the upper floors. I assumed the fat man, whoever he was, would be waiting for me. Finan joined me and the two of us crept up the wooden flight, flinching when the timber creaked. "One man," I whispered.

An open doorway hung with a thick woollen curtain opened to the right of the small landing. I suspected that as soon as I stepped onto that landing a spear would be thrust through the wool, so I reached up with Serpent-Breath and edged it aside. There was no spear thrust. I edged the curtain further aside and heard a stifled whimper. There were more heavy footsteps, suggesting that the fat man was climbing yet more stairs.

"Gunnald?" Finan suggested.

"I suspect so." I said, no longer trying to be quiet. I took the last step and ripped the curtain down. There was a gasp, a scream, and I saw another cage, which held three women who watched me with eyes wide with terror. I put a finger to my lips and they crouched silent, their eyes going to another wooden stairway that led to the top floor. "Gunnald!" I shouted.

There was no answer.

"Gunnald! I came here to keep a promise!" I climbed the stairs, deliberately heavy-footed. "You hear me, Gunnald?"

There was still no answer, just a scuffling sound deep in the attic. This last floor was built under the roof. Beams crossed it. There was little light, but as I reached the top I saw the fat man standing at the far end. He had a sword in his hand. He was shaking. I had rarely seen a man so frightened.

Finan went past me and pushed open the small shutter I had seen from the courtyard, and in the new light I saw heavy timber chests and a sturdy wooden bed heaped with furs. There was a girl half-hidden in the bed, watching us fearfully. "Gunnald?" I asked the man. "Gunnald Gunnaldson?"

"Yes," he said scarce above a whisper.

"I'd drop the sword," I said, "unless you want to fight me?"

He shook his head, but still gripped the weapon.

"My name," I said, "is Uhtred, son of Uhtred, Lord of Bebbanburg."

The sword fell from a nerveless hand, clattering on the wooden floor. Gunnald followed it, dropping to his knees and holding clasped hands toward me. "Lord!"

There was a second shuttered window in the gable facing the river. I walked past the kneeling man and pushed the shutter open to let more light into the room. "I don't like slave-traders," I said mildly as I went back to Gunnald.

"Many don't, lord," he whispered.

"Is she a slave?" I asked, pointing Serpent-Breath at the girl in the bed.

"Yes, lord," Gunnald's whisper was scarcely audible.

"Not any longer," I said. Gunnald said nothing. He was still shaking. I saw a robe or gown on the floor, a threadbare thing of linen. I picked it up with Serpent-Breath's bloodied tip and tossed it to the girl. "Do you remember a slave-trader called Halfdan?" I asked Gunnald. He hesitated, perhaps surprised at the question. His face was round, his eyes small, and his beard too scanty to cover his thick jowls. His hair was thinning. He wore a mail coat, but too small, so he had ripped the sides upward so the mail would cover his belly. A big belly. "We don't see many fat people," I said, "isn't that right, Finan?"

"A few monks," Finan said, "and a bishop or two."

"You must eat plenty," I told Gunnald, "to get a belly like that. Your slaves are all thin."

"I feed them well, lord," he muttered.

"You do?" I asked with pretended surprise.

"Meat, lord. They eat meat."

"Are you telling me you treat your slaves with kindness?" I asked. I crouched in front of him and let Serpent-Breath's tip rest on the floor by his knees. He stared at the blade. "Well?" I prompted him.

"A contented slave is a healthy slave, lord," Gunnald managed to say, his eyes on the blade's drying blood.

"So you do treat them well?"

"Yes, lord."

"So that girl wasn't forced to your bed?"

"No, lord," and again his whisper was almost inaudible.

I stood. "You'll think I'm a strange man, Gunnald," I said, "because I don't like seeing women beaten or raped. You think that's strange?" He just looked at me, then lowered his eyes again. "Halfdan treated women badly," I said. "Do you remember Halfdan?"

"Yes, lord," he whispered.

"Tell me about him."

"Tell you, lord?"

"Tell me about him!" I encouraged him.

He managed to raise his eyes to me again. "He had a yard on the other side of the bridge, lord," he said. "He did business with my father."

"He died, yes?"

"Halfdan, lord?"

"Yes."

"He died, lord. He was killed."

"Killed!" I sounded surprised. "Who killed him?"

"No one knows, lord."

I crouched again. "It was me, Gunnald," I whispered. "I killed him."

The only answer was a whimper. Footsteps sounded on the stairs and I turned to see Father Oda, Vidarr Leifson, and Benedetta come into the attic. Benedetta's hood shadowed her face. Another whimper made me look back to Gunnald who was shivering, and not from the cold. "You, lord?"

"I killed Halfdan," I said. "He was fat too."

That killing had been years before and in a riverside yard not unlike Gunnald's. Halfdan had thought I had come to buy slaves and had greeted me with an effusive politeness. I still remember his bald head, his waist-long beard, his false smile, and his swollen belly. Finan had been with me that day, and both of us had been thinking of the months we had been enslaved together, chained to a bench of a slaver's ship, whipped through the ice-cold seas, and kept alive only by the thoughts of revenge. We had seen our fellow oarsmen whipped to death, heard the women sobbing, and seen children dragged screaming to our owner's house. Halfdan had not been responsible for any of that misery, but he had paid for it all the same. Finan had hamstrung Halfdan and I had slit his throat, and that was the day we freed Mehrasa, a dark-skinned girl who came from the lands beyond the Mediterranean. She had married Father

Cuthbert and now lived in Bebbanburg. Wyrd bið ful ãræd.

"Halfdan," I still crouched close to the shivering Gunnald, "liked to rape his slaves. Do you rape your slaves?"

Gunnald, terrified, retained enough cunning to understand that I had this strange dislike of slavers raping their own property. "No, lord," he lied.

"I can't hear you," I said, standing again, this time taking his abandoned sword with me.

"No, lord!"

"So you treat your slaves well?"

"Yes, lord. I do, lord!" He sounded frantic now.

"I am glad to hear it," I said. I tossed Gunnald's sword to Finan, then drew Wasp-Sting and held the seax hilt first toward Benedetta. "You'll find this easier," I told her.

"Thank you," she said.

Father Oda began to say something, then looked at my face and thought better of it. "One last thing," I said, and turned back to the kneeling Gunnald. I stood behind him and dragged the ragged mail coat over his head so that all he wore was a thin woollen robe. When the coat was free of his face and he could see again, he gasped because Benedetta had pushed back her hood. He stammered something, then, as he saw the hatred on her face and the blade in her hand, the stammering turned into a moan. "You two know each other, I think," I said.

Gunnald's mouth still moved, or at least quivered, but no sound came now. Benedetta turned the sword so that the attic's small light glinted on the steel. "No, lord!" Gunnald managed to say in a panicked voice as he shuffled backward. I kicked him hard, he went still, then moaned again as his bladder gave way.

"*Porco!*" Benedetta spat at him.

"Father Oda," I said, "come downstairs with us. Vidarr, you stay here."

"Of course, lord."

"Don't interfere. Just make sure it's a fair fight."

"A fair fight, lord?" Vidarr asked, puzzled.

"He's got a cock, she's got a sword. Seems fair to me." I smiled at Benedetta. "There's no hurry. We won't leave for a while. Come, Finan! You, girl!" I looked at the bed. "Are you dressed?" She nodded. "Then come!"

There was a coiled whip made of braided leather hanging on a nail driven into the newel post of the stairs. I took it and saw dried blood crusted in the whip's tip. I tossed the whip to Vidarr, then went downstairs.

Leaving Benedetta, Vidarr, and Gunnald in the attic.

And Gunnald was screaming before I reached the middle floor.

"**The church,**" Father Oda said to me when we reached the bottom of the two stairways, "does not condone slavery, lord."

"Yet I've known churchmen who own slaves."

"It is not seemly," he said, "yet the scriptures do not forbid it."

"What are you telling me, father?"

He flinched as another scream sounded, this one more terrible than any that had assaulted our ears as we came downstairs. "Well done, girl," Finan muttered.

"Vengeance must belong to God," Father Oda said, "and only to God."

"Your god," I said harshly.

He flinched again. "In his epistle to the Romans," the priest said, "Paul tells us to leave revenge to the Lord."

"The lord took his time revenging Benedetta," I said.

"And the fat bastard deserves it, father," Finan put in.

"I don't doubt it, but by encouraging her," he was looking at me now, "you have encouraged her to commit a mortal sin."

"Then you can shrive her," I said curtly.

"She is a fragile woman," Oda said, "and I would

not burden her fragility with a sin that separates her from Christ's grace."

"She's stronger than you think," I said.

"She is a woman!" he said sternly. "And women are the weaker vessels. I was at fault," he paused, plainly disturbed, "and I should have stopped her. If the man deserved death then it should have been at your hands, not hers."

He was right, of course. I did not doubt that Gunnald deserved death for a multitude of crimes, but what I had just unleashed in the slaver's attic was cruel. I had condemned him to a long, terrible, and painful death. I could have satisfied justice with a swift killing, as swift as the one I had given Halfdan so many years before, but I had chosen cruelty instead. Why? Because I knew that choice would please Benedetta. Another scream sounded, faded, grew again. "It is not seemly," Father Oda repeated, "that you have put that woman's mortal soul at risk!" He spoke fervently and I wondered if the Danish priest was attracted to Benedetta and that thought gave me a pulse of jealousy. She was beautiful, undeniably beautiful, but there was a darkness in that beauty and an anger in her soul. I told myself she was ridding herself of that shadow with Wasp-Sting.

"You pray for her, father," I said dismissively, "and I'm going to look at the ship that will take us home."

I led Finan into the early sunlight. Gunnald's screams had faded and the loudest noise came from the gulls fighting over a carcass stranded on the mud at the far side of the Temes. A small breeze, too small to be of any use to a sailor, rippled the river. Gunnald, while he still lived, owned two wharves, both protected by walls of wooden staves. His ship was on the lefthand wharf, a long, big-bellied ship, made for distant voyages. She looked heavy. Her timbers were dark, almost pitch-black, and weed was thick at her waterline. A sail was furled on the yard, but its ragged cloth was crusted with bird droppings. I walked down the wharf, then stopped. Finan stopped with me, swore, then began to laugh. "Taking her to Bebbanburg, are we?" he asked.

There was water in the ship's wide belly. The dark of her timbers was not pitch, but rot. There were a half-dozen oars, good only for firewood, their looms warped and their blades cracked. A gull screamed at me. I stepped down onto a bench that creaked alarmingly and prodded the hull with Serpent-Breath, and her blade's tip went into the wood as though it were fungus. This ship could not cross the river, let alone take us home to Bebbanburg.

I had captured a wreck.

Finan was grinning. "It would be quicker to swim to Bebbanburg!"

"We might have to," I answered sourly. "It's my fault. I should have sent Oswi to take a look. Not the boy."

"I think it's aground," Finan said.

I climbed back to the wharf and gazed across the useless ship at the farther berth, which was empty. "Benedetta said he had two ships."

Finan followed my gaze and shrugged. "A second ship isn't much use if it's not here," he said. I made no answer. "Maybe he's sent some slaves to Frankia?" Finan suggested. "They say prices are higher there."

That would explain the empty berth. "How many slaves have we got?"

"A dozen women, four children, and three half-starved young men."

"I expected more."

"So maybe his second ship will be back in a day or two!"

"Maybe," I grunted. I looked beyond the empty wharf and saw there were four guards watching us from the high parapet of the bridge that was a long bowshot away. I waved to them, and after a moment's hesitation, one waved back. I doubted they had heard the commotion as we captured the yard, and though they could probably hear Gunnald's desperate shrieks of pain they would surely not think such sounds unusual coming from a slaver's warehouse.

"So what do we do?" Finan asked.

"We think," I said sharply, but in truth I had no idea what we should do. My father, I thought, had been right. I was impetuous. I had been goaded by the attacks on my ships and, with the excuse of my oath to Æthelstan, I had come south thinking to find Æthelhelm and kill him. Now *Spearhafoc* was gone and I was trapped in an enemy-held city. "We wait for the second ship, I suppose. A pity we can't ask Gunnald where it is."

"We can ask his men, they'll know."

Benedetta was coming down the wharf, her hood still pushed back so that the sun glinted on her long dark hair that had come loose. To my eyes she looked like a Valkyrie, one of the messengers of the gods who take slain warriors to the feast hall in Valhalla. She was unsmiling, blood had splashed onto her gray robe, while Wasp-Sting was coated to the hilt with gore. I looked quickly up to the bridge parapet, wondering what the guards would make of a blood-covered blade, but they had all turned their backs. "I will wash it for you, lord," Benedetta said, showing me the sword.

"Give it to one of the boys to wash," I said. "Tell Aldwyn to scrub it."

"And thank you, lord."

I looked into her gray-green eyes. "Father Oda says I encouraged you to commit a sin."

"That is what I am thanking you for, lord."

"Did you make the bastard suffer?" Finan asked.

"They will have heard his screams in hell," she said.

"Then you did well, so you did!" the Irishman said happily.

"I did what I have dreamed of doing for over twenty years. I am happy." She turned to look into the wreckage. "Is this the boat?"

"No," I said.

"That is good," she said gravely, making both Finan and me laugh.

"It's not funny," Finan said.

"It's not," I agreed, still laughing.

Then someone began hammering on the outer gate, and a moment later Aldwyn came running. "Lord, lord! There are soldiers outside! Soldiers!"

"God help us," Finan said.

Someone had to.

The hammering started again. I had run through the warehouse and into the yard where I opened the small hatch in the gate. Two soldiers only, both wearing mail and both looking bored, and with them were two men, evidently servants, who were standing by a handcart that was loaded with two barrels. "I'm opening the gate!" I called.

"Take your time!" one of the mailed men answered sourly.

Finan and Vidarr were with me. There were also two dead men and two slaughtered dogs sprawled on the stones. I pointed at them, then at the stable, and Finan took one corpse, Vidarr the other, and began dragging them out of sight.

"Hurry!" a voice called from beyond the gate.

"I'm hurrying!" I called, and lifted the first locking bar. I dropped it noisily and saw Vidarr was dragging the dogs into the stable. I lifted the other bar, taking my time, waiting till Finan had closed the stable, then I pulled open the gates.

One of the two men I had supposed were servants took a backward step, evidently surprised by my appearance. "Who are you?" he asked.

"Who are you?" I responded harshly.

"I am the under-steward from the palace," he answered nervously, "delivering the supplies, of course. But where's Ælfrin?"

"Sick," I said, suddenly realizing that I was wearing

my hammer amulet openly. The man who was questioning me saw it too and looked back to my eyes warily.

"Sick?"

"Fever."

"Most of the lads are sweating like pigs," Finan added to my story, "and the slaves too. A couple of them are already dead."

The man took another backward step, as did the two soldiers. Both of the mailed men looked strong and confident, but even the most confident warrior who had experienced the hell of shield walls feared the plague. Finan feared it too and, doubtless remembering the rumors of sickness in the north, made the sign of the cross.

"Did Lord Varin send you?" I asked.

"Of course," the under-steward said. "We couldn't send any in the last two weeks because the pretty boy's men were in charge, but things are normal again now."

"For Christ's sake, hurry," one of the soldiers growled.

"So Gunnald hired you?" the under-steward asked me.

I gestured toward the warehouse. "Go and ask him."

"He's sweating too," Finan said, "God preserve him."

"Four shillings," the man said, evidently tired of the

conversation. He beckoned at the handcart. "Just pay and take the barrels."

"I thought it was just two?" Finan had the wit to bargain. "Gunnald said two shillings."

One of the soldiers stepped toward us. "Four shillings," he snarled. "They hired the two of us to keep your damned food safe, so the price has gone up. Four shillings."

I felt into my rapidly diminishing pouch, gave the under-steward four shillings, and helped Finan and Vidarr carry the two barrels into the yard. They stank.

"Next week!" the under-steward said. He gave a shilling each to the two soldiers, kept two for himself, then all four walked away.

I closed and barred the gates. "What was that about?" I asked.

Finan made a noise of disgust. He had levered the lid from one barrel that was two thirds full of cloudy ale. He dipped a finger and tasted. "Sour," he said, "tastes worse than badger piss."

"You'd know?" Vidarr asked.

Finan ignored that, opening the second barrel and recoiling as the stench in the yard worsened. "Sweet Jesus! We paid silver for this?"

I crossed to the two barrels and saw that the second one was half full of meat, which I thought was pork, though this pork was riddled with rancid fat and crawling with maggots. "Gunnald did say he fed them meat," I muttered.

"Is that tree bark?" Finan was bending over the barrel and poking the rotten meat with a finger. "The bastards mixed this with bark!"

I rammed the lid back into place. "Where do they get this filth?"

The answer was given by one of the captured guards who told us that Gunnald had an arrangement with the palace steward who sold unused ale and food to feed the slaves. "The women cook it in the kitchen," he said.

"They won't cook that," I said and ordered the barrel's contents to be pitched into the river. The captured guard told us more, that Gunnald's son had taken slaves to Frankia and that the ship had been gone now for three days. "Did he go to buy slaves too?" I asked.

"Just to sell them, lord." The captured man's name was Deogol. He was younger than the other three captives and eager to please. He was a West Saxon who had lost a hand fighting when Edward had invaded East Anglia. "I couldn't work at home," he had explained, lifting the stump of his right arm, "and Gunnald gave me work. A man has to eat."

"So Gunnald's son is selling slaves?"

"War isn't good for trade, lord, that's what they say.

Prices are low in Lundene so he's selling the best across the water. All except for . . ." he paused, decided to say nothing, but I saw him glance to where the stairs began.

"Except for the girls who were upstairs?" I asked.

"Yes, lord."

"Why isn't he selling those? They look valuable to me."

"They're his girls, lord," Deogol said miserably. "His father's girls really, but they share them."

"Gunnald Gunnaldson and his son?" I asked, and Deogol just nodded. "What's the son's name?"

"Lyfing, lord."

"Where's his mother?"

"Dead, lord."

"And who rows his ship?"

"Slaves, lord,"

"How many?"

"Just twenty oars," Deogol said, "ten a side."

"So a small ship?"

"But it's fast," he said. "That old one," he jerked his head toward the wreck on the wharf, "needed twice as many men and she was always a pig."

So Gunnald had bought a smaller, lighter vessel that needed fewer men on the oars and, if our captive was right, was fast enough to escape most Frisian or Danish raiders looking for easy prey. And that lighter ship might return any day, but meanwhile I had nineteen freed slaves, four captive guards, a dozen children, my seven men, a priest, Benedetta, and the two horses in the stable to feed. Luckily there were a dozen sacks of oats in the kitchen, a mound of firewood, a stone hearth that still had glowing embers, and a great cauldron. We would not starve. "But it's a pity about the mouse droppings," Finan said, looking at a handful of oats.

"We've eaten worse."

Benedetta, the bloodstains dry on her gown, found her way to the kitchen that was a grimy shed built alongside the wharf. She brought Alaina, an arm around the girl's shoulder. "She's hungry."

"We'll boil some oats," I said.

"I can make oatcakes," Alaina said brightly.

"Then we need some lard," Benedetta said, starting to hunt through boxes and jars stored on a shelf, "and some water. Salt, if there is any. Help me search!"

"I like oatcakes," Alaina said.

I looked at Benedetta questioningly and she smiled. "Alaina's doing well," she said, "she's a good girl."

"And you'll find my mama?" Alaina asked me earnestly.

"Of course he will!" Benedetta answered for me. "Lord Uhtred can do anything!"

Lord Uhtred, I thought, would need a miracle to find the child's mother, let alone escape from Lundene, but for the moment all I could do was wait for the slave ship to return. I ordered the dead bodies brought to the wharf and heaped against the western wall where they were hidden from any inquisitive guard on the bridge. The dead would all be tipped into the river after dark. Gunnald's fat, pale, and blood-streaked corpse was dragged down the stairs, his grimacing eyeless head bumping on each step. I searched his attic lair and found a sturdy box full of money. There were West Saxon and Mercian shillings, Danish hacksilver, and Northumbrian gold, besides Frisian, Frankish, and other strange coins, some inscribed with letters of an alphabet and language I had never seen before. "These are from Africa," Benedetta told me, fingering a big round silver piece. "They are *Saraceni* coins. We used them in Lupiae." She put it back with the rest of the money. "How safe are we?" she asked.

"Safe enough," I said, trying to reassure her and hoping I told the truth. "The East Anglians will think we all escaped on *Spearhafoc*. They won't be searching for us."

"And *Spearhafoc*," she stumbled over the unfamiliar name, "is where?"

"Well on her way home by now, I hope."

"And will your people send help?"

"They won't even know whether we're alive," I said, "so if they've any sense they'll shut the fortress doors, guard the ramparts, and wait for news. That's what I'd do."

"And what do we do?"

"We capture Gunnald's second ship," I said, "and follow *Spearhafoc* home."

"So we stay here till then?"

"Better that than the cellar next to the cesspit."

"Lord!" Beornoth called from the foot of the stairs. "You'll want to see this!"

I went back down to the wharf and followed Beornoth to the end of the westernmost pier where Finan was waiting. The Irishman jerked his head downstream. "Enough of the bastards," he said.

Four ships were being rowed upriver. They looked to be Saxon ships, big and heavy, and all four had crosses on their prows. The tide was ebbing, which made the water seethe through the spaces between the bridge piers, but none of these ships was trying to go upstream because all four had masts crossed by spars on which sails were furled and none of their crews was trying to lower those masts. They began to turn toward the downstream wharves, their oarsmen struggling against tide and current, and as they turned I saw the ships' big bellies were crammed with men and many of those men wore the dark red cloak that was Æthelhelm's mark. "The reinforcements," I said bleakly.

"Enough of the bastards," Finan said again.

My only consolation as I watched my enemy bringing more men to the city was that *Spearhafoc* was not being towed or rowed with them. Not that four such heavily loaded ships would have had a chance of outrunning and capturing my ship, but it suggested Berg and his crew had slipped past them and were on their way north. That thought made me wonder about Bebbanburg and the rumors of plague. I touched my hammer amulet and said a prayer to the gods that my son was safe, that his prisoners were securely held, and that Eadgifu and her children would not sicken. I had saved her sons from Æthelhelm's spite, but had I sent them instead to an agonizing death from the plague?

"What are you thinking?" Finan had seen me touch the hammer.

"That we hide here," I said, "we wait, and then we go home."

Home, I thought wistfully. I should never have left it.

All **we** could do was wait. The ship commanded by Gunnald's son could return at any moment which meant I had to have men watching on the wharf, and other men guarding the courtyard gate, and still others in the warehouse where we had chained the captured guards in one of the slave pens. The slaves themselves were neither chained nor penned, but forbidden to leave because I dared not risk one of them betraying our presence.

We had tipped the naked corpses into the river at night. The falling tide and the current would have taken them eastward, though I did not doubt the bodies would be stranded on a mudbank long before they reached the distant sea. No one would take note. There would be enough corpses this summer as men struggled to take the throne of Wessex.

More ships brought more men to Lundene. They brought reinforcements for Jarl Varin, who still commanded the garrison on Æthelhelm's behalf. We knew that because after two days there was a proclamation bellowed throughout the old city that folk could walk safely after dark and, despite Finan's dour warning, I went that night to a big riverside alehouse called Wulfred's Tavern, though everyone called it the Dead Dane because a falling tide had once revealed a Danish warrior impaled on one of the rotting stakes of an old wharf. For years the dead man's hand had been nailed to one of the tavern's doorposts and everyone who entered would touch a finger. The hand had long gone, though a crude picture of a corpse still decorated the sign hanging above the door. I pushed inside, followed by Father Oda and Benedetta.

Oda had suggested he accompany me. "A priest commands respect," he had claimed, "not suspicion. And Benedetta should come too, as my wife."

I had almost bridled when he spoke of Benedetta as his wife, but had the sense to hide my irritation. "It's not safe for women," I said.

"Women have walked the streets all day," Oda said calmly.

"Benedetta should stay here," I insisted.

"The East Anglians," Oda said patiently, "must suspect there are fugitives still hiding in the city. They will be looking for young men, not for a priest and his wife. You want news, yes? So let us come. Strangers will trust a priest."

"Suppose you're recognized?"

He had shaken his head. "I left East Anglia as a beardless youth. No one will know me now."

I was swathed in a big, dark cloak. I had ransacked both Gunnald's attic and the room beneath where his son lived, and discovered the cloak with its hood. I wore it and belted the cloak with a length of rope, then borrowed a wooden cross from Gerbruht and hung it around my neck. I carried no sword, only a knife concealed beneath the big cloak. "You look like a monk," Finan had said.

"Bless you, my son."

We found a table in a dark corner of the tavern. The room was almost full. There were some local people, women as well as men, sitting at tables to one side of the large room, but most of the customers were troops, almost all wearing swords, who watched us with curiosity, but looked smartly away when Father Oda sketched the sign of the cross toward them. They were here to drink, not to hear a sermon. Some were here for more than a drink and climbed the wooden staircase that led to the rooms where the tavern's whores did their trade. Everyone who climbed the stairs received a chorus of cheers and jeers from their companions, raucous sounds that earned frowns from Father Oda, though he said nothing.

"The men going upstairs—" Benedetta began.

"Yes," Oda said curtly.

"They're young men," I said, "far from home."

A drab girl came to our table and we asked for ale, bread, and cheese. "Is Wulfred still alive?" I asked her.

She peered at me, seeing nothing under the deep shadow of my hood. "He died, father," she said, evidently mistaking me for another priest.

"Pity," I said.

The girl shrugged. "I'll bring you a rushlight," she said.

I made the sign of the cross toward her. "Bless you, my child," I said, and earned a disapproving intake of breath from Oda.

The East Anglians began singing as the evening wore on. The first song was in Danish, a lament by seafarers for the women they had left behind, but then the Saxons in the alehouse drowned the Danes with an old song that was plainly intended for our ears, and Father Oda, hearing the words, frowned into his ale. Benedetta took longer to understand, then gazed at me wide-eyed. "It's called the 'Tanner's Wife,'" I said, beating my hand on the table in time with the song.

"But the song is about a priest?" Benedetta asked. "No?"

"Yes," Father Oda hissed.

"It's about a tanner's wife and a priest," I said. "She goes to him for confession and he says he doesn't understand what she's confessing so he tells her to show him."

"To do it with him, you mean?"

"To do it with him," I said, and to my surprise she laughed.

"I thought we were here to learn news," Father Oda growled at me.

"The news will come to us," I said, and sure enough a moment later, when the rowdy troops had moved to a new song, a middle-aged man with a cropped gray beard brought an ale-jug and a beaker to our table. He wore a sword with a well-worn hilt and had a slight limp that suggested a spear-thrust taken in a shield wall. He looked quizzically at Father Oda, who nodded permission, and the man sat on a bench opposite me. "I apologize for that song, father."

Oda smiled. "I have been with soldiers before, my son."

The man, who looked old enough to be Oda's father, raised his beaker. "Then your good health, father," he said.

"I pray God it is good," Oda answered carefully, "and yours too."

"You're Danish?" the man asked.

"I am Danish," Oda confirmed.

"Me too. Jorund," he introduced himself.

"I am Father Oda, this is my wife and my uncle." Oda was speaking Danish now.

"What brings you to Lundene?" Jorund asked. He was friendly, with no suspicion in his voice, but I did not doubt that the East Anglians had been warned to look for enemies in the city, but, just as Oda had claimed, a priest and his wife looked the most unlikely of enemies and Jorund seemed merely curious.

"We seek a ship to carry us across the sea," Oda said.

"We are going to Rome," I put in, telling the tale we had agreed on.

"We are pilgrims," Oda explained. "My wife ails." He reached out and put a hand over Benedetta's hand. "We seek the blessing of the Holy Father."

"I'm sorry for your wife, father," Jorund said sincerely and, watching the priest's hand, I felt another pulse of jealousy. I looked at Benedetta and she looked back, her eyes sad, and for a moment we held each other's gaze. "It's a long way you have to travel," Jorund went on.

"A long journey indeed, my son," Oda answered, looking suddenly startled because Benedetta had drawn her hand sharply away. "We seek a ship here," the priest went on, "to cross to Frankia."

"There are plenty of ships," Jorund said, "I wish there weren't."

"Why?" Father Oda asked.

"That's our job. Searching them before they leave."

"Searching them?"

304 • BERNARD CORNWELL

"To make sure no enemy escapes."

"Enemy?" Father Oda pretended surprise.

Jorund took a long drink of his ale. "There was a rumor, father, that Uhtredærwe was in Lundene. You know who he is?"

"Everyone knows."

"Then you know that they don't want him as an enemy. So find him, they tell us, find him and capture him."

"And kill him?" I asked.

Jorund shrugged. "Someone will kill him, but I doubt it will be us. He's not here. Why would he be here? It's just a rumor. There's a war coming and that always means rumors."

"Isn't there already a war?" Father Oda asked. "There was fighting here, I'm told."

"There's always fighting," Jorund said morosely. "I mean a proper war, father, a war of shield walls and armies. And it shouldn't be, it shouldn't be."

"Shouldn't be?" Oda inquired gently.

"It's not so far off harvest time, father. We shouldn't be here, not now. We should be at home, sharpening sickles. There's real work to be done! Wheat, barley, and rye don't harvest themselves!"

The mention of barley made me touch my hammer,

only to find the wooden cross. "You were summoned here?" I asked.

"By a Saxon lord," Jorund said, "who won't wait for harvest."

"Lord Æthelhelm?"

"Coenwald," Jorund said, "but he holds land from Æthelhelm so yes, it's Æthelhelm who summoned us and Coenwald has to obey." He paused to pour ale from the jug.

"And Coenwald summoned you?" I asked.

"Didn't have much choice did he? Harvest or no harvest."

"Did you have a choice?" Oda asked.

Jorund shrugged. "We swore fealty to Coenwald when we converted." He paused, perhaps reflecting on how the Danish settlers of East Anglia had lost their war to keep a Danish king. "We fought against him and we lost, but he let us live, he let us keep our land and he lets us thrive, so now we have to fight for him." He shrugged. "Maybe it'll all be over by harvest."

"I pray so," Oda said quietly.

"Maybe there'll be no war?" I suggested.

"When two men want one chair?" Jorund asked scathingly. "Good men will have to die just to decide which royal arse warms the damned thing." He turned as angry voices sounded, then a woman's shriek made me shiver. "Oh god," he groaned.

The angry shouts had come from the upper floor. There was a yelp and then a man was hurled down the stairs. He was a young man who crashed against the steps, bounced, and collapsed on the floor. He did not move. Men stood, either to help him or to protest against the violence, but then all of them went very still.

They went still because a man was coming down the stairs. A big man. The first we saw were his boots, then massive thighs, and then he came into view, and I saw it was Waormund. He was bare chested, his clothes over his arm. He carried a sword belt with a sheathed sword; a big blade for a big man. There was not a sound in the tavern except for those heavy boots on the stairs. He paused after a few steps and his harsh face, blank-eyed and scarred, looked around the room. Benedetta gasped, and I put my hand over hers, warning her to keep silent.

"Scum!" Waormund snarled at the room. "Little Danish bastard thought to use my woman. Told me to hurry! Anyone else in a hurry to use her?" He waited, but no one made a sound. He was terrifying; the width of that muscled chest, the sneer on his face, and the size of the heavy sword had cowed the room into submission. Benedetta was clutching my hand beneath the table now, her grip tight.

Waormund came down the last steps. He paused again, looking down at the youngster who had offended him. Then, very deliberately, he kicked him. Kicked him again and again. There was a yelp from the boy, then no sound except for Waormund's massive boot crashing into the prone body. "East Anglian pussies!" Waormund snarled. He looked around the tavern again, plainly hoping someone would defy him, but still no one spoke or moved. He looked at our corner, but just saw two hooded people and a priest. The rushlight was weak, the room shadowed, and he ignored us. "Danish god-damned pussies!" He was still trying to provoke a fight, but when no one responded he picked an ale pot from the closest table, drained it, and stalked into the night.

Benedetta was crying softly. "I hate him," she whispered, "I hate him."

I held onto her hand beneath the table. Men were helping the fallen youth and conversation was starting again, but subdued now. Jorund, who had stood when the boy was thrown down the stairs, had gone to see what damage had been done and came back a moment later. "Poor boy. Broken ribs, crushed balls, lost half his teeth, and he'll be lucky to keep an eye." He sat and drank some ale. "I hate that man," he added bitterly.

"Who is he?" I asked.

"Bastard called Waormund. Lord Æthelhelm's mastiff."

"And it seems he doesn't like Danes," I said mildly.

"Danes!" Jorund said wryly. "He doesn't like anyone! Saxon or Dane."

"And you?" Father Oda asked. "You fought against the Saxons, yet now you fight alongside them?"

Jorund chuckled. "Saxon and Dane! It's a forced marriage, father. Most of my lads are Saxons, but maybe a third are Danes, and I'm always having to stop the silly bastards from hammering each other senseless. But that's young men, isn't it?"

"You lead men?" I asked, surprised.

"I do."

"A Dane leading Saxons?" I explained my surprise.

"The world changes, doesn't it?" Jorund sounded amused. "Coenwald could have taken my land, but he didn't, and he knows I'm the most experienced of all his warriors." He turned to look at the room. "And most of those lads need experience. They've never seen a proper fight. God help them, they think it's a tavern brawl with spears. Still, I hope to lead every last one of them home, and soon!"

Jorund was a good man, I thought, yet fate, that most capricious bitch, might demand that I face him in a shield wall one day. "I hope you lead them home very soon," I said, "and that you gather your harvest safely."

"I pray the same," Jorund said. "And I pray never to see another shield wall as long as I live. But if it is to be a real war then it won't take long."

"It won't?" I asked.

"It's us and the West Saxons against the Mercians. Two against one, see?"

"Maybe the Northumbrians will fight alongside the Mercians," I suggested mischievously.

"They'll not come south," Jorund said scornfully.

"Yet you say there's a rumor that Uhtred of Bebbanburg is already here," I said.

"If he was here," Jorund said flatly, "he'd have his army of northern savages with him. Besides, there's plague up north." He made the sign of the cross. "We hear tales," he went on, "and they say Jorvik is a city of corpses."

"Jorvik!" I asked, unable to keep the alarm from my voice.

"So they say," Jorund said.

I felt a cold shiver. My hand went to touch my hammer amulet and again found Gerbruht's wooden cross. Father Oda saw the gesture. "I pray God that's just another rumor," the priest said too hurriedly. "You leave the city soon?" he asked Jorund, evidently trying to move the conversation beyond the fear of plague.

"God knows, father," Jorund said, "and God isn't telling me. We stay here, or maybe we don't stay here. Maybe the Mercian lad will make trouble, and maybe he won't. He won't if he has any sense." He poured the last of the jug's ale into our beakers. "I didn't come to bore you with talk of war, father," he said, "but wondered if you'd be kind enough to give us a blessing?"

"With pleasure, my son," Father Oda said.

"I hope you recover, mistress," Jorund said to Benedetta. She had not understood the conversation in Danish, but smiled her thanks to Jorund, who now called the room to silence.

Father Oda gave the blessing, enjoining his god to bring peace and to spare the lives of all the men in the tavern. Jorund thanked him and we left, walking the riverside street in silence for a while. "So they're searching all the ships that leave," Oda said.

"But they don't have men in Gunnald's yard," I said. "Once we get the new ship we'll leave at dawn, hope for an ebbing tide and row hard." I made it sound easy, but I knew better and again went to touch my hammer and found the cross.

We walked a few paces more, then Father Oda chuckled. "What?" I asked.

"Northern savages," he said, amused.

Was that our reputation? If so, it pleased me. But the northern savages, or a handful of them, were trapped, and our savagery would win us nothing unless we managed to escape. We needed a ship.

And next morning she came.

PART THREE
The Field of Barley

Eight

It was late morning and Immar was standing as sentry on the western wharf, or rather he was sitting in the summer sunlight on the western wharf with a pot of sour ale and with two small boys, both from Aldwyn's tribe of orphans, sitting at his feet and listening awestruck to whatever tall tales he told them. Immar was a young Mercian whom I had saved from being hanged the previous year, though he had been forced to watch his father dancing the rope-death on my orders. Despite that experience he had sworn loyalty to me and now wore mail and carried a sword. He had learned his sword-skill remarkably quickly and had proved to be a ferocious fighter on two cattle raids, but he had yet to be tested in a shield wall. Still, the two small boys were captivated by his stories, as was Alaina who had wandered to join them and now listened just as keenly.

"Nice little girl," Finan said.

"She is," I agreed. Finan and I were sharing a bench on the landward wharf, watching Immar and idly discussing the chances of having a west wind instead of the persistent but gentle southeasterly that had blown all night and morning.

"You think her mother is alive?" Finan asked, nodding toward Alaina.

"Mother's more likely to be alive than her father."

"True," he allowed, "poor woman." He took a bite of an oatcake. "Be nice for Alaina if we could find her."

"It would," I agreed. "But she's a tough little girl. She'll survive."

"She made these oatcakes?"

"She did."

"They're horrible," Finan said, throwing the rest of his oatcake into the river.

"It's the mouse shit in the oats," I pointed out.

"We need better food," Finan grumbled.

"What about those two horses in the stable?" I suggested.

"They don't mind eating mouse crap. It's probably

the best food they've had in years! Poor beasts. They need a month or two on good pasture."

"I don't mean that," I said, "I mean why don't we kill the two beasts, skin them, butcher them, and stew them?"

Finan looked at me aghast. "Eat them?"

"Must be enough meat on those two horses to last us a week?"

"You're a barbarian," Finan said. "I'll let you persuade Father Oda."

Father Oda would disapprove of eating horse meat. The church had forbidden its followers to eat the flesh of horses because, the clerics insisted, that flesh only came from pagan sacrifices. In truth we pagans are reluctant to offer Odin a sacrificial horse, the beasts are too valuable, though when times are desperate the gift of a prized stallion might placate the gods. I had made just such sacrifices, though always with regret. "Father Oda doesn't have to eat the stew," I pointed out, "he can live on mouse shit."

"But I can't," Finan said firmly, "I want something decent. There must be fish for sale?"

"Horse meat tastes good," I insisted. "Especially an older horse. My father always swore that an older horse's liver was a meal fit for the gods. He once made me kill a foal just so he could taste the liver, and he hated it, and after that he always insisted on an older horse. But you mustn't overcook it, it's best while it's still a bit bloody."

"Oh, dear God," Finan said, "and I thought your father was a Christian."

"He was, so every time he ate horse liver he added it to the other sins he confessed, and there were enough of those."

"And you'll find your Benedetta won't eat horse meat," Finan said slyly, "she's a good Christian."

"My Benedetta?" I asked.

He just chuckled and I thought of Eadith in far-off Bebbanburg. Was there really plague in the north? And if there was, had it reached my fortress? Jorund had heard a rumor that it was ravaging Eoferwic where two of my grandchildren lived with their father, and I touched my hammer amulet and sent a wordless prayer to the gods. Finan saw the gesture. "Worried?" he asked.

"I should never have left Bebbanburg," I said.

I knew Finan agreed with me, but he had the decency to say nothing of that. He just stared at the glitter of sunlight on the river, then stiffened and put a hand on my arm. "What's happening?"

I came out of my reverie and saw Immar was standing

and staring downriver. Then Immar turned and, looking at me, pointed eastward, and I saw a mast, crossed
with a yard on which a sail was furled, showing above
the eastern palisade. "Come back!" I shouted at Immar.
"And bring the boys! Alaina! Come!"

We had planned to present Gunnald's son with a
small mystery when he arrived. Usually, the captive
guards had told us, there would be at least one man
on the wharf to take the arriving ship's lines. "Lyfing
Gunnaldson needs help, lord," Deogol the one-handed
captive had told me. "He can't handle a ship like his
father. And if there's no one on the wharf he sounds a
horn and we'll run to help him."

"And if no one helps him?" I had asked.

Deogol had shrugged. "He'll get ashore somehow,
lord."

I was insisting that the arriving ship must find the
wharf deserted and that no one should help Lyfing
Gunnaldson tie up. If he saw strangers on the wharf he
would be suspicious, and he would likely draw off until
he saw a familiar face, and I dared not risk it. Better to
let him think the guards were lazy and let him moor
the ship himself.

I was not even sure that the approaching ship was
the one we wanted, but she did have a mast, and no
ship with a mast could get under the bridge, so any that

did come this far upriver were trying to reach one of the very few wharves that lay this close to where the Temes foamed and fell between the bridge piers.

Finan and I went back into the warehouse where Benedetta was playing with the smaller children. Their laughter, I thought, was a rare sound in this grim place and it was a pity to interrupt it. I clapped my hands. "Everyone be quiet now! Not a sound! Beornoth! If any of those bastards makes a noise you can kill them." I meant the four captured guards who were shackled inside the smallest cage. Beornoth would keep the captives quiet, while Father Oda and Benedetta would make sure that none of the children or freed slaves made any noise.

Finan and I stood just behind the half-open door that led to the wharf. Five men, all in mail and all with swords, waited behind us. I took a pace forward, still in shadow, and saw the mast coming closer and then the ship's bows came into sight. A small wooden cross was mounted on her prow. The ship was making painfully slow headway against the tide and the fierce current. "They're tired," Finan said of the oarsmen.

"They've come a long way."

"Poor bastards," he said, remembering our own time chained to the benches when we had hauled on oar looms with callused hands and tried not to catch the eyes of the men carrying whips. "But that's our ship," Finan added grimly.

It was plainly a slave-driven ship because two men with whips were stalking between the benches. Three more men stood at the stern, where one, a fair-haired man wearing high boots and a white jerkin, handled the steering-oar. The other two crewmen were standing at the prow. One was holding a horn, the other had a looped berthing line. "Seven men," Finan said.

I grunted, watching as the ship turned toward the empty wharf. The river was flowing through the bridge arches with violent speed, heaping up on the far side, then churning white as it seethed through the gaps. The speed of the current caught the steersman by surprise and the ship was being swept back downriver. "Pull, you bastards!" the steersman shouted, and the two men with whips lashed the rowers' backs. They were too late. The ship drifted out of sight behind the wall and it was a minute or two before it came back into view. The slaves were pulling harder now, encouraged by the whips, and the steersman had the sense to aim his prow well upriver of the wharf. "Pull!" he shouted. "Pull!" The horn sounded, demanding help, but we stayed in the doorway's deep shadow.

The whips cracked, the rowers heaved on their long oars, and the ship surged toward the wharf, but even so it was being driven downstream. "Pull!" the steersman screamed. The oar-blades dipped, they hauled, and the ship came into the gap between the wreck and the empty wharf, but again the steersman had misjudged, and he was now too far from the empty wharf and the current was driving him back toward the wrecked ship. "Bring in the oars!" he bellowed, not wanting his precious blades splintered against the wreck.

Finan chuckled. The Irishman was no seaman, but he recognized a clumsy display of ship handling when he saw it. The slaving ship drifted and struck, pinned against the wreck, and with no one on the wharf to take the lines. "Ælfrin!" the steersman shouted toward us. "Ælfrin, you lazy bastard! Come here!" Ælfrin, we had learned, had commanded the guards left at the yard and was the first man I had killed. By now his body was somewhere downriver, presumably stranded on a mudbank where the gulls would be feasting on his bloated corpse.

One man had to struggle across the half sunken wreck, taking the bitter end of a line, then walk around to the empty wharf where he hauled the ship's bow into the western wharf. He tied off the line, then caught a second line hurled from the stern and so pulled the ship into its berth. The oarsmen were slumped on their benches. I could see blood on some backs. My own back still carried the scars.

"Ælfrin!" the steersman bellowed toward us, and again there was no answer. I heard a muttered curse, then the clattering sound of heavy oars being stowed amidships. One of the crewmen was unshackling the rowers on the two benches nearest the prow and I remembered my days on the *Trader*, the slave-driven ship where Finan and I had been chained to a bench, and how cautious the crew was when it came time to unshackle us. We were released two at a time and escorted by men with whips and swords to whatever hovel would be our home. It seemed Gunnald's son was just as cautious. Another crewman made sure the two berthing lines were well secured, then added a third.

"Let's go," I said.

I had deliberately waited until the ship was firmly tied to the wharf so it could not back out into the current when the crew saw us. Now, with three lines lashed down, it was too late for them to escape. Nor did they even try. The fair-haired man who had made such a mess of docking the ship just stood at the stern and stared at us. "Who are you?" he shouted.

"Lord Varin's men," I called back, strolling down the wharf.

"Who in God's name is Lord Varin?"

"The man who captured the city," I said. "Welcome to East Anglia."

That confused him and he still just gazed at us as we came closer. Our swords were sheathed and we seemed to be in no hurry. "Where's my father?" he asked, finding his voice again.

"Is he the fat fellow?"

"Yes."

"He's somewhere," I said vaguely. "What are you carrying?"

"Carrying?"

"What cargo?"

"Nothing."

"We were told you sold slaves in Frankia. Did you give them away?"

"Of course not!"

"So you got paid?" I asked, standing by the ship's stern.

Lyfing Gunnaldson saw where the questions were leading and looked uncomfortable. "We were paid," he muttered.

"Then your cargo is money!" I said cheerfully. "Bring it ashore."

He hesitated, looking at his crewmen, but those men were not wearing mail and we were, they had either short-swords or a mariner's knife, and we all carried long blades. Lyfing still hesitated, then he saw me put a hand on Serpent-Breath's hilt and he stepped off the steering platform, reached beneath it, and pulled out a small wooden chest, which, from the effort he needed to lift it, was plainly heavy.

"It's just customs dues," I said reassuringly. "Bring it ashore!"

"Customs dues," he said bitterly, but still obeyed. He clambered up from the ship and dropped the box on the wharf. There was a happy sound of coins. His face, reddened by wind and sun, was soured by resentment. "How much do you want?"

"Open it," I ordered.

He bent to unclasp the iron latch and I kicked him hard in the ribs, drawing Serpent-Breath as I did. I stooped and pulled his seax from her scabbard and tossed the sword into the boat where she fell at the feet of an oarsman who looked scared. One of the men with whips drew his arm back. "Use that whip," I shouted at him, "and I'll strangle you with it!" The man glared at me and bared his teeth. He only had two that I could see, while his scarred face was framed by black greasy ringlets and a beard that fell to his waist. "Drop the whip!" I snarled at him. He hesitated, then reluctantly obeyed.

Lyfing Gunnaldson was trying to get to his feet. I kicked him again and told Immar to stand guard on him. "Kill him if he tries to stand."

"Yes, lord."

It was simple after that. We went on board, disarmed the crewmen, and prodded them up to the wharf. There was no fight in them, not even in the black-bearded man who had wanted to defy me. They still believed we were East Anglians who had taken over their city. One wanted to know when he would get his sword back and I just snarled at him to be silent. "And you all stay where you are!" I called to the slaves on the rowing benches. "Vidarr?"

"Lord?"

"Make sure they stay!" The rowers were shackled with iron rings about their ankles, the rings threaded by long chains that ran from the prow to the ship's stern. The two chains had already been freed from their prow staples and the slaves could have escaped easily enough, but they were weary, they were frightened, and so they stayed. I left two men to make sure the rowers remained quiet, locked our new captives in the same cage as the other guards, then stood at the warehouse door and gazed at the ship. She looked new, her rigging was taut, and her furled sail unfrayed.

I touched my hammer and sent a wordless prayer of thanks because I could take my men home.

"Now what?" Finan had joined me.

"We get the oarsmen off the ship," I said, "and wait for dawn tomorrow."

"Dawn tomorrow?" Finan asked. "Why not go now?"

We were standing in warm sunlight. It was a calm day with no wind to speak of, certainly not the west wind I wanted, but the river was running fast, helped by an ebbing tide, so that even with tired rowers it would be a quick passage to the estuary, and the afternoon could well bring a breeze to take us northward. And like Finan I wanted to go home. I wanted to smell Bebbanburg's sea and rest in Bebbanburg's hall. I had thought to leave in the dawn, shrouded from curious eyes by the remnants of darkness and a river mist, but why not leave now? The city seemed quiet. Jorund had told us the previous night that ships wanting to leave the docks were searched, but no East Anglian soldiers were taking any interest in our wharf. "Why not go now?" I repeated.

"Let's just go home," Finan said forcibly.

So we told everyone; the freed slaves, the children, Father Oda, and Benedetta to board the boat. We had cooked more shit-speckled cakes with the last of the oats and they were carried on board with whatever plunder we wanted from Gunnald's yard. Among that plunder were four good large shields, a dozen mail coats, two boxes of coins and hacksilver, ten leather jerkins, and a heap of other clothing. The last cask of ale was loaded.

The ship was crowded. There were children crammed in the stern, the freed slave girls huddled at the prow, and all of them staring fearfully at the oarsmen who were ragged-haired, filthy, and frightening. "I am your new master," I told those oarsmen, "and if you do what I ask you will all be freed."

There must have been men from several races because I heard muttering as my words were translated. One man stood. "You'll free us?" he sounded suspicious. "Where?"

He had spoken in Danish and I answered in the same language. "In the north."

"When?"

"This week."

"Why?"

"Because you are saving my life," I said, "so as a reward I will give you your life back. What's your name?"

"Irenmund."

I stooped to the deck and picked up one of the short-swords we had taken from the ship's crew, then walked the passage between the slaves. Irenmund watched me suspiciously. He was still shackled, but he was a formidably strong young man. His hair, blond and ragged, hung to his shoulders, his blunt face was fearful, but still defiant. He looked at the sword in my hand, then back to my eyes. "How were you captured?" I asked him.

"We were driven ashore in Frisia."

"We?"

"I was a crewman on a trading ship. Three of us, the master and two seamen. We managed to get ashore and were captured."

"And were sold?"

"We were sold," he said bitterly.

"You were a good seaman?"

"I am a good seaman," he said defiantly.

"Then catch," I said, and tossed the sword hilt first to him. He caught it and looked at me in bemusement. "That's my pledge that I'll free you," I said, "but first you have to get me home. Finan!"

"Lord?"

"Release them all!"

"Are you sure, lord?"

I looked back to the slaves and raised my voice. "If

you stay here in Lundene you will remain slaves. If you come with me you'll be free men, and I swear I will do my best to send you home." There was the sound of iron links rattling on the deck and clanking through the fetters as the long chains were pulled back.

"We'll need a smith to knock those manacles from their ankles," Finan said. "Remember ours? We had sores for weeks afterward."

"I never forget," I said grimly, then raised my voice. "Irenmund! Are you released?"

"Yes."

"Yes, lord!" Finan corrected him.

"Come here," I called.

Irenmund came to the steering platform, the heavy metal rings attached to his ankle fetters clinking as he walked. "Lord?" He said the word uncertainly.

"I am a jarl," I told him, "and I want you to tell me about this ship."

He sneered. "She's stern heavy, lord, and she yaws like a bullock."

"They didn't move the ballast?"

He spat over the side. "Lyfing Gunnaldson knows nothing about ships and I wasn't going to tell him."

"Does the ship have a name?"

"*Brimwisa*," he said with another sneer. The name meant "sea monarch," and, whatever else she was, this ship was no ruler of the waves. "One more thing, lord," Irenmund said hesitantly.

"What?"

He hefted the short-sword. "Five minutes ashore?"

I looked into his eyes, blue eyes in a face hurt by cruelty, and I was about to deny him, but then remembered my own feelings when I had been released from the shackles. "How many of them?"

"Just the one, lord."

I nodded. "Just the one. Gerbruht! Oswi! Vidarr! Go with this man. Let him do what he wants, but make sure he does it quickly."

I moved the children into the bows to help balance the ship and, when Irenmund returned, still holding the sword, though now it was red with blood, we cast off the mooring lines and the tired oarsmen backed the ship gently into the river's current. The stern was immediately swung downstream so that we were pointing westward instead of downriver, but a few strokes of the steerboard oars turned the hull until our cross-decorated prow pointed toward the distant sea. "Slowly now!" I called. "Take her gently! We're in no hurry!"

Nor was I in a hurry. It was better to leave slowly, raising no suspicion that we had cause to flee the city. The wind was no help to us so we rowed only enough to keep our headway, carried more by the ebbing tide and the river's current than by the sweep of oars. Finan came to stand by me. "I've been in some mad places with you," he said.

"Is this mad?"

"A ship of slaves? In a city of enemies? Yes, I'd say it was mad." He grinned. "So what do we do?"

"We get out of the estuary, we turn north, and we pray for a good wind. We should make Bebbanburg in three days, maybe four." I paused, watching swans on the sun-touched water. "But it means I've failed."

"Failed? You're getting us home!"

"I came to kill Æthelhelm and his rotten nephew."

"You'll kill them yet," Finan said.

The sun was warm. Most of the oarsmen were young, stripped to the waist, sunburned and sinewy. Word of Irenmund's revenge had spread through the benches and the rowers were grinning even though they were tired. I had assumed Irenmund had wanted to kill Lyfing Gunnaldson, but instead it had been the burly black-ringleted man whose screams had reached the wharf. "He made a mess of him, lord," Vidarr had told me with indecent relish, "but he was quick." Now Irenmund was back on his bench, hauling the oar, but slowly. The current would carry us till the tide turned, then the hard work would begin unless the gods sent a friendly wind.

Father Oda had been talking to the oarsmen and now joined us. "Mostly Saxons," he said, "but three Danes, two Frisians, a Scot, and two of your countrymen, Finan. And all of them," he added pointedly, looking at me, "Christians."

"You can pray with them, father," I said cheerfully.

We were passing the wharves on the northern bank. Shipping was thick there, though to my relief there were few warriors visible on the wharves. The day seemed lazy and quiet, even the river's traffic was scanty. Nothing was coming upriver against the tide, but we passed a handful of smaller boats that ferried goods to the southern bank. The air smelled cleaner out in the river's center, though the Lundene stench of smoke and shit was still there, but by tonight, I thought, we would be in the open sea beneath the stars. I was going home and my only regret was that my oath was unfulfilled, but I consoled myself that I had done my best. Æthelhelm still lived and his vile nephew was now called King of Wessex, but I was taking my people home.

We passed the Dead Dane and came in sight of my old home, the Roman house on its stone wharf at the river's edge. Gisela had died there and I touched the hammer at my neck. In my heart I believed she was waiting for me somewhere in the realms of the gods. "Three days, you think?" Finan interrupted my thoughts.

"To get home? Yes. Maybe four."

"We'll need food."

"We'll call into a harbor in East Anglia. Take what we need."

"There'll be no one to stop us," Finan said with amusement, "the bastards are all here!"

He was staring at the house, my old house where we had taken refuge when we first arrived in Lundene. A ship was moored there, a long, low ship moored to face upstream, with a high prow on which a cross was mounted. Her mast was raked, giving her a predatory appearance. I guessed she was twice as long as *Brim-wisa*, which made her a much faster ship, and for a heartbeat I was tempted to steal her, but rejected the idea when I saw men come from the house onto the terrace. There were a dozen men, half of them in mail, and they watched as we slid past. I waved to them, hoping the gesture would convince them that we were no threat.

Then one man, taller than the others, came from the house and pushed through his companions. He stood at the edge of the stone wharf and stared at us.

And I cursed. It was Waormund. I stared at him and he stared at me, and he recognized me. I heard his bellow of rage, or perhaps of challenge, and then he was shouting at the men around him and I saw them running toward the lethal-looking ship. I swore again.

"What?" Father Oda asked.

"Speed the rowers," I told Finan.

"Speed them?"

"We're being pursued," I said. I looked up at the sky and saw that darkness was still many hours away.

And we were no longer safe.

The ebbing tide was nearing low water, which meant it was running faster and gave us some help as, with the river's current, it swept us downriver. Finan was hammering the time with a stave and he quickened it, but the oarsmen were too tired after rowing upriver against the ebb. The current, of course, would help our enemy as much as it helped us. I hoped it would take Waormund a long time to assemble sufficient oarsmen, but hope is never something to rely on in warfare. My father had always said that if you hope the enemy will march east, then plan for them marching west.

We passed the old Roman fort that marked the eastern extremity of the old city and I looked back and saw my father had been right. The ship was already pulling away from the wharf, her rowers turning the long sleek hull to follow us. "It's not a full crew," Finan said.

"How many?"

"Maybe twenty-four oars?"

"They'll still catch us," I said grimly.

"That's a big ship for just twenty-four oars."

"They'll catch us."

Finan touched the cross at his neck. "I thought someone said this was a fast ship?"

"For her size, she is."

"But the longer a ship, the faster she is," Finan said unhappily. He had heard me say that too many times, but had never understood why that was true. I did not understand it either, yet I knew the pursuing ship must inevitably catch us. I was steering *Brimwisa* to follow the huge horseshoe bend in the river that would sweep us southward before curving north. I was using the outside of the bend, which was a longer row, but there the current was fastest and I needed all the speed I could find. "There are men at her prow," Finan said, still staring behind.

"They're the ones who'll board us," I said.

"So what do we do? Go ashore?"

"Not yet."

The current was racing us southward. The river was low, with wide stretches of glistening mud on each bank, and beyond them little but desolate marshland where a few hovels showed where folk made a living from trapping eels. I turned and saw our pursuer was gaining on us. I could see the mailed men in the prow, see their shields with Æthelhelm's leaping stag, and see the afternoon sun glinting from spearheads. Those men planned to jump down onto *Brimwisa*'s deck. "How many in the prow?" I asked Finan.

"Too many," he said grimly. "I reckon he has forty men at least."

So Waormund had roughly half his men rowing and the other half armed and ready to overwhelm us. "They'll ram us," I said, "and board us."

"And what do we do? Die?"

"We outrun them, of course."

"But you said they'll catch us!"

"They will!" I could feel the water vibrating through the loom of the steering-oar. That meant we were going fast, but we needed to be faster. "If you want to be free men," I shouted at the oarsmen, "then row as you've never rowed before! I know you're tired, but row as if the devil is at your heels!" Which he was. "Row!"

They put their feeble strength into the oars. Four of my men had taken the places of the weaker oarsmen, and they called the time as the strokes quickened. We had gone around the vast southern bend and were heading northward now. The pursuing ship was a little more than three hundred paces behind us and her rowers, fresher than ours, were pulling faster. I saw the river break white at her cutwater, saw how each pull of the oars surged her a pace nearer. "If we go ashore," Finan began nervously.

"They'll hunt us in the marshes. It won't be pretty."

"So?"

"So we don't go ashore," I said, deliberately confusing him.

"But—"

"Yet," I finished.

He gave me a weary look. "So tell me."

"We won't reach Bebbanburg, at least not for a while."

"Because?"

"See those trees ahead?" I pointed. About a mile ahead of us the river turned east again toward the sea, but on the northern bank was a prominent clump of trees. "Just beyond those trees is a river," I went on, "the Ligan, and it takes us north into Mercia."

"It takes them north too," Finan said, nodding astern.

"Half a lifetime ago," I went on, "the Danes took their ships up the Ligan and Alfred built a fort to block the river. They lost all their ships. That was a fight we missed."

"We didn't miss many," Finan said grumpily.

I turned to look behind and saw that the big ship was now a little more than two hundred paces away. I could see Waormund too, looming above the other men in the prow. He turned and evidently shouted at his oarsmen to row faster. "That ship may be longer than ours," I told Finan, "and she's certainly quicker, but she draws more water. The Ligan is shallow, so if we're lucky," and I touched the hammer, "she'll go aground."

"And if we're unlucky?"

"We die."

I had never sailed the Ligan. I knew the river was tidal for a few miles upstream, and deep enough beyond the tidal head to take boats almost as far as Heorotforda, but I also knew it was a difficult river. The Ligan's last few miles flowed through dense marshland where the river divided into a dozen shallow streams that changed their courses over the years. I had seen ships using those channels, but that had been years before. And we were very close to the tide's ebb, when the water would be at its shallowest. If I was unlucky we would go aground and then there would be blood in the Ligan.

Our rowers were weakening, our pursuers were nearer, and once we turned into the Ligan we would be rowing against the current. "Pull!" I shouted. "Pull! Your lives depend on it! You can rest soon, but pull now!" I could see that the freed slave girls, crouched in the bows with the children, were crying. They knew just what they could expect if the bigger ship caught us.

We were close to the end of the northern reach, but Waormund's ship was now only a hundred paces behind. I prayed he had no bowmen on board. I watched the river's northern bank appear as we began the eastward turn. Trees grew in the marshes and the Ligan's channels threaded those trees. "Poplars," I said.

"Poplars?"

"Just hope the mast doesn't catch on a branch."

"Mary, mother of God," Finan said, and touched his cross.

"Pull! Pull! Pull!" I shouted and heaved the steering-oar over, and the *Brimwisa* turned across the river's current and headed for the Ligan. She slowed immediately, no longer helped by tide or river, and I bellowed at the oarsmen again. The big ship was following us, close enough now for a man to try throwing a spear that fell into our feeble wake just a few paces short. "Pull!" I bellowed. "Pull!"

And we slid out of the Temes into the clearer water of the Ligan and the oarsmen were grimacing, hauling on the looms, and still I bellowed at them as we turned into the widest of the Ligan's channels. To the left, driven deep into the river's margin, were four giant stakes. I wondered if they were markers, or perhaps the remnants of a wharf, then forgot them as the steerboard side oars touched bottom and I hauled the steering-oar toward me and shouted at the oarsmen to keep rowing. There was a small island of reeds ahead. Did I go to the left of it or to the right? I felt panic. It would be so easy to go aground, but just then a small ship nosed into view behind a screen of poplars. The ship was little more than a barge, loaded with hay, and she was aiming toward the easternmost channel. I touched my hammer again and thanked the gods for sending a sign. "Row!" I shouted. "Row!"

The helmsman of the barge would know the river, and know just which channels had enough depth to float his heavily laden barge. He was using the ebbing tide to carry his cargo down the Ligan and, once at the river's mouth he would wait for the flood tide to float him and carry him up the Temes to Lundene. He had four oars, scarce enough to move the vast load, but the tides would do most of his work.

Our rowers could clearly see Waormund's ship, and see the mailed and helmeted men crowded into her prow. The oarsmen were bone-weary, but they pulled hard and we slid up the easternmost channel, passing the hay barge, and again our steerboard oars struck the river bed and I screamed at those rowers to keep pulling. Another spear was thrown and hammered into our stern post. Finan plucked it loose. The men on the hay barge watched us open mouthed. The barge's four oarsmen were so astonished at our sudden appearance that they had stopped rowing to stare at us, while the steersman just gaped and his ship slewed across the river. There was a bellow of anger from behind as Waormund's ship slammed into the barge and veered into the eastern bank. Men lurched forward as the big hull grounded.

And we rowed on, struggling against the current and the last of the ebb. I let the oarsmen slow, content just to make a walking pace as we slid between the marshes. Waormund's ship was aground, but men were already leaping overboard to shove her back into the channel. The hay barge had gone ashore on the other bank and its crew had been sensible enough to leap overboard and flee through the marshes.

"So we're safe?" Finan asked.

"They'll be afloat soon."

"Jesus," he muttered.

I was gazing ahead, trying to pick a course through the tangled waterways. Our oars touched the river's bed every few strokes, and once I felt the shudder of mud beneath the keel and held my breath till we had slid into deeper water. The branch of a poplar brushed our furled sail's yard and scattered leaves on the rowers. Birds fled from us, their wings white, and I tried to discern an omen in their flight, but the gods had given me the gift of the hay barge and offered me nothing more. An otter slid into the water, looked up at me for an instant, then dived out of sight. We were still rowing through marshes, but ahead of us the land rose almost imperceptibly. There were small fields of wheat and rye and I thought of Jorund, whom we had met in the Dead Dane, and how he wanted to be home for the harvest.

"Bastards are coming," Finan said. But the bastards were having a more difficult time than *Brimwisa*, their oars were fouling more often and their pace was slowed by the river's depth. They had a man in the prow who was watching for the shallows and shouting directions. "They'll give up soon," Finan added.

"They won't," I said, because ahead of us the river twisted like a serpent. It flowed south on its way to the Temes, then turned sharply northward before another tight bend brought it south again to where we struggled against the current. We would be well ahead of

Waormund when we reached that first bend, but as we rowed south his ship would be just forty or fifty paces away on the northward reach. "Irenmund!" I shouted.

"Lord?"

"I want you here! Vidarr? Take his oar!" I waited for Irenmund to reach me. "You can steer a ship?" I asked.

"Been doing it since I was eight years old," he said.

I gave him the steering-oar. "Stay on the outside of that bend," I said, "then keep her in the middle of the river."

He grinned, happy to be given the responsibility, and I pulled on my old, battered helmet with its boiled-leather cheek-pieces. Finan pulled on his own helmet and gave me a quizzical glance. "Why that fellow?" he asked softly, nodding at Irenmund. "And not Gerbruht?"

"Because we'll be fighting soon," I said. Gerbruht was a fine seaman, but he was also an immensely strong man who was pulling an oar and we needed all the strength we could find. "Or we will be fighting," I went on, "if Waormund has half a brain."

"He's got tripe for brains," Finan said.

"But sooner or later he'll see his chance."

That chance was caused by how closely the southern

reach lay to the northern. Just a narrow strip of marsh separated the two, which meant that Waormund could send men across the intervening marsh to assail us with spears. Irenmund was already taking us into the bend, keeping to the outside where the water would be deepest, but the current was also fastest there and our progress was painfully slow. Most of our rowers were at the end of their endurance, their faces grimacing as they hauled on the heavy oars. "Not much longer now!" I shouted as I made my way forward to where the children, the women, and Father Oda were sitting on the deck beneath the small prow platform. Benedetta looked up at me anxiously and I tried to reassure her with a smile.

"I want the smallest children under the platform," I told Benedetta, pointing to the small space at the prow, "and the rest on this side of the deck." I was on the larboard side because once we rounded the sharp bend, that side would be facing the enemy ship as it rowed northward. "Immar!" I shouted. "Come here!"

He scrambled back to me and I handed him one of the big shields we had discovered in Gunnald's yard. "The bastards might be throwing spears," I explained, "and your job is to stop them. Catch them on the shield."

Finan, Immar, Oswi, and I had shields. Finan would protect the steering platform, Immar would try to defend the women and children huddled beneath the ship's rail, while Oswi and I must somehow keep spears from striking the rowers. "It would be a long throw," Oswi said dubiously. He was gazing at the enemy ship that was nearing the first bend just as we struggled out of it.

"They won't throw from the ship," I said, "and maybe they won't throw at all." I touched the hammer, hoping I was right.

The helmsman on the enemy ship stayed too close to the inner bank of the curve and I saw the big ship lurch as she ran aground again. For a few heartbeats it just stayed there, then a dozen men leaped overboard. I thought they were about to attempt to push the big ship off the mud, but instead they carried spears and began running toward us.

"Pull!" I shouted. "Irenmund! Keep to the right!" The steerboard oars began fouling the river bed again, but they also found purchase and *Brimwisa* kept moving. The rowers on the larboard benches looked anxiously at the enemy who were stumbling through the marsh's reeds and tussocks. "Just keep rowing!" I called.

"Why?" A bare-chested man with a spade beard

challenged me. He stopped hauling his oar, stood, and looked at me truculently. "They're your enemy, they're not ours!"

He was right, of course, but there was no time to argue with him, especially as some of the oarsmen muttered sullen agreement. I just drew Serpent-Breath, stepped over the next bench, and thrust hard. He had time to look astonished, then his callused hands closed on the long blade that had glanced off a rib and driven deep into his chest. He made a gasping noise, blood bubbled at his open mouth and spilled down his beard as his eyes stared at me beseechingly. I snarled, wrenched the blade sideways and so toppled him over the side. Blood spread on the water.

"Does anyone else want to argue?" I asked. No one did. "Those men," I pointed the blood-streaked blade at our pursuers, "will sell you! I will free you. Now row!" The death of one man spurred the others to renewed effort and *Brimwisa* surged forward against the river's swirling current. "Folcbald," I shouted, "take this oar! Aldwyn!" The boy ran to me and I gave him Serpent-Breath. "Clean it."

"Yes, lord."

"Dip the blade in the river," I told him, "then wipe off every drop of blood and water. Bring it back when it's dry. Really dry!"

I had not wanted to kill the man, but I had sensed resentment among the bone-weary oarsmen who had been trapped in a struggle that was none of their business. The dead man, whose body now floated belly down toward our pursuers, could have roused that resentment into outright refusal. Even now, as the oarsmen pulled desperately on their looms, I saw the distrust on their faces, but then Irenmund, standing proud at the stern, called out. "Lord Uhtred is right! We'd just have been sold again! So row!"

They rowed, but even with the new energy born of fear, they could not outpace the men hurrying across the marsh. I counted them. Twelve men carrying two spears each. Waormund was not among them, he was still on board the pursuing ship that was being heaved off the mudbank. I could just hear him bawling orders.

Then the leading spearman decided to chance his arm. It was a long throw, but he hurled his spear and it soared across the river, aimed at Irenmund, and I heard it thump into Finan's shield. The other men kept coming, then two stopped and threw their spears. One fell short, plunging into the river, the other struck *Brimwisa*'s hull and quivered there.

Waormund had been clever. He had realized that spearmen on foot could catch us and cripple us by slaughtering enough oarsmen, but he had not been clever enough to tell them that their best chance was to throw their spears together. A man can dodge a spear or catch it on his shield, but a shower of spears is far more deadly. One by one the men threw the heavy blades, and one by one we either stopped them or watched them fly high or low. Not every spear missed. One oarsman was hit in the thigh, the blade gouging a deep cut that Father Oda hurried to bandage. Another glanced off the iron rim of my shield and scored a long shallow wound across a man's naked back, but most of the spears were wasted, and still we rowed on, nearing the next bend that would take us north again. North into Mercia.

Waormund had freed his ship and had his men hauling on their oars again, but Irenmund was already taking us into the sharp curve. I saw Beornoth readying to hurl a spear back at the frustrated men who could only watch as we rowed away from them. "No!" I called to him.

"I can skewer one of the bastards, lord!" he called back.

"And give them a chance to throw it back? Don't throw!"

Waormund's men had used all their spears and his only chance now was to row faster, but the deeper draft of his big ship was turning against him and the tide was blessedly low. We turned the bend and headed north and saw our pursuer shudder to another stop. We rowed on, gaining distance with every stroke, still threading the wide marsh, but ahead of us now there were low wooded hills and the smoke from cooking hearths. The river was becoming dirtier, with streaks of foul-smelling brown water. There was a village, I remembered, built where the Roman road from Lundene to Colneceaster forded the Ligan, and I feared that the East Anglians might have left men there to guard the crossing. We were rowing now between thick willow trees that snagged on our mast and yard and I could see the small smoke from the village smearing the sky. Benedetta had come aft to join me as we passed between the village's first small cottages. She wrinkled her nose. "The stink!"

"Tanners," I said.

"Leather?"

"They cure the hides with shit."

"It is filthy."

"The world is filthy," I said.

Benedetta paused, and then, in a lower voice, "I have to say something."

"Say it."

"The slave girls," Benedetta said, nodding toward

the bow where the girls we had freed from Gunnald's warehouse were huddled. "They are frightened."

"We're all frightened," I said.

"But they have been kept from the men. It is not your enemy they fear, but the other slaves. I am frightened of them too." She paused and then, more harshly, "You should not have freed the men with oars, Lord Uhtred. They should all be chained still!"

"I'm giving them freedom," I said.

"Freedom to take what they want."

I gazed at the women. All were young, and the four who had been kept for Gunnald's use were undeniably attractive. They stared back at me with fear on their faces. "Short of killing the rowers," I said, "the best I can do is protect the women. My men won't touch them."

"I'll kill any man who does," Finan put in. He had been listening to our conversation.

"Men are not kind," Benedetta said. "I know."

We passed a wooden church, and beyond it a woman was pulling weeds from a vegetable garden. "Are there soldiers here?" I called to her, but she pretended not to hear and walked toward her thatched hovel.

"Can't see any troops," Finan said, "and why would they have an outpost here?" He nodded ahead to where a ripple of water showed where the road forded the river. "Isn't that the road to East Anglia? They can't be expecting enemies on that road."

I shrugged and said nothing. Irenmund still steered us. A dog chased us along the bank, barking frantically, then gave up the pursuit as we reached the ford. Our keel touched the bottom again, even though we were keeping to the middle of the river, but the ominous scraping died and the slight grounding hardly checked our small speed. "He won't get past that," I told Finan.

"Waormund?"

"That ford will stop him dead. He'll have to wait hours."

"God be praised," Benedetta said.

Aldwyn brought me Serpent-Breath. I checked that the blade was clean and dry, slid the sword into her fleece-lined scabbard, and patted Aldwyn's head. "Well done," I said, then looked behind and could see no sign of our pursuer. "I think we're safe."

"God be praised," Benedetta said again, but Finan just nodded westward.

And on the road to Lundene, at the village's western end, were horsemen. The sun was low, dazzling my eyes, but I could see men hauling themselves into saddles. They were not many, perhaps eight or nine, but two of them wore the distinctive dull red cloaks. "So they did leave sentries here," I said bitterly.

"Or maybe a forage party," Finan said dourly.

"They don't seem interested in us," I said as we rowed on northward.

"You hope," Finan said. Then the horsemen disappeared behind an orchard. The sun might have been low, but it was summer and a long evening lay ahead.

Which could yet bring us death.

Nine

It should have been a pleasant evening. The day was warm, but not too hot, the sun slanted across a green land, and we rowed slowly, almost gently. The oarsmen were near the end of their strength, but I did not demand more effort. We were traveling at a walking pace, content that no one pursued us. True, we had seen a small group of Æthelhelm's men at the village by the Ligan's ford, but it seemed they had taken no interest in us, and no horsemen appeared in the fields to our left and so we went slowly northward between willows and alders, past meadows where cattle grazed, and by small steadings marked by smoke that rose into the windless air. We kept rowing as the shadows lengthened into the long summer evening. Hardly anyone spoke, even the children were quiet. The loudest noises were the creaking of the oars and the splashes of the blades that left ripples which the current swirled downstream. I relieved Irenmund on the steering-oar and he took the oar of a youngster who looked on the point of collapse. Finan squatted beside me on the steering platform, and Benedetta perched on the rail with one hand on the sternpost. "This is Mercia?" she asked me.

"The river is the frontier," I explained. "Which means that is East Anglia," I pointed to the right bank, "and that," I pointed into the setting sun, "is Mercia."

"But if it is Mercia," she went on, "then we will surely find friends?"

Or we would find enemies, I thought, but I said nothing. We were rowing up a long straight river stretch and I could see no sign of any pursuit. I was certain Waormund's ship would not have been able to pass the ford, at least not until the tide rose, and his men, tired from rowing and burdened by mail and weapons, could never catch us on foot. My fear was that Waormund would find horses and then he would be on to us like a stoat slaughtering leverets, but as the sun blazed its last in the west we saw no sign of any horsemen.

We passed by two more villages. The first was on the western bank and was surrounded by the rotting remnants of a palisade and by a ditch that was half filled in. That fallen palisade was a reminder of how peaceful this part of Britain had become. It had been a wild frontier once, the border between the Saxons of Mercia and the Danes of East Anglia. King Alfred had signed a treaty with those Danes, ceding them all the land to the east, but his son had conquered East Anglia, and the river was peaceful again. Now Edward's will, that divided his kingdom between Æthelstan and Ælfweard, might mean that the palisade would need to be repaired and the ditch deepened. The second village was on the eastern bank and had a wharf fronting the river where four barges, each about the size of *Brimwisa,* were tied. None of the barges had a mast stepped, but all were equipped with stout tholes for oars and one had her deck heaped with sawn timbers. Beyond the wharf were felled trunks that two men were splitting with wedges and mauls. "Timber for Lundene," I said to Finan.

"Lundene?"

"The ships don't have their masts stepped," I said, "so they can get under the bridge." The Saxon city beyond Lundene's Roman walls was where the hunger for timber, for new houses, for new wharves, and for firewood, was unending.

The two men splitting the trunks paused to watch us pass. "There's a ford up there," one shouted, pointing north. He spoke in Danish. "Careful now!"

"What's this place called?" I called back in the same language.

He shrugged. "A timber yard!"

Finan chuckled, I scowled, then looked behind, but still saw no pursuing horsemen. At best, I thought, Waormund would return to Lundene and set out in the morning with sufficient men to slaughter us. He would search the river till he found *Brimwisa* and, if she was deserted, scour the nearby countryside. For a moment I even thought of turning the ship and rowing downstream, hoping to reach the Temes and then the open sea, but it would be a night-time journey against the tide with an exhausted crew in a shoaling river, and if Waormund had a shred of sense he would leave his ship with sufficient men to block the Ligan and so trap us.

We crossed the ford north of the timber yard without scraping the shingle, though some of the oars faltered as they struck the river bed. "We must stop soon," Benedetta insisted, "look at the men!"

"We keep going while there's light," I said.

"But they are tired!" she said. I was tired too, tired of trying to escape a predicament all of my own making and anxious because of the horsemen we had seen. I wanted to stop and I feared to stop. The river was wide here, wide and shallow, and Benedetta was right, the oarsmen were near the end of their strength and we were barely making progress against the sluggish current. The sun was low now, touching the crests of distant hills, but outlined against that burning sun I could just see a high thatched roof above a stand of elms. A hall, I thought, and a chance to rest. I pulled the steering-oar toward me and ran *Brimwisa* aground, her bows just nudging the bank.

Finan glanced at me. "Stopping?"

"It'll be dark soon. I want a place to shelter."

"We could stay on the boat?"

"We've come about as far we can," I said. The river was increasingly shallow and for the last few minutes we had been rowing through sinuous water weed and our oars and keel had been constantly scraping the river bed. I decided it was time to abandon *Brimwisa*. "We could wait for the flood tide," I told Finan, "and make a few more miles, but we'll be waiting for hours. Better to walk now."

"And rest first?"

"And rest first," I assured him.

We went ashore, taking with us the captured weapons, clothes, food, mail, and money. I distributed the food, letting everyone take what they could carry. The last things I took were the two long chains that had linked the shackles of the rowers. "Why these, lord?"

Immar asked me after I draped one of the heavy coiled chains around his neck.

"Chain is valuable," I said.

Before we left the river I had Gerbruht and Beornoth, the only two of my men who could swim, take off their boots and mail, then take *Brimwisa*'s bow line across the river. Once there they hauled the ship to the East Anglian bank, tied her to a willow, then half waded and half swam back. It was a small and probably useless precaution, but if Waormund did follow us then he would discover the ship on the eastern bank and might perhaps lead his men across the river and so away from us.

It was twilight as we walked across a lush river meadow that was thick with buttercups, through the elms and so to a large steading, which, like the villages we had passed, had no palisade. Two tethered dogs greeted us with frantic barking. There was a large hall from which smoke rose into the evening, a newly thatched barn, and some smaller buildings that I took to be granaries and stables. The dogs barked more urgently, straining at the thick ropes that held them to the hall, and only stopped when the door was thrown open and four men were outlined against the glow of the fire inside. Three of the men carried hunting bows that had arrows notched on their cords, the fourth held a sword. It was that man who bellowed at the dogs to stop their damned noise, then looked at us. "Who are you?" he shouted.

"Travelers," I called back.

"Jesus, enough of you!"

I gave my sword belt to Finan and, accompanied only by Benedetta and Father Oda, walked toward the hall. As I got closer I saw that the man holding the sword was elderly, but still hale. "I seek shelter for a night," I explained, "and have silver to pay you."

"Silver is always welcome," he said guardedly. "But who are you and where are you going?"

"I am a friend of King Æthelstan," I answered.

"Maybe," he said cautiously, "but you're not Mercian."

My accent had told him that. "I am from Northumbria."

"A Northumbrian is a friend of the king?" he asked scornfully.

"As I was also a friend to the Lady Æthelflaed."

That name gave him pause. He stared at us in the fast fading light and I saw him look down at the hammer amulet hanging from my neck. "A Northumbrian pagan," he said slowly, "who was a friend to the Lady Æthelflaed." He looked back to my face as he lowered the sword. "You're Uhtred of Bebbanburg!" He spoke in a tone of amazement.

"I am."

"Then you are welcome, lord." He sheathed his sword, gestured for his companions to lower their bows, then took a few paces toward us, stopping just a sword's length away. "My name is Rædwalh Rædwalhson."

"You're well met," I said fervently.

"I fought at Fearnhamme, lord."

"A bad fight that," I responded.

"We won, lord! You won!" He smiled. "You are indeed welcome!"

"I might not be so welcome if you know that we're being pursued."

"By those bastards who captured Lundene?"

"They will come," I said, "and if they find us here they'll punish you."

"East Anglians!" Rædwalh said angrily. "They've already sent men to raid our storehouses and steal cattle."

"We have food," I said, "but we need ale and a place to rest. Not in your hall, I can't endanger your household."

He thought for a moment. An elderly woman, I assumed she was his wife, came to the door and watched us. The first bats were leaving the barn, dark against the sky in which the first stars were showing. "There's a place a short mile south of here," Rædwalh said, "and you can rest there safe enough." He looked past me at the motley collection of slaves, children, and warriors. "But you lead a mighty strange army, lord," he went on, amused, "so what in God's name are you doing?"

"You have time for a story?"

"Don't we always, lord?

It had been the mention of Æthelflaed that had un-locked Rædwalh's generosity. The Mercians had loved her, admired her, and now mourned her. It was Æthelflaed who had driven the Danes from Mercia, who had endowed churches, monasteries, and convents, and who had built the burhs that defended the northern frontier. She was the Lady of Mercia, a ruler who had fiercely defended Mercia's pride and Mercia's wealth, and all Mercians knew I had been her friend and a few even suspected I had been her lover. Rædwalh talked of her as he led us south around the flank of a wooded hill, then listened as I told him of our escape from Lundene. "If the bastards come looking for you," he assured me, "I won't say a word. Nor will any of my people. We've no love for East Anglians."

"The man leading the search," I said, "is a West Saxon."

"We haven't much love for them either! Don't worry, lord, none of us have seen you."

The night was bright with moonlight. We were walking the river meadows, and I worried that Waormund might have sent men north on foot to find *Brimwisa*. I saw her mast above the shadowed willows as we went south, but saw no sign of any enemy. "If you want that ship," I said to Rædwalh, "she's yours."

"Never did like ships, lord."

"Her timbers might be useful?"

"That's true! A good ship's timbers will build a couple of cottages. Careful here." We had come to a reed-fringed ditch and, once across, Rædwalh led us west toward low wooded hills. We followed a track that wound through ash and elm to a clearing where an old decaying barn stood gaunt in the moonlight. "This was part of my father's steading," Rædwalh explained, "and part of mine too, but the old fellow who owned the river meadows died ten years back and I bought the land from his widow. She died four years after her old fellow, so we moved into their hall." He pushed open a half-collapsed door. "It's dry enough in there, lord. I'll send ale to you and whatever food the wife can spare. There's cheese, I know."

"You mustn't go hungry because of us," I said, "we just need ale."

"There's a spring back and beyond," Rædwalh nod-ded toward the higher ground to the west, "and the water's safe."

"Then all I need is shelter." I felt in my pouch.

Rædwalh heard the chink of coins. "It doesn't seem right taking money from you, lord, not for a night's shelter in an old barn."

"I stole the money from a slave-trader."

"In that case," he grinned and held out a hand. "And where are you going, lord? If you don't mind me asking."

"Farther north," I said, deliberately vague. "We're looking for King Æthelstan's forces."

"North!" Rædwalh sounded surprised. "You don't need to go north, lord, there's a fair few hundred of King Æthelstan's men in Werlameceaster! Both my sons are there, serving Lord Merewalh."

It was my turn to sound surprised. "Werlame-ceaster?" I asked. "Is that close by?"

"The good Lord love you, lord," Rædwalh said, amused, "no more than two dozen miles from here!"

So Merewalh, my friend, was close, and with him were the hundreds of men he had so foolishly marched out of Lundene. "Merewalh's still there?"

"He was a week ago," Rædwalh said. "I rode there to give the boys some bacon."

I felt a sudden surge of hope, of relief. I touched the hammer. "So where are we?" I asked.

"God love you, lord, this is Cestrehunt!"

I had never heard of the place, though plainly Ræd-walh considered it notable. I felt in my pouch again and brought out a piece of gold. "Do you have a reliable servant?"

"I have six, lord."

"And a good horse?"

"Six of those too."

"Then can one of your servants ride to Werlame-ceaster tonight," I said, holding out the coin, "and tell Merewalh I'm here and that I need help?"

Rædwalh hesitated, then took the coin. "I'll send two men, lord." He hesitated again. "Is there going to be a war?"

"There already is," I said bleakly, "there was fighting in Lundene, and once a war starts it's hard to stop."

"Because we have two kings instead of one?"

"Because we have one king," I said, "and a vile boy who thinks he's a king."

Rædwalh heard the bitterness in my voice. "Ælf-weard?"

"Him and his uncle."

"Who won't stop till they've swallowed Mercia," Rædwalh said sourly.

"But what if Mercia swallows Wessex and East Anglia?" I asked.

He thought about that, then crossed himself. "I'd rather there was no war, lord. There's been too much. I don't want my sons in a shield wall, but if there has to be war than I pray young Æthelstan wins it. Is that why you're here, lord? To help him?"

"I'm here," I said, "because I'm a fool."

And I was. I was an impetuous fool, but the gods had brought me close to Æthelstan's forces, so maybe the gods were on my side.

The morning would tell.

I would not allow a fire. If Waormund had sent men to follow us through the night then a fire, even inside the old barn, would betray us. We ate stale oatcakes and dried fish, drank the water from the spring that Rædwalh had said was pure, and then I ordered the oarsmen to sleep at one end of the old barn, the women and children at the other, while I and my men would stay between them. I put our plunder, the spare clothes, mail coats, money, and spears with the women. Then I made all my men draw their swords. A small moonlight leaked through the barn's splintered roof, just enough light so that the oarsmen could see the glint of swords. "I'm chaining you," I told them. There was silence for a couple of heartbeats, then a growl. "I'm freeing you too!" I quietened them. "I promised it and I keep my promises. But this night you wear the chains, maybe for the last time. Immar, Oswi! Do it."

That was why I had brought the chains. The oars-men were bone-tired, and that might be enough to keep them sleeping all night, but Benedetta's warning had stayed with me. Men whose ankles were linked by chain would find it impossible to move silently, and any attempt to remove the chain would surely alert us. Benedetta and the women watched as Oswi and Immar threaded the links. There was no way of stapling the chains, so they just tied clumsy knots in their ends.

"Now sleep," I told them, then watched as they sullenly settled on the rancid straw before I took Finan out into the moonlight. "We're going to need sentries," I said. We were gazing across the meadows to where the moon-touched river slid silver between the willows.

"You think the bastards are following us?"

"They might be, but even if they're not—"

"We need sentries," he interrupted me.

"I'll take the first part of the night," I said, "and you the second. We each need three men with us."

"Out here?" he asked. We were standing just out-side the barn.

"One man out here," I said, "and you or me inside with the other two."

"Inside?"

"Do you trust the slaves?" I asked.

"They're chained," he said.

"And desperate. They know we're being pursued. Maybe they think it's better to run now than wait for Waormund's troops to capture us. And they know we have money, women, and weapons."

He thought for a heartbeat, then, "Jesus," he said quietly, "you really think they'll dare attack us?"

"I think we should be ready if they do."

"And there's near thirty of them. If they all attack us . . ." his voice trailed away.

"Even if only half," I said, "or maybe I'm imagining it."

"And if they do attack?"

"Put them down hard and fast," I said grimly.

"Jesus," he said again.

"And warn all our men," I added.

We went back inside. Moonlight came through the ragged holes in the shattered roof. Men were snoring. I could hear a child crying, and Benedetta singing softly to her. After a while the crying ended. An owl hooted in the woods beyond the barn.

I put Oswi outside the barn and sat inside with Beornoth and Gerbruht, the three of us leaning against the wall in dark shadow. None of us spoke and my thoughts drifted as I fought against sleep. I remembered the Lundene house where I had lived with Gisela and I tried to conjure her face in my memory, but it would not come. It never did. Stiorra, my daughter, had resembled her mother, but Stiorra was dead too, and her face was just as elusive. What I could remember was Ravn, the blind skald, who was father to Ragnar the Fearless. It had been Ragnar who had captured me when I was a child, who had enslaved me and then made me his son.

Ravn had been a great warrior till a Saxon sword took his eyes, and so he had become a skald. He had laughed when I said I did not know what a skald was. "You would call a skald a scop," he had explained.

"A shaper?"

"A poet, boy. A weaver of dreams, a man who makes glory from nothing and dazzles you with its making."

"What use is a poet?" I had asked.

"None at all, boy, none at all! Poets are quite useless! But when the world ends folk will remember our songs, and in Valhalla they will sing those songs and so the middle-earth's glory will not die."

Ravn had taught me about his gods and, now that I was as old as Ravn had been when I knew him, I wished I had asked him more, but I did remember him saying that he believed there was a place in the afterworld for families. "I will see my wife again," he had told me wistfully, and I had been too young to know what to say and too foolish to ask him more. All I had wanted to hear was his tales of battle, but now, in the moonlit barn, I clung to those few words spoken so long ago and dreamed of Gisela waiting in some sunlit hall to welcome me. I tried again to summon her face, her smile. I saw her in my dreams sometimes, but never when I was awake.

"Lord," Beornoth hissed, elbowing me.

I must have fallen half asleep, but woke abruptly. Serpent-Breath was drawn, lying hidden in the straw beside me and I instinctively took her hilt. I looked to my right where the rowers had bedded down. I could see none moving and could hear nothing but snoring, but after a moment I also heard low muttering and assumed that sound had alerted Beornoth. I could make out no words. The muttering stopped then started again. I heard the filthy straw rustling and the clink of the chains. That sound had not stopped all night, but sleeping men move their feet and I had dismissed it. The moon was low in the sky, so little light leaked through the barn's broken roof, but all the rowers appeared to be sleeping. I listened, trying to distinguish the noise a chain might make if it were being slowly drawn through the ring of an ankle fetter, but all I heard were snores. An owl called. One of the children at the other end of the barn cried in her sleep and was hushed. A chain clinked again, stopped, and then sounded louder. The straw rustled, then went quiet. I waited, tense, my hand tight on Serpent-Breath's hilt.

Then it happened. A big man, little more than a shadow in the darkness, stood and charged toward me. He bellowed a challenge as he lunged at me. The chain clattered behind him. I shouted too, a wordless shout of rage, and I lifted Serpent-Breath and let the big man run onto the blade. I was trying to stand, but the weight of the man pushed me against Beornoth and we both fell back. Serpent-Breath had gone deep, I had felt her punch through layers of muscle, but the man, still roaring, swung at me with a seax, which must have been the blade I had given to Irenmund, and I felt my mail rip and a sharp pain score across my left shoulder. I had been driven down to the barn's floor. I was still gripping Serpent-Breath and was suddenly aware of warm blood soaking my right hand. Beornoth was shouting, children were screaming, I heard Finan curse, but I could see nothing because I was still trapped beneath the big man who was breathing gutturally, gasping into my face. I heaved him off me, managed to get to my knees, and ripped Serpent-Breath up. I should have been using Wasp-Sting because there was no room to wield the long blade, but before I could free the sword, two more men came at me, their faces distorted by fear and rage. The big man was dying, but had my left leg in his grip. I twisted Serpent-Breath in his guts just as one of the two men lunged at my belly and in the moonlight I saw a small knife in his hand. I twisted away and the dying man's grip tripped me so I fell again and the man with the knife followed me down, snarling, the knife aimed at my right eye. I held his wrist with my left hand, the right still holding Serpent-Breath, and the knife-man snarled again and used his strength to drive his blade down. He had been pulling an oar and his strength was prodigious. I wanted to slash his neck with Serpent-Breath, but the second man was trying to tug the sword away from me, and I remember thinking that this was a futile way to die. The first man was inching the knife closer. In the dim moonlit barn I could see it was not really a knife, but a ship's nail, a spike, and he was grunting with the effort of trying to push it into my eye while I was trying to thrust his hand away and still keep hold of Serpent-Breath.

It was a battle I was losing. The spike came nearer and nearer and he was stronger than me, but then, quite suddenly, his eyes went wide, he stopped snarling, his hand lost all its strength, and the long nail fell, just missing my eye. He began to vomit blood, great gouts of blood that were black in the night, blood spurting with extraordinary force to blind me, blood warm on my face as the man choked and gurgled from the sudden slash in his gullet. At almost the same instant the second man let go of both my arm and of Serpent-Breath's crosspiece.

A woman shrieked like a demon in pain. I was standing, shouting as much from fear as relief. The barn stank of blood. The man who had tried to take Serpent-Breath was backing away, a spear threatening him. He had been wounded in the ribs, presumably by the spear, and I finished him by slicing Serpent-Breath back-handed and so opening his gullet. The big man who had started the fight was still gripping my leg, but feebly, and I stabbed down with my blood-soaked blade and pierced his arm, then, filled with rage, I rammed Serpent-Breath through his eye and deep into his skull.

There was a moan, some gasps from the women and cries from the children, then silence.

"Anyone wounded?" Finan called.

"Me," I said bitterly, "but I'll live."

"Bastards," Finan spat.

Ten of the oarsmen had been persuaded that their best chance lay in killing us and now all ten were either dead or dying in the blood-reeking barn. The rest were huddled against the far wall. Irenmund was one of them. "We didn't know, lord—" he began.

"Quiet!" I silenced him, then stooped and plucked the seax from the dead man's hand. "How did he get this sword?" I demanded of Irenmund.

"I was sleeping, lord." He sounded terrified. "He must have stolen it, lord!"

The big man had stolen the seax and then, slowly and quietly, he had undone the knots in one of the chains. He had loosened it link by link, working through the dark, until he reckoned he could move unhindered. Then he had attacked.

It had been Benedetta who had shrieked like a demon in pain, not because she was hurt, but in astonishment as she had lunged the spear into the ribs of the man trying to take Serpent-Breath. She still held the weapon, her eyes wide in the moonlight, but her astonishment was nothing compared to mine because beside her was little Alaina, also holding a spear, and it was Alaina who had thrust her blade into the throat of the man trying to stab me with his makeshift knife. She appeared quite unconcerned, but just looked up at me proudly. "Thank you," I said hoarsely.

Two of the other girls had seized spears and helped my men woken by the sudden fight. The freed slaves should have overwhelmed us, but the chain had hindered them and they had only the one sword and two makeshift knives, and my men were given just enough time to seize their own weapons.

"That was too close," I told Finan as the dawn showed a sullen gray in the east.

"How's your shoulder?" he asked.

"Cut deep, feels stiff, but it'll mend."

"The women saved us."

"And a child."

"She's a little wonder," Finan said.

I nearly died that night and it was a child with a spear who saved me. I have been in too many battles and stood in too many shield walls, but that night I felt the despair of death come as close to me as ever I felt it. I still remember that spike getting inexorably nearer to my eye, still smell the man's rancid breath, still feel the terror of losing Serpent-Breath and thus being denied my place in Valhalla, but then a child, a seven-year-old girl, had driven death away.

Wyrd bið ful āræd.

There was no sign of any pursuit in the dawn, but that did not mean our enemies had given up the chase. There was a mist over the river meadows and that mist, together with the trees on the higher ground and the hedgerows in the fields beyond, could have hidden a dozen scouts who were looking for us. Rædwalh came with the rising sun, riding a big gray mare and bringing a gift of hard cheese and bread. "I sent two men to Werlameceaster last night, lord," he told me, "they haven't come back."

"Did you expect them to?"

"Not if they've any sense, lord." He stared toward the river mist. "We've seen no East Anglians for a couple of weeks so they should have had no trouble. I dare say they'll be coming back with Merewalh's men. And you, lord, what will you do?"

"I won't stay here," I said.

Rædwalh looked at the children who were wandering around the door of the old barn. "You won't get far with those little ones."

"With a spear up their backsides?" I asked, which made him laugh. "And I've left you a problem," I went on.

"A problem, lord?" I led him into the barn and showed him the slaughtered oarsmen. He grimaced. "Aye, that's a problem."

"I can drag the corpses into the wood," I offered, "let the beasts have at them."

"Maybe better in the river," he suggested, and so I ordered all ten corpses to be stripped naked and dragged down to the river.

Then we walked toward Werlameceaster. Rædwalh
had given me directions to follow a wagon track until
we reached the great road, then to keep on westward.
"The great road?" I had interrupted him.

"You must know it, lord!" he said, sounding astonished at the possibility that I did not. "The road from
Lundene to the north!"

I did indeed know that road. It had been made by the
Romans and it led from Lundene to Eoferwic and beyond that to Bebbanburg. I had ridden that road more
times than I could remember. "Is it close?" I asked.

"Close?" Rædwalh had laughed. "You could spit on
it from the other side of these woods. You only need
reach the road," he had continued, "then walk two or
three miles north and you'll come to a crossroads—"

"I don't want to spend any time on the road," I had
interrupted him.

"Not if you want to stay hidden," he had noted
shrewdly. My curious group of warriors, freed slaves,
women, and children would be noticeable, and travelers would talk. If our pursuers came from Lundene
then they would use the old Roman road and would
question everyone they met, so the fewer people who
saw us the better.

"So I cross the road?"

"You cross the road and keep going westward!

You'll find plenty of woodland to hide in, and if you go a small way north you'll find a good track that leads all the way to Werlameceaster."

"Is it busy?"

"Maybe a few drovers, lord, maybe some pilgrims."

"Pilgrims?"

"Saint Alban is buried in Werlameceaster, lord." Rædwalh had made the sign of the cross. "He was executed there, lord, and his killer's eyes popped out, and quite right too."

I had given Rædwalh another gold coin and then we had left. The sky was almost cloudless and as the sun rose so did the warmth. We went slowly and cautiously, pausing among trees to wait for the Roman road to be empty before we crossed, then following hedgerows and ditches that led us westward. Alaina insisted on carrying the spear she had used to kill the man trying to pierce my throat. The weapon was far too big for her, but she dragged the hilt along the ground with a stubborn look on her face. "You'll never take it off her now," Benedetta said with a smile.

"I'll put her in the next shield wall," I said.

We walked on in silence, dropping into a shallow valley filled with trees. We followed a forester's track that led through thick stands of oak, ash, and coppiced beech. A black scar showed where a charcoal maker had burned his fierce fire. We saw no one and heard nothing except our own footfalls, the song of birds, and the clatter of wings through leaves. The woodland ended at a dry ditch beyond which a field of barley climbed to a low crest. Barley. I touched my hammer and told myself I was being a fool. We had passed two other such fields and I had told myself I could not spend the rest of my life avoiding barley fields. Finan must have known what I was thinking. "It was only a dream," he said.

"Dreams are messages," I said uncertainly.

"I dreamed you fought me over ownership of a cow once," he said. "What sort of message was that?"

"Who won?"

"I think I woke up before we found out."

"What dream?" Benedetta asked.

"Ah, just nonsense," Finan said.

We were following a blackthorn hedge that marked the field's northern boundary, a hedge dense with bindweed and bright with cornflowers, with poppies and pink bramble blossom. North of the hedge lay a field that had been cut for hay. The stubble dropped gently to the road that led to Werlameceaster. We saw no travelers. "Wouldn't it be easier to walk on the road?" Benedetta asked.

"Yes," I said, "but that's where the enemy will look for us."

She thought about that as we climbed the last few paces to the low crest. "But they are behind us, yes?"

"They're behind us," I said confidently, then turned and pointed east to where the road came from the woods. "We'll see them come from there."

"You're sure now?" Finan asked.

"I'm sure," I said, and then suddenly I was not sure at all. I still stared at where the road came from the stunted beeches, but I was thinking of Waormund. What would he do? I despised the man, knew him to be cruel and brutal, but had that opinion made me think him stupid? Waormund knew we had escaped up the River Ligan, and he knew too that we could not have gone too far upriver on the low tide before our ship grounded. But when we had abandoned *Brimwisa* I had not known how close we were to Werlameceaster. I had left the ship on the eastern bank, hoping to mislead Waormund, but now I doubted that he had even bothered to search upriver for us. It did not need a clever man to work out where we would be going. Waormund knew we needed allies and he knew too that I could not expect to find any in East Anglia, but westward, scarcely a morning's walk from the river, lay an army of Æthelstan's men. Why would Waormund bother to follow us when he could lie in wait for us? I had been searching the eastern and southern ground for any sight of a scout, looking for the glint of sunlight glancing off a helmet or spear-point, but I should have been staring westward. "I'm a fool," I said.

"And is that supposed to surprise us?" Finan asked.

"He's ahead of us," I said. I did not know why I sounded so certain, but the instinct of too many years, of too many battles, and of too much danger was convincing me. Or perhaps it was simply that of all the possibilities the one that scared me most was to have Waormund readying an ambush ahead of us. Prepare for the worst, my father had liked to say, though on the day of his death he had ignored that advice and been cut down by a Dane.

I halted. To my right was the hedgerow, to my left the big field of barley that was almost ready for harvest, while ahead was a long, gentle slope that dropped to another belt of woodland. It all looked so peaceful. Buntings flew among the barley, a hawk soared high overhead, and a small breeze stirred the leaves. Far to the north a drift of smoke showed where a village lay in a hazed hollow. It seemed impossible that death stalked this summer land.

"What is it?" Father Oda had joined us.

I did not answer. I was gazing at the belt of woodland that lay like a wall across our path, and I felt despair. I had seven men, a priest, four women, some freed slaves, and a group of frightened children. I had no horses. I could send no scouts to search our path, I could only hope to hide, yet here I was on the high swell of sunlit land, in a field of barley, and my enemy was waiting for me.

"What do we do?" Father Oda tried a different question.

"We go back," I said.

"Back?"

"Back the way we came." I turned to stare east, at the woods where we had passed the black scar of the charcoal makers. "We go back to the trees," I said, "and look for somewhere to hide."

"But—" Oda began.

And was interrupted by Benedetta. "*Saraceni*," she hissed. Just that one word, but a word suffused with fear.

And the one word made me turn to see what had alarmed her.

Horsemen.

"Merewalh's men!" Father Oda said. "Praise God!"

There were maybe twenty horsemen on the pilgrim track, all in mail, all with helmets, and half of them carrying long spears. They were at the place where the road disappeared into the western trees and they had paused there, gazing ahead.

"They are not the enemy?" Benedetta asked.

"They're the enemy," Finan said in a low voice. Two more men had come from the wood, and both wore the red cloaks of Æthelhelm's troops. We could see them through a gap in the hedge, but it seemed that for the moment they had not seen us.

"Back!" I snarled. "Back! All of you! Back to the trees." The children just stared at me, the freed slaves looked confused, and Father Oda opened his mouth as if to speak, but I snarled again, "Run! Go! Now!" They still hesitated until I stepped threateningly toward them. "Go!" They ran, too frightened to stay. "All of you, go!" I was talking to my men who, with Benedetta, had stayed with me. "Go with me!"

"Too late," Finan said.

Waormund, I assumed he was one of the horsemen on the road below us, had done what I would have done in his place. He had sent scouts up through the trees and they now appeared where the barley field ended. There were two of them, both mounted on gray horses, and both were staring along the hedgerow to where I stood on their skyline. One of them lifted a horn and blew it. The mournful sound faded, then came again.

More men appeared on the road. There were forty now, at least forty.

"Go," I said to my men, "you too, Finan."

"But—"

"Go!" I howled the word at him. He hesitated. I untied the heavy money pouch from my belt and forced it into his hands, then pushed Benedetta toward him. "Keep her alive, keep her safe! Keep my men alive! Now go!"

"But, lord—"

"They want me, not you, now go!" He still hesitated. "Go!" I howled the word like a soul in pain.

Finan went. I know he would rather have stayed, but my rage and the demand that he protect Benedetta persuaded him. Or perhaps he knew that it was pointless to die while there was a chance of life. Someone had to take the news to Bebbanburg.

Everything ends. Summer ends. Happiness ends. Days of joy are followed by days of sorrow. Even the gods will meet their end in the last battle of Ragnarok when all the evil of the world brings chaos and the sun will turn dark, the black waters will drown the homes of men, and the great beamed hall of Valhalla will burn to ashes. Everything ends.

I drew Serpent-Breath and walked toward the scouts. Nothing good would come to me, but fate had led me to this moment and a man must endure his fate. There is no choice, and I had invited this fate. I had tried to keep an oath made to Æthelstan, and I had been impetuous and foolish. That was the thought that would not leave my mind as I walked between the summer-bright hedge and the tall stand of barley. A field of barley, I thought. And I thought that I was a fool and I was walking toward a fool's end.

And maybe, I thought, this foolish decision would not save my men. It would not save Benedetta. It would not save the girls or the children. But it was the last slender hope. If I had fled with them then the horsemen would have pursued us all and cut down every man. Waormund wanted me, he did not want them, and so I had to stay in the barley field to give Finan, Benedetta, and all the rest their one slender hope. Fate would decide, and then I stopped beside a patch of blood-bright poppies because the scout's horn had drawn the enemy from the road and they were spurring up the slope toward me. I touched the hammer about my neck, but I knew the gods had deserted me. The three Norns were measuring my life's thread and one of those cackling women held a pair of shears. Everything ends.

And so I waited. The horsemen filed through a gap in the hedge, but rather than ride straight to me they swerved into the tall barley, the big hooves trampling the stalks. I had my back to the hedge and the horsemen made a wide half circle around me. Some held spears that they pointed at me as if they feared I would charge them.

And the last horseman to come was Waormund.

I had met him only once before that fight in the old house beside Lundene's river, and at that first meeting I had humiliated him by slapping his face. It was an ugly face, a flat face slashed from his right eyebrow to his lower left jaw by a battle scar. He had a bristling brown beard, eyes dead as stone, and a thin-lipped mouth. He was a huge man, taller even than me, a man to place at the center of a shield wall to terrify an enemy. This day he rode a great black stallion, the bridle and saddle trimmed with silver. He leaned on the pommel, staring at me, then smiled, except the smile looked more like a grimace. "Uhtred of Bebbanburg," he said.

I said nothing. I gripped Serpent-Breath's hilt. I prayed that I would die with the sword in my hand.

"Lost your tongue, lord?" Waormund asked. I still said nothing. "We'll cut it out before you die," he promised, "and cut your balls off too."

Everything dies. We all die. And all that is left of us is reputation. I hoped I would be remembered as a warrior, as a just man, and as a good lord. And perhaps this miserable death by a hedge would be forgotten. My screams would fade, and reputation would echo on in the songs men sang in the hall. And Waormund? He had a reputation too, and his renown was cruelty. He would be remembered as a man who could dominate a shield wall, but who delighted in making men suffer and in making women suffer. Yet just as I was known as the man who had killed Ubba by the sea and as the warrior who had slain Cnut, so Waormund would be known as the man who had killed Uhtred of Beb-banburg.

He dismounted. He wore mail beneath the red cloak. Around his neck was a silver chain, and his helmet was ringed by silver, the symbols that showed he was one of Lord Æthelhelm's commanders, a warrior to lead war-riors, a man to fight his lord's battles. For a moment I dared hope he would face me in single combat, but instead he gestured for his troops to dismount. "Take him," he said.

Eight long ash-hafted spears surrounded and threat-ened me. One blade, its edge touched by rust, was at my throat. For a heartbeat I thought to raise Serpent-Breath and beat that spear away and hack at the men who faced me, and perhaps I should have fought, but fate had me in her grip, fate told me I had come to the end, and everything ends. I did nothing.

A frightened man stepped between the spears and

took Serpent-Breath from me. I resisted, but the rust-edged spear-blade pricked my throat and I let my sword go. Another man came from my left and kicked my legs, forcing me to my knees. I was ringed by enemies, Serpent-Breath was gone, and I could not fight back.

Everything ends.

Ten

It seemed I was not to die by the hedge. Waormund wanted reputation. He wanted to be known as Waormund Uhtredslayer, and a killing by a hedge would not inspire the poets to write songs about his prowess. He wanted to carry me in triumph to his master, to Æthelhelm my enemy, and he wanted the news of my death to be carried along the Roman roads till all Britain knew and feared the name of Waormund Uhtredslayer.

Yet if my death was not to be swift, I was still to be humbled. He walked toward me slowly, relishing the moment. He said nothing, just nodded grimly to a man standing close behind me. I thought for a heartbeat that was my end, that a knife was about to slice my throat, but instead the man just lifted off my helmet, and Waormund slapped me.

That was revenge for the slap I had given him years before, but this slap was no mere insult as mine had been. It was a fearful blow that threw me sideways, as bad and painful a blow as the stone that had been hurled from Heahburh's high wall to split my helmet and lay me low. My sight suddenly blackened, my head spun, while my skull filled with sound, darkness, and pain. And that, perhaps, was a blessing, because I was not really aware as they ripped the hammer amulet from about my neck, unbuckled my sword belt, took Wasp-Sting, stripped my mail coat, tugged off my boots, slit my shirt, then kicked my naked body. I could hear men's laughter, felt the warmth as they pissed on me, and then I was forced to my feet, my head still ringing, and they lashed my wrists in front of me and tied the rope to the tail of Waormund's horse. They wove the stallion's tail into two plaits that they tied into a loop of the rope to make sure I could not drag the tether loose.

Waormund, towering above me, spat into my face. "Lord Æthelhelm wants to speak with you," he said, "and his nephew wants to make you scream."

I said nothing. There was blood in my mouth, one ear was pain, I was staggering with dizziness. I suppose I must have looked at him, one of my eyes half-closed,

SWORD OF KINGS · 391

because I remember he spat again and laughed. "King Ælfweard wants to make you scream. He's good at that." I said nothing, which angered him and he hit me in the belly, his face distorted with hatred. I folded over, breathless, and he seized my hair and dragged my head up. "The king will want to kill you, but I'll make it easy for him first." He reached out and forced my jaw open, paused, then spat into my mouth. That amused him.

He had tossed Wasp-Sting and her scabbard to one of his men, but kept my sword belt with Serpent-Breath's scabbard for himself. He took off his own belt and sword, tossed them to a tall warrior, then buckled my belt about his waist. He took Serpent-Breath from the man who had disarmed me and ran a finger up the blood groove in her blade. "Mine," he said, almost crooning with joy, "mine," and I could have wept. Serpent-Breath! I had owned her almost all my life, and she was a sword as fine as any in the world, a sword forged by Ealdwulf the Smith and given the sorcerous spells of a warrior and of a woman, and now I had lost her. I looked at her bright pommel where Hild's silver cross glinted and all I could feel was despair and an impotent hatred.

Waormund laid my own sword's blade against my neck and for a brief moment I thought his anger would make him cut, but instead he just spat again and then slid Serpent-Breath into her scabbard. "Back to the road!" he called to his men. "Mount up!"

They would ride east to find the great road that led south to Lundene, the Roman road I had crossed that morning. Waormund led them through a gap in the hedge, though the gap was thick with brambles and the thorns ripped me as I stumbled after his horse. "Tread in my horse's dung, earsling!" Waormund shouted back at me.

The stubble of the pasture cut my feet as I staggered downhill. Twenty men rode ahead, Waormund followed, and another twenty rode behind us. Two horsemen, both with spears, flanked me. It had to be near midday, the sun was high and bright, and the road rutted with dried mud. I was thirsty, but all I could swallow was blood. I stumbled and the horse dragged me for a dozen paces, the mud and stones lacerating me until Waormund stopped, turned in his saddle, and laughed as I struggled to my feet. "Keep up, earsling," he said and kicked his feet so the stallion jerked ahead and I almost fell again. The sudden jolt started blood from the wound in my left shoulder.

The road led through the coppiced beeches. Finan was hidden somewhere in this wood and I dared to hope that he would rescue me, but he had just six men, and Waormund had over forty. Waormund must have known that I had not been alone and I feared he would send men to find my companions, but it seemed he was content with his prize, his reputation was assured, and he would ride in triumph to Lundene where my enemies would watch me die in misery and pain.

We passed two priests and their two servants who were walking west toward Werlameceaster. They stood at the side of the road and watched me stumble by. "Uhtred of Bebbanburg!" Waormund boasted to them. "Uhtred the Pagan! On his way to death!" One of the priests made the sign of the cross, but neither spoke.

I staggered again, fell again, and was torn by the road again. I did it twice more. Slow them down, I was thinking, slow them down, though what that would achieve other than delaying my death I did not know. Waormund became angry with me, but then ordered one of his men to dismount and I was draped over the empty saddle, though still tied to his stallion's tail. The dismounted man walked beside me and amused himself by slapping my naked arse, crowing with laughter with each slap.

We went faster now that I could no longer stumble, and the Roman road soon came in sight. It ran north and south through a wide and shallow valley, while far beyond it I could glimpse a silvery stretch of the River Ligan. The land here was good and plump, rich with pastureland and thick crops, with orchards heavy with ripening fruit, and stands of valuable woodland. Waormund ordered his men to trot, forcing my arse-slapping guard to hold onto the empty stirrup as he ran beside the horse. "We'll make Lundene by nightfall!" Waormund shouted at his men.

"Use the river, lord?" a man suggested. I gave a croak of laughter to hear Waormund addressed as "lord." He did not hear me, but the man whose horse carried me did and he slapped me again.

"I hate boats," Waormund snarled.

"A ship might be quicker, lord?" the man suggested. "And safer?"

"Safer?" Waormund sneered. "We're not in danger! The only troops Pretty Boy has near here are at Werlameceaster, and they're useless." He turned in his saddle to enjoy looking at me. "Besides," he went on, "what do we do with the horses?"

I wondered how he had found the beasts. He had followed me up the river and there had been no horses in his big ship, yet now he had mustered forty or more. Had he somehow gone all the way back to Lundene to find the horses? That seemed unlikely. "We could take the horses back to Toteham, lord?" the man suggested. "And you take the earsling to Lundene by river?"

"Those lazy bastards in Toteham can piss into the wind," Waormund growled, "and we'll keep their damned horses."

I had no idea where Toteham was, but plainly it was not far away. I knew that Merewalh was in Werlame-ceaster, and I supposed that Æthelhelm had sent troops to watch him and harass his forage parties. Maybe those troops were at Toteham where Waormund had found his horses, but what did any of that matter? I was bloody, bruised, and naked, a captive of my enemy, and doomed.

I closed my eyes lest any of my enemies saw tears. There was a clatter of hooves on stone as the leading horsemen reached the Roman road and there we turned southward, going toward Lundene. The road had no hedges here. To the right a long slope of grassland that had been cut for hay led to a wooded crest, while to the left was another field of stubble and beyond that was the low wooded hill where we had fought the slaves in the moonlit barn. The man slapped my arse again, and again he laughed, and I kept my eyes tight shut as if I could blot out the pain with darkness. But I knew there was more pain to come, nothing but pain and death in Lundene where Urðr, Verðandi, and Skuld, the three pitiless Norns who spin our lives at the foot of Yggdra-sil, would cut my thread at last.

Then Finan came.

Waormund reckoned that Æthelstan had no forces closer to Lundene than the garrison at Werlameceaster, which is why he rode southward without any scouts ranging the pastures and low wooded hills on either side of the Roman road. So far as he knew this was safe ground and all he could think of was the joy of his triumph and the sweet revenge of my death.

But Rædwalh's two servants had reached Werlameceaster in the night, and Merewalh, who had fought beside me in Æthelflaed's service, had sent sixty men to rescue me, and those horsemen did have scouts riding ahead. They had seen Waormund's men, but being uncertain how many warriors the West Saxon led, they had followed cautiously. They had seen my capture, but had not known it was me, and so they had followed Waormund farther eastward and, in the wood of coppiced beech, had found Finan and the rest of my company.

Now, caution swept to the wind, they came from a wood to the west of the Roman road. They came at a gallop, the high sun reflecting off spear-points, from sword-blades, and from shields bright painted with Æthelstan's symbol of a dragon clutching a lightning bolt. Their horses' hooves threw up great clods of pastureland, the thunder of the horses suddenly loud.

Waormund's men were tired, their horses white with sweat. For a few heartbeats they just stared in disbelief, then men dragged swords from scabbards and turned to face the charge, but Waormund just went on staring. I heard shouting, though whether it was bellows of surprise from the West Saxons or war cries from the Mercians, I could not tell, but the shouts seemed to startle Waormund who suddenly turned his horse away from the attackers and spurred it toward the field of stubble that lay between the road and the tree-covered hill. His stallion, checked by my weight that was still tied to its tail, reared. Waormund savaged the spurs back, the horse screamed, then bolted. My horse followed, but then it was my turn to scream as I was dragged from the saddle. Behind me were other screams as the Mercian horsemen slashed into the West Saxons. I saw none of it, did not see the blood on the Roman stones nor the men in their death throes. I was being dragged across the dry stubble, being lacerated by the short, sharp stalks, bouncing and sobbing as the horse fled, hauling on my tether in an attempt to prevent my arms

398 · BERNARD CORNWELL

being wrenched from their sockets, and as I sobbed I half saw another horse come alongside me, saw the earth flung up by giant hooves, and saw the sword lifted above me.

Then the sword sliced down. I screamed. And I saw nothing.

Not far from Bebbanburg is a cave where the Christians claim Saint Cuthbert's body was hidden when the Danes sacked Lindisfarena and the monks fled with the saint's corpse. Others say that Saint Cuthbert lived in the cave for a time, but whichever story is true, whether Saint Cuthbert was alive or dead, the Christians revere the cave. Sometimes, when hunting deer or boar, I will pass the cave and see the crosses made from twisted grass or reeds that are left by people praying for the saint's help. It is a sacred place and I hate it. We call it a cave, but in truth it is a massive ledge of rock jutting from a hillside and supported by one small stone pillar. A man can shelter from a storm beneath that ledge. Perhaps Saint Cuthbert did, but that is not why I hate the place.

When I was a child, maybe six or seven years old, my father had taken me to Saint Cuthbert's cave and forced me to crawl under that vast ledge of rock. He had five men with him, all warriors. "You stay there, boy," he had said, then taken a war hammer from one of his men and struck the pillar a great ringing blow.

I had wanted to scream in terror, imagining the massive rock crushing me, but knew I would be beaten bloody if I made a sound. I cringed, but stayed silent. "You stay there, boy," my father had said again, then using all his strength he hit the pillar a second time. "One day, boy," he had continued, "this pillar will crumble and the rock will fall. Maybe that day is today." He hammered it again, and again I kept silent. "You stay there, boy," he had said a third time, then mounted his horse and rode away, leaving two men to watch me. "Don't talk to the boy," he had ordered them, "and don't let him leave," nor did they.

Father Beocca, my tutor, was sent to rescue me at nightfall and discovered me shaking with fear. "Your father does it," Beocca had explained to me, "to teach you to conquer your fear. But you were in no danger. I prayed to the blessed Saint Cuthbert."

That night and for many nights after I dreamed of that great lump of rock crushing me. It did not fall fast in my dreams, but came slowly, inch by ponderous inch, the stone groaning as it descended so inexorably, and in my dream I was powerless to move. I would see the rock coming, know that I was going to be slowly crushed to death, and I would wake screaming.

I had not had that nightmare for years, but I had it that day, and again I woke screaming, only now I was in a farm cart, cushioned on straw and cloaks, my body covered by a dark red cloak. "All's well, lord," a woman said. She was riding in the cart with me as it lurched along the rough road to Werlameceaster.

"Finan," I said. The sun was in my eyes, too bright. "Finan."

"Aye, it's me," Finan answered. He was riding alongside the cart.

The woman bent over me, shadowing my face. "Benedetta," I said.

"I'm here, lord, with the children. We're all here."

I closed my eyes. "No Serpent-Breath," I said.

"I do not understand," Benedetta said.

"My sword!"

"You'll have her again, lord," Finan called.

"Waormund?"

"The big bastard escaped, lord. Rode his horse straight into the river. But I'll find him."

"I'll find him," I croaked.

"You'll sleep now, lord," Benedetta said and she laid a gentle hand on my forehead. "You must sleep, lord, you must sleep."

I did sleep, and at least that was an escape from the

pain that filled me. I remember little of that day after the sight of Finan's bright sword slashing down to sever the rope that had tied me to Waormund's stallion.

I was taken to Werlameceaster. I do remember opening my eyes and seeing the Roman arch of the eastern gate above me, but I must have slept again, or else the pain just drove me to unconsciousness. I was put on a bed, I was washed, and my wounds, and they were many, were smeared with honey. I dreamed of the cave again, saw the rock coming to crush me, but instead of screaming I just woke shaking to see I was in a stone-walled room lit by stinking rushlights. I was confused. For a moment I could only think about rushlights and how bad they smelled when the fat used to smear them was rancid, and then I felt the pain, remembered my humiliation, and groaned. I wanted the blessing of sleep, but someone put a damp cloth on my forehead.

"You're a hard man to kill," a woman said.

"Benedetta?"

"It is Benedetta," she said. She gave me weak ale to drink. I struggled to sit up and she put two straw-filled bags behind me.

"I'm ashamed," I said.

"Hush," she said and held my hand. It embarrassed me and I took my hand away.

"I'm ashamed," I said again.

"Of what?"

"I am Uhtred of Bebbanburg. They humiliated me."

"And I am Benedetta of nowhere," she said, "and I have been humiliated all my life, raped all my life, enslaved all my life, but I am not ashamed." I closed my eyes to stop myself crying, and she took my hand again. "If you are powerless, lord," she went on, "then why be ashamed of what the strong inflict on you? It is for them to be ashamed."

"Waormund," I said the name quietly, as if testing it.

"You will kill him, lord," Benedetta said, "as I killed Gunnald Gunnaldson."

I let her hold my hand, but I turned away from her so she would not see my tears.

I was ashamed.

Next day Finan brought me my mail coat, he brought me Wasp-Sting, with a sword belt to which he had attached Wasp-Sting's scabbard, and he brought me my boots and my old shabby helmet. All that was missing was my torn mail coat, the hammer amulet, and Serpent-Breath. "We took all these off the dead, lord," Finan explained, placing Wasp-Sting and the helmet on the bed, and I was glad it was not my fine war-helmet, the helmet that was crested by the silver wolf, because the wolf of Bebbanburg had been humiliated. "Six or seven of the bastards got away," the Irishman said.

"With Serpent-Breath."

"Aye, with Serpent-Breath, but we'll fetch her back."

I said nothing to that. The knowledge of my failure was too harsh, too strong. What had I thought when I sailed from Bebbanburg? That I could pierce the West Saxon kingdom and cut out the rot that lay at its heart? Yet my enemies were strong. Æthelhelm led an army, he had allies, his nephew was King of Wessex, and I was lucky to be alive, but the shame of my failure galled me. "How many dead?" I asked Finan.

"We killed sixteen of the bastards," he said happily, "and we have nineteen prisoners. Two of the Mercians died, and a couple have nasty injuries."

"Waormund," I said, "he has Serpent-Breath."

"We'll fetch her back," Finan said again.

"Serpent-Breath," I said quietly. "Her blade was beaten out on Odin's anvil, tempered by Thor's fire, and quenched in the blood of her enemies."

Finan looked at Benedetta, who shrugged as if to suggest my mind was wandering. Perhaps it was. "He must sleep," she said.

"No," Finan answered. "He must fight. He's Uhtred

of Bebbanburg. He doesn't lie in a bed feeling sorry for himself. Uhtred of Bebbanburg puts on his mail, straps on a sword, and takes death to his enemies." He stood in the room's doorway, the sun bright behind him. "Merewalh has five hundred men here, and they're doing nothing. They're sitting around like turds in a bucket. It's time to fight."

I said nothing. My body ached. My head hurt. I closed my eyes.

"We fight," Finan said, "and then we go home."

"Perhaps I should have died," I said, "maybe it was time."

"Don't be such a pathetic fool," he snarled. "The gods didn't want your rotten carcass in Valhalla, not yet. They haven't done with you. What is it you like to tell us all the time? Wyrd bið ful ãræd?" His Irish accent mangled the words. "Well, fate hasn't finished with you, and the gods didn't leave you alive for no reason, and you're a lord, so get on your damned feet, strap on a sword, and take us south."

"South?"

"Because that's where your enemies are. In Lundene."

"Waormund," I said, and flinched inwardly as I remembered what had happened beside the hedge in the field of barley. Remembered Waormund and his men laughing as they pissed on my bruised, naked body.

"Aye, he'll be in Lundene," Finan said grimly. "He'll have run home to his master with his tail between his legs."

"Æthelhelm," I said, naming my enemies.

"We're told he's there too. With his nephew."

"Ælfweard."

"That's three men you have to kill, and you'll not do that while your arse is in bed."

I opened my eyes again. "What news from the north?"

"None," Finan said curtly. "King Æthelstan blocked the great road at Lindcolne to keep the plague from spreading south. Every other road too."

"The plague," I repeated.

"Aye, the plague, and the sooner we're home to find out who's dead and who lives the better, but I'll not let you slink home like a beaten man. You fetch Serpent-Breath, lord, you kill your enemies, and then you lead us home."

"Serpent-Breath," I said, and the thought of that great blade in my enemy's hands made me sit up. It hurt. Every muscle and bone hurt, but I sat up. Benedetta put out a hand to help me, but I refused it. I

swung my legs onto the floor rushes and, with an agonizing lurch, stood. "Help me dress," I said, "and find
me a sword."

Because we were going to Lundene.

"No!" Merewalh said the next day. "No! We are not
going to Lundene."

There were a dozen of us, sitting just outside Werlameceaster's great hall, which looked much the same
as Ceaster's hall, which was no surprise because both
had been built by the Romans. Merewalh's men had
dragged benches into the sunlight where the twelve
of us sat, though around us, sitting in the dust of the
big square that lay in front of the hall, were close to
a hundred men who listened. Servants brought us ale.
Some chickens scratched by the hall door, watched by
a lazy dog. Finan sat to my right while Father Oda was
to my left. Two priests and the leaders of Merewalh's
troops made up the rest of the company. I hurt still.
I knew my body would hurt for days. My left eye was
still half closed and my left ear clogged with scabbed
blood.

"How many men garrison Lundene?" Father Oda
asked.

"At least a thousand," Merewalh said.

"They need two thousand," I said.

"And I have only five hundred men," Merewalh said, "and some of those are ill."

I liked Merewalh. He was a sober, sensible man. I had known him since he was a youngster, but his beard and hair had turned gray now and his shrewd eyes were surrounded by deep wrinkles. He looked anxious, but even as a young man he had always appeared worried. He was a good and loyal warrior who had commanded Æthelflaed's household troops and had led them with unshakable loyalty and an admirable caution. He was no risk-taker, and perhaps that was good in a man who saw defense as his deepest responsibility. Æthelstan plainly trusted him, which was why Merewalh had been given command of the fine troops who had captured Lundene, but then Merewalh had lost the city, tricked by a false report that an army was advancing through Werlameceaster.

Now he held these walls instead of Lundene's massive ramparts. "What are your orders now?" I asked him.

"To stop reinforcements reaching Lundene from East Anglia."

"Those reinforcements don't go by road," I said, "they go by ship, and we saw them arrive. Ship after ship loaded with men."

Merewalh frowned at that, but it was surely no surprise to him that Æthelhelm was using ships to strengthen Lundene's garrison. "Mercia has no ships," he said as if that excused his failure to stop the reinforcements.

"So you just guard the roads coming from East Anglia?" I asked.

"Without shipping? That's all we can do. And we send patrols to watch Lundene."

"And to watch Toteham?" I pressed him. I was not sure where Toteham was, but from what I had overheard it must have been between Lundene and Werlameceaster.

My assumption proved to be right because the question provoked an awkward silence. "Toteham has only a small garrison," a man called Heorstan finally said. He was a middle-aged man who served as Merewalh's deputy. "They're too few to cause us trouble."

"Small?"

"Maybe seventy-five men?"

"So the seventy-five men at Toteham don't cause you trouble," I said caustically, "so what do they do?"

"They just watch us," one of Merewalh's warriors answered. He sounded surly.

"And you just ignore them?" I was looking at Merewalh.

There was another awkward silence and some of the

men sitting in the sunlight shuffled and stared at the dusty ground, suggesting to me that they had already proposed attacking Toteham and that Merewalh had rejected the idea.

"If Æthelhelm sends an army out of Lundene to attack King Æthelstan," one of the priests spoke up, evidently trying to save Merewalh from embarrassment, "we are to follow them. Those are also our orders. We are to fall on their rear as the king assaults their vanguard."

"And where is King Æthelstan?" I asked.

"He guards the Temes," Merewalh said, "with twelve hundred warriors."

"Guards!" the priest stressed the word, still attempting to defend Merewalh's inactivity. "The king watches the Temes as we watch the roads to Lundene. King Æthelstan insists that we do not provoke a war."

"There's already a war," I put in harshly. "Men died two days ago."

The priest, a plump man with a circlet of brown hair, waved as if those deaths were trivial. "There is skirmishing, lord, yes, but King Æthelstan will not invade Wessex, and thus far the armies of Lord Æthelhelm have not invaded Mercia."

"Lundene is Mercian," I insisted.

"Arguably, yes," the priest said irritably, "but since the days of King Alfred it has been garrisoned by West Saxons."

"Is that why you left?" I asked Merewalh. It was a brutally unkind question, reminding him of his foolishness in abandoning the city.

He flinched, conscious of all the men who sat listening to our discussion. "You've never made a bad decision, Lord Uhtred?"

"You know I have. You just rescued me from one of my worst."

He smiled at that. "Brihtwulf did," he said, nodding at a young man sitting to his left.

"And he did it well," I spoke fervently, earning a smile from Brihtwulf, who, on Merewalh's orders, had led the men who had rescued me. He was the youngest of Merewalh's commanders and had brought the largest number of troops, well over a hundred men, which should have qualified him to be Merewalh's deputy, but his youth and inexperience had counted against him. He was tall, dark-haired, strongly built, and newly wealthy, having inherited his father's estates just two months before. Finan approved of him. "He's got more silver than sense," the Irishman had told me, "but he's a belligerent bastard. Keen to fight."

"Brihtwulf rescued you," Merewalh went on, "and

are you now trying to rescue me from my bad judgment?"

"It was not bad judgment," Heorstan said firmly. It was plain that Merewalh's deputy supported his commander's cautious approach. "We had no choice."

"Except the invading army didn't exist!" Brihtwulf commented savagely.

"My scouts were certain of what they saw," Heorstan responded angrily. "There were men on the road from—"

"Enough!" I interrupted him with a snarl. It was not really my place to command this assembly, but if they started arguing over past mistakes we would never agree on the future. "Tell me," I said, turning to Merewalh, "if there's no war, what is there?"

"Talking," Merewalh said.

"At Elentone," the plump priest added.

Elentone was a town on the Temes, the river that was the border between Wessex and Mercia. "Is Æthelstan at Elentone?" I asked.

"No, lord," the priest answered. "The king thought it unwise to go himself, so he sent envoys to speak for him. He is at Wicumun."

"Which is close by," I said. Wicumun was a settlement among the hills north of the Temes, while Elentone was on the river's southern bank, both towns an easy march west of Lundene. Was Æthelstan truly seeking a treaty with his half-brother, Ælfweard? It was possible, I supposed, but at least he had shown sense in not risking capture by crossing into his half-brother's country. "So what are these envoys talking about?" I asked.

"Peace, of course," the priest said.

"Father Edwyn just came from Elentone," Merewalh explained, nodding toward the priest.

"Where we were searching for agreement," Father Edwyn said, "and praying there will be no war."

"King Edward," I said harshly, "did something stupid. He left Wessex to Ælfweard and Mercia to Æthelstan and both want the other one's country. How can there be peace without war?" I waited for an answer, but no one spoke. "Will Ælfweard give up Wessex?" Again there was silence. "Or will Æthelstan agree to let Ælfweard rule Mercia?" I knew no one would answer that. "So there can't be peace," I said flatly, "and they can talk as much as they like, but undoing Edward's stupidity will be decided with swords."

"Men of goodwill are trying to forge an agreement," Father Edwyn said weakly.

I let those words fall flat. These men did not need me to tell them that Æthelhelm's goodwill extended no further than his family. The warriors around Merewalh still stared at the ground, apparently unwilling to revive an old argument about what Merewalh should be doing with his troops. Yet it was plain to me, and it was probably plain to Merewalh too, that he was being too cautious.

"Who has the most troops?" I asked. "Æthelhelm or Æthelstan?"

For a moment no one responded, even though they all knew the answer. "Æthelhelm," Merewalh finally admitted.

"So why is Æthelhelm talking?" I asked. "If he has more men, why isn't he attacking?" No one answered again. "He's talking," I went on, "because that gives him time. Time to assemble a great army in Lundene, time to bring all his followers from East Anglia. And he'll go on talking until his army is so large that Æthelstan will have no chance to defeat it. You say King Æthelstan is guarding the Temes?"

"He is," Merewalh said.

"With twelve hundred men? Who are all scattered along the river?"

"They must guard all the bridges and fords," Merewalh admitted.

"And how many West Saxons guard the southern bank of the Temes?"

"Two thousand? Three?" Merewalh suggested uncertainly, then challenged me. "So what do you think King Æthelstan should do?"

"Stop talking and start fighting," I said, and there were murmurs of agreement from the men on the benches. I noticed it was the younger men who nodded first, though a couple of older warriors also muttered approval. "You say he's at Wicumun? Then he should attack Lundene before Æthelhelm attacks him."

"Lord Uhtred is right," Brihtwulf spoke. His flat statement had prompted no response and, emboldened by that silence, he continued. "We're doing nothing here! The enemy isn't sending men by road so we're just getting fat. We need to fight!"

"But how?" Merewalh asked. "And where? Wessex has twice as many men as Mercia!"

"And if you wait much longer," I retorted, "they'll have three times as many."

"So what would you do?" Heorstan asked. He had not liked the way I had peremptorily cut him off earlier, and the question was almost a sneer, certainly a challenge.

"I would cut off the heads of Wessex," I answered. "You say Æthelhelm and his earsling nephew are in Lundene?"

"We were told so," Merewalh answered.

"And I was in Lundene not long ago," I went on,

"and the men from East Anglia don't want to fight. They don't want to die for Wessex. They want to get home for the harvest. If we cut off Wessex's two heads they'll thank us."

"Two heads?" Father Edwyn asked.

"Æthelhelm and Ælfweard," I said harshly. "We find them, we kill them."

"Amen," Brihtwulf said.

"And how," Heorstan asked, still with challenge in his voice, "would we do that?"

So I told him.

"I was a big baby," Finan told me later that day.

I stared at him. "Big?"

"So my ma said! She said it was like giving birth to a pig. Poor woman. They said she squealed horribly when she squeezed me out."

"I'm fascinated," I said.

"And I'm not really a big fellow at all. Not tall like you!"

"More like a weasel than a pig," I said.

"But there was a wise woman at my birth," Finan ignored my sarcasm, "and she read the blood."

"She read the blood?"

"To see the future, of course! She looked at the blood on my wee body before they washed it away."

"Your wee body," I said, and laughed. The laughter made my cracked ribs hurt. "But that's sorcery," I went on, "and I thought you Irish were all Christians?"

"So we are. We just like to improve it with a touch of harmless sorcery." He grinned. "And she said I'd live a long life and die in my bed."

"That's all she said?"

"That's all," Finan said, "and that wise woman was never wrong! And I'm not likely to go to bed in Lundene, am I?"

"Stay out of bed," I said, "and you'll live forever." And I should have avoided barley, I thought.

I knew why Finan was telling me of the wise woman's prophecy. He was trying to encourage me. He knew I was reluctant to return to Lundene, that I had pressed Merewalh to attack simply because men expected me to lead them into battle. Yet the truth was that I only wanted to go home, to ride the great road to Northumbria and so gain the safety of Bebbanburg's walls.

Yet much as I wanted the comfort and safety of home, I wanted to salvage my reputation too. My pride had been hurt and my sword stolen. Finan, who had wanted to go home for so long, was now pressing me to take up the fight again. Was it his reputation too? "It's a huge risk," I told him.

"Of course it's a risk! Life is a risk! But are you going to let that bastard Waormund boast of defeating you?"

I did not answer, but I was thinking that we must all die, and when we die all that remains of us is reputation. So I must go to Lundene whether I liked it or not.

Which was why one hundred and eighty of Merewalh's men were scraping their shields that afternoon. We had no lime and not nearly enough pitch, so instead of trying to repaint the shields men were using knives and adzes to scratch off Æthelstan's symbol of the dragon and lightning strike. Then, once the willow boards were scraped clean, they used red hot-irons to burn a dark cross into the pale wood. It was a crude symbol, nothing like the triple-crown badge that many East Anglians carried, nor like Æthelhelm's symbol of the leaping stag, but the best I could devise. Even I would carry a shield with the Christian cross.

Because we would go to Lundene under a false badge, pretending to be East Anglians come to reinforce the swelling garrison. Merewalh and Heorstan had opposed the plan, but their protests had become weaker as other men urged that we should attack instead of just waiting in Werlameceaster for other men to decide the conflict. Two arguments had persuaded them, and I made both of them, though in my heart I did not really trust either. I wanted to go home, yet the oath bound me, and Serpent-Breath drew me.

My first argument was that if we waited then Æthel-helm's forces must inevitably grow stronger, and that was true, yet already we were woefully outnumbered by his garrison in Lundene. Merewalh had given me one hundred and eighty men and we would assault a city garrisoned by at least a thousand and, quite probably, two thousand.

Those odds should have dissuaded any man from following me, but I had made a second argument that had convinced them. I spoke of the East Anglians we had met in the Dead Dane tavern, how they had been reluctant to fight. "They were only there because their lord demanded their presence," I had said, "and not one wanted to fight."

"Which doesn't mean they won't fight," Merewalh had pointed out.

"But for who?" I had retorted. "They hate the West Saxons! Which was the last army to invade East Anglia?"

"The West Saxon."

"And East Anglia," I had argued, "is a proud country. It has lost its king, it has been ruled by Danes, but now Wessex has imposed a king on them and they don't love him."

"But will they love us?" Merewalh had asked.

"They will follow the enemy of their enemy," I had said, and did I believe that?

It was possible that some East Anglians would fight on the side of Mercia while others might refuse to fight altogether, but it is hard to persuade men to rebel against their lord. Men hold land from their lord, they look to their lord for food in hard times, for silver in good times, and even if that lord served a harsh and cruel king, he is still their lord. They might not fight with enthusiasm, but most would fight. I knew that truth, and Merewalh knew it too, yet in the end he was persuaded. And perhaps that persuasion did not come from my arguments, but rather from a passionate speech given by Father Oda.

"I am an East Anglian," he had said, "and a Dane." There had been murmurs at those words, but Oda stood tall and stern. He had presence, an air of authority, and the murmurs had faded. "I was raised a pagan," he had continued, "but by the grace of our Lord Jesus Christ I have come to His throne, I have become one of His priests and one of His people. I am one of Christ's people! I have no country. I fled East Anglia to live in Wessex, and there I served as a priest in the house of

Æthelhelm." Again there were murmurs, but low and cut short when Oda lifted a hand. "And in the house of Æthelhelm," he had continued, making sure that his voice was heard throughout the whole square, "I looked upon the face of evil. I saw a lord without honor and a prince in whom the devil has found a home. Ælfweard," he spat the name, "is a boy of cruelty, a boy of deceit, a boy of sin! And so I fled again, this time to Mercia, and there I found a prince of God, a man of honor, I found King Æthelstan!" And then the murmurs were approving, but again Oda had held up a hand to still the crowd.

"The East Anglians will fight!" he had continued. "But what is East Anglia? Is it a country? Their last Saxon king died a generation ago, they have been ruled by the Danes and now by West Saxons! They are a people without a country and they yearn for a country and in our scripture Saint Peter tells us that those who have no country belong to the country of God. And in that country God is our lord, God is our ruler, and Æthelstan of Mercia is His instrument. And the dispossessed of East Anglia will follow us! They will fight for our god because they want to dwell in God's country and be God's people! As are we!"

I had just stared in amazement because men were standing and cheering. I needed to say nothing more because the gamble of leading a few men on a desperate mission to Lundene had been turned into a holy duty. If men had their wish they would have ridden for Lundene that very moment, expecting Æthelhelm's East Anglian troops to change their allegiance as soon as we showed our banners.

Even Merewalh had been persuaded, but his natural caution still ruled him. "We might succeed," he allowed, "if God is with us. But King Æthelstan must know."

"So tell him."

"I already sent a messenger."

"So Æthelstan can forbid it?" I challenged him.

"If he wishes, yes."

"So we must wait for his answer?" I asked. "And wait while his advisers debate?"

I had sounded scornful, yet a part of me almost wanted Æthelstan to forbid the madness, but again it was Father Oda who urged boldness. "I believe God wishes us to conquer," he had told Merewalh, "even if a pagan leads us."

"Even if I lead them?" I asked.

"Even so," he had spoken as though there was a stench in his nostrils.

"You believe it is God's will?" Merewalh had asked the priest.

"I know it is God's will," Oda had said fervently, and so now men scraped shields and burned crosses onto the willow boards. And, watching them, I wondered if I was again making a terrible mistake. The enemy in Lundene was so numerous, and Merewalh had given me just one hundred and eighty men, and sense told me I was being an impetuous fool, yet whenever I felt a temptation to abandon the foolishness a small voice told me that success was possible.

Æthelhelm was gathering his troops in Lundene because there he was safe behind sturdy Roman walls in a city large enough to quarter his growing army. And doubtless he hoped that Æthelstan would attack him there because there is no quicker way to destroy an enemy's army than to kill it as it assaulted stone walls. Æthelstan could hurl his men at Lundene's Roman battlements and they would die in their hundreds and the survivors would be hunted and slaughtered across the length and breadth of Mercia. Ælfweard would take the thrones of Wessex, Mercia, and East Anglia, and call them Englaland, before taking his new and even bigger army north to my country of Northumbria.

Yet it was not just numbers. The men of East Anglia might follow Æthelhelm and acknowledge his nephew as their new king, but they did not love either man. Most East Anglians had obeyed Æthelhelm's summons because to disobey it would be to invite punishment. They were a conquered nation and they harbored a sullen resentment for their conquerors. If I could pierce into the heart of Lundene and cut out the center of Æthelhelm's forces they would not want revenge on me. Yet half of that army in Lundene were West Saxons, and how would they respond? I did not know. I did know that many West Saxon lords resented the power and reach of Æthelhelm's wealth, that they despised Ælfweard as a callow and vicious youth, yet would they welcome Æthelstan?

So yes, there was a chance, if a despairingly small chance, that a sudden lunge into the heart of Lundene would undo the damage made by Edward's will. Yet I knew that the real reason I wanted to go back was because my enemy was there. The enemy who had humiliated me, the enemy who was doubtless boasting of his triumph over Uhtred of Bebbanburg, the enemy who held my sword.

I was going for revenge.

Finan was not with me that afternoon as we scraped and branded the shields. I had sent him with two of our men and a pair of Brihtwulf's warriors to wait on the road to Lundene. I had told them to hide themselves beside that road and, just two miles south of Werlameceaster, they had found a spinney of blackthorn and hazel that offered them cover. They waited and did not return until the sun was low in the west, casting long shadows from Werlameceaster's ramparts.

I was in the hall with Merewalh, Heorstan, and Brihtwulf. The two older men were nervous. Merewalh had accepted my plan after Father Oda's fiery sermon, but now he was finding nothing but difficulties. The enemy was too strong, Lundene's walls too high, and the chance of success too low. Heorstan agreed with him, but was less certain that we must fail. "The Lord Uhtred," he said, half bowing his head toward me, "has a reputation for winning. Perhaps we should trust him?"

Merewalh looked at me mournfully. "But if you're defeated before I can bring my troops into the city?" he asked hesitantly.

"I die," I said curtly.

"And Brihtwulf and his men die with you," Merewalh said unhappily, "and they are my responsibility too."

"We surprise the enemy," I said. "We're planning a night attack when most are sleeping, just as they surprised us when they captured the city. We get inside and we open the gate to you and your men."

"If you assault the gate—" Merewalh began.

"We don't assault the gate," I interrupted him. "They'll think we're East Anglian troops come to reinforce them."

"After dark?" Merewalh was intent on finding problems and, if I was honest, there were many. "Men usually don't travel after dark, lord. What if they refuse to open the gate?"

"Then we wait till morning," I said. "In fact it might be even easier in daylight. We'll have crosses on our shields. We just have to persuade them we're East Anglians, not Mercians."

It was at that moment that Finan came into the hall with one of Brihtwulf's warriors. Both men looked hot and tired, but Finan was grinning. The four of us fell silent as the two men paced toward us. "Six men," Finan said as they reached us.

Merewalh looked puzzled, but I spoke before he could question Finan. "Did they see you?" I asked.

"They were riding too hard." Finan found a half-filled pot of ale on a table and drank, before offering it to his companion. "And they didn't see a thing."

"They didn't see us," Brihtwulf's man confirmed. His name was Wihtgar, and he was a lean, dark-faced man with a long jaw and just one ear. The missing ear had been sliced off by a Danish axe in a skirmish and the puckered scar left by the axe was half hidden by long greasy black hair. Brihtwulf, whom I liked, had told me Wihtgar was his best and most vicious warrior and, looking at the man, I believed it.

Merewalh was frowning. "Six men?" he asked, confused by the brief conversation.

"An hour or so ago," Finan explained, "we saw six men riding south, and all of them from this garrison."

Merewalh looked indignant. "But I ordered no patrols! Certainly not this late in the day."

"And all six were Heorstan's men," Wihtgar added menacingly. We had sent two of Brihtwulf's men with Finan because they would recognize any horsemen from Merewalh's forces.

"My men?" Heorstan took a backward step.

"Your men," Wihtgar said, "your men," he repeated, then named the six. He spoke the names very slowly and very harshly, all the while staring into Heorstan's bearded face.

Heorstan looked at Merewalh, then gave a weak smile. "I sent them to exercise the horses, lord."

"So the six have returned?" I asked.

He opened his mouth, found he had nothing to say, then realized silence would condemn him. "I'm sure they've returned!" he said hurriedly.

I slid Wasp-Sting from her scabbard. "So send for them," I growled.

He took another backward step. "I'm sure they'll return soon . . ." he began, then fell silent.

"I'm counting to three," I said, "and if you want to live you will answer my next question before I reach three. Where did they go? One," I paused, "two," I drew Wasp-Sting back, ready to lunge.

"Toteham!" Heorstan gasped. "They went to Toteham!"

"On your orders?" I asked, still pointing Wasp-Sting toward his belly. "To warn Æthelhelm's troops?" I pressed him.

"I was going to tell you!" Heorstan said desperately, now looking beseechingly at Merewalh. "Lord Uhtred's plan is madness! It will never work! I didn't know how to stop our men being slaughtered in Lundene so thought I would warn Æthelhelm and tell you afterward. Then you'd have to abandon this madness!"

"How much money has Æthelhelm been paying you?" I asked.

"No money!" Heorstan gabbled. "No money! I was just trying to save our men!" He looked at Merewalh. "I was going to tell you!"

"And it was your scouts that drew the garrison out of Lundene," I accused him, "with false stories of an army approaching Werlameceaster."

"No!" he protested. "No!"

"Yes," I said, and touched Wasp-Sting's sharp tip to his belly, "and if you want to live, you'll tell us how much Æthelhelm paid you." I pressed the seax against him. "You do want to live? You'll live if you tell us."

"He paid me!" Heorstan said, now in terror. "He paid me gold!"

"Three," I said, and drove Wasp-Sting into his belly. Heorstan half folded over the short blade and then, ignoring the agony in my shoulders, I used both hands to rip the seax upward and he made a mewing sound that turned into a choking scream that faded as he collapsed slowly, his blood reddening the floor rushes. He stared up at me, his mouth opening and closing and his eyes full of tears. "You said I could live!" he managed to gasp.

"I did," I answered, "I just didn't say how long you could live."

He lived a few painful minutes longer, finally bleeding to death. Merewalh was shocked, not by Heorstan's death, he had seen enough killing not to be worried by the spreading blood and choking breaths, but by the revelation that Heorstan had betrayed him. "I thought him a friend! How did you know?"

"I didn't know," I answered, "but if our plan was to be betrayed we needed to know. So I sent Finan south."

"But it is betrayed!" Merewalh protested. "Why didn't you stop the men?"

"Because I wanted the men to reach Toteham," I said, cleaning Wasp-Sting's blade on a scrap of cloth, "of course."

"You wanted them . . ." Merewalh began. "But why? In God's name why?"

"Because the plan I told you and Heorstan was false. That was what I wanted the enemy to hear."

"Then how do we do it?" Merewalh asked.

So I told him. And next day we rode to war.

PART FOUR

Serpent-Breath

Eleven

The dawn brought a mist that lingered above the meadows, drifted across the Roman walls, and was lost in the smoke from Werlameceaster's hearths. Men walked horses in the town's streets where a priest offered blessings outside a small wooden church. Scores of warriors knelt to receive a muttered prayer and a touch of his fingers on their foreheads. Women carried buckets of water from the town wells.

No one had tried to leave the town during the short summer night. Merewalh had doubled the number of sentries who guarded Werlameceaster's gates and paced its walls. Those men would stay in the town as a small garrison while the rest of us, one hundred and eighty men under my command and two hundred led by Merewalh, assaulted the enemy in Lundene.

I had long been awake as the dawn silvered the mist. I had pulled on my mail coat, buckled the sword belt with its borrowed blade, and then had nothing better to do than sit and watch the men who must fight and the women they would leave behind.

Benedetta joined me on the bench, which stood in a street leading from the wide square in front of the great hall. She said nothing. Alaina, who now followed Benedetta everywhere, sat on the street's far side and watched us both anxiously. She had found a kitten that she petted, though she never took her eyes from us.

"So you will go today," Benedetta finally said.

"Today."

"And tomorrow? The day after?"

I had no answer to her implied questions, so said nothing. A crow flew down from a rooftop, pecked at something in the square, and flew again. Was that an omen? I had tried to read every sign that morning, watched every bird in the mist, had tried to recall my dreams, but nothing made sense. I drew the borrowed sword and gazed at its blade, wondering if there was some message in the dull steel. Nothing. I laid the sword down. The gods were silent.

"How are you feeling?" Benedetta asked.

"Just a bit sore," I said, "that's all." My body felt

stiff, my shoulders were sore, the muscles of my arms ached, my skin's lacerations stung, the inside of my cheek was swollen, my head throbbed, and my ribs were bruised if not broken.

"You should not go," Benedetta said firmly and, when I did not reply, repeated herself. "You should not go, it is dangerous."

"War is dangerous."

"Father Oda," she said, "was speaking to me last night. He said the thing you plan is madness."

"It is madness," I agreed, "but Father Oda wants us to attack. He was the one who persuaded Merewalh to attack."

"But he said it is the madness of God, so you will be blessed." She sounded dubious.

The madness of God. Was that why my own gods had sent me no sign? Because this was the madness of the Christian god, not of my gods? Unlike the Christians, who insist that all other gods are false, even insisting that they do not exist, I have always acknowledged that the nailed god has power. So perhaps the Christian god would give us victory? Or perhaps my gods, angered that I harbored that hope, would punish me with death.

"But God is not mad," Benedetta went on, "and God will not want you dead."

"Christians have been praying for my death for years."

"Then they are mad," she said with great certainty and, when I smiled, she became angry. "Why are you going? Tell me that! Why?"

"To fetch my sword," I said, because I did not really know the answer to her question.

"Then you are mad," she said with finality.

"It doesn't matter if I go," I said, speaking slowly, "but I should not be taking other men with me."

"Because they will die?"

"Because I will lead them to their deaths, yes." I paused and instinctively touched my hammer, but of course it was gone. "Or perhaps to a victory?" I added.

She heard the doubt in my last few words. "In your heart," Benedetta pressed me, "which do you believe?"

I could not admit the truth, which was that I was sorely tempted to tell Merewalh that we should abandon the assault. The easy course was to let Æthelhelm and Æthelstan battle out their quarrel while I went north, went home, went to Bebbanburg.

Yet there was a chance, a slight chance, that what we planned could end the war almost before it had begun. Merewalh was to lead two hundred horsemen south to attack Æthelhelm's small garrison at Toteham, then ride on toward Lundene. He would be close to the city by nightfall and would doubtless encounter forage parties who would flee to tell Æthelhelm's men that an enemy force was approaching. Then, as dark fell, his men would light fires, as many as they could, on the heaths that lay some three miles north of the city. The glow of those fires would surely convince the city's garrison that a besieging force had come and, in the dawn, they would be gazing northward, readying to send patrols to discover the enemy's strength and ensuring that the walls were fully manned.

And it was then that I planned to lead the smaller force into the city and give the enemy a gut-stroke like that which had killed Heorstan. But just as flesh closes around a sword, sometimes making it almost impossible to drag the trapped blade free, so Æthelhelm's men would close on us and outnumber us. It was Father Oda's conviction that the East Anglians would change sides, but I reckoned that would only happen if we had first killed or captured Æthelhelm and his nephew King Ælfweard. That was why I was going, not just to retrieve Serpent-Breath, but to kill my enemies.

"The enemy knows you're coming!" Benedetta protested.

I smiled at her. "The enemy knows what I want them to know. That's why we let Heorstan's men ride south yesterday, to mislead the enemy."

"And that will be enough?" she asked. "To mislead them? You will win because of that?" She was scornful. I said nothing. "You lie to me because you are not well! Your ribs! You are hurting. You think you can fight? Tell me what you believe!"

And still I said nothing, because lurking in my heart was the temptation to break my oath to Æthelstan. Why kill his enemies even if they were mine? If a great war broke out between Wessex and Mercia then my country would be safer. For all my adult life I had watched Wessex grow stronger, defeating the Danes, subduing Mercia, and conquering East Anglia, and all in pursuit of King Alfred's dream that there should be one country for all the folk who spoke Ænglisc, the language of the Saxons. But Northumbria also spoke that language, and Northumbria was my land, and Northumbria was ruled by the last pagan king in Britain. Did I want to see Northumbria swallowed into a greater land, a Christian land? Better, I thought, to let Æthelstan and Ælfweard fight it out, to let them weaken each other. And all that was true, except I had given my oath and I had lost my sword. Sometimes we do not know why we do the things we do, we are driven to it by fate, by impulse, or by mere stupidity.

"You're not speaking," Benedetta said accusingly, "you're not answering me."

I stood and picked up the sword that I would carry to the fight and felt the sharp loss of the sword I wished I was carrying. I pushed the blade into its scabbard. "It's time to go."

"But you—" she began.

"I swore an oath," I interrupted her harshly, "and I lost a sword."

"And what of me?" she asked, almost crying. "What of Alaina?"

I stooped and looked into her beautiful face. "I will come for you," I said, "and for the children. When it's over we'll all go north."

I thought of Eadith in Bebbanburg and thrust that uncomfortable thought away. For a heartbeat I was tempted to touch Benedetta's cheek, to assure her I would come back, but instead I turned away.

Because it was time to fight.

Or it was time, rather, to ride the pilgrim road again, to cross the great road, and so to the River Ligan, and that meant passing the hilltop where Waormund had humiliated me. I could barely bring myself to look up the slope to the hedgerow, nor look at the dry ruts in the road that had lacerated me. I hurt. Finan rode to my right with his battered helmet hanging from his saddle pommel and a broad-brimmed rye straw hat shading his eyes from the rising sun. Wihtgar, with whom Finan seemed to have struck up a friendship, rode beyond Finan, and the two were arguing about horses, Wihtgar maintaining that a gelding could outrun a stallion any day, to which Finan, of course, retorted that the horses of Ireland were so swift, so brave, that no horse in the world could outrun them, though he allowed that Sleipnir might. Wihtgar had never heard of Sleipnir, so Finan had to explain that Sleipnir was Thor's horse and ran on eight legs, to which Wihtgar retorted that Sleipnir's dam must have been a spider, which made them both laugh.

In truth I knew Finan was talking to distract me. He had deliberately said Sleipnir was Thor's horse when he knew full well he was Odin's stallion, and he was thus inviting me to correct him. I kept silent.

Merewalh had ridden first, but he and his two hundred men had turned south on the great road and were long out of sight when we crossed and kept riding eastward. We numbered one hundred and eighty men, of whom sixty were Brihtwulf's troops, led by Brihtwulf himself, and by Wihtgar, who was his most experienced warrior. A dozen servants, brought to take the horses back to Werlameceaster, accompanied us with packhorses on which we had loaded barrels of ale and boxes of oatcakes. My few men, all on captured West Saxon horses, rode behind me, but the rest of the troops were Mercians who had wanted to come with us, inspired or convinced by Father Oda's sermon. The priest was also with us, though I had not wanted his company. "You're a priest," I had told him, "and we need warriors."

"You need the living Christ at your side," he had responded fiercely, "and you need more."

"More gods?" I had needled him.

"You need an East Anglian," he had ignored my taunt. "You're pretending to be Æthelhelm's men and you know nothing of his eastern estates, nothing of his tenants. I do."

He had been right, and so he rode with us though he refused both a mail coat and a weapon. I carried a long plain sword with an ash handle. The blade, which Merewalh had given me, had no name. "But it's a fine sword, lord," he had assured me, and so it was, but it was no Serpent-Breath.

Once at the Ligan we turned south. Wihtgar had sent scouts ahead who came back to say there were no red-cloaked troops at the village where the ford crossed the Ligan. "No ship either," one of the scouts reported. I had supposed that the ship in which Waormund had been pursuing us would be grounded at the ford, and so it probably had been, but she was evidently gone. "Did you cross the ford?" I asked.

"No, lord. We did what we were told to do. Look for the enemy in the village. We were told they left two days ago."

That, if true, was a relief. I did not mind if Merewalh's two hundred men were discovered by Æthelhelm's forces, indeed we wanted them to be discovered. We wanted the troops garrisoning Lundene to be watching northward, watching Merewalh, while my smaller force went southward. But to go southward we needed ships and we needed to stay unseen.

We splashed across the ford to the Ligan's East Anglian bank, then turned south again, riding to the big timber yard where, on our voyage upriver in *Brimwisa*, I had seen four barges being loaded with split timbers.

Three of the barges were still there. They were flat-bottomed, made for river work, with a wide beam, a blunt prow, and a steering-oar with a blade the size of a small barn door. All three possessed masts, but the masts were stepped, lying lengthwise in the wide flat bellies of the craft along with their shrouds, a sail yard each, and three neatly furled sails. There were no benches for oarsmen, instead the rowers stood and used the dozen tholes on each side for their long, heavy oars. They were horrible, clumsy looking boats, but they would get us to Lundene. I dismounted, flinching because of the pain in my ribs, and walked toward the barges.

"You can't take them!" An irate elderly man stormed out of a house built next to a vast open shed where timbers were seasoning. He spoke Danish. "You can't take them!" he repeated.

"Are you going to stop us?" It was Wihtgar who snarled that response, and in Danish too, which surprised me.

The man took one look into Wihtgar's scarred face and all defiance fled. "How do I get them back?" he pleaded.

I ignored the question. "Lord Æthelhelm needs them," I said, "and doubtless he'll return them."

"Lord Æthelhelm?" The elderly man was confused now.

"I'm his cousin, Æthelwulf," I said, using the name of Æthelhelm's younger brother who I hoped was still a prisoner in Bebbanburg, then had an impulse to touch my hammer to ward off the thoughts of plague in the north. I had no hammer, but I did have my pouch of money that Finan had returned, and so I gave the man hacksilver. "We're joining my cousin in Lundene," I told him, "so look for your ships there." I saw a thin silver chain under his jerkin, reached out to free it, and found he was wearing a silver hammer. He edged back, alarmed. Our shields were burned with crosses and he plainly feared Christian vengeance. "How much?" I asked.

"Much, lord?"

"For the hammer?"

"Two shillings, lord."

I gave him three, then hung the hammer around my neck and touched it with a forefinger. It was a consolation.

One of the barges was half loaded with stacks of split timber and we unloaded it, then waited for the tide to turn. I sat on a thick oak trunk, gazing across the river, which swirled slow and sluggish. Two swans drifted upstream on the flood tide. I was thinking of Eadith and of Benedetta when a voice interrupted my thoughts. "You said we were Lord Æthelhelm's men, lord?" Wihtgar was standing over me.

"I didn't want him complaining to Æthelhelm," I explained. Not that the elderly man was likely to send a messenger to Lundene, but nor did I want news spreading through the neighborhood of a Mercian force taking boats. "Besides," I went on, "we are Æthelhelm's men now, or we are until we start killing them." We had plenty of captured red cloaks, and we had the charred crosses on our shields. I looked up at Wihtgar. "So you speak Danish?" That was unusual for a Saxon.

He gave me a lopsided grin. "Married to one, lord." He touched the wrinkled scar where his left ear had been. "Her husband did this. He got my ear, I got his woman. A fair exchange."

"Indeed," I said. "Did he live?"

"Not long, lord." He patted the hilt of his sword. "Flæscmangere saw to that."

I half smiled. Flæscmangere was a good name for a sword, and the butcher's blade, I thought, would soon be busy in Lundene.

It was midday before the ebb started, but even before the tide turned, when it was slack water, we untied the ships, poled them off the wharf, and started downriver. It was another bright summer's day, too hot to wear mail. The sun dazzled from the river's ripples, a lazy west wind stirred the willow leaves, and slowly, slowly, we lumbered downstream. We used the oars, but clumsily, because the Mercians were not used to rowing. I had put Gerbruht on the second barge and Beornoth on the third because they were both Frisian seamen and both knew boats. Their barges lumbered behind ours, the oars splashing and clashing, and mostly it was the river's current and the fall of the quickening tide that took us southward.

We reached the Temes in the late afternoon and it was there that I discovered the purpose of the four great posts buried in the river bed where the Ligan's channels joined the greater river. A hay barge was moored to one of the posts. The crew, just three men, were waiting for the tide to turn and, rather than run aground, they were floating, tethered to the post, which meant they did not have to wait for the flood tide to lift them from the mud, but could take advantage of the first strong tidal surge to carry them toward Lundene. We moored with them, then waited again.

The sun blazed. There was hardly a breath of wind now. No clouds. Yet to the west there was a great dark smear in the sky, ominous as any thunderhead. That was the smoke of Lundene. It was a city, I thought, of darkness. I wondered if the smoke lingered above Bebbanburg, or whether a sea breeze was blowing it inland, and then I touched my new hammer to avert the curse of plague. I closed my eyes and gripped the hammer so tightly that it hurt my fingers. I prayed to Thor. I prayed that my lacerations would heal, that my ribs would stop hurting with every breath, and that my torn shoulder would let me wield a sword. I prayed for

Bebbanburg, for Northumbria, for my son, for all the folk at home. I thought of Berg, with his strange cargo of a fugitive queen and her children. I prayed there was no plague.

"You're praying," Finan accused me.

"That the sky stays cloudless," I said, opening my eyes.

"You're worrying about rain?"

"I want moonlight," I said. "We'll be going upriver after sundown."

It was still full daylight when the tethered boats swung ponderously to the new tide. We unmoored from the massive posts and used the big oars to take us into the Temes, then let the tide carry us. The sinking sun was hazed by the great smear of smoke as slowly the western sky turned into a furnace.

There was little river traffic, just two more hay barges and some fishing craft. Our long sweeps creaked in their tholes, giving us just enough speed for the steering-oar to bite. The sky slowly darkened, pricked with the first stars, and a half-moon was bright over-head as the sun died in scarlet glory. By now, I thought, Merewalh's men had swept the enemy out of Toteham and had harried them south. The fires would soon be lit on the heaths, telling Æthelhelm that an enemy had come. Let him stare north, I prayed, let him stare north as we crept westward through the night.

Toward the city of darkness.

We reached the city without going aground, the flooding tide carrying us safely in the deepest channels. We were not alone. Two ships passed us, close together, their oar-blades flashing in the moonlight, and both ships were crammed with men. The leading ship hailed us as she passed, wanting to know where we were from, and Father Oda called back that we were Ealhstan's men from Herutceaster. "Where's Herutceaster?" I muttered to him.

"I made it up," he said loftily. "They won't know."

"Let's hope we're not too late!" a man from the second ship shouted. "All those Mercian girls just waiting for us!" He jerked his hips and his tired oarsmen managed a cheer, then the two ships were past us and became mere shadows on the moon-glossed river.

We could smell the city from miles away. I gazed north, hoping to see the glow of fires from Merewalh's men, but saw nothing. Nor, truly, did I expect to. The heaths were far off, but Lundene was coming ever closer. The flood was nearing its end and we quickened the big oars as we rowed past the city's eastern bastion. A torch burned there and I saw a dull red cloak and the red reflection of flame from a spear-point. The wharves, as ever, were dense with shipping, while a long ship with a high prow on which a cross was mounted was moored to the stone wall where Gisela and I had lived. It was Waormund's ship, I was certain, but no one watched from the stone terrace. A light flickered behind a shutter of the house, then we were past and I could hear men singing in the Dead Dane tavern. Once past the tavern I searched the wharves for a place to berth. There was no empty space, so we moored the three barges outboard of other ships, men jumping from our decks to lash our clumsy craft to the landward hulls. A man crawled from beneath the steering platform of the ship I had chosen. "Who are you?" he asked irritably.

"Troops from Herutceaster," I said.

"Where's Herutceaster?"

"North of Earsling," I said.

"Funny man," he growled, saw that Vidarr was doing no damage to his ship, but merely tying off our lines, and so went back to his bed.

There were sentries on the wharves, but none near us, nor did those who had seen us arrive take much notice. One sauntered down the long landward wharf where torches burned feebly in brackets mounted on the river wall. He stared across the intervening ships and saw that our barges were filled with troops, some wearing the distinctive red cloak, and so wandered back to his post. It was evident no one saw anything remarkable in our arrival, we were just the latest of Æthelhelm's levies to come from his estates in East Anglia. "I wonder how many troops are here?" Father Oda said to me.

"Too many."

"Full of comfort, aren't you?" he said, making the sign of the cross. "We need to know what's happening."

"What's happening," I said, "is that Æthelhelm is gathering the biggest army he can possibly muster. Two, three thousand men? Maybe more."

"He'll find it hard to feed that many," Oda said.

That was true. Feeding an army was a much harder task than assembling one. "So perhaps he plans to march soon," I guessed, "then overwhelm Æthelstan by sheer numbers and so be done with it."

"It would be good to know if that's true," the priest said and, without another word, he climbed up onto the next ship.

"Where are you going?" I called after him.

"To find news, of course." He crossed the two ships that lay between our barge and the wharf and I saw him walk toward the nearest group of sentries. He talked to them for a long time, then made the sign of the cross, presumably giving them a blessing, before walking back. I helped him down onto our deck.

"The sentries," he said, "are East Anglians. And they're not happy. Lord Varin is dead."

"You sound sorry too."

"I did not dislike Varin," Father Oda said carefully. He brushed his black robe, then sat on the barge's low rail. "He was not a bad man, but he was killed for allowing you to escape. He hardly deserved that fate."

"For allowing me to escape! He was put to death?"

"You sound surprised."

"I am!"

Oda shrugged. "Æthelhelm knows you swore an oath to kill him. He fears that oath."

"He fears a pagan's oath?"

"A pagan's oath," Oda said sharply, "has the devil's force, and a man is wise to fear Satan."

I looked across the river at the few flickering lights showing in the settlement on the southern bank. "If letting me escape deserves death," I said, "then surely Æthelhelm should kill Waormund too?"

Oda shook his head. "Waormund is beloved of Lord Æthelhelm and Varin was not. Waormund is a West Saxon and Varin was not." He paused and I listened to the water rippling past the hull. We were well down-

452 • BERNARD CORNWELL

stream of the bridge, but I could still hear the river pouring ceaselessly through the narrow arches. "The boy was allowed to kill him," Oda went on bleakly.

"Ælfweard?"

"It seems Lord Varin was tied to a post and the boy was given a sword. It took some time." He made the sign of the cross. "Men were made to watch, and were told it was the fit punishment for a lack of vigilance. And Lord Varin was not even given a Christian burial! His corpse was thrown to the dogs, and what the dogs left was burned. And to think that Ælfweard is a grandson of King Alfred!" He said the last words bitterly, then added, almost as an afterthought, "The sentries believe the army will march soon."

"Of course it will," I said. Æthelhelm had assembled a massive army and he needed to feed it, and the easiest way to do that was to march into Mercia and steal whatever food could be found. For the moment his troops would be surviving on the supplies they had discovered in Lundene's storehouses and on what food they had brought with them, but hunger would come soon enough. Doubtless Æthelhelm still hoped that Æthelstan would assault Lundene and that he could slaughter the Mercians beneath the city walls, but if Æthelstan did not oblige him then he would be forced to leave the city and seek to destroy the enemy in battle. And the West Saxons, I reflected bitterly, must be confident. They had the bigger army, much the bigger army, and that army would march soon.

"The signal," Father Oda went on, "will be the ringing of the city bells. When they sound, the troops must assemble at the old fort."

"Ready to march," I grunted.

"Ready to march," Oda confirmed. "But it is an unhappy army."

"Unhappy?"

"The East Anglians are treated as serfs by the West Saxons, and the Christians are unhappy too."

I snorted a humorless laugh. "Why?"

"Because the archbishop," Oda began, then stopped.

"Athelm?"

"They say he's a prisoner in the palace here. An honored one, perhaps." He paused, frowning. "But still they dared lay hands on Christ's servant!"

I had long suspected that Athelm, the Archbishop of Contwaraburg, was an opponent of Æthelhelm and his family, even though Athelm was himself a distant cousin to the ealdorman. Perhaps that kinship explained his hostility, a hostility born of knowing Æthelhelm and his nephew only too well. "They won't dare kill the archbishop," I said.

"Of course they will," Oda said brusquely. "They'll

say he's sick," and once again he made the sign of the cross, "then claim he died of a fever. Who is to know? But it won't happen yet. They need him to place the helmet on the boy's head." Ælfweard would not be properly king until that ceremony was performed, and Æthelhelm would surely insist that Archbishop Athelm lift the gem-encrusted helmet of Wessex. Any lesser bishop would be seen as a poor substitute, calling into question Ælfweard's legitimacy.

"Has the Witan met?" I asked. Ælfweard needed the Witan's approval before he could receive the royal helmet.

Oda shrugged. "Who can tell? Maybe? But my suspicion is that Æthelhelm is waiting until the Witan of all three kingdoms can meet. He wants to proclaim Ælfweard as the king of all the Saxons." He turned, frowning, as sudden loud voices sounded from the sentries, but it was only the arrival of two girls. Whores, I assumed, from one of the river taverns. "Æthelhelm has the support of the West Saxon lords, of course," Oda went on, "and the East Anglians are too frightened to oppose him, but to get the Mercian support he needs to crush Æthelstan. Once that's done he'll kill the Mercian lords who defied him and appoint new men to their estates. Then Æthelhelm's family will rule all Englaland."

"Not Northumbria," I growled.

"And how will you oppose his invasion? You can raise three thousand warriors?"

"Not even half that number," I admitted.

"And he'll probably come with more than three thousand," Oda said, "and what will you do then? You think your walls at Bebbanburg can defy that army?"

"It won't happen," I said.

"No?"

"Because tomorrow I kill Æthelhelm," I said.

"Not tonight?"

"Tomorrow," I said firmly. Oda lifted a quizzical eyebrow, but said nothing. "Tomorrow," I explained, "is when Heorstan's men would have told Æthelhelm to expect us. He expects me to try to force an entry through one of the northern gates, so they'll be watching from the northern ramparts."

"Meaning they'll be awake and alert," Oda pointed out.

"As they will be tonight, too," I said. Night is when evil stirs, when spirits and shadow-walkers haunt the world, and when a man's fear of death is felt most keenly. Æthelhelm and Ælfweard would be deep in the palace, and their red-cloaked guards would be all around them. No stranger would be permitted through the palace archways except perhaps those who brought an urgent message, and even they would be disarmed beyond the gates. The corridors and great hall would be full of household warriors, both Æthelhelm's and the royal guards. We might just succeed in breaking through one gate, but would then find ourselves in a maze of passages and courtyards swarming with enemies. Come morning, when the dawn chased the evil spirits back to their lairs, the palace gates would open and Æthelhelm would surely want to watch from the northern wall. It was there, I thought, that I would have to find him.

"And how will you kill him tomorrow?" Oda asked.

"I don't know," I said, nor did I. In truth my only plan was to wait for an opportunity, and that was no plan at all. It was not a cold night, but still, thinking of what I had promised to do next day, I shivered.

The dawn came early, a summer dawn with another cloudless sky smeared only by the city's smoke. I had slept badly. We had unrolled the barge's sail and laid it on the deck, set sentries, and then I had worried through the short night. My ribs hurt, my shoulders ached, my skin was sore. I must have dozed, but I was still tired when the sunrise brought a freshening southwest wind, and I took that wind as a sign from the gods.

Back in Werlameceaster my plan had seemed possible. Not likely, perhaps, but possible. I had thought that if Æthelhelm's men were watching for me from Lundene's northern wall we could climb the hill from the river, and then what? I had imagined discovering Æthelhelm and his nephew somewhere close to the walls, and that a sudden assault would overcome his guards and give us the chance to slaughter both. Their deaths, I had hoped, would be enough to rouse the East Anglians who, once we had opened a gate to let Merewalh's men into the city, would help chase the West Saxons out of Lundene. Æthelhelm ruled by fear, so to remove that fear was to destroy his power, but now, as the sun climbed higher, I felt nothing but despair. Lundene was a city crammed with my enemies, and my feeble hopes depended on persuading some of those enemies to fight for us. It was madness. We were in a city garrisoned by thousands of the enemy, and we were one hundred and eighty men.

Brihtwulf and Wihtgar had walked into the city at dawn. I had not known they were going and would have stopped them for fear that one of Heorstan's six men might recognize them, but they returned safely to report that there had been frequent fights during the darkness. "West Saxons against East Anglians," Brihtwulf said.

"Just tavern fights," Wihtgar said dismissively.

"But men died," Brihtwulf added.

Both men sat on my barge's deck and began to stroke their sword-blades with sharpening stones. "Not surprising, is it?" Brihtwulf said. "The East Anglians hate the West Saxons! They were enemies not too long ago."

It had not been that many years since the West Saxons had invaded East Anglia and defeated the Danish jarls. Those jarls had been squabbling, unable to choose their own king after the death of Eohric who, twenty years before Edward's death, I had cut down in a ditch. I remembered Eohric as a fat, pig-eyed man who had squealed as we hacked him with our blades, and the squealing had only stopped when Serpent-Breath delivered the killing stroke.

And so had died the last true Danish King of East Anglia. Eohric had tried to preserve his kingdom by pretending to be a Christian, thus averting the power of Wessex, though I remember his hand desperately clutching the hilt of his broken sword in his death throes so that he would be taken to Valhalla. He had ruled a country of his own people, the Danish settlers, but they were outnumbered by Saxon Christians who should have welcomed King Edward's troops. And many did welcome the West Saxons, until tales of rape, theft, and murder soured the conquest. Now those East Anglians, both Danish and Saxon, were expected to fight for Wessex, for Æthelhelm and for Ælfweard.

"God-damned West Saxons," Wihtgar snarled, "strutting about as if they own the city."

"They do own it," Finan said drily.

Finan, Brihtwulf, and Wihtgar were talking together while I mostly listened. Brihtwulf described how he had been challenged as he returned to the wharf. "Some arrogant bastard said we were going the wrong way. He said we should go to the walls."

"And you told him what?" I asked.

"That we'd go where we damn well liked."

"And maybe we should go," I said.

Brihtwulf looked puzzled. "Already? I thought you told Merewalh to wait till past noon."

"I did."

Wihtgar glanced at the sky. "Long time till noon, lord."

I was sitting on the great oak block where the barge's mast would be stepped. "We have a westerly wind," I said, "and it's brisk."

Brihtwulf glanced at Wihtgar, who just shrugged as if to say he had no idea what I was talking about. "A westerly?" Brihtwulf asked.

"A westerly wind lets us leave the city," I explained. "We can steal three ships, fast ships, and we sail downriver."

There was a pause, then Brihtwulf spoke with evident disbelief. "Now? We leave now?"

"Now," I said.

"Jesus," Finan muttered. The other two just stared at me.

"Father Oda believes there may be three thousand men in Lundene," I went on, "so even if we succeed in opening a gate for Merewalh, we'll be outnumbered by what? Five men to our one? Six to one?" The numbers had haunted me through the short summer night.

"How many of those are East Anglians?" Brihtwulf asked.

"Most of them," Wihtgar muttered.

"But will they fight against their lords?" I asked. Brihtwulf had been right when he said that the East Anglians hated the West Saxons, but that did not mean they would lift a sword against Æthelhelm's troops. I had sailed to Cent hoping to raise a force of Centishmen to fight Æthelhelm, and that had failed, now I was pinning my hopes on East Anglians, a hope that seemed as frail as that which had faded in Fæfresham. "If I lead you into the city," I said, "and even if we succeed in opening a gate for Merewalh, we all die."

"And we just abandon Merewalh?" Brihtwulf asked indignantly.

"Merewalh and his horsemen will retreat north," I said, "and Æthelhelm won't pursue too far. He'll fear a trap. And besides, he wants to destroy Æthelstan's army, not a handful of horsemen from Werlameceaster."

"He wants to kill you," Finan said.

I ignored that. "If Merewalh sees horsemen coming from the city he'll retreat. He'll go back to Werlameceaster." I hated abandoning the plans that we had persuaded Merewalh to join, but all night I had brooded, and the dawn had brought me to my senses. It was better we should live, than die uselessly. "Merewalh will survive," I finished.

"So we just . . ." Brihtwulf began, then paused. I suspect he was about to say that we would just run away, but he curbed the words. "Then we just go back to Werlameceaster?"

"Serpent-Breath," Finan muttered to me.

I smiled at that. In truth I was wondering whether the west wind was truly a sign from the gods that I should abandon this reckless adventure and instead seize three good ships and fly in front of the wind to the sea and safety. I remember Ravn, the blind poet and father to Ragnar, often telling me that courage was like a horn of ale. "We begin with a full horn, boy," he had told me, "but we drain it. Some men drain it fast, maybe their horn was not full to begin with, and others drain it slowly, but courage lessens as we age." I was trying to persuade myself that it was not a lack of courage that made me want to leave, but rather prudence and an unwillingness to lead good men into a city filled with enemies, even if those good men wanted to fight.

Father Oda joined us to sit on the great oak block. "I said a prayer," he announced.

You need to, I thought, but stayed silent.

"A prayer, father?" Finan asked.

"For success," Oda said confidently. "King Æthelstan is destined to rule over all Englaland and we today make that possible! God is with us!"

I was about to give him a sour answer, about to confess that I doubted our success, but before I could say a word the first church bell sounded.

There was only a handful of bells in Lundene, perhaps five or six churches had raised or been given enough silver to buy them. King Alfred, when he had decided to rebuild the old Roman city, had wanted to hang bells at each gate, but the first two had been stolen within days, and so he decreed that horns be used instead. Most churches simply hung a metal rod or sheet that could be beaten to summon the faithful to worship, and now, together with the few bells, all of them began to sound, a cacophony that panicked birds into the sky.

None of us spoke as the clangor went on. Dogs howled.

"That must," Brihtwulf broke our silence, paused, then raised his voice so he could be heard, "that must be Merewalh."

"It's too early," Wihtgar said.

"Then Æthelhelm is assembling his army," I said, "ready to march. And we're too late."

"What do you mean?" Father Oda asked indignantly. "Too late?"

The bells were surely summoning Æthelhelm's army, which meant he would be leading that horde out of the city to attack Æthelstan's weaker forces. We were all standing now, gazing north, though there was nothing to be seen there.

"What do you mean?" Father Oda insisted. "Why are we too late?"

But before I could say a word in answer there was a bellow of anger from farther down the wharves. The shout was followed by more yelling, by the clash of blades, then by hurried footsteps. A man appeared, running for his life. A spear followed him, and the spear, with deadly aim, struck him in the back. He took a few stumbling steps, then collapsed. He lay for a heartbeat, the spear's shaft wavering above him, then tried to crawl. Two men in red cloaks appeared. One seized the spear's haft and drove it downward, the other kicked the wounded man in the ribs. The man jerked, then shuddered. The clangor of the bells was lessening.

"You will go to the walls!" a voice shouted. More men in red cloaks appeared on the landward wharf. They were evidently searching the ships, rousting out men who had slept on board, then herding them through the gaps in the river wall and so into the city. I assumed the dying man who still shuddered on the wooden planks had defied them.

"Do we kill them?" Finan asked. The red-cloaked men, I could see about thirty of them, had not yet reached our three barges. "They're here to stop men leaving," Finan guessed, and I guessed he was right.

I gave him no answer. I was thinking of what Briht-wulf had said, how the East Anglians hated the West Saxons. I was thinking of Serpent-Breath. I was thinking of the oath I had given to Æthelstan. I was thinking that Brihtwulf despised me for being a coward who wanted to run away. I was thinking that fate was a malevolent and capricious bitch, and I was thinking that we must slaughter the men in red cloaks and steal three good ships to make our escape from Lundene.

"You! Who are you?" A tall man in Æthelhelm's red cloak was staring at us from the wharf. "And why aren't you moving?"

"Who are we?" Brihtwulf muttered, looking at me.

It was Father Oda who answered. He stood, his pectoral cross bright above his black robes, and shouted back, "We are Lord Ealhstan's men from Herutceaster!"

The tall man did not question either name, both of which were Oda's inventions. "Then what in Christ's name are you doing?" he snarled. "You're supposed to be on the walls!"

"Why did you kill that man?" Oda demanded sternly.

The red-cloaked killer hesitated, plainly offended at being questioned, but Oda's natural authority and the fact that he was a priest made the man reply, if surlily. "Him and a dozen others. The bastards thought they'd run away. Didn't want to fight. Now for God's sake, move!"

The clamor of the bells, the death of the men on the wharf, and the anger of the man shouting at us seemed an enormous commotion in response to Merewalh and his two hundred men. "Move where?" Brihtwulf called back. "We only arrived last night. No one told us what to do."

"I'm telling you now! Go to the walls!"

"What's happening?" Father Oda shouted.

"Pretty Boy has come with his whole army. Seems he wants to die today, so move your East Anglian arses and do some killing! Go that way!" He pointed west. "Someone will tell you what to do when you get there, now go! Move!"

We moved. It seemed that the west wind was indeed an omen.

Because it had brought Æthelstan from the west. He had come to Lundene.

So we would fight.

Twelve

"Pretty boy?" Brihtwulf asked as he paced beside me.

"He means Æthelstan."

"Why pretty boy?"

I shrugged. "Just an insult."

"And he's come to attack Lundene?" Brihtwulf asked, astonished.

"So he said, who knows?" I had no answer, unless the garrison had mistaken Merewalh's two hundred men for Æthelstan's army, which seemed unlikely.

Two horsemen in red cloaks spurred past us, going west. "What's happening?" Brihtwulf shouted at them, but they ignored us. We had gone through one of the gaps in the river wall and were walking west along the street beyond. We passed Gunnald's yard, the gates shut, and I had a sudden image of Benedetta in her cowled gown. If I lived through this day, I thought, I would go to Werlameceaster and find her, and that made me think of Eadith, and I pushed that uncomfortable thought away just as we reached the slight bend in the street where it led up to the northern end of the great bridge.

"It has to be Æthelstan," Finan said. He was staring south across the wide river.

Merewalh had sent a messenger to Æthelstan, seeking permission for this madness, but had the message encouraged Æthelstan to join it? I stared at the troops on the opposite bank of the Temes. There were not many in sight, perhaps forty or fifty showing between the houses of Suðgeweork, which was the settlement built at the bridge's southern end, but those men were plainly there to threaten the high wooden-walled fortress that protected the bridge itself. A dozen spearmen were hurrying south across the bridge, presumably to reinforce the fort's garrison.

The men among Suðgeweork's houses were too far away for me to make out any symbol on their shields, though I could see they were in mail and wore helmets. If they were Æthelstan's men then they must have crossed the river above Lundene and marched down-

stream to surround the Suðgeweork fort. Those men, or
at least the ones I could see, were not enough to capture
the fort's ramparts, and I could see no ladders, but their
very presence was sufficient to draw defenders away
from the walls of Lundene.

There were a score of men still manning the barricade at the bridge's northern end. They were commanded by a red-cloaked man on horseback who stood
in his stirrups to watch the southern bank, then turned
as we drew near. "Who are you?" he shouted. Father
Oda gave his usual reply, that we were Lord Ealhstan's
men from Herutceaster, and again the names provoked
no curiosity. "What are your orders?" the man asked
and, when none of us answered, he scowled. "So where
are you going?"

I nudged Brihtwulf. I was too well known to too
many men in Wessex and had no desire to draw attention to myself. "We don't have orders," Brihtwulf
answered, "we just got here."

The horseman put two fingers between his lips and
gave a piercing whistle to draw the attention of the men
crossing the bridge. "How many do you need?" he
shouted.

"Many as you've got!" a man yelled back.

"Lord who?" the horseman asked, spurring
toward us.

"You," I muttered to Brihtwulf, who stepped forward.

"I am Ealdorman Ealhstan."

"Then take your men across the bridge now, lord," the man ordered with scant courtesy, "and stop the bastards taking the fort."

Brihtwulf hesitated. Like me he had not imagined for a moment that we would go to the southern bank of the Temes. We had come to kill Æthelhelm and Ælfweard and those two would be here, on the northern bank, but suddenly I knew that fate had offered me a chance of pure gold. "Over the bridge," I muttered to Brihtwulf.

"For God's sake, hurry!" the horseman said.

"What's happening?" Finan called.

"What do you think, grandpa? The pretty boy is here! Now move!"

"I'll kill that earsling," Finan muttered.

I kept my head down. I was wearing the helmet I had kept on board *Spearhafoc*, the helmet that had belonged to my father. I had laced together the thick cheek-pieces of boiled leather to hide my face, yet I still feared that one of the West Saxons would recognize me. I had fought alongside them often enough, though on this hot day I was not dressed in my usual fine mail and crested helmet. Finan and I filed through the small gap in the barricade and the men who guarded it jeered us. "Keep walking, grandpa!"

"East Anglians!"

"Mud babies!"

"Hope you bastards have learned to fight," another added.

"Enough!" the horseman silenced his men.

We started across the bridge's uneven planks. The piers had been built by the Romans and I guessed they would stay solid for a thousand years, but the roadway was constantly being repaired. The last time I had been on the bridge it had had a great jagged gap where the Danes had ripped up the timber road. Alfred had repaired the damage, but still some planks were rotten and others moved alarmingly as we trod on them. There were gaps between the roadway's timbers through which I could see the seething river churning white as it was channeled between the stone piers, and I wondered, as I did so often, how the Romans had built so well. "What in God's name is Æthelstan doing?" Finan asked me.

"Capturing Lundene?" I suggested.

"How in God's name does he hope to do that?"

It was a good question. Æthelhelm had sufficient

men to defend Lundene's walls, yet Æthelstan had evidently appeared in front of the ramparts, and that could only mean that he meant to make an assault. The last I had heard was that Æthelstan was at Wicumun, which lay a long day's march west of Lundene. I stared upriver as we crossed the bridge, but could see no movement beyond the city's wall where the River Fleet poured the filth of tanneries, slaughteryards, and sewage into the Temes. The Saxon town, built beyond the valley of the Fleet, showed no sign of an army come to assault the city, but undoubtedly something had caused the city bells and horns to sound the alarm.

"He'll never get across those walls," Finan said.

"We did."

"We got through them," Finan insisted, "we never tried to cross the ditch and wall. Still, it was a rare fight!"

I instinctively touched my chest where Thor's hammer was hidden beneath the mail. It had been years since Finan and I, with a small band of men, had used deceit to capture the Roman bastion that guarded Ludd's Gate, one of Lundene's western gates, and we had defended that bastion against a furious Danish assault. We had held the bastion and we had returned the city to Saxon rule. Now we had to fight for the city again. "Æthelstan must know the East Anglians are unhappy," I said, "so maybe he's relying on that?"

"If the East Anglians change sides." Finan sounded dubious.

"If," I agreed.

"They won't fight unless they see we're losing," Brihtwulf put in.

"Then we mustn't lose," I said. We had gone around two hundred paces, perhaps a third of the way across the long bridge. Father Oda had filed through the barricade last, lingering to talk with the horseman who commanded its guard, and he now hurried to catch up with us. "It seems King Æthelstan is to the northwest of the city," he said.

"So he's threatening the fort?" I asked.

"They've seen his banners," the priest said, ignoring my question, "and it appears he is here in force."

"The fort is the last place I'd assault," I said sourly.

"Me too," Brihtwulf muttered. He was walking beside me.

"And surely," Oda went on, "we'll be of no use to the king if we're south of the river?"

"I thought you Danes were supposed to be good at warfare?" I said.

Oda bridled at that, but decided to take no offense.

"It is the fate of Englaland," he said as we neared the southern end of the bridge. "That's what we decide today, lord, the fate of Englaland."

"And that fate," I said, "will be decided here."

"How?"

So I told him as we walked. We were not hurrying, despite the horseman's last urgent request. As we neared the southern bank I could see more of the troops who still watched the fort from Suðgeweork's houses, but they were making no apparent effort to assault the strong wooden ramparts. At the bridge's end was a timber gateway with a fighting platform from which Æthelhelm's flag with its leaping stag flapped in the brisk wind. Beneath it the gates were open and a harassed-looking man was beckoning to us. "Hurry!" he called plaintively. "Up to the ramparts!"

"Up to the ramparts!" I echoed to my men.

"Thank God you're here," the harassed man said as we passed.

"Onto the ramparts!" Brihtwulf called.

I stepped aside, drawing Finan with me. I beckoned for my six men, Oswi, Gerbruht, Folcbald, Immar, Beornoth, and Vidarr to join me, then let the rest of the men pass us by. The fort was not large, but a quick look around the walls showed only about forty spearmen on the fighting platforms. A dozen guarded the wooden arch above the gate that led south, a gate that probably needed twice that number if it was to be adequately defended. No wonder the harassed man had been pleased to see us. "Who are you?" I asked him.

"Hyglac Haruldson," he answered, "and you?"

"Osbert," I said, using the name I had been given at birth before the death of my elder brother made my father give me his own name.

"East Anglian?" Hyglac asked. He was younger than me, but still looked old. He had sunken cheeks because of missing teeth, a short gray beard, gray hair showing beneath his helmet, and deep lines around his eyes and mouth. It was a warm morning, too warm to be wearing leather-lined mail, and his face was running with sweat.

"East Anglian," I said, "and you?"

"Hamptonscir," he said shortly.

"And you command the fort?"

"I do."

"How many men do you have?"

"Till you came? I had forty-two. We were supposed to have more, but they never came."

"We're here now," I said, looking at my troops who were climbing the ladders that led to the timber ramparts, "and if I were you I'd shut the bridge gates." Hyglac frowned at that. "I'm not saying it's likely," I went on, "but a small group of men could sneak around the fort and climb up to the bridge."

"I suppose they're better closed," Hyglac allowed. He did not sound convinced, but was so relieved that we had arrived to bolster his garrison that he would probably have agreed to fight stark naked if I had suggested it.

I told Gerbruht and Folcbald to push the great gates shut so that the men guarding the barricade at the bridge's northern end could see nothing of what happened inside the small fort. "Are all your men West Saxons?" I asked Hyglac.

"All of them."

"So you're one of Lord Æthelhelm's tenants?"

He seemed surprised to be asked. "I hold land from the abbot at Basengas," he said, "and he ordered me to bring my men." Which meant that the abbot at Basengas had received gold from Æthelhelm, who had always paid generously for the clergy's support. "Do you know what's happening?" Hyglac asked.

"Pretty boy is to the city's northeast," I said, "that's all I know."

"Some of them are here too," Hyglac said, "too many! But you're here, thank God, and they'll not capture us now."

I nodded south. "How many are out there?"

"Maybe seventy. Maybe more. They're in the alleys, they're hard to count."

"And they haven't attacked?"

"Not yet."

"Do you have horses?" I asked Hyglac.

"We left them in the city," he said. "There's a stable there," he nodded toward the smaller of the two thatched buildings that lay inside the fort. "If you need it," he added, perhaps thinking we had horsemen following us across the bridge.

"We came by boat," I said. Both buildings looked new and both were made of stout timbers. I assumed the larger was to house the garrison, which in peacetime would surely not number more than twenty men, just sufficient to stand guard over whoever collected the custom dues from the merchants entering or leaving the city. I nodded toward the larger building. "That looks sturdy enough."

"Sturdy?" Hyglac asked.

"To keep prisoners," I explained.

He grimaced. "Lord Æthelhelm won't like that. He says we're not to take prisoners. We're to kill them all. Every last man."

"All of them?"

"More land, you see? He says he'll share out Mercian land to us. And give us all of Northumbria too!"

"All of Northumbria!"

Hyglac shrugged. "Not sure I want to be part of that war. They're god-damned savages in Northumbria."

"They are," Finan said fervently.

"I still need a place to keep prisoners," I said.

"Lord Æthelhelm won't like that," Hyglac warned me again.

"You're right," I said, "he won't, because you're the prisoners."

"Me?" He was certain he had misheard or, at the least, misunderstood.

"You," I said mildly. "I'm giving you a choice, Hyglac." I spoke softly, reasonably. "You can die here, or you can give me your sword. You and your men will be stripped of your mail, your weapons and boots, then put into that building. It's that or death." I smiled. "Which is it to be?"

He stared at me, still trying to understand what I had said. He opened his mouth, revealing three crooked yellow teeth, said nothing and so closed it.

I held out my hand. "Your sword, Hyglac."

He still seemed dazed. "Who are you?"

"Uhtred of Bebbanburg," I said, "lord of the Northumbrian savages." For a moment I thought he was going to piss himself with terror. "Your sword," I said politely, and he just gave it to me.

It was that easy.

A warrior called Rumwald led the Mercians who had threatened Suðgeweork's fort. He was a short man with a round cheerful face, a straggling gray beard, and a brisk manner. He had led one hundred and thirty-five men into the fort. "You had us worried, lord," he confessed.

"Worried?"

"We were about to assault the fort, then your men showed up. I thought we'd never capture the place after that!"

Yet captured it was, and we now had a little more than three hundred men, ten of whom I would leave to guard Hyglac's garrison, who were safely imprisoned inside the larger of the two buildings. The West Saxons had been surly, resentful, and outnumbered, but they had little choice except to surrender, and once they had been disarmed and shut away we had opened the fort's southern gates and shouted at the Mercians to join us. Rumwald had been reluctant to let his men approach the fort, fearing a trap, and in the end Brihtwulf had walked without shield or sword to persuade his fellow Mercians that we were allies.

"What were you supposed to do after capturing the fort?" I asked Rumwald. I had learned that he and his men had crossed the Temes at Westmynster, then walked along the river's southern bank.

"Tear up the bridge, lord."

"Tear up the bridge?" I asked. "You mean destroy it?"

"Rip up the planks, make sure the bastards couldn't escape." He grinned.

"So," I said, "Æthelstan really means to assault the city?" I had half convinced myself that the Mercian army had come merely to scout the city, to unsettle Æthelhelm, and then withdraw.

"God love you, lord!" Rumwald said happily. "He plans to assault once you open a gate for him."

"Once I open . . ." I began, then ran out of words.

"He got a message, lord, from Merewalh," Rumwald explained. "It said you would open one of the northern gates, and that's why he's come! He reckons he can take the city if there's an open gate, and he doesn't want half Æthelhelm's army to escape, does he? Of course he didn't mean this gate!" Rumwald saw my confusion. "You did mean to open a gate, lord?"

"Yes," I said, remembering my wish, not two hours before, to flee Lundene. So Æthelstan now expected me to unlock the city for him? "Yes," I said again, "I do mean to open a gate. Do you have a banner?"

"A banner?" Rumwald asked, then nodded. "Of course, lord. We have King Æthelstan's banner. You want me to tear that rag down?" He nodded at Æthelhelm's banner of the leaping stag that still flew above the fort's northern arch.

"No!" I said. "I just want you to bring the flag with us. And keep it hidden till I tell you."

"So we're going into the city, lord?" Rumwald asked. He sounded excited.

"We're going into the city," I said. I did not want to, the night's dread was still lurking inside me, making me fear that this was the day when the vast boulder of Saint Cuthbert's cave would finally fall on me.

I left Rumwald and climbed the ladder that led to the fighting platform above the bridge's entrance, and from there I stared across the river. The city smoke was being blown eastward and there was little sign that anything happened beneath that perpetual pall of smoke. There was still a squad of soldiers guarding the barricade at the bridge's northern end, while another score of soldiers guarded the downstream wharves, presumably to stop men from deserting. I could see into Gunnald's slave-yard where the only ship was the wreck and where no men moved. More usefully I could see up the hill that climbed from the bridge and could even see men slumping on benches outside the Red Pig tavern. If, as Father Oda had said, this was the day that would decide the fate of Englaland, then it all looked peaceful, strangely so. Finan joined me. He was hot and had taken off his helmet and was wearing his ragged rye-straw hat again. "Three hundred of us now," he said.

"Yes," I answered. Finan leaned on the wooden parapet. I was searching the sky for an omen, any omen.

"Rumwald reckons Æthelstan has twelve hundred men," Finan remarked.

"Fourteen hundred if Merewalh has joined him."

"Should be enough," Finan said, "so long as the East Anglians don't fight too hard."

"Maybe."

"Maybe," Finan repeated, and then, after a pause, "horsemen." He pointed and I saw two horsemen riding down the hill toward the far end of the bridge. They paused by the Red Pig and after a moment the men lounging on the benches stood, picked up their shields, crossed the street, and vanished into the western alleys. The horsemen came on down to the bridge, reining in at the barricade. "Those earslings at the barricade aren't doing any good," Finan said. I supposed they were there to stop men crossing the river to escape the battle, but if any man did try to flee they would only reach Suðgeweork's fort, which they must assume was still under Æthelhelm's control. The small force at the barricade was pointless, and it seemed the horsemen had come to order them away. "Pity," Finan said.

"Pity?"

"I wanted to slaughter that bastard for calling me grandpa. Now he's gone." The men had indeed been ordered away from the barricade. The horsemen accompanied them westward and we watched till they disappeared up a side street. "Nothing to stop us now," Finan said, and I knew he sensed my reluctance. My ribs hurt, my shoulders hurt. I gazed at the smoke-smeared sky, but saw no omen, good or bad. "If we meet Waormund," Finan said quietly, "I'll fight him." And I knew from those words that he did not just sense my reluctance, he sensed my fear.

"We must go," I said harshly.

Most of Rumwald's troops carried shields that bore Æthelstan's badge of the dragon with its lightning bolt. It was horribly dangerous to show that shield inside the city, but I could not ask men to fight without shields. It was a risk we must take, though I also took care to make sure some men wore the red cloaks we had captured, and for others to carry the shields we had taken from Hyglac's garrison, which showed a fish and a cross, evidently the badge of the Abbot of Basengas. I was fearful that when men in the city saw us crossing the bridge they would realize we were the enemy and would send a force to oppose us, but perhaps the red cloaks and the sight of Æthelhelm's banner still flying above Suðgeweork's fort would deceive them. I had known when I first decided to cross to the southern bank that returning over the river would be a dangerous moment, but I had wanted the men besieging the fort to join us. The easy capture of the fort had swollen our numbers, but we were still a pitifully small force. We needed to reach a gate, and if Æthelhelm's men suspected that the three hundred soldiers crossing the bridge were a threat then we would end up being slaughtered in Lundene's streets. I told the men to straggle, to take their time. Attackers would have hurried, but we walked slowly, and all the while I watched the street beyond the abandoned barricade and watched the men on the wharves. They saw us, but none showed alarm. Rumwald's men had vanished from between the houses across the river, so did those red-cloaked troops think the Mercians had withdrawn? And that we were coming to reinforce Æthelhelm?

And so three hundred men, at least a third of whom displayed Æthelstan's badge, filed through the barricade, which I had ordered left intact in case we needed to retreat. The sun was high and hot, and the city still and silent. Æthelhelm's men, I knew, would be on the northern walls, watching Æthelstan's army, while the citizens of London, if they had any sense, would be behind barred doors.

It was time to leave the bridge and to climb up into the city. "Keep your men closed up now!" I told Briht-wulf and Rumwald.

"Should we tear up the bridge roadway, lord?" Rumwald asked eagerly.

"And trap ourselves on this side of it? Leave it alone." I started climbing the hill, Rumwald keeping pace with me. "Besides," I went on, "if any of Æthel-helm's men try to escape across the bridge they'll have to fight through that closed gate."

"We only left ten men there, lord." Rumwald, for the first time, sounded anxious.

"Six men could hold that gate forever," I said dismissively. And how likely was it that we would have a victory that forced Æthelhelm's great force to flee in panic? I said nothing of that.

"You think six men are enough, lord?" Rumwald asked.

"I know so."

"Then he'll be king!" Rumwald had regained his

optimism. "By sundown, lord, Æthelstan will be King of Englaland!"

"Not of Northumbria," I growled.

"No, not Northumbria," Rumwald agreed, then looked up at me. "I've always wanted to fight alongside you, lord! It'll be something to tell my grandchildren! That I fought with the great Lord Uhtred!"

The great Lord Uhtred! I felt a vast weight on my heart when I heard those words. Reputation! We seek it, we prize it, and then it turns on us like a cornered wolf. What did Rumwald expect? A miracle? We were three hundred in a city of three thousand, and the great Lord Uhtred had a battered body and a fearful heart. Yes, we might open a gate, and we might even hold it long enough to let Æthelstan's men into the city, but what then? We would still be outnumbered. "It's an honor to fight beside you," I told Rumwald, merely saying what he would like to hear, "and we need a horse."

"A horse?"

"If we capture a gate," I said, "we have to send word to King Æthelstan."

"Of course!"

And at that moment a horseman appeared. He came from the top of the hill, his gray stallion stepping carefully on the old paving slabs. He turned toward us and I held up a hand to check our progress close beside the empty benches outside the Red Pig. "Who are you?" the horseman called as he approached.

"Lord Ealhstan!" Brihtwulf came to stand on my right. Finan, who had been walking behind me, stood on my left.

The horseman could see red cloaks, he could see the fish symbol on Rumwald's borrowed shield, but he could not see Æthelstan's dragon shields because we had placed those men at the back.

"East Anglians?" The horseman curbed the stallion just in front of us. He was young, his mail was finely made, his horse's trappings were polished leather studded with silver, and his sword was in a silver-coated scabbard. A thin gold chain circled his neck. His horse, a fine stallion, was nervous and stepped sideways, and the rider patted it with a gloved hand on which two rings glittered.

"We're East Anglians and West Saxons," Brihtwulf said arrogantly, "and you are?"

"Edor Hæddeson, lord," the horseman said, then glanced at me, and for a heartbeat there was a startled look on his face, but it vanished as he looked back to Brihtwulf. "I serve in Lord Æthelhelm's household," he explained. "Where's Hyglac?" He had evidently recognized the fish shields.

"He stayed at the fort," Brihtwulf said. "The pretty

488 · BERNARD CORNWELL

boy's troops gave up and walked back westward, but Hyglac kept enough men there in case they come back."

"They went westward?" Edor asked. "Then that's where we need you, all of you!" He patted his skittish horse's neck again and looked back to me. If he served in Æthelhelm's household then it was likely he had seen me at one of the meetings between King Edward and my son-in-law, Sigtryggr, but I had always been in my war-glory, my arms thick with the rings of silver and gold. Now I wore ragged mail, carried a shield scarred with the cross, and my face, still lacerated from Waormund's treatment, was half hidden by the leather cheek-pieces of my rust-touched helmet. "Who are you?" he demanded.

"Osbert Osbertson," I said, then nodded at Brihtwulf. "I'm his grandfather."

"Where do you need us?" Brihtwulf asked hurriedly.

"You're to go west." Edor pointed to a side street. "Follow that street. You'll find men at the far end, join them."

"Æthelstan's going to attack there?" Brihtwulf asked.

"Pretty boy? Christ no! We're going to attack him from there."

So Æthelhelm planned to attack Æthelstan's army,

maybe not in hope of crushing the enemy, but at least to drive him away from Lundene and inflict casualties in the process. I felt in my pouch, took a step closer to Edor's horse and bent down, grunting from the pain in my ribs. I touched the stone of the road, then straightened, holding a silver shilling. "Did you drop this?" I asked Edor, holding the bright coin toward him.

For a heartbeat he was tempted to lie, then greed conquered honesty. "I must have," he lied, then reached down for the coin. I dropped the silver, seized his left wrist, and pulled hard, sending an agonizing lance of pain through my shoulder. Finan's sword, Soul-Stealer, was already sliding from its scabbard. The horse, alarmed, stepped away, but that only helped me pull Edor out of the saddle. He shouted in rage or alarm. He was falling, but his left foot was trapped in the stirrup and he was being pulled away. My shoulder, torn from being dragged behind Waormund's horse, felt as if a red-hot poker was being thrust into the joint. Then Wihtgar seized the stallion's reins, Soul-Stealer sliced down with the sun reflecting bright from her blade, and suddenly there was blood on the road. Edor was on the ground, coughing blood, moaning, and then Soul-Stealer struck again, point first, to pierce mail, leather, and ribs. Edor gave a high pitched gasp, his left hand seemed to reach toward me, made a clutching motion, then fell. He lay still, his eyes gazing sightless at the cloudless sky. Finan crouched, snapped the gold chain and tugged it free, unbuckled the rich sword belt with its weapon, then worked the rings off Edor's gloved fingers.

"Jesus," Rumwald breathed.

"The horse is yours," I told Brihtwulf, "you're Lord Ealhstan, so mount up. Gerbruht!"

"Lord?"

"Drag that thing into an alley." I nudged Edor's corpse with my foot.

"No one saw a thing!" Rumwald said in amazement.

"Of course they did," I said, "they just don't want us to know they saw us." I looked along the windows of the street and could see no one, but I was certain folk were watching us. "Just pray they don't send word to Æthelhelm." I turned. "Oswi!"

"Lord?"

"Take us to the nearest gate to the north, and I want to avoid the palace."

"The Crepelgate, lord," Oswi said, then led us confidently, taking us through a maze of small streets and alleys. The Roman buildings gave way to newer houses, all made of timber with thatched roofs, then those houses ended and we were at the top of the city's low eastern hill, and in front of us was a wasteland of ruins, hazel saplings, and weeds. I could see the palace a long way to the west, close to it were the remnants of the amphitheater and, beyond that ruin, the fort at the city's northwestern corner.

And in front of us were the walls.

They are extraordinary, those walls. They ring the whole city, are built of dressed stone, and are three times the height of a tall man. Towers are built every two or three hundred paces, and the seven gates are flanked by great stone bastions. The walls have stood for three or four hundred years, perhaps longer, and for most of their length the ramparts still stand as the Romans built them. Some gaps have appeared across the years, and many of the towers have lost their roofs, but the gaps have been plugged with great timbers and the roofs replaced with thatch. There are stone stairs leading up to the ramparts and, where the wall has fallen into the ditch and been repaired in timber, there are wooden fighting platforms. Lundene's wall is a marvel, making me wonder, as so often, how the Romans had ever lost Britain.

And in front of us, too, were men. Hundreds of men. Most were on the ramparts, from where they gazed northward, but some, too many, were behind the gate. From where we stood we could only see one gate, the Crepelgate, with its two massive bastions looming over the roadway and Æthelhelm's banner flying from the nearest tower, while beneath it, amid tall weeds and the rubble of old walls, were troops. I could not see how many, they were sitting on crumbling walls or resting, but I could see enough to know they were too many. "They expect Æthelstan to attack here?" Brihtwulf asked.

"They probably have forces waiting inside each gate," I said. "How many can you see?" Brihtwulf, high in his saddle, could see more than us.

"Two hundred?"

"We outnumber them!" Rumwald said excitedly.

"And how many on the gate ramparts?" I asked, ignoring Rumwald.

"Thirty?" again Brihtwulf sounded uncertain.

"And how far away are Æthelstan's men?" I asked, though I did not ask it of Brihtwulf or of anyone else because the question was unanswerable until we had climbed the ramparts and could see the country to the north.

"So what do we do?" Brihtwulf asked.

I touched my mail where it covered the silver hammer. I looked westward, but knew that the next city gate was built into the walls of the fort, and that would mean first capturing an entrance to the fort. It was this nearest gate, I thought, or else abandon the whole madness. "What we do," I answered Brihtwulf, "is what we came to do. Wihtgar! Take forty men. You'll climb the stairs to the right of the gate." I looked up at Brihtwulf. "I need thirty of your men for the steps to the left. I'll lead them." He nodded, and I turned to Rumwald. "And I'll need your banner. You take every man that's left and follow Brihtwulf to the gate. You tell the bastards you've been ordered to make a sally north-ward. They probably won't believe you so you can start killing them, but open the damned gates first. And once the gate is open," I looked up at Brihtwulf again, "you will ride like the wind to find Æthelstan."

"And if the king doesn't come in time?" Father Oda asked.

"We die," I said brutally.

Oda made the sign of the cross. "The Lord of Hosts is with us," he said.

"He damned well better be," I said grimly. "So let's move."

We moved.

The city had seemed deserted as we came up from the river, but now we could see men all along the walls, others waiting just inside the gate, and small groups of men, women, and children watching from the edge of the wasteland. Many of those city folk were accom-

panied by priests, presumably hoping that the clergy-
men could protect them if the Mercians invaded the
city. They might be right, I thought. Æthelstan was
famously as pious as his grandfather Alfred, and would
doubtless have given his troops dire warnings against
offending his god.

We followed a track eastward until we reached a
fine new church, the lower walls of stone, the upper of
bright timber, which stood at the edge of the houses.
We turned north at the church to follow a road of beaten
earth that led to the gate. Two goats cropped weeds on
the verge where Roman stonework was half buried.
A woman watched us, made the sign of the cross, and
said nothing. The men resting inside the gate stood as
we came nearer. Many of their shields were unpainted,
just bare wood, while others were decorated with a
cross. None showed the leaping stag. "East Anglians?"
Finan muttered to me.

"Probably."

"They look like the fyrd to me," Finan said, meaning they were not household warriors, but plowmen
and carpenters, foresters and masons, dragged from
their fields or workshops to fight for their lord. Some
had spears or swords, but many carried only an axe or
a reaping hook.

Brihtwulf rode ahead, tall on his stolen horse, pointedly ignoring the first men who stood to question his coming. I trudged behind, sweat trickling down my face, sometimes glancing up at the men on the ramparts. They were watching us too, but not with any alarm because most of them would have no idea what was happening. They knew Æthelstan's forces were near, they had heard the commotion of the city bells, but ever since that first excitement they would have been told little and understood less. They were hot, they were thirsty, they were bored, and we were just more troops coming to wait in the hot sun for something to happen.

"This way!" I called to the men who would follow me. "Up the steps!" I slanted off the road and headed for the stairs leading up to the rampart on the left of the gate. Immar was behind me, carrying Æthelstan's banner that was tightly furled on its pole. "You can't fight holding that thing," I told him, "so stay out of trouble." Hulbert, one of Brihtwulf's men, would turn left at the rampart's top and, with ten men, defend our backs as we captured the gate itself.

Brihtwulf had reached the great archway where he was challenged by an older man who leaned over the arch's rampart. "Who are you? What do you want?"

"I'm Ealdorman Ealhstan." Brihtwulf curbed his horse and stared up at the man. "And I want the gates opened."

"For God's sake why?"

"Because Lord Æthelhelm wants it," Brihtwulf called. He was keeping both hands on his saddle's pommel. His shield, fire-scarred with the cross, hung at his back. His sword hung low to his left.

"I was told not to open the gates to the Lord God Almighty Himself!" the man answered.

"He can't come," Brihtwulf said, "so Lord Æthelhelm sent me instead."

"Why?" The older man had seen me and my men start up the stairs. "Stop!" he shouted at me, holding out a warning hand. I stopped halfway up the time-worn stairs, the shield heavy on my back. The troops on the gate's rampart were not from any fyrd, they were in good mail and carried spears and swords.

"The pretty boy," Brihtwulf shouted, "is over there." He pointed vaguely northwest. "We're sending men out of the western gates to give him a spanking, but we need to keep him in place. If he sees another force coming from this gate he won't know which one to defend against. Of course you can always go and ask Lord Æthelhelm himself."

The man had been looking down at Brihtwulf, but

now glanced at us to see that I had only paused for a heartbeat and then kept climbing and had now reached the ramparts. He frowned, but I gave him a friendly nod. His shield, showing Æthelhelm's leaping stag, was propped against the inner parapet. The men below, I thought, might be from the East Anglian fyrd, but the shield betrayed that the spearmen on the ramparts were West Saxons and probably fiercely loyal to Æthelhelm. "Hot day!" I said to the older man, my voice muffled by the laced cheek-pieces, then walked to the outer parapet. I leaned on the sun-warmed stone and for a moment everything to the north appeared as I remembered it. Beneath the walls was a scum-covered ditch crossed by a stone bridge. A small crowd had gathered beyond the bridge. There were merchants come from the north with packhorses, folk from the villages with eggs or vegetables to sell, all of them barred from entering the city, but unwilling to leave. Small hovels lined the road, and a graveyard had spread into parched pastureland, beyond which were woods thick with summer leaves. A village lay a mile or so to the north where smoke rose into the west wind. Then more woods before the land climbed to a bare hilltop. Other villages, betrayed by smoke, lay hidden in the woods to the west. A small child drove a flock of geese across the pasture and I fancied I could hear her singing, but perhaps that was my imagination. A man, seeing me appear on the wall, shouted that he wanted to bring his packhorses into the city, but I ignored him, gazing instead into the heat-hazed distance. And then I saw them. I saw horsemen shadowed by trees, scores of horsemen.

"Merewalh?" Finan suggested.

"Æthelstan, I hope," I said fervently, but whoever the far horsemen were, they were just watching.

"So will you please open the damned gate?" Briht-wulf demanded loudly and angrily from beneath us.

"Twenty-eight men up here," Finan said, still talking low. He meant twenty-eight men on the gate's parapet, most of them crowded onto the half-circles of the twin bastions that jutted out to the ditch's edge. I nodded.

Wihtgar and his men had reached the parapet at the far side of the gate. The older man looked at them, frowned, turned back to me, then saw that Immar was carrying the furled banner. "Is that a banner, boy!" he demanded.

"Will you open the gate?" Brihtwulf called.

"Show me the banner, boy!"

I turned and held out a hand to Immar. "Give it to me," I said. I took the staff and unrolled a foot or so of the flag, then tossed it at the older man's feet. "Look for yourself," I said, "it's the dragon of Wessex." And so it would be, I thought, if the gods were with me today. The man leaned down to the staff and I took a step toward him.

Finan put a hand on my arm. "You're still slow, lord," he said in a very low voice, "let me."

He kept his hand on my arm, watching as the older man took hold of the flag's edge to unroll it. All of his men were watching as he pulled to reveal the dragon's clawed forelegs. He pulled again, about to reveal the lightning bolt in the dragon's grip. Then Finan moved.

And it began.

Finan was the fastest man I have ever seen in a fight. He was thin, lithe, and moved like a wildcat. I have spent hours practicing sword-skill with him and I reckon he would have killed me nine times out of ten, and the older man never stood a chance. He was looking up in surprise as Finan reached him, Soul-Stealer was already out of her scabbard, but Finan just kicked him under the chin, jerking his head back, then the blade swung in a savage back cut that threw the man sideways, throat severed and blood spurting high over the inner parapet, and Finan was already threatening the men watching from the bastion. They were not ready, any more than the older man whose life pulsed away onto Æthelstan's banner had been ready. They were still lowering their spears as Finan attacked, and my borrowed sword was only halfway out of her scabbard as he thrust Soul-Stealer into a man's belly and ripped her sideways.

"Open the gate!" I shouted. "Open it!"

I shrugged the shield off my shoulder. Wihtgar was attacking from the far side of the gate. The fighting had started so fast, so unexpectedly, and our enemy was still confused. Their leader was dead, they were suddenly assailed by swords and by Folcbald wielding a massive axe. Hulbert and his Mercians were attacking westward, driving the defenders on the ramparts away from the gate, while I joined Finan in clearing the bastions and the fighting platform above the arch. We were desperate. We had managed to cross an enemy-held city, we had reached this gate without being discovered, and now we were surrounded by enemies, and our only hope of living was to kill.

There is pity in war. A dying boy, gutted like a beast and calling for his mother is pitiable, regardless that a moment before he had been screaming curses and trying to kill me. My borrowed sword was no Serpent-Breath, but she went through the boy's mail and leather easily enough, and I cut off his yelps for his mother with a downward thrust through his left eye. Beside me Finan, screaming in his Irish tongue, had put two men down and his blade was red to the hilt. Gerbruht, bellowing in his native Frisian, was swinging an axe against men who had not been given time to retrieve their shields. We were thrusting the West Saxons back into the half circle of the bastion, and they were screaming for mercy. Some had not even had time to draw their swords and they were so packed together that their spearmen could not lower their weapons. "Drop your blades," I bellowed, "and jump into the ditch!"

All that mattered was to clear the gate's parapet. Wihtgar, with his Mercians, was savaging the enemy on the eastern side of the archway, and his sword, Flæscmangere, was as red as Finan's Soul-Stealer. I ran back to the steps and saw that Rumwald's men were thrusting the confused East Anglians away from the gate's arch, but Brihtwulf, his stallion white-eyed and frightened, was still inside the closed gates. One locking bar had been freed from the iron brackets, but the second was high and heavy. "Hurry!" I bellowed, and four men used spears to push the bar upward. It fell with a crash, making Brihtwulf's horse rear, then the huge gates were pushed outward on squealing hinges. "Go!" I called. "Go!" And Brihtwulf kicked his heels and the stallion bolted across the bridge. The folk waiting outside scattered.

Rumwald had made a shield wall across the road. Behind it were bodies, some moving, most motionless in puddles of their blood. Father Oda was shouting at the East Anglians, telling them their war was over, that God Almighty had sent King Æthelstan to bring peace and plenty. I let him harangue them and went back to the parapet where terrified West Saxons, relieved of their weapons, were being forced to jump off the high bastion into the filth of the flooded ditch. "The shit will kill them if they don't drown," Finan said.

"We have to barricade the parapet," I said, "both ways."

"We will," Finan said.

We had taken the twin bastions and the arch's fighting platform between them, and Rumwald's men, beating swords against shields, were driving back a larger number of East Anglians who seemed reluctant to fight and equally reluctant to surrender. I knew we would be attacked down there soon, but the immediate danger came from the men manning the walls on either side of the gate. For the moment, dazed and confused by our sudden assault, they were holding back, but other men were running along the walls, coming to retake the gate.

They were coming because Immar had pulled down the leaping stag and hoisted the blood-drenched banner of King Æthelstan. The dragon and the lightning bolt now flew above the Crepelgate, and revenge for that was coming.

The Crepelgate. Under the pitiless midday sun we had to hold the gate, and I remembered that Alfred, distressed by the number of maimed and blinded folk in Lundene, many of them men he had led into battle, had issued a decree allowing cripples to beg from travelers at this gate. Was that an omen? We had to defend the gate now and the fight would surely make more cripples. I touched the silver hammer, then cleaned the blood from my borrowed sword and slid her back into her scabbard.

And knew she must be drawn again soon.

Thirteen

The enemy's first response was ragged, brave, and ineffectual. The troops manning the long stretches of the wall on either side of the captured Crepelgate attacked along the ramparts, but a shield wall of just four men could easily defend the width of the fighting platform. A dozen men, arrayed in three ranks, would be an even more formidable obstacle, but the day's heat and the undoubted ferocity of the enemy's attacks would wear that small force down fast, so I had men bringing stones from the nearby ruins. We piled them on the fighting platform to make two crude barricades, and by the time the wall's defenders to our west had organized a disciplined assault, our makeshift wall was already knee high. Gerbruht and Folcbald led that defense, using the spears we had captured from the West

Saxons, and within a short time the knee-high wall was heightened by mail-clad corpses. Wihtgar, to the east, faced less opposition, and his men went on piling stones.

Brihtwulf had left the city and vanished among the far trees, but neither he nor any of Æthelstan's men had reappeared. Inside the gate the East Anglians had retreated fifty or more paces, and Father Oda was still shouting at them, but they had not dropped their shields nor lowered their banner, which showed a crudely embroidered boar's head.

Everything was now happening either very fast or painfully slowly. It was fast on the wall's top where we piled still more stones as vengeful West Saxons assaulted both crude barricades, but it was slow inside the city where Rumwald's shield wall stood ready to defend the open gate against an East Anglian force that showed no desire to attack. Yet I knew it was there, on the road between the rubble and weeds of the ruined city, that this fight would be decided.

The West Saxons on the eastern reach of the wall had been reluctant to attack at first, and had given Wihtgar's men the chance to make their stone barrier chest high. The enemy there hurled spears over the crude wall, but after the first attackers tried to clamber over the heap of stones and were met by spears thrusting from below, they were more cautious. Yet to the west the fighting was far more vicious. The pile of stones was broad there, but only knee high, and the enemy kept coming, urged on by a black-bearded man in polished mail and wearing a glittering helmet. He shouted his troops forward, though I noted he never joined them as they charged with shields held high and spears leveled. He was screaming at them to kill, to charge faster, and that was a mistake. Men hurried to cross the crude barrier and their haste made them trip on the stones and they came to our shield wall raggedly only to be met by swords, spears, and axes. Their fallen bodies made an ever-growing barrier on top of the first, a new barrier made worse by the men dying in agony who were trodden underfoot by other men trying to cross the blood-soaked obstacle.

"The wall will hold," Finan told me. We were standing halfway up the steps, he was watching the fight above as I stared west toward Lundene's higher hill.

"The men need ale or water," I said. The day was getting hotter. Sweat was stinging my eyes and trickling inside my mail.

"There'll be ale in the guard house," Finan said, meaning one of the chambers inside the twin bastions. "I'll have it sent up here."

A spear struck the stone between us. The West

Saxons on the western wall had seen us, and several had hurled spears, but this was the first to reach us. It skidded off the step and fell down to the road. "Bastards will give up soon," Finan said.

He was right. The men attacking us along the wall were tired of dying and had become aware that other men would do the fighting instead, and those men were appearing, heralded by blasts from horns that made us all gaze across the northern stretch of Lundene. Closest to us the land was a ruin of old walls, then it dropped to where the Weala brook flowed toward the Temes. Beyond it the land rose to Lundene's western hill on which stood the ruins of the amphitheater and, on the amphitheater's farther side, the walls of the old Roman fortress. And a stream of men was coming from that fort. Many were mounted, most were on foot, but all were in mail, and even as Finan and I watched, a group of horsemen came through the gate surrounded by standard-bearers, their flags bright in the noonday sun.

"Jesus," Finan said quietly.

"We came here to fight," I said.

"But how many men does he have?" Finan asked incredulously, because the procession of mailed warriors seemed unending.

I made no answer, instead I climbed back to the wall's top and stared across the pastureland to the far woods where no horsemen were in sight. For now, it seemed, we were alone, and if Æthelstan's men did not come from those distant woods we would die alone.

I sent half the men who had been defending the barricades down to stiffen Rumwald's shield wall, then took one last glance northward to see no sign of Æthelstan or his men. Come, I urged him silently, if you want a kingdom, come! Then I went down the steps to where a battle must be fought.

It would be a battle, I thought bitterly, to decide which royal arse would warm a throne, and what business did I have deciding the throne of Wessex? Yet fate, that callous bitch, had tied my life's threads to King Alfred's dream. Was there really a Christian heaven? If there was then King Alfred would be gazing down on us even now. And what would he want? Of that I had no doubt. He wanted a Christian country of all the men who spoke the Ænglisc tongue, and he wanted that country led by a Christian king. He would be praying for Æthelstan. So damn him, I thought, damn Alfred and his piety, damn his stern face, always so disapproving, damn his righteousness, and damn him for making me fight for his cause a lifetime after his death. Because today, I thought, if Æthelstan did not come, I would die for Alfred's dream.

I thought of Bebbanburg and its windswept ramparts, I thought of Eadith, of my son, and then of Benedetta, and I wanted to ignore that last regret and so I shouted at Rumwald's men to get ready. They were in three ranks and had made a small half-circle about the open gate. It was a perilously small shield wall and was about to be attacked by the might of Wessex. It was no longer time to think, to indulge in regrets or to wonder about the Christian heaven, but time to fight. "You're Mercians!" I shouted. "You've defeated the Danes, you've fought off the Welsh, and now you'll make a new song of Mercia! A new victory! Your king is coming!" I knew I lied, but men facing battle do not want truth. "Your king is coming!" I shouted again. "So stay firm! I am Uhtred! And I am proud to fight alongside you!" And the poor doomed bastards cheered as Finan and I pushed through the ranks to stand where the shield wall barred the road.

"You shouldn't be here," Finan muttered.

"I am here."

And I hurt still from the beating Waormund had given me. I hurt all over. I hurt and I was tired, while the weight of the shield made my left shoulder feel as if an auger was twisting into the joint. I lowered the shield to rest it on the roadway, then looked westward, but none of the troops coming from the fort had yet appeared out of the Weala's shallow valley. "If I die . . ." I began in a very low voice.

"Quiet," Finan snarled, then, much lower, "you shouldn't be here. Go to the rear rank."

I gave him no answer, nor did I move. In all my years I had never fought anywhere except the front rank. A man who leads others to death's doorway must lead, not follow. I felt stifled, and so I undid the knot that held the boiled-leather cheek-pieces and let them swing free so I could breathe more easily.

Father Oda paced in front of our wall, talking now to us and seemingly oblivious of the East Anglians behind him. "God is with us!" he called. "God is our strength and our shield! Today we shall strike down the forces of evil! Today we fight for God's country!"

I stopped paying attention because, not far to the west, the first banners were appearing above the lip of the Weala's valley. And I could hear drums beating. The heartbeat of war was coming nearer. A man a few paces away in our front rank bent over and vomited. "Something I ate," he said, but that was not true. Our shields were propped against legs that trembled, there was bile in our throats, our stomachs were sour, and our laughter at bad jests was forced.

The first men of Wessex appeared from the shallow

valley, a line of gray sparked with spear-points. The East Anglians who had faced us so irresolutely began to edge backward, as if making room for the approaching horde. We had been right, I thought ruefully. The East Anglians did not want to fight, neither for the West Saxons nor, it seemed, for us either.

The enemy who had come from the fort were getting closer. Their banners were bright; banners with crosses, with saints, with the dragon of Wessex, with Æthelhelm's leaping stag and, leading all of them, a banner I had never seen before. It was being waved from side to side so we could see it clearly and it showed a dull gray dragon of Wessex beneath a leaping stag embroidered in deep scarlet. A small cross showed in the upper corner.

"God is with us!" Oda shouted. "And your king is coming!"

I hoped he was right and dared not leave the shield wall to find out. The gate was open and we just had to keep it open until Æthelstan arrived.

Rumwald stood to my right. He was shaking slightly. "Keep together!" he called to his men. "Stand fast!" His voice was uncertain. "He is coming, lord?" he asked me. "Of course he's coming. He won't let us down." He talked on, saying nothing of importance, just talking to cover his fear. The drums became louder. Horsemen rode on the flanks of the approaching West Saxons and still more footmen came, their spears thick. I could see the leaping stags on the shields now. The front rank, that was ragged because men were stepping over the remnants of walls, numbered about twenty, but there were at least twenty ranks behind. It was a daunting mass of household warriors who advanced in front of a group of horsemen, and there were still more ranks behind those mounted men. They had begun shouting, though they were still too far away to hear their insults.

I picked up my shield, wincing at the stab of pain, then drew Wasp-Sting, and even that short blade felt heavy. I beat her against the shield. "Æthelstan is coming!" I shouted. "Æthelstan is coming!" I remembered the boy I had taught how to kill, a boy who, on my command, had killed his first man. He had executed a traitor in a ditch where bog-myrtles grew. Now that boy was a warrior king, and my life depended on him. "Æthelstan is coming!" I shouted again, and kept clashing Wasp-Sting's blade on the ironbound boards of willow. Rumwald's men took up the chant and began to beat their swords on shields. The second rank just shouted. They carried spears with shafts axe-hacked to half their length. A spear needs two hands, but a short spear can be wielded with one hand. They would close up behind us and thrust the spears between our shields. The fighting on the walls had stopped because the enemy there, frustrated by our makeshift barriers, was content to watch as the larger force overwhelmed us. Wihtgar had brought twenty men down from the ramparts and now waited with them under the gate's arch, ready to reinforce any part of our shield wall that looked to be fragile. I wished I had Wihtgar beside me instead of Rumwald, who still chattered needlessly, but Rumwald had provided most of the men for this fight and I could not deny him his place of honor beside me.

Honor was his word, not mine. "It's an honor to stand in a shield wall with you, lord," he had said more than once. "I shall tell my grandchildren!" And that had made me touch the silver hammer that I had pulled out from under my mail. I touched it because my grandchildren were in Eoferwic and we had heard no denials of the rumors of plague in the north. Let them live, I prayed, and I was not the only man praying in that shield wall, nor was I the only one praying to Thor. These men might all call themselves Christians, but many warriors had a lurking fear that the older gods were just as real, and when the enemy is coming near and the drums of war are beating and the shields are heavy then men pray to any god and every god.

"God is our shield!" Father Oda had come inside

our half-circle of men and was now standing on the steps leading to the ramparts. "We must prevail!" he shouted hoarsely, and he needed to shout because the West Saxons were very near now. A horseman was leading them across our front, driving the East Anglians still farther away.

I gazed at our enemy. Good troops, I thought. Their mail, their helmets, and their weapons looked well maintained. "Æthelhelm's household warriors?" I muttered to Finan.

"Looks like it," he said. It was too hot for men to wear Æthelhelm's red cloaks, and besides a cloak is an encumbrance in battle, but all the shields were painted with the leaping stag. They stopped forty paces away, too far for a spear's throw, turned toward us, and began beating swords against their shields. "Four hundred of them?" Finan suggested, but they were just the beginning because still more men came to beat their blades on shields, some painted with the stag and others with the badges of West Saxon noblemen. This was the army of Wessex, forged by Alfred to fight the Danes and now arrayed against their fellow Saxons, and all led by the men on horseback who, under their gaudy banners, rode to confront us.

Æthelhelm, wearing a red cloak despite the heat, sat on a magnificent bay stallion. His mail had been cleaned and polished, and on his chest was a cross of gold. His face was hidden by the gold-encrusted cheek-pieces of his helmet, which was crested with a golden stag. The hilt of his sword glittered with gold, his stallion's bridle and girth were decorated with small golden plates, and even his stirrups had golden decorations. His eyes were shadowed by his lavish helmet, but I did not doubt he was looking at us with contempt. On Æthelhelm's right, mounted on a tall gray stallion and draped in a white cloak edged with red, was his nephew Ælfweard, who alone among the horsemen wore no helmet. He had a vacant, slack-mouthed moon face that now showed excitement. The boy could not wait to see us slaughtered and doubtless expected to help kill whichever of us survived the coming onslaught, but his lack of a helmet suggested his uncle wanted the boy to take no part in the fighting. He had a coat of shining mail and a long scabbard criss-crossed with golden strips, but what caught the eye was what he wore in place of a helmet. He was wearing King Alfred's crown, the golden crown studded with the emeralds of Wessex.

Two priests mounted on geldings and six spearmen on stallions waited behind Æthelhelm. The spearmen were plainly guarding Ælfweard and his uncle, as was the horseman whose tall stallion stood to Æthelhelm's left, a horseman who looked too big for his horse. It was Waormund, a looming and baleful figure who, in contrast to the other horsemen, was shabby. His mail was dull, his stag-painted shield was deeply scored by blades, and his battered helmet had no cheek-pieces. He was grinning. This was Waormund's delight. He had an enemy shield wall to break and men to kill and, as if he could not wait for the slaughter to begin, he swung himself out of the saddle, looked at us derisively, and spat.

Then he drew his sword. He drew Serpent-Breath. He drew my sword, the whorls on her steel blade reflecting a lance of sunlight to dazzle me. He spat toward us a second time, then turned and swept Serpent-Breath up in a salute to Ælfweard. "Lord King!" he bellowed.

It seemed to me that Ælfweard giggled in reply. He was certainly laughing as his troops all shouted the same words, "Lord King! Lord King!" They chanted it, still beating their swords against their shields until Æthelhelm held up a leather-gloved hand to silence them and kicked his stallion forward.

"He doesn't know you're here," Finan muttered to me. He meant Waormund. My cheek-pieces were open, but I was holding the shield high, half obscuring my face.

"He'll find out," I said grimly.

"But I fight him," Finan insisted, "not you."

"Men of Mercia!" Æthelhelm shouted, then waited for silence. I saw him glance up to the western walls and gaze intently for an instant, and I realized he was watching for a signal that Æthelstan's forces were coming. He looked back to us, betraying no alarm. "Men of Mercia!" he called again, then beckoned for a standard-bearer to come forward. The man waved his flag slowly, the new flag on which the stag of Æthelhelm dominated the dragon of Wessex.

Æthelhelm has loosened the gold-chased cheek-pieces of his helmet so that men could see his narrow face; a handsome face, long and commanding, clean shaven and with deep-set brown eyes. He pointed to the flag. "That flag," he called, "is the new flag of Englaland! It is our flag! Your flag and my flag, the flag of one country under one king!"

"King Æthelstan!" a man shouted from our ranks.

Æthelhelm ignored the shout. I saw him glance again to the walls, then look back to us unperturbed. "One country!" he said, his voice easily carrying to the men on the ramparts. "It will be our country! Yours and mine! We are not enemies! The enemy are the pagans, and where are the pagans? Where do the hated North-men rule? In Northumbria! Join me and I promise that every man here will share in the wealth of that heathen country. You will have land! You will have silver! You will have women!"

Ælfweard grinned at that and said something to Waormund, who gave a bark of laughter. He still held Serpent-Breath. "Your king," Æthelhelm pointed to his grinning nephew, "is King of Wessex, King of East Anglia, and he offers you pardon, mercy, and forgiveness. He offers you life!" Again a quick glance at the far walls. "Together," Æthelhelm went on, "we will make one country of all the Saxons!"

"Of all Christians!" Father Oda called. Æthelhelm looked at the priest and must have recognized him as the man who had fled his service in disgust, but he betrayed no annoyance, just smiled. "Father Oda is right," he shouted, "we will make a country for all Christian men! And Northumbria is the land of Guthfrith the Pagan and together we shall take his land, and you, the men of Mercia, will be given their steadings, their woodlands, their flocks, their herds, their young women, and their pastures!"

Guthfrith? Guthfrith! I stared at Æthelhelm in a daze. Guthfrith was Sigtryggr's brother, and if he was indeed king, then Sigtryggr, my ally, was dead. And if he was dead and if it was the plague that had killed him, then who else had died in Eoferwic? Sigtryggr's heir was my grandson who was too young to rule, but Guthfrith had taken the throne? "Lord," Finan muttered, nudging me with his sword arm.

"Fight me here," Æthelhelm called, "and you fight against God's anointed king! You fight for a bastard, born to a whore! But drop your shields and sheathe your swords and I will grant you the land of our real enemy, the enemy of all Christian Englaland! I will give you Northumbria!" He paused, there was silence, and I realized that Rumwald's men were listening, and that they were almost persuaded that the lies Æthelhelm told were the truth. "I will give you wealth!" Æthelhelm promised. "I will give you the land of Northumbria!"

"It's not yours to give," I snarled. "You faithless bastard, you earsling, you son of a poxed whore, you piece of slug shit, you liar!" Finan tried to restrain me, but I shook him off and stepped forward. "You are slime from a cesspit," I spat at Æthelhelm, "and I will give your lands, all of them, to the men of Mercia!"

He stared at me. Ælfweard stared and Waormund stared and slowly it dawned on all three that, disheveled as I was, I was their enemy. And for a heartbeat I swear I saw fear on Æthelhelm's face. It came and it went, but he did edge his horse backward. He said nothing.

"I am Uhtred of Bebbanburg!" I was talking to the West Saxons shield wall now. "Many of you have fought under my banner. We fought for Alfred, for Edward, for Wessex, and now you would die for that piece of weasel shit!" I pointed Wasp-Sting at Ælfweard.

"Kill him!" Ælfweard squealed.

"Lord?" Waormund growled to his master.

"Kill him," Æthelhelm snapped.

I was full of anger. Guthfrith ruled? Grief was thick inside me, threatening to overwhelm me, but I was angry too. Angry that Æthelhelm should think to give away my land, that his filthy nephew would be king of Bebbanburg's fields. I just wanted to kill.

But Waormund wanted to kill too, and he was the bigger man, and I remembered his speed in a fight. He was skilled too, as skilled as any man with a sword, a spear, or an axe. He was younger, he was taller, he out-reached me, and he was probably faster. I might have matched him for speed if my body had not been racked by his horse dragging me across fields, but I was sore, I ached, and I was weary.

But I was also angry. It was a cold anger holding grief at bay, an anger that wanted to destroy both Waormund and his reputation that had been made at my expense. He was walking slowly toward me, his heavy boots crunching the gravel of the road leading to the gate, his scarred face grinning. He carried no shield, just my sword.

I let my shield drop to the road, put Wasp-Sting into my left hand, and drew the borrowed sword with my right. Finan made one last effort to stop me, coming toward me with an outstretched arm.

"Step back, Irish scum," Waormund growled, "you're next."

"My fight," I told Finan.

"Lord . . ."

"My fight," I said again, louder.

It occurred to me as I walked slowly toward my enemy that Æthelhelm had made a mistake. Why had he waited? Why had he not tried to overwhelm us and close the gates? And by letting Waormund fight me he gave Æthelstan more time to reach us. Or perhaps Æthelhelm knew more than I did, that the men he had sent to the western gates were already fighting the Mercian army beyond the walls, and that Æthelstan was too busy to come. I saw Æthelhelm look again to the walls, but again he showed no alarm. "Kill him, Waormund!" he called.

"Cripple him!" Ælfweard commanded in a high voice. "I must kill him! Just cripple him for me!"

Waormund had stopped. He beckoned me with his left hand. "Come!" he crooned as if I were a child. "Come and be crippled."

So I stopped and stood still. If Æthelstan was to come then I must give him as much time as I could. And so I waited. Sweat stung my eyes. The helmet was hot. I hurt.

"Frightened?" Waormund asked, then laughed. "He's frightened of me!" He had turned and was shouting to the West Saxons behind Æthelhelm. "That's Uhtred of Bebbanburg! And I've already beaten him once! Dragged him naked at my horse's arse! And this is his sword!" he held Serpent-Breath high. "It's a good sword." He turned his dull, cruel, animal eyes to look at me. "You don't deserve this blade," he snarled, "you gutless turd."

"Kill him!" Æthelhelm called.

"Cripple him!" Ælfweard demanded in his shrill voice.

"Come, old man," Waormund again beckoned me, "come!"

Men watched. I did not move. I held my sword low. She did not have a name. Sweat ran down my face. Waormund charged.

He charged suddenly and, for a big man, he was quick. He held Serpent-Breath in his right hand, his left hand empty. He wanted the fight to be over swiftly and I was not making it easy by standing still, and so he had decided to charge me, to swing Serpent-Breath in one mighty blow to batter down my parry and then hit me with his full weight so that I would be thrown to the ground where he could disarm me, then give me to Ælfweard's mercy. So do the unexpected, I told myself, and took a half step to my right, which he did expect, then hurled myself straight at him. I hit him with my left shoulder and the pain was sudden and fierce. I had hoped Wasp-Sting would pierce his mail, but he moved into me at the very last instant and her lunge slid past his waist as we collided and I smelled the ale on his breath and the stink of the sweat-soaked leather under his mail coat. It was like throwing my weight against a bullock, but I had been expecting the impact and was ready for it, Waormund was not. He staggered slightly, but still kept his footing then turned fast with Serpent-Breath swinging. I parried her with Wasp-Sting, saw his left hand reaching for me, but he was still off balance and I stepped away before he could grasp me. I turned to lunge with the borrowed sword, but he was too quick and had backed away.

"Hurry!" Æthelhelm called. He must have realized that this fight was wasting time, time he might not have, but he also knew that my death would dispirit the Mercians and make them easier to slaughter, so he would let Waormund finish me. "Get it done, man!" he added irritably.

"Piece of northern shit," Waormund said, then sneered, "they're all dead in the north! You will be soon." He took a half step toward me, Serpent-Breath raised, but I did not move. I had been watching his eyes and knew it was a feint. He stepped back. "Good sword this," he said, "better than a turd like you deserves." Then he came for me again, for real this time, lunging Serpent-Breath and again hoping to knock me off my feet with his weight, but I used my long-sword to throw Serpent-Breath off to my right and stepped left. He back-swung the blade as he turned toward me, I parried with my sword and felt the jolt of steel on steel, then I stepped to the right, still close to him, stepping into his sword arm, and I kept moving, and as I moved I stabbed Wasp-Sting at his belly.

I knew at that moment I was making a mistake, that he had fooled me, that I was doing just what he wanted. I suddenly remembered the fight on the terrace above the Temes and how he had gripped my mail coat. That was how he fought. He wanted me close so he could grab hold of me and shake me as a terrier shakes a rat. He wanted me close where his height, weight, and strength could overwhelm me, and now I was very close. I was passing him, still going to my right, and I saw his left hand reaching for me and I almost pulled away, but the thought was too late, I was committed and so I thrust the seax. I ignored the fiery pain in my left shoulder and I just rammed Wasp-Sting as hard as I could. It hurt, that thrust, it hurt terribly. The effort to drive Wasp-Sting deep made me gasp aloud, but I kept thrusting her, ignoring the pain.

Waormund had been reaching to grip one of my cheek-pieces, but Wasp-Sting was quicker. She pierced mail and leather. She broke through thick muscle. She buried half her length in his gut, and his reaching hand fell away as he turned quickly, grimacing, so quickly that he tore Wasp-Sting's hilt from my hand so that she stayed in his belly, blood just showing in the links she had pierced. I backed away. "You're slow," I said, the first words I had spoken to him.

"Bastard," he spat and, ignoring the seax in his gut, came for me again. He was angry now. He had been contemptuous before, but now he was nothing but fury, hacking Serpent-Breath in savage short strokes, her blade ringing on my blade as he forced me to retreat by the sheer weight of the blows. But his anger was hot, it made him unthinking, and the blows, though brutally hard, were easy enough to parry. I taunted him. Called him a beef-witted piece of shit, said his mother had shat him instead of giving birth, that through all Britain men called him Æthelhelm's arse-licker. "You're dying, you maggot," I mocked him, "that blade in your belly is killing you!" He knew that was probably true. I have seen men recover from ghastly wounds, but rarely from a gut stroke. "It will be a slow painful death," I told him, "and men will remember me as the man who killed Æthelhelm's arse-licker."

"Bastard!" Waormund was almost crying in his fury. He knew he was probably doomed, but at least he could kill me first and so salvage his reputation. He swung again and I parried Serpent-Breath and felt the force of the blow shudder up my arm. Serpent-Breath had shattered many a blade, but by a miracle my borrowed sword had not broken from any of his blows. He lunged fast, I twisted away, almost tripped on a loose stone, and Waormund was bellowing now, half rage and half pain. Wasp-Sting was deep in his entrails, she had ripped them open, and the blood at his belly was welling through the mail to drip on the road. He tried to pull her free, but the flesh had closed on her blade, gripping it, and his attempt only hurt him, and he left her there, lunged again, but slower, and I knocked his thrust aside and lunged in turn, aiming for his face, then dropping my blade to strike Wasp-Sting's hilt. That hurt him, I saw it in his eyes. He swayed back, stumbled, and then found a new fury and a new energy. He attacked frantically, driving me back with swing after massive swing, grunting with each huge effort. I parried some blows, stepped away from others, content now to let Wasp-Sting kill him slowly and so buy us time. Waormund was weakening, but his strength was prodigious and I was being forced back toward Rumwald's shield wall. The Mercians had cheered when they saw me stab Wasp-Sting into Waormund's gut, but now they were silent, awed by the sight of the giant warrior, a sword-hilt sticking from his belly, attacking with such demented anger. He was in pain, he was slowing, but still he tried to hack me down.

Then a horn sounded to the west. An urgent horn. It was being blown from the ramparts, and the sound half checked Waormund. "Now!" Æthelhelm bellowed. "Now!"

He was telling his shield wall to advance, telling them to kill us, telling them to close the gate.

But Waormund had momentarily turned at the sound of his master's voice and my borrowed sword, with its edges nicked by the violence of Serpent-Breath's attacks, slid through his tangled beard and into his throat. Blood jetted into the hot air. He looked back to me, all strength gone, and for a heartbeat he just stared at me in apparent disbelief. He opened his mouth as if to speak, but blood spilled from his lips and then, oddly slowly, he fell to his knees on the dusty gravel that was soaked with his blood. He still looked at me, only now it seemed he was begging for pity, but I had no pity. I struck Wasp-Sting's hilt again and Waormund whimpered, and then fell sideways.

"Kill them all!" Æthelhelm bellowed.

I just had time to drop the blood-tipped borrowed sword, stoop and prise Serpent-Breath from Waormund's weakening fingers. Then I ran, or at least stumbled, back to the shield wall where Finan handed me my fallen shield. The drums began to beat again. The horn still sounded its urgent warning. And the warriors of Wessex were coming to kill us.

They came slowly. The poets tell us that men charge into battle, welcoming the slaughter as eagerly as any lover, but a shield wall is a fearsome thing. The men of Wessex knew they would not break us with a wild charge, but would only reach the gate behind us by keeping their ranks tight and their shields overlapped and firm, and so they walked to us, their faces watchful and grim above the iron rims of their stag-painted shields. Every third man carried a shortened spear, the others came with either a seax or an axe. I had left

Wasp-Sting in Waormund's belly, and I needed her. A long-sword is no weapon for a shield wall, but Serpent-Breath was in my hand and she would have to serve.

"Our king is coming!" I shouted. "Hold them!"

"Kill them!" Ælfweard's high-pitched voice screamed. "Slaughter them!"

The West Saxon spears were lowered. I had thought their rear ranks might throw spears, but none came, though Wihtgar's men hurled spears over our heads. The blades thumped into West Saxon shields. "Break them!" Æthelhelm shouted, and they came forward, still cautiously, men stepping around Waormund's massive corpse. Their shields made a constant clatter, edge touching edge. They were close now, so close. They stared into our eyes, we stared into theirs. Men took a breath, steeling themselves for the clash of shields. Harsh voices were ordering them onward. "Kill them!" Ælfweard shouted excitedly. He had drawn a sword, but was staying well back from the fight.

"For God and for the king!" a West Saxon shouted, and then they came. They screamed, they shouted, they charged the last two paces, and our shields met with a thunder of clashing wood. My shield was pressed back, I heaved. An axe hacked at the rim, narrowly missing my face, a warrior with gritted teeth and a badly mended helmet was grimacing at me, just inches from my face. He was trying to thread a seax past my shield's edge as the axeman attempted to pull my shield down, but the axe's blade slipped from the rent it had made and I heaved again, pushing the grimacing man back, and Finan must have lunged his seax into him because he sank down, giving me space enough to lunge Serpent-Breath at the axeman.

Men were shouting. Blades were clashing. Priests were calling on their god to kill us. A Mercian spearman behind me thrust past my shield. I heard Æthelhelm's voice, touched with panic, yelling at his men that they must close the gate. I looked up when he shouted and caught his eye an instant. "Close the gate!" His voice was shrill. I looked away from him as an axe thumped on my shield. I shook the blade off as a Mercian spearman thrust a spear past me. I rammed Serpent-Breath forward, felt her strike wood and lunged again, but my elbow was jarred by Rumwald who had staggered against me. He was whimpering, then his shield fell and he sank down, the spearman behind me tried to take his place, but Rumwald was thrashing wildly, suddenly screaming in agony, and so stopped him. A West Saxon spear pierced Rumwald's mail, then a merciful axe split his helmet, shattered his skull. The spearman lunged at Rumwald's killer, but a West Saxon seized the ash shaft and tugged until Serpent-Breath skewered his armpit.

"Kill them!" Ælfweard screeched. "Kill them! Kill them! Kill them all!"

"You must close the gate!" Æthelhelm bellowed.

"God is with us!" Father Oda's voice was hoarse. The men in our rear rank were shouting, encouraging us to kill. Wounded men moaned, the dying screamed, the battle stench of blood and shit filled my nostrils.

"Hold them!" I bellowed. A spear or a seax scored across my left thigh, Finan lunged. The spearman from the second rank had stepped across Rumwald's body and his shield touched mine. He lasted maybe long enough to lunge his spear once, then the axe drove into his shoulder, opening him deep and he fell beside his lord, and the axeman, a fair-haired man with a blood-spattered beard, swung his blade at me and I raised the shield to block the blow, saw the wood split where the blade struck, swung the shield down, and drove Serpent-Breath at his eyes. He jerked away, another man had taken the dying Mercian's place and he stabbed with a shortened spear, driving the blade into the axeman's groin. The axe dropped, the man shrieked in agony and, like Waormund, fell to his knees. There were dead and dying men between us and the enemy, who had to step on the bodies to reach us and try to stab and lunge and hack their way to the gate. The drums still pounded, shields were splintering, the West Saxons were driving us back by weight of numbers.

Then there was a bellow behind me, a cheer, a clatter of hooves, and something slammed into my back, throwing me to my knees and I looked up to see a horseman thrusting a long spear over my head. More horsemen came. The Mercian cheers grew. I managed to stand. Finan had thrown down his seax and drawn Soul-Stealer because the horsemen were driving the West Saxons back, giving us space for longer blades. "Break them!" another voice shouted, and I had a glimpse of Æthelstan, his helmet a glory of polished steel circled with gold, thrusting his stallion into the West Saxon ranks. The warrior king had come, glorious in gold, ruthless in steel, and he hacked with a long-sword, beating down his enemies. His men spurred to join him, spears stabbing, and suddenly the enemy broke.

They just broke. The longer spears of the Mercian horsemen had reached deep into the West Saxon ranks and on another day, on another battlefield, that would not have mattered. Horses are easy to wound and a panicked horse is no help to his rider, but on that day, by the gate of cripples, the horsemen came with a savage fury, led by a king who wanted to fight and who led his men from the front. There was blood on his stallion's chest, but the horse kept plunging, rearing, flailing with heavy hooves, and Æthelstan kept shouting his men onward, his long-sword reddened, and our shield wall, saved from death, found new passion. Our line, so short and so vulnerable, now surged forward. Brihtwulf had returned and joined the charge, bellowing at his men to follow, then Æthelstan's horsemen split the enemy shield wall and the West Saxons broke in panic.

Because a king had come and a king now fled.

"Sweet Jesus," Finan said.

We were sitting on the lowest step of the stairs leading to the ramparts that were rapidly emptying of the enemy. I lifted off my helmet and dropped it on the ground. "It's so damned hot," I said.

"Summer," Finan said bleakly.

Still more of Æthelstan's men were streaming through the gate. The East Anglians who had first threatened us had dropped their shields and seemed to have no interest in what happened in the city. A few had wandered back to the gate in search of ale, and they took no notice of us and we took no notice of them. Immar had brought me Wasp-Sting. She lay on the ground in front of me, waiting for her blade to be cleaned, while Serpent-Breath lay on my knees and I kept touching her blade, scarce able to believe I had found her again.

"You gutted that bastard," Finan said, nodding toward Waormund's corpse. There were perhaps forty or fifty other corpses left from Æthelhelm's shield wall. The wounded had been helped into the shade where they groaned.

"He was fast," I said, "but he was clumsy. I didn't expect that. I thought he was better."

"Big bastard though."

"Big bastard," I agreed. I looked down at my left thigh. The bleeding had stopped. The wound was shallow and I started laughing.

"What's funny?" Finan asked.

"I swore an oath."

"You always were an idiot."

I nodded agreement. "I swore to kill Æthelhelm and Ælfweard, and I didn't."

"You tried."

"I tried to keep the oath," I said.

"They're probably dead by now," Finan said, "and they wouldn't be dead if you hadn't taken the gate, so yes, you kept your oath. And if they're not dead they soon will be."

I stared across the city where the killing continued. "It would be nice to kill them both though," I said wistfully.

"For Christ's sake, you've done enough!"

"We've done enough," I corrected him. Æthelstan and his men were hunting through the streets and alleys of Lundene, seeking out Æthelhelm, Ælfweard, and their supporters, and those supporters were few. The East Anglians did not want to fight for them, and many of the West Saxons simply threw down their shields and weapons. Æthelhelm's vaunted army, as large an army as had been seen in Britain for many a year, had proved as fragile as an eggshell. Æthelstan was king.

And that evening as the smoke above Lundene glowed red in the light of the sinking sun, the king sent for me. He was King of Wessex now, King of East Anglia, and King of Mercia. "It is all one country," he told me that night. We were in the great hall of Lundene's palace, originally built for the kings of Mercia, then occupied by Alfred of Wessex, then by his son, Edward of Wessex, and now the property of Æthelstan, but Æthelstan of what? Of Englaland? I looked into his dark, clever eyes, so like the eyes of his grandfather

Alfred, and knew he was thinking of the fourth Saxon kingdom, Northumbria.

"You swore an oath, lord King," I reminded him.

"I did indeed," he said, not looking at me, but gazing down the hall where the leaders of his warriors were gathered at two long tables. Finan was there with Briht-wulf, as were Wihtgar and Merewalh, all drinking ale or wine because this was a feast, a celebration, and the victors were eating the food that had belonged to the defeated. Some of the defeated West Saxons were there too, those who had surrendered quickly and sworn allegiance to their conqueror. Most men still wore their mail, though Æthelstan had stripped off his own armor and wore a costly black coat beneath a short cloak dyed a deep and rich blue. The cloak's hems were embroidered with gold thread, he had a gold chain about his neck from which hung a golden cross, and about his head was a simple gold circlet. He was no longer the boy I had protected through the long years when his enemies had tried to destroy him. Now he had the stern face of a warrior king. He looked like a king too; he was tall, straight-backed, and handsome, but that was not why his enemies had called him Faeger Cnapa. They had used that derisive name because Æthelstan had let his dark hair grow long and then twisted it into a dozen ringlets that were threaded with gold wires. Before the feast, when I had been summoned to share the high table, he had seen me staring at the glittering strands beneath the golden circlet and he had given me a defiant look.

"A king," he had said defensively, "must appear kingly."

"He must indeed, lord King," I had said. He had looked at me with those clever eyes, judging whether I mocked him, but before he could say more I had dropped to one knee. "I take pleasure at your victory, lord King," I had said humbly.

"As I am grateful for all you did," he had said, then raised me up and insisted that I should sit at his right hand where, gazing down at the celebrating warriors, I had just reminded him of the oath he had sworn to me.

"I did indeed swear an oath," he said. "I swore not to invade Northumbria while you live." He paused and reached for a silver jug that was etched with Æthelhelm's stag. "And you can be sure," he went on, "that I am mindful of the oath." His voice was guarded and still he looked into the hall, but then he turned to me and smiled. "And I thank God that you do live, Lord Uhtred." He poured me wine from the jug. "I am told you rescued Queen Eadgifu?"

"I did, lord King." I still found it strange to address him as I had addressed his grandfather. "So far as I know she's safe at Bebbanburg."

"That was well done," he said. "You can send her to Cent and assure her of our protection."

"And for her sons too?"

"Of course!" He sounded annoyed that I had even asked. "They are my nephews." He sipped wine, his eyes brooding on the tables below us. "And I hear you hold Aethelwulf as a prisoner?"

"I do, lord King."

"You will send him to me. And release the priest." He did not wait for my assent, but simply assumed I would obey him. "What do you know of Guthfrith?"

I had expected the question, because Guthfrith, brother to Sigtryggr, had taken the throne in Eoferwic. Sigtryggr had died of the plague and that was almost all the news Æthelstan knew of the north. He had heard that the sickness had ended and he had ordered the roads to Eoferwic to be opened again, but of Bebbanburg he could tell me nothing. Nor did he know of the fate of his sister, Sigtryggr's queen, nor of my grandchildren. "All I know, lord King," I answered him carefully, "is that Sigtryggr wasn't fond of his brother."

"He's a Norseman."

"Of course."

"And a pagan," he said, glancing at the silver hammer I still wore.

"And some pagans, lord King," I said sharply, "helped keep the Crepelgate open for you."

He just nodded at that, poured the last of the wine into his goblet, then stood and hammered the empty jug on the table to silence the hall. He hammered it at least a dozen times before the noise subsided and the warriors were all looking at him. He raised his goblet. "I have to thank the Lord Uhtred," he turned and inclined his head to me, "who this day gave us Lundene!"

The warriors cheered and I had wanted to remind the king that Brihtwulf had helped, and poor Rumwald had died helping, and so many good men had fought at the Crepelgate where they had expected to die for him and some had, but before I could say anything Æthelstan turned to Father Oda who sat on his left. I knew he was inviting the Danish priest to serve in his household, an invitation I knew Oda would accept.

Æthelhelm was dead. He had been caught trying to escape through one of the western gates, and Merewalh, who had joined Æthelstan's army, had been one of the men who pierced him with a spear. Ælfweard had become separated from his uncle and with just four men tried to escape across Lundene's bridge only to find the fort at the southern end barred to him by the handful of men we had left there. He had begged them to let him pass, had offered them gold which they accepted, but when he rode through the opened gate they had hauled him from his horse and taken both his gold and his crown. His four men had just watched.

Now, after the feast, when men were singing and a harpist playing, Ælfweard was brought to Æthelstan. Candles lit the hall, the shadows thrown by their flickering flames leaping about the high rafters. The boy, he was twenty years old but looked six or seven years younger, was escorted by two warriors. He looked terrified, his moon face crumpled by crying. He no longer wore his fine mail, but was dressed in a grubby shift that hung to his knees. He was pushed up the stairs of the high table's dais, and the harpist stopped playing, the singing died, and Æthelstan stood and walked to the front of the table so that every man in the now silent hall could see this meeting of the half-brothers. One was so tall and commanding, the other looked so pathetic as he dropped to his knees. One of the two men guarding Ælfweard was holding the crown the boy had worn in the battle, and Æthelstan now held out his hand and took it. He turned it in his hands so that the emeralds flashed in the candlelight, then he held it out to Ælfweard. "Wear it!" he told his half-brother. "And stand."

Ælfweard looked up but said nothing. His hands were shaking.

Æthelstan smiled. "Come, brother," he said and held out his left hand to help Ælfweard to his feet, then gave him the crown. "Wear it proudly! It was our father's gift to you."

Ælfweard had looked astonished, but now, grinning because he believed he would be King of Wessex still, albeit in submission to Æthelstan, he put the crown on his head. "I will be loyal," he promised his half-brother.

"Of course you will," Æthelstan said gently. He looked at one of the guards. "Your sword," he commanded, and when he had the long blade in his hand, he pointed it at Ælfweard. "Now you will swear an oath to me," he said.

"Gladly," Ælfweard bleated.

"Touch the sword, brother," Æthelstan said, still gently, and when Ælfweard put a tentative hand on the blade Æthelstan just lunged. One straight, savage lunge that shattered his half-brother's ribcage, drove him back with Æthelstan following, and then the sword pierced Ælfweard's heart. Some men gasped, a serving girl screamed, Father Oda made the sign of the cross, but Æthelstan just watched his brother die. "Take him to Wintanceaster," he said when the last blood had pulsed and the last twitch ended. He tugged the blade free. "Bury him beside his father."

The emerald-encrusted crown had rolled under the table where it struck my ankle. I retrieved it and held it for a few heartbeats. This was the crown of Wessex, Alfred's crown, and I remember the dying king telling me it was a crown of thorns. I placed it on the linen cloth that covered the board and looked at Æthelstan. "Your crown, lord King."

"Not until Archbishop Athelm consecrates me," Æthelstan said. The archbishop, who had been held in the palace as a privileged prisoner, sat at the high table. He looked confused, his hands shaking as he ate and drank, but he nodded at Æthelstan's words. "And you will come to the ceremony, Lord Uhtred," Æthelstan demanded, meaning that I should attend the solemn moment when the Archbishop of Contwaraburg placed the royal helmet of Wessex on the new king's head.

"With your permission, lord King," I said. "I would go home."

He hesitated a moment, and then nodded abruptly. "You have my permission," he said.

I was going home.

In time we heard that Æthelstan was crowned. The ceremony was performed at Cyningestun, on the Temes, where his father had been given the royal helmet of Wessex, but Æthelstan refused the helmet, instead insisting that the archbishop place the emerald crown on his gold-threaded hair. The ealdormen of three kingdoms acclaimed the moment, and Alfred's dream of one Christian kingdom thus came one step nearer.

And now I sat on Bebbanburg's high rock, the flame-lit hall behind me and the moon-silvered sea before me, and I thought of the dead. Of Folcbald, killed by a spear thrust in the shield wall by the Crepelgate. Of Sigtryggr, felled by fever and dying in his bed with a sword in his hand. Of his two children, my grandchildren, both dead. Of Eadith, who had gone to Eoferwic to care for the children and had caught their plague and now was buried.

"Why did she go?" I had asked my son.

"She thought you would want her to go."

I had said nothing, just felt guilt. The plague had not reached as far north as Bebbanburg. My son had barred the roads, threatening travelers with death if they tried to come onto our land, and so the sickness had ravaged the land from Lindcolne to Eoferwic, and then spread through the great vale of farms that surrounded the city, but it had been kept from Bebbanburg. The plague had died itself by the time we reached Eoferwic on our journey north.

And Guthfrith was king there, his election supported by the Danish jarls who still ruled much of Northumbria. I had met him briefly. Like his brother Sigtryggr he was a thin, fair-haired man with a handsome face, but unlike Sigtryggr he was sour and suspicious. The night I met him, when he reluctantly feasted me in his great hall, he had demanded my allegiance, had demanded that I swear an oath to him, but he had not demanded it instantly, suggesting that when the feast was over there would be time enough for that brief ceremony. Then he had drunk mead and ale, had demanded more mead, then cheered raucously when one of his men bent a serving girl over a table. "Bring her here!" he shouted. "Bring the bitch here!" But by the time the girl had been dragged to the platform where we ate, Guthfrith was vomiting into the rushes and he slept soon after. We left in the morning, mounted on horses taken from Æthelhelm's beaten army, and I had sworn no oath.

I had ridden home with my men. With Finan, an Irishman, with Gerbruht, a Frisian, with Immar, a Dane, with Vidarr, a Norseman, and with Beornoth and Oswi, both Saxons. We were seven warriors, but we were brothers too. And with us rode the children we had rescued in Lundene, a dozen of the slaves we had freed from Gunnald's ship, and Benedetta.

And Eadith was dead.

And I was at home at last, where the sea wind swept across the rock and where I thought of the dead, where I thought of the future, and where I thought of the three kingdoms that were now one and wanted a fourth.

Benedetta sat beside me. Alaina, as ever, was near her. The child crouched, watching as Benedetta took my hand. I gripped hers, maybe too hard, yet she did not complain or take it away. "You did not want her dead," she said.

"But I did," I spoke softly and bleakly.

"Then God will forgive you," she said, and leaned her head on my shoulder. "He made us," she added, "so He must take us as we are. That is His fate."

I had come home.

Historical Note

Edward the Elder, as he is now known, died in July 924. He had reigned for twenty-five years, succeeding his father, Alfred, as King of Wessex in 899. In the regnal lists he is usually followed by Æthelstan, but there is plenty of evidence that Ælfweard, half-brother to Æthelstan, ruled Wessex for about a month following his father's death. If that is true, as for fictional purposes I have plainly assumed it is, then Ælfweard's death was extremely convenient for Æthelstan who thereby became the king of the three southern kingdoms of Saxon Britain: Wessex, East Anglia, and Mercia.

Much of the novel is fictional. We do not know how Ælfweard died, and his death probably took place at Oxford rather than Lundene, and it took another month before the West Saxons accepted Æthelstan as their new king. He was crowned at Kingston upon Thames that same year and was the first king to insist on being invested with the crown rather than with a helmet. Much of the reluctance to accept Æthelstan as king surely arose from the rumor that Edward had not married his mother, that he was indeed a bastard.

Edward's reign left much of southern England free of the Viking scourge. King Alfred's strategy of building burhs, which are heavily fortified towns, had been adopted by Edward and by his sister Æthelflaed in Mercia. East Anglia, which had been a Danish kingdom, was conquered and its towns fortified. Edward built more burhs along the Welsh border and in the north of Mercia to deter raids from western Northumbria where there were powerful Norse settlements. Sigtryggr, a Norseman, was King of Northumbria, ruling from York, and for purely fictional purposes I have brought his death forward by three years.

King Alfred undoubtedly dreamed of a united England, or Englaland, which would be one realm of everyone who spoke the "Ænglisc' tongue. That sounds simple, though in truth an inhabitant of Kent would have found the English speech of a Northumbrian difficult to comprehend and vice versa, but nevertheless it was the same language. Nor was that ambition restricted to language. Alfred was famously pious, a man dedicated to the church, and all Christian folk, whether Saxon, Dane, or Norse, were included in his dream. Conversion was just as important as conquest. Æthelstan, when he assumed the throne of his father, inherited a much wider realm, a kingdom that included most English speakers, but there was still that awkward kingdom to the north, a kingdom that was part Christian and part pagan, part Saxon and part settled by Danes and Norsemen: the kingdom of Northumbria. That country's fate must wait for another novel.

Æthelstan ruled for fifteen years and completed the unification of the English-speaking peoples. He never married and so left no heirs and was succeeded first by Edmund, the eldest son of Edward and Eadgifu, then by Edmund's younger brother, Eadred. I have set the battle at the end of the novel at the Crepelgate, Cripplegate, and though the name does stretch back to Saxon times I invented Alfred's decree allowing the severely handicapped the right to beg at that gate.

Sword of Kings is fiction, yet I hope it echoes a process that is little known: the creation of a country called England. Its birth is still some time off, and will prove bloody, but Uhtred will live to see it.

About the Author

BERNARD CORNWELL is the author of the acclaimed *New York Times* bestsellers *Waterloo*, *1356*, *Agincourt*, and *The Fort*; the bestselling Saxon Tales, which include *The Last Kingdom*, *The Pale Horseman*, *Lords of the North*, *Sword Song*, *The Burning Land*, *Death of Kings*, *The Pagan Lord*, *The Empty Throne*, *Warriors of the Storm*, *The Flame Bearer*, and, most recently, *War of the Wolf*; and the Richard Sharpe novels, among many others. He lives with his wife on Cape Cod and in Charleston, South Carolina.